Miguel de Cervantes Saavedra, Gordon Willoughby James Gyll

Galatea

A pastoral romance

Miguel de Cervantes Saavedra, Gordon Willoughby James Gyll

Galatea
A pastoral romance

ISBN/EAN: 9783337018665

Printed in Europe, USA, Canada, Australia, Japan

Cover: Foto ©Andreas Hilbeck / pixelio.de

More available books at **www.hansebooks.com**

GALATEA.

A PASTORAL ROMANCE.

BY

MIGUEL DE CERVANTES SAAVEDRA

LITERALLY TRANSLATED FROM THE SPANISH BY

GORDON WILLOUGHBY JAMES GYLL,

AUTHOR OF "A TRACTATE ON LANGUAGE," "THE HISTORY OF WRAYSBURY, HORTON, AND COLNBROOK, BUCKS," ETC.

LONDON: GEORGE BELL AND SONS, YORK STREET, COVENT GARDEN.

1883.

LONDON:
PRINTED BY WILLIAM CLOWES AND SONS, LIMITED,
STAMFORD STREET AND CHARING CROSS.

TRANSLATOR'S PREFACE.

In this translation of the Galatea of Cervantes, the object
has been to convey the story in language as closely as possible to the original. The translator fears he may not alway
have succeeded in completely rendering the narratives of
the various incidents which characterise this simple pastoral
epic, and that also he may have to apologise for somewhat of
roughness in his transfusion of the poetry, which has found
its equivalent, where the lines have been long, in blank
verse. The other portions of the poetry he has rendered
literally, but wherever the two dialects assimilated he has
thought it sufficient to furnish only a kind of metrical
rhythm.

This elegant and simple production, the earliest from
the pen of the eminent poet and novelist of Spain, pour-
traying young, fresh, and vivid scintillations of genius, has
never been translated into any language. We have only
its shadow in the French production of Florian, which is
based on the Spanish story, and though written in an engaging and graceful style, is not that mature and elegant
child of the brain of Cervantes which is now for the first
time presented to the English reader.

It has been asserted that in the Galatea all the characters
are strictly innocent; there are, however, occasional cases
of homicide and abduction, while envy and jealousy, the
never failing vices of nature in all conditions of life, are
found in contrast with the more ennobling and elevating
virtues.

This kind of composition seems to have been peculiarly in the vein of Cervantes, who had previously tried "his 'prenticed hand" at another pastoral epic, the Filena, but which, although he states that it had been generally read, soon disappeared, and is now rarely found, not having been printed in the collected works of the author, who probably felt that the Filena was a failure, although with pride he averred "resono por las silvas,"—it reverberated in the groves. But as he was unwilling to allow his epic talent to be quenched, he judiciously selected Galatea as a new and happy medium of success.

The distance between these two pastorals must have been very marked; Galatea possessing all the good properties which should stamp such a pastoral—for the rural characters are nicely defined; modesty and grace with simplicity prevailing. The texture is simple, yet rich, the figures are adapted to the ideas, while the general diction is at once plain, modest, and artless, furnishing a supplement to the graces of conception.

This eminent man, Cervantes de Saavedra, whose name is synonymous with fertility and fancy, and which will ever survive in his Don Quixote and Galatea, did not slide softly into old age. He died hardly in 1616, tempest-beaten, about the same time with our great dramatic poet, having attained the nominal period allotted to humanity.

He was to Spain what Sir Walter Scott became in England; the minds of both instinctively gravitating towards romances and novels. Poetry too was the affection of both. Cervantes constantly introduced sweet snatches of songs into all his compositions. The Galatea is replete with various forms of verse and rhythm in upwards of one hundred and fifty songs, diffused through its six cantos, styled in Spanish tercets, redondillos, octaves, and lines, like the Alexandrine, extending to twelve and more syllables.

The compositions are cast in lyrics and iambics, without being quite of a dithyrambic character, furnishing relief to the prose, and evincing the skill and tendency of the bard in all effusions relative to love, the master passion of our existence, without which all would be arid and disappointing to the eagle spirit of the child of song.

The most esteemed poems in Galatea are in the Cancion style, some being iambic, some trochaic, but all subsiding in rhyme. The dactylic stanza is also found, and assonances take place of rhyme, common in most dialects excepting English, the finest of languages for oratory and poetry, owing to its innate robustness and ductility and its almost entire freedom from inflection.

Spanish poetry is perhaps more decidedly national than any recognised in Europe, and Cervantes is the Spanish high priest. He may be said to belong to the whole world as one of the great parent geniuses who have nursed and nourished the universe of literature—a poet and a versifier of a high class, composing in modulated prose and well-constructed verse, presenting resistless charms of rhythmical harmony in most species of composition.

Among the earliest of Cervantes' poetic pieces were his "Sonnets" and the "Filena," all delivered to the Spanish world of literature soon after he had attained his majority. From being a poet and a romancer, he became a son of Mars, and his zeal in his new profession honourably swelled his renown. At the famous battle of Lepanto, in 1571, the Trafalgar of the time, where Turks and Christians engaged in the furious close of naval war, and the combined fleets of Spain and other maritime states, under John of Austria, won that celebrated victory, Cervantes was but twenty-five years old. He had there the misfortune to lose his left hand and a part of his arm. He remarks, in his writings, that the scars which a soldier shows in his face and breast, are stars which guide others to the haven of honour, and the desire of just praise.

This honourable mutilation constrained him to return homewards, and that circumstance was the precursor of future fame.

He now felt the divine energy of genius within him, and eventually his name filled Spanish literature, which he flooded with a golden light by virtue of that moral purity which enriched his labours, and that simple, soft, yet touching eloquence which is the mistress of the affections. Adventures, intrigues and surprises are inventions prominent and prevailing in all his writings, conciliating, informing and moving as became the qualities of a bard whose flight is epic

Nature had endowed him with the sterling gift of genius, the groundwork of great undertakings. The utmost stretch of human study, learning and industry, which masters everything besides, can never attain to this. Invention is the foundation of poetry. Yet did evil fate pursue him, that inheritance of man. Having lost his hand, on his return, as he hoped to participate the charms of his native country, the ship in which he had embarked was captured by an Algerian corsair, not an uncommon event in those Mediterranean waters, where the confraternity of *sea-soli citors* abounded until they were dispersed, in 1816, by Admiral Lord Exmouth, with the destruction of the fleet and arsenal of Algiers.

The bard was sold for a slave, to which untoward fact he feelingly adverts in his general works, describing his own sufferings under feigned names and events.

The captivity extended over seven years, and in his novel of 'The Captive' he has enumerated sundry casualties which had befallen him whilst in Turkish durance. He was eventually ransomed. He revisited Spain in 1581, and then he consecrated himself to what he was best fitted by a bounteous nature, the pride and passion of authorship,—for with him fame was the wise man's means.

In his retirement he composed his 'Galatea,' which disclosed a talent and usefulness worthy his subsequent reputation.

In his comedy styled 'Trato de Argel,' he has detailed life in Algiers, a memento of his own experience and woes, while he mourned his protracted captivity.

His principal work, and the wonder of time, 'Don Quixote,' he did not commence until he had compassed half a century of existence, but to what cause the world is beholden for this fantastic creation has been left to surmise. In it he discovered and displayed the natural bent of his genius, a produce of his wisdom so novel, that it has been translated more frequently than perhaps any other known work. Whatever is effected in literature or the fine arts is amenable to the rigour of criticism, sometimes to the unnecessary and ungracious snarl of the would-be fastidious. Here envy abounded, that infirmity which is a reigning vice and feeds especially on exalted merit and flourishing fortune. Cervantes, however, reaped his harvest of praise, yet was his material position not much improved, for he continued to drift through comparative penury to the grave, in addition to his frequent collisions with exasperated enemies.

A *littérateur* styled Avellanada had the effrontery to venture on a continuation of Don Quixote, and this kindling just indignation in Cervantes, he exercised his withering scorn upon the temerarious interloper who dared to link his insignificance to the author's immortality. It had a crushing effect, for Avellanada's continuation fell almost still-born, while that of Cervantes has augmented and enriched the original, and invested the composer with imperishable renown wherever literature is cultivated.

Poverty, which is said to whet the brain, drove Cervantes to write for the stage. His histrionic capacity seems not generally to have been effulgent. He composed thirty pieces, of which few only are extant. The best of his surviving dramas, perhaps the foremost of all, is his 'Numancia,' a very noble production, emulative of the fire of Æschylus, despite the rigid dramatic canons of Aristotle. Like our own bard of Avon, he would not be subservient to theory.

According to the world's verdict, he succeeded better in romances. The work known as Persíles and Sigismunda, a kindly pastoral, completed his sublunary toils; for to it he wrote a dedication only a few days antecedent to his end.

Through the ingratitude of his countrymen the place of Cervantes' sepulture is scarcely known.

DEDICATED BY CERVANTES,

To His Excellency DON JOSEPH MOÑIÑO, Count of Florida Blanca, Knight of the Grand Cross of the Royal Order of K. Charles III.

Most Excellent Sir,

I submit to your Excellency the " Six Books of the Galatea," the earliest production of the wisdom of Miguel de Cervantes, divided into two parts. Also another work which contains the famous "Voyage of Parnassus," to which I have annexed the " Tragedy of Numantia, and the Comedy of the Trades of Argel," which two works have never before been printed. These three books are of the same size and form as the " Labours of Persiles and Sigismunda, and the Novels," which I had also the honour to present to your Excellence, and shortly will follow the " History of Don Quixote," to complete the edition.

I trust the urbanity of your Excellence will graciously accept this small offering, which your much obliged and grateful Servant consecrates to you,

ANTONIO DE SANCHA.

DEDICATION

To the ILLUSTRIOUS SEÑOR ASCANIO COLONA,

Abbot of Santa Sofia.

The courtesy of your Worship has been such towards me that it has removed the apprehension which I might have reasonably entertained in presuming to offer to you these the first fruits of my narrow wit.

But reflecting that your Worship not only came to Spain to illuminate her foremost Universities, but to be the pole-star to all, that they might walk in the path of whatsoever science they profess (especially the poetic profession), I was desirous not to lose this guide, for I am conscious that in it, and by it, I shall find a secure harbour and a favourable reception.

Acquiesce then in my desire which I send before me, and may you accord to me some consideration in this my minute service. But should I not deserve it for this, grant it to me for having followed during several years the victorious standards of that sun of the army, whom heaven yesterday removed from our sight, but not from the memory of those who have endeavoured to retain it in all those things so worthy of it, viz., the excellent member of the Society of Jesus. Superadding to this the effect which certain things caused in my mind, as in prophecy I have heard often said of this member of the Jesuits to Cardinal Aquaviva, having been his chamberlain in Rome, which things I now find not only accomplished, but that all the world are enjoying the virtue, Christianity, magnificence and benevolence of that man whose works gave daily proof from what a worthy stock he was derived, which for ancestral remoteness competes with the origin of Rome's greatness and its magnates, whilst in worth and in deeds of heroism the same identity is re-cognised in a yet loftier career.

All this do numberless histories verify, replete with acts of honour, deducible from the trunk and branches of the royal house of Colona, under whose strength and character I place myself for a shield against those murmurers whose property is never to pardon.

Therefore, if your Worship forgive this assurance, I have no other fear or wish but that the Lord may guard your illustrious presence with an increment of dignity and position, which all we your adherents desire.

Illustrious Sir, I kiss your hand, and am your ever faith-ful servant,

MIGUEL DE CERVANTES SAAVEDRA.

THE COMMISSION.

By order of the Lords of the Royal Council, I have seen this work, entitled "The Six Books of Galatea;" and my opinion is, that it may be printed, being a loving treatise, and of a lively fancy, without affecting any one in either its verse or prose.

Indeed it is a composition of much value, for its style is chaste and the romance a neat invention, divested of all impropriety or aught adverse to morality. Hence may we assign to the Author the premium of his toil, which is in his application for this license, which we confer.

Done at Madrid, 1 Feb. 1634.

TO CURIOUS READERS.

The occupation of writing eclogues at a time when poetry is so forsaken I suspect will not be estimed for a so laudable exercise, but that it will be indispensable to give some especial satisfaction to those who follow the different tastes of natural inclination; for they who are of a different persuasion rate this employment as little less than labour lost and time also.

Yet as it behoves no one to try to satisfy wits who are enshrouded in such narrow limits, I would feign reply to those who exempt from passion, but on a surer foundation, are induced to acknowledge no difference in poetry, in the belief that those who in this age treat of it, publish their works without due consideration, borne away by the power which the passion for these compositions alone is accustomed to excite in their authors.

For myself, I can truly allege what predilection I have entertained for poetry, for when I was scarce emancipated from my youthful shackles, I gave way to these identical pursuits, so that I cannot deny but that the studies of this faculty (in bygone times with reason well appreciated) carry with them more than a moderate share of profit, such as enriching the poet relatively to his mother tongue, and so to rule over the artifices of eloquence therein comprised, with a view to higher aims and of more serious import; to open the way by the imitation of him, that narrow souls who in brevity of language seek that the fertility of the Castilian dialect should accomplish all, may understand that there is an open field, easy, spacious, whereby with facility and sweetness, with gravity and eloquence they may move with freedom, showing the diversity of acute conceptions, weighty yet elevated, which, in the richness of the Spanish genius, the favourable influence of heaven has with such effect, in various parts, produced, and is producing hourly in this our happy age, of which I bear sure testimony, and that some I know who with justice, and despite the bashfulness which accompanies me, might in security pass through a so dangerous career.

Still are human difficulties so common and yet so different, and the aim and acting so various, that some, with a desire for glory, venture, while others, through dread of disgrace, dare not publish that, which once committed to the world, must encounter the judgment of it, dangerous and most times deceptive.

I, not because I think it reasonable that I may be trusted, have given proof of boldness in the publication of this book, but because I would not determine of two evils which was the greater; or he who with levity, desiring to impart the talent which he has early received from heaven, ventures to offer the fruit of his intelligence to his friends and country; or he who quite scrupulous, lazy and late, never satisfied with what he does or understands, holds only for an accomplishment that which he never attains, and never determines on publishing his works or communicating anything, so that as the boldness and confidence of one may be condemned for a licentious excess, which is granted with safety, so the suspicion and tardiness of another is vicious, for either late or never does he benefit by the fruit of his genius and study those who hope and desire his aid and corresponding example to the end that they may make advances in his exercises.

Avoiding these two *dilemmas*, I have not published anything before this work, nor did I wish to lock it up, my understanding having wrought it out for a higher end than mere personal satisfaction.

I know well that what is wont to be condemned is that excess in the matter of style which appertains to it; the very prince of Latin poetry was blamed for making some of his eclogues more elevated than others.

Hence I have no fear that I shall be criticised because some philosophical reasons are interspersed with certain amorous arguments of shepherds, who rarely rise in discourse beyond country affairs, and this, too, with a congenial simplicity. Yet noting (as in this work is found) that many of the disguised shepherds are so only in attire, this objection is cleared.

The remaining objections must be placed to the account of the invention and disposition of the piece, and these are palliated, for it is a prudent motion, and it is the author's wish to be pleasant, and having done so in this particular and to the best of his power, he may have been successful.]

Yet if this section of the work does not realise his most earnest wish, he offers henceforward others of better taste and of a wider range of wit.

CONTENTS.

BOOK I.

BOOK II.

BOOK III.

BOOK IV.

BOOK V.

BOOK VI.

sis of the eldest swains.—Nocturnal repast, and the visitors remain
during night around Meliso's tomb.—A mass of fire appears, which
Telesio approaches to discover the cause of the phenomenon.—In
the centre arises a graceful nymph.—Her vesture.—The vision opens
its arms on both sides, and delivers an address, in which she adverts
to the lofty origin of poesy.—Declares herself to be the goddess of
song, Calliope, and particularises the poets to whom she has been especial patroness.—Finally she seizes a harp, at whose sounds the
heavens cleared up, and a novel splendour illumined the earth.—She
sings the deeds of all illustrious Spanish bards, with some specifications to the extent of one hundred and ten stanzas of eight lines
each.—At the close, the burning element, whose flames had diverged,
reunited, and the nymph disappeared in the awful blaze.—Telesio
descants on the immortality of the soul, and the good which lives
after we are interred. — Exhorts the multitude to return to their
homes, treasuring the memory of what the muse had inculcated.—
Adjourn to the streamlet of Palms.—On the suggestion of Aurelio,
Erastro awakened his rebeck, and Arsindo his pipe, and lending a
hand to Elicio, he ventured on a dithyrambic ode, which was followed by Marsilio, in an equally impassioned mood.—This fired up
Erastro who added to the harmony.—Crisio's love state impels him
to give vent to his feelings.—Damon and Lauso, bringing up the
rear, so that in broken air trembling, the wild music floats.—Galatea's voice could not be suppressed, and the general chorus was completed by the exquisite singing of Nisida and Belisa.—Meeting at the
palms.—Aurelio proposes efforts of wit, riddles, conundrums, &c.,
himself giving the example.—The rest followed, and there is as much
wit displayed in propounding as unravelling riddles.—A sudden
sound is heard on Tagus' banks, and two swains are seen to hold
down a young shepherd, who attempted suicide by drowning ; it was
Galercio, brother of Artidoro.—Teolinda addresses Galatea.—A piece
of paper falls from the bosom of the suicide, which was placed on a
tree to dry.—Gelasia's cruelty was the cause of the sad attempt.—
She sings some verses with marked apathy.—Lenio also recites
verses.—Galatea inquires about Artidoro, on which some explanation
ensues.—Teolinda melts in tears.—Songs of Galercio to Gelasia.—
Interlocution of Thirsis and Elicio.—Galatea disconcerted at her
friend's farewell.—Letter of Galatea to Elicio, and his reply, which
was entrusted to Maurisa.—Swains propose addressing Galatea's
father about the forced marriage of his daughter.—Elicio's song. —
In the morning Elicio receives his friends.—They agree, if Aurelio
did not consent to revoke his decree respecting Galatea's marriage,
that they would use violence to counterwork it, for they could not

GALATEA.

BOOK I.

1. WHILST to the sorrowful and mournful plaints,
   Of the too ill assorted sound of my set strain,
   In bitter echo of the exhausted breast
   Reply the mountains, meadows, plain and stream.
   To deaf and hasty winds complaints we throw
   Which from the burning and the frigid breast
   Arise to my discomfort—asking in vain
   Aid from the stream, the hill, meadow and plain.

2. Augment the humour of my wearied eyes,
   The water of this stream, and of this mead
   The variegated flowers brambles are
   And thorns, which in my soul entrance have found.
   The lofty mount lists not to my *ennui*,
   The very plains are wearied with the same;
   Not e'en a slight cessation of my pain
   Is found in mount, in plain, in mead or rill.

3. I thought the flame which in my soul awakes
The winged boy—the noose with which he binds—
The subtle net wherewith the gods he takes,
The fury and the vigour of his shaft,
Which would offend, as it offended me.
And me subjects to one who unequal is—
But 'gainst a soul which is of marble framed,
Nor net, nor fire, noose, arrow compass can.

4. Yet in a fire I burn and am consumed,
And round my neck I meekly place the noose,
Fearing but little the invisible net,
The shaft's dread vigour gives me no alarm,
To such extremity am I arrived for this,
To such a grief, a misadventure such,
That for my glory and my solace too
I bear the net, the arrow, noose and fire.

Thus sang Elicio, a shepherd, on the banks of the Tagus, to whom Nature had been as liberal as fortune, and love had been wanting, although the course of time, the consumer and restorer of all human actions, had brought him to a crisis, in which his wish had placed him on account of the incomparable beauty of Galatea, one without an equal, as shepherdess, born in the same coasts; and although she had been educated in rustic and pastoral exercises, yet was she so exalted in intelligence that discreet women, brought up in royal palaces and used to the judicious conduct of a court, considered themselves fortunate to resemble her in discretion as well as beauty, by reason of the many and rich gifts with which heaven had adorned Galatea.

She was beloved, and with a sincere earnestness, too, by many shepherds and herdsmen, who fed their flocks on Tagus' banks.

Among these the gay Elicio presumed to solicit her with a pure and anxious love such as the virtue and propriety of Galatea allowed.

We must not infer that Galatea disregarded Elicio, or that she actually loved him, for sometimes as one overwhelmed by his many services, with an honest zeal she raised him upwards, and again, without rendering reason, she would so neglect him that the enamoured shepherd could scarce comprehend his lot. The good qualities of Elicio were not to be despised—neither were the beauty, grace and goodness of Galatea not to be loved.

In fine, Galatea did not reject Elicio, nor could Elicio, nor ought he, nor wished he, to forget Galatea. It seemed to Galatea that as Elicio showed her so much preference it would be excess of ingratitude if she did not requite his honest thoughts. Elicio concluded, since Galatea did not disdain his services, that his desires tended to a favourable issue ; and when these thoughts reanimated hope, he was so content and emboldened in himself, that a thousand times he wished to disclose to Galatea what he with such difficulty had concealed.

But the perspicacity of Galatea detected in the motions of his countenance what Elicio contained in his soul, and she evinced such condescension that the words of the enamoured shepherd congealed in his mouth, and he remained in the joy alone of a first motion, though it appeared to him that he had done an injury to her, even to treat of what might not have the semblance of rectitude.

With these downright (antibaxos) strokes of his life the shepherd passed it so uncomfortable that he thought even the loss of her might be a gain, instead of feeling what had caused his miscarriage.

So one day, having reviewed his sentiments variously, and being in a delightful meadow, invited by solitude, and the murmurs of a brawling brook which through it ran, drawing from his scrip a polished rebeck, whereby he communicated his plaints to heaven, at the top of his voice he sang the sequent verses :—

> 1. Amorous thought
> If you appreciate yourself as mine,
> Move with such an air
> That no coyness humble you ;
> Or contentment make you proud.
> Secure a mean, if you find yourself
> Capable of such constancy—
> Fly not joy,
> Much less close the gate
> To the grief which love imparts

2. If you wish that of my life
 The career finish not,
 Remove it not so ashamed.
 Or raise it where it hopes not,
 Let there be death in the fall.
 This vain presumption
 In two things it will stop—
 One in thy destruction,
 The other that your heart
 Will pay for these doubts.

3. From it wert thou born, and in birth
 Thou sinnest, and it paid itself—
 Thou fliest it, and if I pretend
 To gather you up in it even a little,
 I do not reach you, or understand
 This dangerous flight
 Whereby you mount to heaven—
 Unless thou art fortunate
 There will be lodged on the soil
 My ease and thy repose.

4. Thou wilt say who well employs himself
 And delivers himself to chance,
 That it is not possible he
 Of such an opinion be madly judged
 From the sprightliness in which it is arrayed
 In that lofty occasion
 There is a glory without equal,
 In holding such presumption—
 And the more so if it agree
 With the soul and the heart.

5. So I understand it,
 But I would undeceive you,
 Which is a sign of boldness,
 To have less part in love
 Than the humble and bashful,
 You rise behind a beauty
 Which cannot be greater—
 I understand not your capacity
 Which can hold love
 With so much inequality.

6. But if a thought verges
   Towards an exalted subject,
   Contemplate it, and it withdraws itself,
   Not being assured
   As to its touching a point so high;
   Much more is love born
   Joined with confidence,
   And in it feeds and banquets.
   When hope fails
   It vanishes like a cloud..

7. Then thou who seest so far
   Into the core of what thou **desirest**,
   Hopeless, yet constant
   If in this career you die
   You will drain ignorance,
   But nothing comes of it
   In this amorous enterprise
   Whence the cause is sublimated,
   Death is an honourable life,
   And suffering extreme joy.

Scarce had ceased the agreeable song of Elicio, when the voice of Erastro sounded on his right hand side; he, with his flocks of goats, had settled in that place.

Erastro was a rustic shepherd, yet did not his rusticity and wild lot so far prevail as to prevent the entrance of love into his hardy breast, there to take up possession; having sought more than his very life the beauteous Galatea, to whom he proffered his court when occasion presented. Though a very rustic, yet was he a true lover, and so discreet in all lovers' ways, that when he discoursed thereon it would seem that Love himself appeared, and through his tongue gave utterance. Nevertheless with all this, for Galatea heard all, stories of diversion abounded.

The rivalry of Erastro gave Elicio no pain, for he understood from the wit of Galatea that she aspired to higher things rather than pity and envy towards Erastro. Pity in observing that at last he loved, and that it was not possible to reap the fruit of his wishes. Envy in appearing, perhaps, that he had no such understanding as would give way to a soul which would feel the disdain or favours of Galatea, so that some might terminate, and some drive him frantic. Erastro approached, with his dogs, the faithful guardian of his simple sheep, who, under his protection, were secure from the fleshy teeth of hungry wolves, rejoicing in them, and calling them by their names, giving to each such a title as each merited. One he styled Lion, another Hawk. This was termed the strong, that the spotted, while they, as if endued with reason, by moving their heads on approach, reciprocated the feeling which they had evoked.

So came Erastro, and by Elicio agreeably received, was also interrogated if in any other part he had determined to pass the sultry season, as all was ready for him should it not be disagreeable to him to pass it in his company. "With no one could I pass it better than with you, Elicio, were she not as hardened to my requests as is an entire grove of oaks to my complaints (si ya ni fuese con aquella que es-ta tan enrobrescida á mis demandas, quan hecha encina á tus continuos quexidos)."

Immediately the two sat them down on the small grass, while their flocks rambled at will, eating the tops of the tender herbs of the grassy plain, with their cud-chewing teeth. And as Erastro, by many recognised signs, knew clearly that Elicio loved Galatea, and that the merit of Elicio was of many more carats in value than his own; in token that he admitted this fact in the midst of his talk, among other reasons he put to him the following remarks—

"I know not, gallant and amorous Elicio, if the love I bear to Galatea has been the cause of annoyance to you, and if so, pardon me, for I never intended any harm, nor did I request aught of Galatea but permission to serve her.

"A madness and foul disease consumes and affects my wanton kids and my tender lambkins. When they quit the udder of their beloved mothers they find not herbs enough to support them, but bitter *tueras* and venomous oleanders.

"And I have tried a thousand times to blot it from my memory, and oft have been to doctors to seek remedies for my solicitude, and the cause for which I suffer. Some order all sorts of love potions, others commend me to heaven, which cures all disorders, and say that is a madness only.

"Suffer me, good Elicio, that I request you, since you are

sure that if you, with your skill and extreme grace and intelligence, cannot assuage my ills, much less can I soften them with my simplicity. This licence I beg, and am in debt to your desert, for should you not give it to me, it would be as impossible to cease living as it would be for water not to moisten, or the sun with its well-combed locks not to illuminate us."

I cannot help laughing, Elicio, at the reasons of Erastro, and at the politeness with which he asks to love Galatea—and thus he replied :—

"It does me no harm, Erastro, that you love Galatea. Your condition afflicts me, for which your reason and unfeigned words can effect nothing.

"May heaven aid your wishes in proportion as you have sincerity in them, and henceforth you will not find in me any obstacle to your loving Galatea, for I am not in so forlorn a condition but I can find occasion for my purposes.

"On the contrary, I request you by what you owe to the goodwill I evince towards you, that you deny me not your conversation and friendship, for as far as I am concerned, you are quite safe. Let our heads and our ideas coalesce.

"Then, by the sound of my pipe will be announced pleasure or pain, according as the gay or sorrowful countenance of Galatea directs.

"I with my rebeck in the soft stilly night or evening during the heat of the *siesta* in the fresh shade of green trees wherewith our banks are adorned, I will try to remove the heavy charge of your toils, by giving notice to heaven of my own.

"And in virtue of my proposition, and my sincere friendship, whilst the shades of these trees become wider, and the sun westward declines, let us unite our instruments, and really begin the exercises which henceforth we must entertain."

Scarce had this proposal been made, than with an indication of extreme content at discovering so much friendship in Elicio, that he brought forth his pipe, and Elicio his rebeck, whilst one responding to the other, they sang as follows :—

ELICIO.

1. Blandly, sweetly, reposedly,
   Ungrateful love, that day you subjected me,
   When the rays of gold, and the noble front
   Of the sun I contemplated, which the sun obscured—
   Thou cruel solace, like the serpent
   Concealed in the ruddy tangles of the thicket,
   I who came to view the sun in masses,
   Came too to imbibe his rays through my eyes.

ERASTRO.

2. Astonished I remained, and appalled,
   As a hard rock, voiceless,
   When of Galatea the extreme
   Courtesy I beheld—her grace, her beauty,
   On my left side Love settled,
   With his arrows of gold (oh hard death)
   Making a door whereby might enter
   Galatea, and my soul surprise.

ELICIO.

3. By what miracle, Love, openest thou the breast,
   Of the wretched lover who pursues thee ;
   And the inward wound which thou hast made,
   An increase of glory thou shewest to him who follows—
   How is the ill thou makest a provision ?
   How in thy death lives joyous life,
   How the soul which experiences such results ?
   The cause is known, the manner rests unknown.

ERASTRO.

4. One sees not so many countenances displayed
   In a broken mirror, or framed by art ;
   If we look and see ourselves reflected,
   We discern a multitude in each and every part.
   How many cares on cares arise
   All from one cruel care which will not
   From my soul—o'ercome by its own rigour,
   Until it separate in union with existence.

ELICIO.

5. The driven snow and coloured rose,
   Which e'en the summer destroys not, or the winter,

The sun of two morning stars, where reposes
Soft love, and where eternally will dwell
The voice as that of Orpheus, all powerful
To suspend the rage of Hell.
And other things to see, tho' blind,
Have furnished me with aliment for an invisible fire.

ERASTRO.

6. Two beauteous apples, beauteous in colour,
Such seem to me two cheeks
And the arches of two raised eyebrows.
Such wonders as never Iris reached.
Two rays, two extraordinary threads,
Of pearls, 'twixt scarlet, as if one may say
A thousand graces which have no equal
Have infused o'er me a loving gale.

ELICIO.

7. I burn, yet consume I not; I live and die,
Far am I from myself, yet near.
On one thing only do I hope, and yet despair—
Heaven I ascend, and yet the abyss descend.
I love that I hate—meek and yet fierce.
Love engenders paroxysms,
And with contrarieties, by degrees
My latest agonies do I approach.

ERASTRO.

8. I promised you, Elicio, I would tell you
All that in my life is left
To Galatea, that she may return to me,
My heart and soul, which she has robbed me of.
And after the flock, I would join
My dog, Hawk, to the spotted one.
And as she must be a goddess,
The soul will require her above all things.

ELICIO.

9. Erastro, the heart which in exaltations,
Is doomed by fate, or lot, or not,
To desire its overthrow by force or art;
Oh, human diligence is madness—
One should be content with their lot—

For tho' one die without it, I imagine
There is in this world no happier life
Than for a cause so sacred thus to die.

Whilst Erastro was preparing to pursue his song in succession, and they were seated by a steep mountain which lay at their shoulders, they heard a no slight voice and rush, and both getting on their feet to see what was the matter, they saw that from the mountain a shepherd issued, at a smart running pace, with a naked weapon in his hand, and his colour quite changed; and behind him came another shepherd who overtook the first, who seizing him by the hair of his skin garment, raised his arm as high as he could and dealt him a blow, burying the weapon twice in his body, saying, " Take this, O wretched Leonida, the life of this traitor, which in vengeance I sacrifice for thy death ;" and this was effected with such despatch that neither Elicio nor Erastro could prevent it, for they just arrived as the stricken shepherd exhaled his last breath, embarrassed by these few and ill-arranged words :—

" You will let me satisfy, O Lisandro, heaven with a repentance more exemplary than the wrong I did you, and then you will take my life, which now for the reason I have stated, ill at ease with the flesh, separates from it ;" and so without power to add more, he closed his eyes in eternal night.

From these words Elicio and Erastro inferred that the other shepherd had not perpetrated the signal and cruel murder without just cause. And the better to get information, they sought it from the homicide ; but he with retreating steps abandoning the dead shepherd, to the wonder of the two observers, turned back to regain the mountain. But Elicio desirous of pursuing him, to ascertain from him what he wanted, saw him sally out of the wood, and standing at some space from them, in a raised voice, said—" Pardon me, gentle shepherds, if I have not been in your presence what you sought to have seen, because a just and mortal anger which I entertained against the traitor would not let me exercise more moderate discourse. What I suggest is, if you would not irritate the Deity who dwells in highest heaven, that you should not carry out the obsequies and accustomed rites in favour of the traitorous soul of that body which you have before you—or even give it sepulture, if it is not customary to bury traitors in your country." This finished, he turned round at full speed to regain the mountain, so that Elicio lost all hope of overtaking him, however he tried. Hence the twain, with bowels yearning, returned to perform the pious office, and give burial as best they could to the wretched corse, which had just completed its short existence. Erastro went to his cabin hard by, and collecting sufficient implements, made a grave in the same place where the body lay, and giving a parting adieu, they lodged the body in it.

And not without compassion for these sorrowful affairs, they returned to their flocks, re-collecting them in haste, and the sun being on the point of going down, they repaired to their usual lodgings, where, despite anxiety and retirement, nothing could prevent Elicio from meditating on the motives which had impelled the two shepherds to come to such a desperate encounter; grieving he had not effectually pursued the homicide and had ascertained from him what he desired. Imbued with this thought, and more which love had awakened, having left his flock in security, he issued from his cabin, as his wont was, and in the radiance of the beauteous Diana, which appeared in the sky, he rushed into the thick of a wood to seek some solitary spot, where in the silence of the moon with great tranquillity he might give rein to his amorous fancies, it being a fact that solitude is the great awakener of reminiscences joyful or sorrowful. So moving gently on, in the fruition of a mild zephyr which met his face, replete with the fragrant smell of flowers which were concentrated there, and thus passing through them, enshrouded in a delicious robe of air, he heard a noise as if from one in deep anguish, and holding his breath awhile that the noise should not interrupt the sound, he perceived there to issue from some closely pressed brambles which lay adjacent, a very lugubrious voice, and though interwoven with deep sighs, he understood what was enunciated :—

" Cowardly, yet daring arm, mortal enemy to your own self-respect ; see now how nothing is left to take vengeance, but yourself. To what use the protraction of an abhorred life ? If you think our ill is one which time can remedy you are deceived; for there is no remedy more remote from cure than our own misfortune. For he who could have done it good, found life so short, that in his tender years he offered it to the fatal knife, which took it on account of the treachery of the wicked Carino. This had in part appeased the soul of Leonida, if she dwells in heavenly mansions, and retains a lust of vengeance.

" Ah, Carino, Carino, I appeal to you in the heavens, if just complaints are there heard—that they admit no extenuation, if you advance any for the treachery you have practised on me, and that they permit your body to lie unburied, even as your soul was wanting in mercy.

" And thou, beauteous and ill-attained Leonida, receive as the token of the love I bore you in life, the tears which for your death I shed, and ascribe it to no slight feeling my not parting with my life, such as I felt for your death; a small recompense as to what I owe and ought to feel is the grief which ends so briefly. You will see, if you observe, how this afflicted body will one day perish gradually of woe, for its greater affliction and sensibility—like to moistened and illumined powder, which devoid of noise or flame, consumes itself, without leaving aught save the track of burnt ashes.

" Grieve as much as possible, O, soul of my soul, that I cannot enjoy you in life, or perform thy obsequies, or do justice to your goodness and virtue. Still I promise and swear that the little time—and short it is to be—that this, my impassioned soul, may moisten the heavy charge of this miserable body, and the exhausted voice retain the breath which supports it, to treat of nothing in my doleful and bitter ditties but thy praises and merits."

At this juncture the voice ceased, by which Elicio clearly defined it to be the voice of the homicide, at which he was glad to think that he could at length learn what he had so desired from him; and being anxious to advance nearer, he turned to stop, as it seemed to him that the shepherd gently made a rebeck speak, and he wished, first, to listen if she should also answer to it. Delay was not long, when, with a melodious and well-adjusted voice, he heard the sequent strains—

LISANDRO.

1. Ah ! adventurous soul,
Which, from a human veil,
Free flies, full of life, to the lofty region ;
Leaving in the dark
Dungeon of discomfort
My life—though it goes with thee—
Without thee, dark hast thou left
The clear light of day.
To earth beat down
The well-founded hope
In the more firm seat of joy ;
In fine, with your flight
Grief remained quick ; life was death.

2. Involved in thy spirits,
Death has seized
The excess of beauty—
The light of those eyes
Which seen in thee
Continued riches enclosed,
With the ready lightness
Of lofty thought,
And the enamoured breast,
Glory is dissolved
Like wax before the sun, or clouds the winds.
And all my venture
The stone of my grave shuts up.

3. How could the hand,
Inexorable and savage,
And the intent cruel, wicked,
Of brother's vengeance
Leave free and destitute
My soul of beauteous mortal veil ?
Why disturb the repose
Of our hearts ?
Which could we not accomplish it,
Or be joined
In honest and holy ties.
Ah ! cruel hand, disdainful ;
How hast thou ordained that living I should die ?

4. In eternal grief,
   My wretched soul,
   Years will pass, months and days;
   While age, firm and lasting,
   Will not dread
   The obstinacy of time.
   With sweet delights
   Wilt thou see the glory fixed,
   Of which thy commendable life
   Finds thee so worthy.
   If in thy memory thou canst hold her,
   And not lose her from earth.
   Thou shouldest preserve her
   Whom I so much adore.

5. But how simple have I been,
   Blessed and pure soul,
   To ask that you remember
   Not even joking me
   Who have so much
   Desired you.
   Now know I that my complaint
   Will go on in favours, eternising itself;
   Better is it that thinking
   I am of thee forgotten.
   My wound presses me;
   Make it so to slacken
   With the grief which is
   Yet left in life,
   With such excess of ill lot,
   That death itself no ill considered is.

6. Rejoice in holy chorus,
   With other holy spirits,
   O soul, in that ever-during
   Security.
   Lofty, rich treasure,
   Rewards, thanks, so many,
   That it rejoices not to eschew
   The good path
   There I hope to enjoy.
   If I am conducted by thy steps,

With thee in the entire peace
Of eternal spring.
Without alarm, surprise, or deviation,
To this it leads me.
Then will it be a deed
Worthy thy works ;
Then you celestial souls
Regard the good I covet,
And to so good desire enlarge the wings.

Thus ceased the voice, but not the sighs, of the unfortunate man who had just sung, and both were stimulants to extend the wish to ascertain who he was.

So, bursting through the spiny brambles, to ascertain the exact spot whence the sound issued, he abutted on a little meadow like a theatre, surrounded by thick and intricate shrubs, wherein he espied a shepherd, who, in a state of excitement, stood with his foot advanced, and the left hand behind, and the right raised as if to make a cast. This was truly so, for the noise Elicio had made in struggling through the bushes, thinking it to be some wild animal, from which shepherds must defend themselves, he adjusted himself to throw a heavy stone, which he held in his hand. Elicio, perceiving his object from his position, before he effected it, said :—"Assuage your breast, wretched herdsman, for he who comes brings his provision to do what you require, and the desire of learning your misfortune has moved him to tears, though it may destroy the case, which, being alone, it may secure to you." With these mild and polite words, Elicio calmed the hind, who, with no less blandness, replied, saying, "I accept your kind offer, whomsoever thou art, gentle shepherd ; but if, by chance, you would know what I have never revealed, you may remain unsatisfied." "You speak truth," answered Elicio, "but for the words and complaints which this night I have heard you indicate clearly that you are not deeply afflicted ; still, you shall not the less satisfy my wishes by telling me your hardships, and declare to me your contentment also, and thus I give you up to fortune, and trust you will not deny me what I solicit, unless your not knowing me restrains ; although, to assure you, and to move you, I vow I have not a soul so content as

not to feel the misery you should recount to me.   This I say
because I know there is nothing more excusable and yet
baneful than for the wretch to recapitulate his woes to one
who overflows with placid content."

"Your excellent reasons oblige me," rejoined the hind,
"that I should satisfy you; yet do not imagine that these
complaints arise from a pusillanimous soul (which you have
just heard), though I may be reluctant to divulge them."

At this Elicio rejoiced, and after some reciprocal politeness, Elicio giving tokens of his being a real friend of the
shepherd, and he recognising a friendly intent, was induced
to acquiesce in what Elicio had asked.

Hence both sat on the soil, Diana reflecting on them the
rays which rivalled those of her brother; then the hind,
with evidence of deep emotion, thus began his narrative—

"On the banks of the Betis, mighty river, which enriches
the vast Vandalia, was born Lisandro (for that is my unfortunate name), and of noble parentage, as it pleased heaven,
though I might have been the offspring of a humbler stock.
Oft nobleness of lineage supplies wings and power to the
soul to elevate her eyes beyond where humble lot has cast
it, and of such boldness succeed similar calamities with
what you shall hear, if with attention you listen.   In the
same hamlet was also born a shepherdess, by name Leonida,
the paragon of beauty, and sucq as the world rarely produces, and of a birth correspondent in nobility with her
beauty and virtue.   It came to pass that both parents, being
the principals of the locality in whom resided the government that envy, the mortal enemy of tranquillity, on some
differences came to a quarrel, and even a mortal strife, so
that the inhabitants were divided into two sects, one following mine, the other her parents, and with such rooted
rancour and bad spirit, that no human interposition sufficed
to allay its venom.   Fate decreed, as if to throw off all
prospect of restoration to amity, that I should fall violently
in love with the handsome Leonida, daughter of Parmindro,
head of the opposite faction.   Such was my love, though I
adopted all means to detach it from me, that I fell prostrate
before it.   A mountain of difficulties uprose, which prevented the execution of my desires, such as the opposition
of Leonida, the inveterate hatred of our parents, the few

opportunities, or rather the absence of them; and withal, when I added the eyes of imagination to the rare beauty of Leonida, some difficulty was eased off, so that I thought I might pare away the sharp corners of the diamond, facets as it were, to touch my amorous and honest thoughts. Having combated with myself some days to see if I could divert my mind from the attempt, and seeing it to be hopeless, I gathered up all my industry, to find means of conveying to her the secret of my breast—but as all beginnings are difficult, those of love exceed in that, until it, when it desires to prove favourable, opens a remedy where all access seems intercepted; thus did it appear in my case. Still guided by my own cogitations, I concluded that no better medium did contribute to my hope than that of establishing an acquaintance with the parents of Silvia, a shepherdess and firm friend of Leonida, who unitedly visited the village cottages.

Now Silvia had a relative styled Carino, a close companion of Crisalvo, brother to the dear Leonida, whose whimsical manner and asperity had earned for him the reputation of cruel, and so was he accounted by all who knew him, and not the less so by Carino, Silvia's relative, a companion of Crisalvo, who, from being a sort of compound, and very acute, she gave the *sobriquet* of sharp, with whom, and with Silvia (as it served my purpose), by means of little gifts and dainties, I founded a friendship in appearance at least, so on Silvia's side it became deeper than I desired, for the presents she had received from me my ill-fortune converted to my present wretchedness.

Now this maiden was of rare beauty, and with such gracefulness, that even the savage heart of Crisalvo was melted to love, and this I found to my discomfort, for in some days after, and relying on Silvia's freedom, an opportunity arising in my tenderest accents, I disclosed the nature of my wounds, adding that being both profound and dangerous, I trusted to find in her some solace for them, averring how honourable were my professions, my purpose being marriage with the lovely Leonida—hence I inferred that she would deign to take my case into her keeping.

In fine, to avoid prolixity, love suggested such terms that being convinced thereby, and more by the sufferings I underwent than evidence in my face, she courteously took charge of my love affairs and offered to communicate my feelings, promising to superadd all she could realise as to my wishes, despite the difficulty arising from the hostility of our parents, which, however, might be extinguished by this union.

Moved by this good feeling, and softened by the tears I shed, as heretofore related, she ventured to be my advocate, and inquiring what method she would adopt with Leonida, she ordered me to write a note which she would present at the earliest opportunity.

This seemed very acceptable, and that same day I sent one, which being the result of my agreeable interview with her, I committed to memory, though I cannot revert to it now in the hour of my grief. Silvia got the note, and I waited a moment to deliver it to Leonida. "No," said Elicio, stopping the reasons of Lisandro; "it is not right that you let me omit mention of the note you sent to Leonida—as being the first, and finding you so smitten at that time, it should have been discreet—and since you admit to me that you have it in remembrance, and the joy you have experienced, you will not refuse to declare it to me." You say well, my friend, that I was then as deep in love as I am now in discontent and despair, so that I seemed not to desire to say aught, though Leonida assured he gave credence to all which the note contained. If you are studious to know its contents, this is a version of it :—

LISANDRO TO LEONIDA.—" Whilst I was capable (though with extreme sorrow) of resisting, with my own faculties, the amorous flame which I entertained for thee, O lovely Leonida, it consumed me. I have never been bold enough, respecting the exalted courage which I recognise in you, to reveal to you the love I bear you. Not the less is that virtue consumed which till now has made me bold, and I have been constrained to discover my wound, and to try writing as the first and last remedy. What may be the first you know, and the second dwells in your hand, whence I hope to realise what your compassion promises and my honest desires merit. What they are, and the end they aim at, you will learn by Silvia, who will deliver this to you—and as she has undertaken to do so, know they are just in proportion to your deservings."

This epistolary effusion of Lisandro did not appear ill-timed to Elicio, who prosecuting the narrative of his loves, said—"A few days only and that identical note reached the lily-white hands of Leonida by the compassionate agency of Silvia my constant friend, who, in her commission, introduced things which in a great measure tempered the anger and change which the letter had produced in Leonida, suggesting as a consequence of marriage that the family feud might end, and that the object should be not to reject the suit—the more so as one could not compassionate her beauty, or die without respect to one who loved her as I did, adding other reasons with which Leonida was acquainted."

But not to let it be thought she surrendered at the first assault and that all was finished at the first advance, she gave not so agreeable a response to Silvia as she desired. However by the intercession of Silvia to which she forced her, she did reply as follows :—

LEONIDA TO LISANDRO—"Should I understand, Lisandro, that your temerity arose from a defect of propriety in myself, would I execute the punishment I deserve, so to be assured of this from what I know of myself, I think your boldness proceeds more from ill-balanced thoughts than love—and though they be as you allege, do not think your advances to me can alleviate them, as Silvia would insinuate, for I complain of being induced to reply to you, as well as of your assurance in writing to me ; silence had been the fittest reply. If you withdraw from what you have commenced you will act discreetly, for I would have you to know that I count more on my own honour than on your vanities."

This was the reply of Leonida, which, united to the hopes which Silvia imparted, though somewhat indefinite, made me conclude myself amongst the most fortunate of my sex.

Pending these transactions, Crisalvo was not deficient in soliciting Silvia by various messages, presents, and services, but his bearing was rough and untutored that he could extort not the smallest favour, from which circumstance he lost all patience, and resembled a bull vanquished and fretted with cruel darts (agarrochado)—on account of his loves he had established a friendship with the cunning

Carino, Silvia's relative,—from being a mortal enemy owing to a certain wrestling match they had one feast day before the whole village, at which many lusty Swains attended, when Crisalvo got down Carino and ill-treated him, which gave rise to a perpetual enmity, and not a less one was entertained also against my other brother, for opposing him in his amours, and carrying from him the fruits which Carino expected. This rancour and settled ill-will Carino concealed till time favoured him with an opportunity to avenge himself on both through the means of a very cruel artifice. He was my friend—for the admission to Silvia's house was no impediment—Crisalvo loved him that he might advance his suit with Silvia, and such was the amity, that whenever Leonida visited Silvia, Carino was a companion—on which account it seemed good to Silvia, being my friend, to avow the love which I entertained for Leonida, which went on then so briskly by the intervention of Silvia that time and place alone were wanting to cull the fruit of our immaculate desires, the which being known to Carino, he chose me as instrument for a disgraceful treason. For one day (playing the loyal with Crisalvo and infusing into him an idea that he more highly prized his friendship than the honour of his parentage) he said to him that the principal cause why Silvia neither loved nor encouraged him was from her being enamoured of me, and of that he was convinced; and that now as our loves were known, that had he not been blinded by passion he had discovered it by a thousand signs—and, to certify the more what he averred, that henceforth he should look to him, because he plainly perceived that without any impediment, she accorded to me unusual favours. On this representation Crisalvo became furious, as it seemed he was by what ensued. From this juncture Crisalvo employed spies to observe what took place between Silvia and me, and as I had frequent cause to be alone with her, not on account of love for her, but for that which related to my own interests, these were assumed by Crisalvo as being favours which arose from pure friendship, and which Silvia offered to me. Hence the indignation of Crisalvo attained such a point that often he essayed to kill me, as I thought, not on account of love matters but by reason of the ancient family enmity.

/ Seeing, however, he was Leonida's brother, I took great care not to offend him, knowing for certain, if I married his sister, our opposition would cease. This he regarded not, he even thought that I malevolently courted Silvia to spite him and not for love. The end was that he lost his reason from annoyance and rage, though he was scarce a reasonable being, and there needed no great effort to consume all he had—and it drove him so far out that he began to detest Silvia in an inverse ratio with his former predilection for her, because of her presumed preference for me, as he averred; so in whatsoever company he was he jeered Silvia and gave her ugly epithets. The world, however, knowing his intractableness and Silvia's blandness, it all went into thin air. Such being the case, Silvia concerted with Leonida that both should wed, and to effect it nicely that one day Leonida should come with Carino to a certain house, and not return to her parents' house that night, and that with Carino she should repair to a hamlet some half league off, where some of my rich relatives dwelt, in whose house with greater quiet the affair might be consummated. For if in the event the parents of Leonida were not satisfied, at least, she being away, the plan would be easiest to accomplish. This appointment arranged, and notice given to Carino, he offered with much cheerfulness to remove the willing Leonida to the other hamlet.

The services I did for Carino out of pure good will, the words of kindness I uttered, the embraces which I gave him, one had supposed had quenched in a heart of steel all covert ill-feeling. Yet did this traitor Carino, turning his back on my kindness, efforts, and promises, regardless of what he owed me, conceive the treason which I will recount. \ Carino being cognisant of the wish of Leonida, and seeing it to be in conformity with that of Silvia, planned on the first approach of darkness, how he should undertake to conduct Leonida in as secret and honourable a way as possible. After this concert which you have heard, he went to Crisalvo as I since learned, and he told him that his relative Silvia was so forward in her amours with me, that on a certain night he had determined to force her from her parent's house, and remove her to another village where my parents dwelt, and where he might perpetrate vengeance on both;

on Silvia for the little respect she had to his services, on me for the ancient enmity and the disgust I had caused in drawing him from Silvia. Hence Carino learned to cajole and say what he pleased, and with a heart cruel as his own, induced bad thoughts in him. The day having arrived which I deemed to be most to my content, failing to tell Carino not what he had done, but what he ought to do, I went to the other hamlet to give orders how to receive Leonida— and it was recommended to Carino to leave her as a poor simple lamb is left to hungry wolves, or a gentle dove in the claws of a fierce hawk who would tear it in pieces. Ah friend! at this point of imagination, I know not how to collect force to sustain life, or thought to reflect on it, much less language to express it. Oh evil-counselled Lisandro! Know you not the double conditions which bound Carino? But who would trust to words which were not reinforced by deeds? woe to thee ill attained Leonida—what evil have I touched by your preference of me. In fine, to end with the tragedy of my disgrace, know thou, discreet shepherd, that the night which Carino set aside for the abduction of Leonida to the village where I expected her, he called to another shepherd, who was an enemy, though he concealed his aversion under his accustomed dissimulation, whose name was Libeo, and asked him to be his companion that night, for that he resolved to abduct a shepherdess, so attractive, to the hamlet which I told you of, where he trusted to make her his wife. Libeo, both gallant and amorous, made no objection to become his companion. Leonida dismissed Silvia with tumultuous clasps and loving tears, as presuming this to be the last farewell. She should then have reflected on the treason against her parents, and not what Carino had arranged, and how bad an account of her was rife in the village. Now passing over all these thoughts, and impelled by the love which overcame her, she surrendered herself to the custody of Carino, and that he would bear her whither I expected. How oft does it recur to my memory, at this point, what I dreamed that day, which I had thought most lucky, if in it I had closed my existence! I remember that quitting the village a little ere the sun departed from our horizon, I found myself at the foot of an ash tree on the very spot that Leonida should pass, expecting that the night would close in to advance my object and to receive her, not knowing how, I fell asleep—and scarcely surrendering my eyes to that influence, it seemed to me that the tree against which I leaned, yielding to the fury of a stiff wind which blew, deracinating the deep roots from the earth, it fell on my body, and trying to elude the heavy weight, I rolled from side to side. So standing in this predicament, I imagined that I saw a white deer close by, to whom I offered supplications that as well as it could it might avert from me the impending danger; and while soliciting the animal to be moved by compassion, at the same instant a fierce lion rushed from the wood, and seizing the deer with his sharp claws took it off into the thicket, and now that by a heavy labour having escaped, I went to seek the deer in the mountain, and there found her mangled and rent into a thousand pieces, whereon such grief seized me that my soul was shocked by reason of the compassion the deer had evinced towards me, so that in my sleep I wept sore, and the tears awakened me. Perceiving my cheeks to be tinged with moisture, I was beside myself, when I reflected on what I had dreamed; yet was the hope of seeing Leonida so high, that I considered my dream but as a stroke of fate, which awaking I should realise. When I opened my eyes, night began to close in all its darkness, and with such thunder and lightnings, as to facilitate the horrors which were to be transacted in it. As Carino issued from the house of Silvia with Leonida, he delivered her to Libeo, ordering him to accompany her to the village I mentioned, and as Leonida was surprised to see Libeo, Carino declared that he was no less my friend than his, and with all security she could go with him until he gave me news of their arrival. The simple then enamoured one believed the words of the false Carino, and with less mistrust than was judicious, conducted by the plausible Libeo, continued her steps to her destruction, hoping only to find satisfaction. Carino advanced from the two, as I said, and reported to Crisalvo what had occurred, and what with the other four relatives on the same road took place, and all were surrounded on every side by wood, and remained concealed, and told them how Silvia came up, and that I alone accompanied her, and that they should rejoice at the good opportunity which fortune had put into their power to avenge themselves of the injury they had received, and that it would be on Silvia, though a relative, the first who should experience the edge of their steel. The five cruel butchers quickly appeared to dye themselves in the innocent blood of the pair, who without suspicion of a treason of such magnitude came that way, and having reached the point of ambush, the perfidious homicides fell on them and enclosed them. Crisalvo joined Leonida, mistaking her for Silvia, and with injurious and heated language, and beset by the hellish rage which mastered him, with six mortal stabs left her extended on the soil, at the same time that Libeo, with the four others, thinking it was on me they struck with reiterated slashes, reeled to earth. Carino, discerning how well his traitorous intent had succeeded, without asking questions, went off incontinently before them, and the five traitors in themselves content, as if they had enacted some valorous exploit, returned to the hamlet, and Crisalvo went to Silvia's house to inform the parents of the event to aggravate their grief and sensibility, saying they must now bury their daughter Silvia whose life he had taken, because she had paid more attention to the frigid solicitations of his enemy Lisando than to his repeated services. Silvia, who felt all that Crisalvo said, averred that she was still in being, and free from all imputation, but that she grieved at the murder no less than if it had been her own death ; and with this she told him that her sister Leonida had left the house that night in an unusual apparel. Crisalvo, surprised to see Silvia alive, fearing most assuredly she lay dead, with no slight bound made off for her house, and not finding there her sister, in the most profound confusion and rage returned alone to see who it was he had murdered, for Silvia it was not.

During the passage of these events I stood in extreme anxiety awaiting Carino and Leonida, and thinking them later than they should be, I desired to go out and find them, and to learn the cause of their delay that night. When I was not far on the road, a voice of woe struck my ear, saying, " Oh Sovereign Creator of Heaven, withdraw thy arm of justice, and open the fonts of mercy, in favour of the soul now about to render account of the offences it has offered to you !"

Ah, Lisandro, Lisandro, how will the friendship of Carino cost your life, since it is not possible that the grief of my having lost it for thee will end it. Oh cruel brother, that without hearing my exculpations, is it possible you would make me pay the penalty of my error?

When I heard this reasoning, by the voice I recognised directly that of Leonida, and the presage of my misfortune; and with this emotion I groped about to find where Leonida was involved in her own blood, and, discovering the spot, I fell immediately on her corpse in extremity of suffering, saying, "What woe is this, my beloved? Oh, my soul! what hand was it that respected not so much loveliness!" By these sounds I was recognised by Leonida, and raising with vast trouble her exhausted arms, I fixed them round my neck, and fastening them as best I could, joining her mouth to mine, with weak and ill-enunciated reasons, she spoke only thus to me—" My brother has slain me—Carino sold—Libeo is lifeless; may God give you, Lisandro mine, long and happy years, and permit me to enjoy in another life the repose which has been denied me here." And again joining her mouth to mine, having closed her lips to confer on me her first and last kiss, she re-opened them only to exhale her soul, and she was left dead in my arms. When I felt this, abandoning myself on the corpse, I remained motionless, and if I was yet alive it were as dead. Who seeing us in this predicament would not call to mind the woeful story of Pyramus and Thisbe? However, returning to my self-possession, I opened my mouth to fill the air with my lamentations and sighs, and I perceived some one advancing with quickened steps, and on his approach, though the night was obscure, the eyes of my soul gave me to understand that it was Crisalvo, and so it was. He turned round to certify if by chance it was Leonida his sister whom he had killed. So soon as I was sure it was him, and while he did not regard it, I fell on him like a wrathful lion, and giving him two wounds I heaved him to the earth, and before he breathed his last I dragged him where Leonida was, and putting in the dead hand of Leonida a dagger which her brother had, the same that murdered her, helping her to it, thrice was it plunged into his heart— and so, consoling myself with Crisalvo's death without delay, I took on my shoulders Leonida's body, and bore it to the village where her parents dwelt, and, recounting the mischance, solicited for the corpse honourable burial; and then I resolved to execute vengeance on Carino, as I had done on Crisalvo, and as that occurred by his absence from the village, my just wrath was delayed till I found him at the wood, though six months have intervened since the event, and now he has paid the price of his treason, and no longer further vengeance rests within me, save on myself, as against a life which I breathe unwillingly. This shepherd is the cause of the lamentations you have heard.　If it seems to you reason good for such sentiments, I leave them to your judgment.　And so he ended the discourse, and gave vent to such copious tears that Elicio could not restrain the flux of his own; but when in time the grief of one which oppressed him was mitigated and softened into sighs, and in the other the sense of compassion, Elicio began with the soundest reason to console Lisandro, though his grief was so far beyond counsel as its success had evinced, so that among other things he said to him, and what concurred with Lisandro's feelings, was, that ills without remedy should be without regard, and that from the very high and virtuous condition of Leonida it was to be believed that she had enjoyed a calm existence, and that one should rather rejoice at the good she had attained, than be wretched at what she had lost.

To this replied Lisandro—"I know your reason carries force enough with it to cause me to accept such conclusions, yet do neither they nor what the world could say, suffice to assuage me; with Leonida's decease begin my misfortunes, and these will cease not till I go to her, and since this can only be by my death, he who shall procure me that alternative will be my truest friend."　Elicio, however, did not wish to superinduce more mental anguish by his advice, though he did not so reckon them, only he adjured him to accompany him to his cabin, in which what he might wish would be found, proffering his friendship in aught that could serve him.　To this Lisandro agreed, and though he desired not to visit Elicio, yet he consented, swayed by his importunities.　Thus they both arose and wended towards Elicio's cabin, where they passed the remainder of the night.

Now when the brilliant Aurora had left the couch of her jealous husband, and gave tokens of the coming day, Erastro arose and commenced putting in order the cattle of Elicio and his own, to conduct them to their usual pasture. Elicio invited Lisandro to join him, and the three shepherds coming with the gentle flock of sheep to a watercourse below, on mounting one side they heard the sound of a dulcet pipe, which by the enamoured shepherds, Elicio and Erastro, was recognised for that of Galatea, and in brief space from the hill top they discerned some sheep, and near them Galatea herself, whose attractiveness was such that it were better to imagine it, as words were inadequate to do it justice. She came, vested in mountaineer's attire, with hair floating in the wind, so that Apollo might envy her, for casting his light on her, it was somewhat obscured, and the rays which darted from the obscuration represented another sun. Erastro was dumb with astonishment, nor could Elicio avert his eyes. Now, as Galatea saw the flocks of Elicio and Erastro were blended with hers, evinced no disposition to continue with them all that day, she called to the tender ewe-lamb in her hand, and to the others which followed behind, to go to another part, where the shepherds were not. Hence Elicio, seeing what Galatea did, without tolerating such disdainful conduct, approaching the spot where the shepherdess was, said to her—"Suffer, beautiful Galatea, that your flock unite with ours ; but if you dislike the company, select what you do like, that by thy absence our sheep may not lack pasture, for I, who am born to serve thee, think more of them than my own ; and so despise me not thus overtly, for my free will towards you deserves it not, as your course was towards the pebble fountain, and now you see me you turn aside ; and if this be, as I have a shrewd idea it is, tell me where, now and henceforth, you would pasture your flock, and then I swear I will never there obtrude mine." "I promise you," said Galatea, "that it is not to avoid your company or that of Erastro, that I have changed the course which you imagined I had pursued, for my purpose is to pass here the evening with my companion, Florisa, who attends me, near to the brook of palms, for only yesterday we agreed so to do, and feed our flocks, and as I came along thoughtlessly tuning my pipe, the gentle ewe took the road towards the pebble stream, as the most accustomed. For the good will you bear me, and your considerate offers, thanks; but do not infer that your suspicions are well-grounded." "Alas, Galatea!" answered Elicio, "and how do you feign it should appear, having so little need for artifice, for in fact I entertain no other desire than what you desire. Go now, then, to the stream near the palm-trees, to the wood of counsel (al soto de consejo) or to the fountain of pebbles, and be assured you will not go alone, for my heart will bear you company, and if you see it not it is because you desire it not, as having no wish to furnish balm to it." "Until now," replied Galatea, "I think I see the first heart, and so I conclude I have incurred no wrong in not supplying a remedy." "I know not how you can allege this," replied Elicio, "heavenly Galatea, for you see it to wound it, and not to cure." "You remove evidence from me," rejoined Galatea, "in saying that I am armed (for to women no arms are allowed), have wounded no one." "Yes, discreet Galatea," said Elicio, "how you play with that which makes my heart suffer, and what invisibly inflicts wounds, and with your beauty alone for weapons. Still I murmur not so much at the woe you have caused me, as at your indifference to my pain." "I should consider it less even if I found it more again," retorted Galatea. Now, at this juncture of time arrived Erastro, and observing that Galatea went away and left them, said to her—"Whither go you, or rather fly, handsome Galatea? If from us who adore you, you fly, who can hope your company? Oh, enemy! how volatile you make off, triumphing over our ardent wishes; may heaven destroy the good I entertain for you if I do not long to see you in love with one who esteems your complaints as you requite mine; and do you smile, Galatea? I weep at your acts." Galatea could not reply to Erastro, because she was engaged in conducting her flock to the brook of palms, and lowering her head from afar, in token of taking leave, she retired, and when she found herself alone, and had reached the spot where her companion Florisa thought she would be, with the consummate voice which nature gave her, she warbled this sonnet :—

Far off from fire, noose, cold, or from the dart
Of love, which burns, presses, enflames and chills,
For such flame no proclivities has my heart,
Or with such knot will e'er rest satisfied.
Consume, bind, freeze, slay, press,
Take any wish you choose,
But as for arrow, snow, or net, hope not
My soul in any such a heat to melt;
Its fire will petrify my chaste purpose,
The knot will break by force or art,
Snow will dissolve my burning zeal,
The arrow my thoughts will blunt;
And thus I shall not, in security, fear
The blaze of love, the snare, the dart, the cold.

With juster reason may you stop brutes, move trees, and force stones to listen to the sweet song and delicious harmony of Galatea, as when to the harp of Orpheus, the lyre of Apollo, and the music of Amphion, Troy walls and those of Thebes founded themselves without the artificer's intervention, and the Sisters, dark indwellers of profound Chaos, were softened at the exquisite voice of the incautious lover. When Galatea finished her song, and reached the place where Florisa was, by whom she was welcomed with a smile, and to whom Galatea imparted her meditations, and as they let the cattle move at their own free will to feed on the verdant spot, invited by the clearness of the liquid element, they resolved to refresh their beauteous countenances (though such a proceeding did not contribute to enhance their beauties, as in many persons such alternatives are adopted, whereby nature's claims are martyrised for the semblance of beauty). Equally beautiful after the bathing did they remain as before, save that by applying their hands to their cheeks they became of a more roseate hue, so that an indescribable beauty supervened, and chiefly to Galatea, in whom were concentrated the three graces whom the ancients depicted in a state of nature, as being the mistresses of beauty. Now began they to cull various flowers from the green meadows, wherewith to weave chaplets to arrest the wanderings of their dishevelled hair, which floated on their alabaster shoulders. Thus were these two shepherdesses engaged, when unexpectedly they discerned a shepherdess moving towards them, of graceful air and gesture, at which they were not a little surprised, for they were sure she was no inhabitant of their village, or of any of the circumjacent hamlets; hence they wondered, and perceived her approach behind them, and though they were not far off, she appeared so absorbed and even transported by her reflections that she did not discern them, though they wished to present themselves to her. From space to space she stopped, and upturning her eyes heavenward, gave sighs so piteous and profound, that her very inwards seemed to be disturbed, wreathed her lily-white hands, and let furtive tears course down her innocent cheeks, resembling liquid pearls. By these external indications of woe in the shepherdess, Galatea and Florisa perceived how some inward grief oppressed her weighted soul, and to ascertain how this would end the two hid themselves under some adjoining myrtles, and thence, with unspeakable curiosity, observed the actions of the maiden, who, approaching to the margin of the streamlet, stopped to view attentively the current, and falling on the banks as if exhausted, hollowing one of the palms of her fair hands, she brought up some pure water, and so laving her precious eyes, with a low and meek voice, she said—"Oh, clear and fresh water, how little can your frigidity temper the heat of my most secret emotions. Vain indeed to hope from you, or even from all the waters of the ocean-stream that remedy of which I stand in need, for were all applied to my consuming heat, it would produce no other effect than a drop of fluid on a burning forge, which absorbs and aggravates the flame. Ah, wretched eyes! causes of my destruction, on what powerful occasion did I raise them to my great fall. Oh, fortune! enemy of my ease, with what velocity hast thou hurled me from the summit of my content, to the abyss of misery. Oh, cruel Sister! how did not the meek and loving presence of Arsildo appease the fury of thy unenamoured breast? What words could I address to you that you should retort so bitterly? Certain it is, sister, that your estimate of him and mine widely differ, for were it not so, you had been like subject to his influence as I am." All this, uttered by the shepherdess, was mingled with tears; neither could any heart have remained unmoved on hearing such passionate language. Now, her afflicted breast being somewhat assuaged, at the noise of the liquid lapse of waters, arranging herself apropos, she sang two couplets of verse with a soft and delicate voice—

1. Now is all hope departed,
   I alone can myself console;
   Time which passes and flies,
   Will soon my life require.

2. Two things there are in love,
   Affecting both its taste;
   Desire of improvement one,
   The other is the hope
   Which restraint or fear imposes.
   The two possess
   My breast, and I see not,
   Rather in my afflicted soul,
   For love despatches all,
   Still is my hope lost.

3. Should desire fail
   When hope minishes.
   Contrariwise to me it appears,
   For the more it strives to hide itself
   The bigger bulk it shows;
   No caution avails
   With wounds which irritate me,
   For in this amorous school
   A thousand ills do martyr me,
   One good alone consoling.

4. Scarce had attained
   The good unto my thought,
   When heaven, lot, and fate,
   With a slight motion
   Arrested my poor soul.
   If any grieves
   For my bitter woe
   Let the ship strike sail,
   And we may lighter move,
   For time not only passes, but e'en flies.

5. Who would not consume
   With the burdens I suffer?
   In them one sees entirely
   How with lead they weighted are,
   And yet are pleasures of wing.
   And with such a fall
   My happy new action is,
   In it there is respite,
   For what suspends all hope
   Will life too soon arrest.

Soon terminated the song of the shepherdess, but not the tears with which it was solemnized, whereby both Galatea and Florisa were moved to compassion and issued from their concealment, and with loving and courteous expressions saluted the woe-begone shepherdess, saying among reasons—"As the heavens, lovely shepherdess, shew themselves favourable to that which you desire to seek, and by them you can attain your wishes, so now inform us, if it is not distasteful, what chance or destiny has brought you to this spot, for we infer from our discourse that before this we have never seen you; and having listened to what you have sung, and concluding by it that your heart does not enjoy that solace which it so much needs, and by the tears which have been shed as your speaking eyes give proof, by the law of politeness we are constrained to obtain for you that counsel which is within our power. Should your grief be such that it accepts no consolation, at least you will recognise in us the spirit to serve you."

"I know not in what way to requite you," replied the shepherdess of the woods, "my charming maidens, for the courteous offerings you have made me, save by silence; and yet by accepting and appreciating them at their true value, and not refusing what of my own knowledge you might wish, it might be better to pass over in silence the character of my misfortune than divulge it, which might also savour of levity."

"Neither your face nor the graceful acts," answered Galatea, "which naturally belong to you, betray a dull intelligence, actuated by which you would do aught to damage your character by a revelation; and seeing that your appearance and speech have made such an impression on us, that we are convinced of your discretion, prove it by recounting to us your life, if your mischances correspond with your discretion."

"As to my belief," rejoined the shepherdess, "both were equal, did not my lot award to me more judgment, that I might be more sensitive as to my griefs. I do clearly perceive, however, that my woes overbalance my discretion, for my policy is quite overcome, nor can I devise how to remedy it; and though experience undeceives us, should you listen to me, lovely shepherdess, I would recount in brief all I can, how from the surplus of intelligence, which you judge me to have, has arisen the woe which has caused this condition of things." "With nothing more, O discreet wood-nymph, will you satisfy our desires," rejoined Florisa, "than by replying to our interrogations." "Let us retire," said the shepherdess, "from this spot, and seek another, where, unseen and undisturbed, I may reveal to you what it grieves me to have promised, for I foresee that in a brief space you will abandon the good opinion you entertained of me; however, I delay in opening my thoughts, unless your hearts have been pierced with an infirmity analogous to that I suffer." Desirous the nymph should fulfil her promise, the three arose and repaired to a secret locality apart, which the two wood-nymphs knew, where, beneath the grateful shade of an overtopping myrtle, unobserved the three might rest, whence, with grace and feeling, the forest shepherdess started her narrative—

"On the banks of the famous Henares (near Alcalà, in Castile), which to the gilded Tajo, offers a fresh and charming tribute, was I born and bred, in no such low position, so as to predicate of me the humblest of our village. My parents were labourers, and used to field employ, in which I followed them, having in charge a few simple sheep for the common pasture (dehesa conceyil) in our village, and thus were my ideas so level to my vocation that nothing gave me more pleasure than witnessing the increase of my flock, and thinking only how I could secure for my sheep more fertile soil, with a clear and running stream; hence I had not nor could have other case than what related to my pastoral charge. Woods were my companions, in whose solitude oft invited by the harmony of the sweet feathered tribe, I took leave of the voice for a thousand honest songs without any mixture of sighs or reasons which would indicate love or passion. Woe is me! how oft to content myself alone, and to play with time, I traversed from bank to bank, from valley to valley, culling there the white lily, there the flower de luce, again the red rose, with the sweet-smelling pink, making with these odoriferous flowers a woven garland wherewith to adorn and bind up my hair; then admiring myself in the clear, tranquil waters of some fountain, I was so charmed with myself that I would not have changed my condition for any other. And what mockery have I not made of some girls who, trusting to detect in me some sympathy with them in their love-stricken breasts, with abundance of tears and sighs, have disclosed to me how they were equally enamoured. I remember how, one day, a young shepherdess came to me, and casting her arms round my neck, and joining her pretty face to mine, her eyes representatives of fountains, said—'Ah, sister Teolinda,' for that is the appellative of this unfortunate being before you, 'I believe the end of my career is arrived, for love has not recompensed me as my desires merited.' I, struck by the extremities of the case, presuming that some dire evil had happened to her by loss of cattle, or death of parents, wiping her eyes with the sleeve of my robe, I asked her to tell me what the distress was of which she so complained. She, permitting her tears to fall, and giving no truce to her sighs, said to me—'What greater ill, O, Teolinda, would you have happen to me than that the chief herdsman of the village has absented himself without hinting to me one word about it, one whom I love more than my own eyes; and of having witnessed, this morning, in the possession of Leocadia, daughter of the principal shepherd, a roseate girdle, which I had given to that treacherous Eugenio; so my suspicions of their mutual exchanges of love were confirmed.' When I had ceased to hear her complaints, I declare, friends and noble ladies, that I could not restrain myself from smiles, and I said to her—'On my faith, Lydia,' for so she was styled, 'I thought you had cause to complain of a much deeper wound. But now I know how irrelevant are your love motives when you take notice of such trifles. Now tell me, by your life, dear Lydia, of what great value is a carnation-coloured cincture, that it should so disgust you to see it possessed by Leocadia, or if Eugenio did give it her? Better attend to your honour, and what concerns the pasture of your flock, and not interpose yourself in these lovefooleries, for, as far as I can see, you draw therefrom only a diminution of honour and ease too.' When Lydia heard this reply, so contrary to what she hoped from my mouth and sympathetic condition, down fell her head, and adding tears to tears, and sobs to sobs, she left me, and at a short distance, turning her head, she said,—'I only pray Heaven, Teolinda, that in a brief space you may see yourself in a state compared to which you may call mine happy, and that love may treat you so that you may recount your losses to him who will estimate them, and so may you thus feel how poignant you have made mine.' Thus she made off, and I was left laughing at her vagaries. But oh, wretched woman, now I know how I am accelerating the curse, for I am actually communicating my pain to one who is sorry to have learned it."

So Galatea replied, "Would to heaven, discreet Teolinda, that as you will find in us compassion for your misfortune, you could procure a remedy which will destroy the suspicion you entertain in us." "Your attractive persons and conversation, dear shepherdess," said Teolinda, "inspire me with such a hope—but my misfortune induces fear; yet come what come may, I must soon recount to you all I promised."

"With the liberty I have addressed you, and in the exercises I have mentioned, I passed my life so joyful and calmly that I knew not what desire was until vindictive love came to exact strict account of the little he could claim, and he ended by leaving me his slave, nor do I think he is yet paid, or advancing to satisfaction. It fell out that one day, (and it had been for me one of the most venturous of my life, had not time and opportunity diminished my joys,) I was going with some other shepherdesses of our hamlet, to cut sticks and collect reeds and flowers, and green swordflags to adorn the temple and ways of our locality (for a festive day was at hand, and to force the inhabitants by promise and vow to keep it), we chanced to pass altogether by a most engaging thicket which was situated between the hamlet and the rivulet, where we met a band of well-conducted shepherds, who during the ardours of the day rested for their *siesta*; they when they saw us rose to meet us, and divining our purpose with courteous words persuaded us, and even constrained us to advance no further—for some of them carried boughs and flowers for which we also went. Thus persuaded by requests, we yielded to what they desired, and soon six of the youths, distinguished by their bills, quitted us with great satisfaction to bring the verdant spoils which we were in quest. We who were also six in number, joined the shepherds' stand, who received us with all becomingness, especially one forester who was there, known personally to some of us, but of such sweet deportment, and so brisk too, that all our party admired him, whilst I was subject to him. I know not what I say, shepherdesses, but as soon soever as my eyes beheld him, my heart melted within me, and through my vein rushed a chill which enflamed me, and not knowing how, my heart bounded to think my eyes should be set on a face so bewitching as that of the unknown shepherd; and in brief, without previous experiments in love I discerned that it was Love which had assaulted me—and soon had I wished to complain of it, had time and opportunity supplied the means. Finally then, as now, I remained vanquished and depressed, yet with more confidence of recovery than now I entertain.

"Oh, how often then did I wish to join Lydia, and to say to her, Pardon me, dear sister, for the rude reply I made you lately, for I must acknowledge that now I have more experience of the complaint than yourself. At one thing I am surprised that so many being around me, no one divined by the motions of my face the secrets of my heart, and this induced the other shepherds to turn towards the forester, and ask him to finish a song which he had begun ere we came up. He, without further solicitation, continued his imperfect strain in a voice so exquisite and wondrous that all listeners were transported with the effect. From this moment I began to abandon myself to all that love exacts—without retaining in myself any other wish in life, and as I was more enraptured at the hearing than the rest, I could not but mark deeply the purport of the words, for love had so made me his slave, that my soul had been delivered up, had he but treated of that passion, or had I imagined his thoughts were so engaged, or that mine desired the same thing. What he then sang was only certain praises of pastoral life, and the quiet state of the country and advice useful for the preservation of flocks. Of this I remained content, as it seemed to me that if a shepherd was in love, of naught but that delicious passion would he treat; as it is the condition of lovers to think their time ill-spent, save in what exalts and praises the cause of their sorrow, or contented hurts them. See now, ladies, in how brief a space I became mistress in the school of love. When the shepherd ceased singing, and the discovery of those who brought boughs were simultaneous, who I saw at a distance looking like a little mountain moving along stately, and covered with trees. Coming near to us all the six raised their voices, one responding to the other with signs of satisfaction, and with a noisy outbreak began a regular pastoral. In this state they advanced quicker than I wished, for they prevented my seeing the forester. Having laid down their green charge, we observed that each bore a beauteous garland, clasping his arms snake-wise, and composed of divers agreeable flowers, which with apt and gracious words they presented to each of us, and offered also to bear the boughs to the village. We, delighted with their urbanity, wished to retire, when Eleuco, an ancient hind who was a bystander, said, 'It will be well, engaging shepherdesses, that you pay us for what our hinds have done for you, leaving us the garlands which you take superfluously from what you came to seek; but with this condition, that you bestow them on whom you like best.' 'If by so slender a recompense you should be satisfied with us,' replied one of the damsels, 'I am for my part content,' and so catching up the garland with both hands she put it on the head of a youngster, her cousin; the others, guided by her example, gave theirs to the different youths, who were also relatives. I who remained the last, and had no doubt, evincing a certain negligence, advanced to the forester, and setting my garland on his brow, said, 'This I give you, good shepherd, for two reasons: one on account of the song you gave, so satisfactory to all; and the second reason is, because in our village we are wont to honour strangers.' All the bystanders' actions denoted satisfaction at this behaviour. But what shall I tell you of what my inmost soul felt when so near to him who had stolen it, save that I had freely given up any thing I had desired for the liberty of embracing his neck in my arms, as I then surrounded his temples with the garland? The shepherd bowed to me, and with engaging words thanked me for the favour I had conferred on him, and in taking his leave, with a low voice, and with furtive glances, said to me, 'I have paid you better than you think, adorable shepherdess, for the garland you gave me ; take it with you, and if you can estimate its value, you will know that you still remain in my debt.' I had earnestly desired to reply, but the haste of my companions was such that the opportunity did not revert. So I returned to the village in a far different frame of mind from that I came out, and I really was surprised at myself. Company became painful to me, and every thought which obtruded itself, save only the shepherd, I quickly discarded, as unworthy to occupy a place overflowing with love-thoughts. I cannot imagine how in so short a time I could transform myself into a different being, for I had hitherto not lived in myself, but in Artidoro, as the half of my soul was styled, in which I went in quest. Wheresoever I turned my eyes there was his visage ; what I listened to, quickly sounded in my ears as his melodious voice ; my feet no sooner moved than I thought to find my life. Apples yielded not their wonted taste, nor did my hands perform their accustomed offices. In fine all my senses were exchanged from my former self ; even my soul wrought for what it was not accustomed. Considering the new Teolinda which had been born in me, and in contemplating the graces of the shepherd which were left on my soul, that day passed off, and the night before the solemn festival, which arrived and was kept with the highest rejoicings and applauses by all the inhabitants of our village, and solemnised in the circumjacent localities. After the sacred oblations were offered in the temple and all due ceremonies fulfilled, in a narrow spot opposite the temple within the shade of four ancient and leafy elms, all the populace united. There was a race, and space was assigned for foreign and native competitors to indulge in exercise, in honour of the feast. Soon lusty and active shepherds presented themselves, who, giving proofs of youth and capacity, commenced various games—now drawing the heavy bar, now displaying the lightness of their pliant limbs in old-fashioned leaps, now discovering increased strength and active adroitness in close involved wrestling, again exercising their swift feet in extended careers, each trying to be such that he should merit the first prize which the superintendent of the village had set aside for those who excelled in these sports. Now in all these of which I have made mention, and in others which I omit, for fear of prolixity, none of the far and near competitors came up to Artidoro, whose very presence did honour to the feast, and who carried off the prizes by the verdict of the judges. Such, shepherdess, was his skill and gallantry, and such the laudation of all beholders, that I felt proud, and an unaccustomed happiness wantoned in my breast by reason of my having occupied my thoughts on him. Yet it gave me great discomfort that Artidoro, as a foreigner, had to quit our village, and if he went without knowing what part of me he bore away—that is, my very soul, what a void would be mine in his dear absence, or how could I forget my sufferings, having none but myself to participate the complaints. Thus involved in these ideas, the feast and rejoicings ceased ; and Artidoro desiring to take leave of the shepherds, his friends all collectively asked him to stay during the octaves of the festival, unless something more to his taste prevented.

" ' Nothing would give me greater pleasure, kind shepherds,' replied Artidoro, ' than to serve you in that or in any way which you would please, but as I am bound to seek for a brother who ought to have arrived at our village, I will comply with your request, seeing how great is the advantage.'

" All rejoiced and rested satisfied with his stay. The more I reflected how in eight days I could not find occasion to disclose to him what I could not conceal. All that night we passed in dances and games, and in recounting each to each the evidences of physical power we had witnessed in the shepherds that day, adding, such danced better than such, though A exercised more versatility than B. Mingo got down Bras, yet the latter excelled the former in the course ; but in fine, all concurred that the forest hind had borne off the bell, whose praise was one strain of unanimity for especial graces—all which laudations redounded to my deep satisfaction. The morning after the feast, ere the fresh Aurora had lost the dew adorned with seed-pearl (aljoforado) from her lovely locks, and Phœbus had ceased displaying his rays on the misty mountain-tops, we, some dozen of us, shepherdesses, the *elite* of the village, our hands in union, to the chime of a bag-pipe (gayta) and of an oaten-pipe making in and out caperings, sallied from the village to a green meadow, not remote, giving unfeigned content to those who witnessed our tangled dance. Now chance, up to that point, had well adjusted my advances, decreed that in this same mead all the identical hinds should assemble, and with them Artidoro, who on sight of us, tuned their tambourines to the cadence of our oaten-pipe, and with the same measure and dance came out to receive us, blending one with the other confusedly, and yet in time, changing sound and changing dance, so that it was necessary that the women should dis-unite and give their hands to the men; and it was my good fortune to find Artidoro for a partner. I cannot say how, dear ladies, you will estimate that conjuncture, but I must add, that I was so disconcerted that I could not conform to the steps of the dance, so that Artidoro had to move me towards himself with a soft violence, not to interrupt the symmetry of the measure, and so availing myself of the moment, I said, 'In what has my hand offended! Artidoro, that you press it?' He whispered in a tone inaudible to all but me: 'Rather what has my soul done, that you ill-treat it?' 'My offence is obvious,' said I very meekly, 'but thine it is not possible to discern.' 'Here stands the mischief,' replied Artidoro, 'you contribute to do it, and you fail to apply the remedy.' So ceased our reasonings, for the measure done, I rested content and pensive at what Artidoro said; and though I held all for amorous remarks, no assurance of the fact followed. Soon all of us of both sexes were on the grass, and having recovered ourselves from the lively pas-times, the antique Elenco, tuning up his instrument, a re-beck in unison with the oaten-pipe of another shepherd, asked Artidoro to sing something, for he seemed the wor-thiest so to do, to render thanks to heaven, to fail of which had been a deep ingratitude. Artidoro receiving Elenco's praises, commenced singing some verses which reviving in me those hints which had passed between us, I committed them to memory, and to this moment hold them fast, which though it may give affliction to hear them, only because by your hearing them you will better appreciate the position into which love has cast me. I will recite them in all their perfection :—

1. In a sharp closed dark night,
   Without ever seeing the wished-for day,
   Bitter complaints increase continual;
   From pleasure far, smile or content,
   Deserveth he to be, in living death,
   Who loveless passes life.

2. What can be the most cheerful life,
   Without a shadow of brief thought—
   Oh semblance natural of death—
   If in these so many hours the day but lasts—
   Then silence to the grief of anguish full,
   Love's sweet smile admits not?

3. Where blind love dwells, dwell smiles;
   Where it dies, dies our very existence too—
   To wails converts the sapid pleasure,
   And in the ever-during darksome night
   Of peaceable day the clear night,
   To live without, why that is bitterness!

4. The dreadful circumstance of death
   Flies not the lover, ere with smiles
   He longs for the occasion, and day hopes
   When he may offer up his treasured life,
   Until he sees the latest tranquil night
   To amorous fire and dulcet wail made o'er.

5. The wail of love, the wail calls not—
   Nor should death death invoke;
   Night should give no title to dark night—
   Or smile solicit smile.
   Life should exist in its own certainty,
   Alone should wanton in its joyousness.

6. Oh for me venturesome in this day in truth,
   When I may put restraint on grief,

And rejoice to have sacrificed my life
To her who could or life or death confer.
But what hope have I, barren smiles except—
From face the sun exceeding, and to night turns
Into clear day, has turned my dark night.
Love—my griefs accumulated into smiles,
And my approach of death to life prolonged.

" These were the verses, splendid shepherdesses, which with marvellous grace, and to the no less satisfaction of those who heard them, that day sang my Artidoro, about which act and the reasons to which I have already adverted, I seized the opportunity of imagining if by chance my appearance had caused any new amorous accident in Artidoro's breast, and how my suspicion was not proved vain until I found he did not return to the village to convince me of it." At this point of the love narration came Teolinda, when the shepherdesses heard a frightful noise of hinds and barking dogs, which caused them to end the discourse commenced, and stop to peep through the boughs, and so they perceived on a verdant meadow, which lay on the right, a pack of dogs crossing it, and pursuing a timid hare, which in all haste entered the thick brambles for protection, and in a short space at the same spot where the hinds were, they viewed it enter and go directly to the side of Galatea, quite exhausted from its long chase, and thus almost secure against the imminent dangers, dropped down on the soil nearly breathless, and as if he would speedily expire. The dogs, by smell and track, followed the hare close to where the women stood; Galatea, taking the panting leveret into her arms, stopped the vengeance of the hungry hounds, as it seemed unjust to her to leave the animal to chance. Some other hinds joined them in pursuit of their dogs and the timid creature, among them Galatea's father, out of respect for whom Galatea, Florisa, and Teolinda advanced to pay him merited courtesy. He and his companions were struck with Teolinda's comeliness, and in them it awakened a desire to know who she was, for in her they recognised a stranger. This meeting with Galatea and Florisa did not a little disconcert them, as it took from them the pleasure of hearing about the success of Teolinda's loves, whom they solicited not to leave them for some days, if it did not interfere with the accomplishment of her desires. "Quite the contrary; to see if my desires can be satisfied, I find it convenient to remain on this bank a day or two, and so not to leave imperfect my story in its course. I am obedient to your will."

Galatea and Florisa embraced, and were reassured of each other's friendship, and each promised to advance their mutual interests to the best of their power. During this process, the father of Galatea and the other hinds having spread their long, loose coats on the banks of the clear streamlet, and taking from their scrips some apples, invited Galatea and her companions to the repast, which they accepted; so down seated they satisfied hunger, as the close of the day had brought on fatigue also. Whilst the rural parties mutually entertained each other, the time came to return to the hamlet. Speedily Galatea and Florisa, turning to their flocks, collected them, and in Teolinda's company and the rest of the party, they all retired slowly to their dwellings. At the break of the hill where that morning they had met Elicio, and heard the pipe of the disappointed Lenio, a shepherd, in whose breast never love remained; and so satisfied and cheerful was he, that in what conversation or company soever he was, his sole object was to speak disparagingly of love and lovers, and in this strain flowed all his ditties, and for this sullen state he was known, spurned by some of his companions, so by some he was appreciated.

Galatea and her friends stopped to hear if Lenio, as usual, had a song to recite, and soon observing that he gave his instrument to a companion, at its sound he sung what now follows :—

LENIO.

1. A vain, careless thought,
   A lofty, foolish fancy.
   Something indescribable
   Which memory creates,
   Wanting reality, quality, and base.

2. A hope which the wind raiseth;
   A grief with reverse of gladness;

  A night confused without day ;
  A blind error of the mind.

3. These are the roots whence rise
  The ancient celebrated chimera,
  Which love for a name supports
  In every soil.

4. But the soul which in love is delighted,
  Deserves to be exiled from the land,
  Not even to heaven admitted.

While Lenio was singing what we just heard, both Elicio and Erastro, with their wind instruments, came up, in company of the much-to-be-lamented Lisandro, and it seemed to Elicio that the evil which Lenio spoke of, love, as far as it extended with reason, went to show clearly his deception ; and availing himself of the same ideas as are found in the verses which he had recited, when Galatea, Florisa, and Teolinda arrived, and the other herdsmen, to the sound of the rebeck of Erastro, Elicio beegan this strain :—

1. He deserves who on the soil,
  And in his breast doth love conceal,
  That he should be expelled from heaven's height
  And not be tolerated e'en on earth.

2. Love, which is perpetual virtue,
  With many others which it reaches too,
  By one similitude or another
  Ascendeth to the first and infinite cause,
  And he deserves whose zeal
  Him banishes from such love,
  That he should be expelled from heaven's height,
  And not be tolerated e'en on earth.

3. A handsome countenance and figure,
  Though obnoxious to mortality,
  Is a copy and a seal
  Of beauty divine ;
  And he who on this soil the beautiful,
  Repudiates and hurls it to the ground,
  Let him an outcast from high heaven be,
  And be not suffered upon earth to dwell.

4. Love its own folds within,
   With admixture of contingencies,
   Is as suitable to earth
   As rays are of the sun ;
   And he who entertains mistrust
   Of love, which truly so much good conceals,
   Deserves no prospect of heaven
   Or that the firm-set earth should him endure.

5. Well knows he that love
   Is full of endless good ;
   But of evil good ariseth,
   What good is becoming better,
   So he who damages a hair,
   In pure amorous war,
   Should never sight of heaven's bliss attain,
   Or be on earth maintained.

6. Love is infinite,
   If its basis is sound,
   But what soon ends
   Is passion, and not love.
   Its elevation without flight,
   Solely to will confining,
   May a sun's ray destroy him,
   And cover him no earth.

No small gratification possessed the hinds when they saw how furiously Elicio stood his ground ; not the less did the loveless Lenio adhere fixedly to his own notions, ere he desired to return to the song, and to evince in what he enunciated of how small significance were the reasonings of Elicio to obscure the truth, which he stoutly maintained. Yet did Galatea's father (whose august name was Aurelio) remark, " Disconcert not thyself to make appear in thy song what thy heart feels. The road to the village is short, and it seems to me that more time is needed than you compute, to defend you from the swains advanced against you. Hold thy thoughts for a more opportune crisis, for some day will Elicio and them join with other herdsmen at the fountain of stones or the palm brook, where more commodiously you may broach the point, and clear up your diversity of opinion."

"What Elicio holds is but opinion," answered Lenio, " but mine is certified truth, which sooner or later, in forcing verity, constrains me to espouse it, yet will a time not fail, as you remark, more expedient for this effect." " This will I obtain," rejoined Elicio, " for with a genius so rare as yours, friend Lenio, it grieves me that it should fail to attain the point, which is the true character of love, of which you are the avowed enemy." " You are in error, Elicio," retorted Lenio, " if you imagine that by some painted and fantastic words you can induce me to change, what I consider it unmanly to change." " So much the worse is it," rejoined Elicio, " to be obstinate in wrong, as it is wholesome to persevere in good ; and by my elders I have heard say, that it is a quality of the wise to embrace counsel." " This I deny not," again said Lenio, " did I conclude my opinion to be untenable, yet as neither experience nor reason inform me of the contrary up to this point, I infer my notion to be right, as I hold yours to be the contrary." " If the heresies of love are to be chastised," said Erastro, " at this season, from now, I should begin, dear Lenio, to cut wood wherewith to burn that vast heresy and enemy which love comprises." " And should I meet nothing of love but what you follow, and are of the group of the enamoured," again said Lenio, " it would demand one hundred tongues to renounce it, if so many could be acquired." " And now does it appear to thee, Lenio," answered Erastro, " that I am not calculated for love ?" " Contrariwise," said Lenio. " Such of your mental and physical qualities are its favoured ministers, for he who is lame, by the least defect is discovered, and he whose judgment is wanting differs little from an idiot, so those who follow the banners of your valorous captain. I, in my deductions, hold them to be no great characters, for had they so been, immediately that the poison of love assailed them, they had thrown it off."

Great was the annoyance to him at what Lenio said, but he furnished this rejoinder :—" In my idea your grotesque notions merit only words for reply, still I hope some day you may pay for it, and really find neither defender nor defence."

" If I understood from you, Erastro," remarked Lenio, " that you were as valiant as amorous, thy menaces would really infuse fear in me, but as I discern you are in the rear of some affections and in advance of others, laughter takes the place of dread."

And thus was exhausted Erastro's patience, and despite the presence of Lisandro and Elicio, who were arranged in their midst, he answered Lenio with dumb significance, for his tongue really refused to do its office in the perturbation of his vexed wrath.

Great was the satisfaction which all experienced from the quarrel of the hinds, and the more anger and annoyance Erastro evinced, the more it was imperative on Galatea's parent to attempt some reconciliation, though Erastro—not losing the respect of that lady's father in no way—contributed to it. So soon as the question was finished, all jovially repaired to the hamlet, and on their transit thither, the nonpareil Florisa, at the sound of the instrument of Galatea, set up this strain—

1. May my dear lambkins grow ;
   In the enclosure of verdant pastures,
   And in the ardent heat, and in frigid winter,
   Abundance find of fodder and cool streams !

2. May he remember in sleep nights and days together,
   In all that to the pastoral state relates,
   Without love's cares, how slight soever,
   Being felt, or its oft told triflings avowed !

3. May this announce love's thousand 'vantages,
   May that its vanities make known,
   And I know not if both may not perish !

4. Nor victor shall I know to award the crown,
   This I know of the elect of love, for it
   How few there are ; how many have to mourn.

Short was the road to the shepherds, allured and entertained by the charming voice of Florisa, who ceased not her song till she neared the village and the cottages of Elicio and Erastro, who, with Lisandro, dwelt there, taking leave first of Aurelio, of Galatea and Florisa, who, with Teolinda, came to the village, and each of the residents to his own home. That very same night the mournful Lisandro asked permission of Elicio to visit him, and as far as in him lay in

unison with his desires, to finish what, to his idea, remained
of his life.   Elicio, with all available reasons, and with the
truest evidence of friendship, could only let him remain with
him some days, and then the unlucky hind, embracing
Elicio, with floods of tears and sighs, took leave, promising
to inform him all about his condition, and having accompanied Elicio some half league from his cottage, returned to
renew the embrace, and thus, with reiterated offers of
friendship, they again separated, which quite unnerved
Elicio ; so he repaired to his own cot, to drift through the
night in amorous illusions, and to hope the next day to
revisit Galatea, the cause of the woe, who, having reached
her own village, and longing to hear the result of Teolinda's
loves, effected it so that they should be alone that night,
and thus Florisa and Teolinda, realising the convenience to
be desired, the lovelorn shepherdess pursued her narrative,
as it is disclosed in the second book of this pastoral.

BOOK II.

Pursuance of Teolinda's adventures.—Her ditty.—Lamentation of Artidoro inscribed on the barks of trees.—The three shepherdesses retire to rest.—Florisa tunes her instrument, to which Teolinda sings.—Interrupted by the sounds of a pipe and a rebeck.—Responsive songs of Damon and Thirsis.—Colloquy of Thirsis and Damon. —Retire to a village to be present at the marriage preparations of Duranio and Silveria.—Surprised by a ditty from Elicio.—Erastro strikes into the conversation.—Songs of Erastro, Elicio, Damon, and Thirsis.—Taken unawares by a song from an unknown voice of a youth found in a disconsolate situation.—Erastro consoles him.— The youth's narrative.—His journey and his recognition of his friend Timbrio, whom he discovered bound in fetters and ready for execution.—Addresses and rescues him.—Is himself captured and lodged in prison.—Timbrio fell amongst thieves, and was seized as one of them.—Love of Timbrio for Nisida.—Verses of Silerio to Timbrio.—Verses by Silerio in praise of Nisida's beauty.—Note of Timbrio to Nisida.—Conversation of Aster and Nisida.—Love of Silerio for Nisida.—His verses.—Love for Blanca, sister to Nisida.— Silerio sings, and whilst pursuing his story is astonished by hearing some music, and seeing some swains, in the midst of whom was a youth crowned with flowers, who turns out to be Daranio.—Progress to the village.—Lenio's song.—Advance of Galatea, and Erastro's song to her.

FREE and detached from that which appertained to night with the flocks, they managed to withdraw and be alone with Teolinda, where no one could interpose, to hear the conclusion of the love tale. Hence to a little garden went they, which belonged to Galatea, and sitting, all three, below a green and flourishing vine tree, which most intricately—by means of nets or poles—was interwoven. Teolinda, turning to repeat some words already spoken, pursued her narrative :—

"The dance being over with the song of Artidoro, as before stated, sweet shepherdesses, it was the opinion of all that we should repair to the hamlet, and in its temple offer the wonted sacrifices, and in this mind the solemnity of the festival gave us a certain latitude. So regardless of the gathering, with such freedom we rejoiced, both sexes in one concentrated mass, with becoming gladness returned to the hamlet, each discoursing on what pleased him best.　My fate and care so ordained it, and also the solicitude of Artidoro, that without any artificial arrangements we two separated, so that *en route* we could speak of what we listed, each regarding only what had reference to each.

" Finally, I, to sweep away obstacles, as one says, spoke thus,—' The days you have spent in our village will be years to you, for in your own village you have enough to occupy you, and that, too, with superior satisfaction.'　' All I can hope in my life would I exchange,' replied Artidoro, ' for the days I have passed in the village, were truly years, and greater contentment is not attainable.'

" ' Is all this satisfaction due to our *fête*, then ?' remarked I.　' It is not so quite, but the contemplation of the personal charms of the soft sex in your village.'　' Truly,' again said I, ' there must be an equivalent in your village also. Certainly we are not deficient, but yours abounds with beauty, so that in only one whom I have seen, a comparison with her makes them plain enough.'　' Your politeness extorts from you, O Artidoro, this sentiment, for I am persuaded that in this village there is not anyone so supereminent as you allege.　Much better is my opinion,' said he, ' because I have taken a very minute look into other villages.'

" ' Peradventure your observation was taken from afar, and distance might lend enchantment to the view,' rejoined I.　' In like manner,' said he, ' that thou whom I see and admire now, the same I might have witnessed in another, and have been pleased with the delusion, although her condition and her beauty may not have corresponded.　This does not affect me, although she may be announced, and be admitted to pass for a superior beauty.'　' By so much the more,' said Artidoro, ' I would you had not been the subject of comparison.'　' But how would you lose again,' remarked I, ' if as I am not what you avow another were ?'　' My gain I can appreciate,' said he.　' As to my loss, I am doubtful, and in fear.'

" ' You know well,' added I, ' how to play the lover.' ' Say rather, Teolinda, it is thou, who love inspirest,' he rejoined.　To this remark I again ventured ' I am ignorant

which of the two, or if not both, are in delusion.' Again
he spoke. 'That I am not deceived, I am sure, but your
deception, or wish to deceive yourself, rests with you wholly,
whenever you make experiment of the pure will which I entertain for your service.' 'I will give you requital for that,'
said I, seeing it would not answer to hesitate in the matter.

"At this exact juncture came up Eleuco, the herdsman,
and in a high tone said—'Holloa, my fine shepherds and
shepherdesses, let the village feel that we are come, by en-
toning some pastoral ditty to which we may give response, for
see how the indwellers turn out to participate in our fête.'

"And as we acquiesced in the suggestion of Eleuco,
quickly the hinds gave me their hands to enact a beginning,
and profiting by the occasion, and by what had passed with
Artidoro, I set up this strain—

1. In all matters of love
   Nothing to perfection can pretend,
   The honest love, and secret.

2. To attain the sweet
   Savour of love, if you would reach it,
   The door thereto is secret—
   But virtue is the key
   And this entry no one knows,
   Except the discreet worshipper,
   He must be both discreet and virtuous.

3. Human beauty to love
   May be reprehensible,
   If such propensity be not meted
   By virtue and reason's force ;
   Love of such a quality
   Quick touches in effect
   What honest is and secret.

4. It is an admitted fact,
   Which no one dares gainsay,
   That sometimes speech doth lose
   What silence had secured.
   And he who could enamoured be,
   Will never find himself perplexed
   If honesty and secrecy prevailed.

5. How a talkative organ
   And temerarious looks
   Infinite annoyances can cause,
   Into confinement lap the soul
   By so much grief diminishing;
   The pressure is relaxed
   When honesty and secrecy prevail.

"I know not, my charming companions, if, in what you have heard, I succeeded; but this I do know, that it was approved by Artidoro; for during the remainder of his visit in our hamlet, though he spoke to me very oft, it was with so much deference, honesty, and purity, that neither lazy eyes nor scandalous tongues discovered, even faintly, the wherewithal to reproach us. But in the fear which I entertained that the term of Artidoro's stay completed, he would return to his own village, I, at the cost of my modesty, took care that my heart should not conceal what I might prudently avow in his absence. Hence the evidence of my eyes assuring me how amorously his met mine, how tongues could not remain silent, or fail to indicate by words what those speaking organs and that pure spirit of sense, the eye, so clearly announced.

"Now you must be informed, choice friends, that one day, being alone with Artidoro, with tokens of an inflamed desire and yet modesty withal, he revealed to me the depth of his true love, still it behoved me to play the receding part and the coy, and although I apprehended he would quit the place, I did not desire to rebuff him, or give him his *congé*, though it was obvious to me that the distaste which sometimes occurs in early love is the cause why a good beginning is often abandoned by those who are inexperienced in the tender passion; hence I ventured an answer in unison with my own wishes. Waiting, in concert with others, till he should depart from the hamlet, and in a few days afterwards, with a third person of integrity, he should send to demand me for his wife from my parents; with this he concurred so cheerfully, that he allowed that day to have been of peculiar good augury when his eyes lighted on my person. I knew that for myself I would not exchange my contentment with aught imagination could suggest; safe in the valour and capability of Artidoro, and in the conviction that these attributes would induce my parents to accept him for a son-in-law. In this fortunate crisis of which you have heard, shepherdesses, stood our amours, and only two or three days remained ere Artidoro left, when fortune, as if no end was to be to this condition of things, ordained that a sister, somewhat junior to myself, returned to our village, from the house of an aunt who had been indisposed ; and when you consider what strange and unexpected cases do happen in this sublunary state, I request you courteously to attend to one which will fill you with surprise, and it is, that this my sister, who till then had been away, seemed to me in face, figure, sprightliness, and airyness of manner, so like myself, if I can boast of these qualities, that not only our neighbours, but our very parents have mistaken us, and have addressed one for the other, so that to prevent this deception, we were obliged to wear different attire. In only one thing, I believe, did nature make us different, which was in some conditions relative to a certain asperity which she had, for she was less compassionate than discreet, whilst I was one who would rather weep all my life out. It fell out, that immediately on my sister's return to the hamlet, with the desire she entertained of renewing her gentle pastoral exercise, she rose earlier than I liked, and with the sheep which I was wont to tend, she repaired to the mead, and although I wanted to follow her, to obtain a sight of my Artidoro, I know not how, but my mother detained me that day at home, which was of my joys the last. That evening my sister, having penned her flock, whispered to me in secret that she had something most important to impart. I, who thought the communication would be very different, from the fact arranged that we should be alone, when she with a visage something changed (I standing suspended on her words) spoke thus—

" ' I know not, sister, what I think of your discretion, nor do I know if I ought to withhold what I cannot conceal, to ascertain if you can exculpate me from the blame which I presume you entertain against me, although, as a younger sister, I was forced to address you with more deference, yet will you pardon me, for in what I have this day seen, you will perceive cause for exculpation.'

" This announcement being made to me, I had not wherewithal to reply, but let her run on as her discourse tended. ' You must know, sister,' pursued she, ' that this morning, on quitting with our flocks the mead, and I accompanying them alone on the margin of the cool Henares' water, while passing the Almeda, a shepherd appeared before me, whom I can aver with truth I never before saw in these parts, and with a most extraordinary ease of manners made me such amorous advances that a confusion of face surprised me, quite ignorant of what reply I should venture. He, not warned by the annoyance which my face denoted, approached nearer, saying—" What silence is this, lovely Teolinda, last refuge of a soul which worships thee?" And shortly he raised my hands to kiss them, accompanying the action with a series of pretty, soft, alluring expressions which bore the semblance of being studied for the purpose. Soon I took up the discourse, perceiving how he had fallen into a common error, which was that he thought his conversation was with you. Whence my suspicion, that if you, dear sister, have never seen him or treated him courteously, he had not presumed thus to act ; so that I put on such a face of disgust that he could scarce find a word to follow. Yet finally did I answer in a style which his temerity deserved, and in a strain such as you, sister, had adopted, had such a liberty been offered to you ; and had not the shepherdess Licea just then arrived, I had added such cutting reasons as had caused him seriously to repent his unsolicited advances ; and the best of it is, that I would not undeceive him, but left him to conclude that it was with Teolinda he was speaking. In fine, he quitted me, calling me an ingrate, unthankful, and unknowing ; and from his countenance I inferred, sister, that he will never venture to address us, even though he should find either of us alone.

" ' Now, what I want to know is, who is this hind, and what conversation you have held together, and whence arises the airiness of manner emboldening such a deportment.' To your discretion, my prudent ladies, I leave it to imagine my feelings consequent on the story recounted by my sister. Still, dissembling all I could, I said ' the greatest possible reward hast thou given me, sister Leonarda,' for that was the appellative of the disturber of my quiet, ' in relieving me by thy sharp remonstrances from the *hauteur* and restlessness which this hind has ventured according to your report. He is a stranger of about eight days standing in this locality, into whose brain such arrogance and madness have entered, that he has done to me also what you have seen ; giving out that he has my good good-will, and although I have undeceived him, it may be, despite the bitter encounter you have had with him, that he will yet prosecute his vain endeavours, and in verity, sister, I hope the day will soon arrive to warn him that unless he departs from his vanity, he may expect nothing but a reiteration of what he has heard.' Now this is as true as truth, dearest friends, and I awaited patiently for the dawn to carry out my resolve—to go alone in quest of my Artidoro, and impart to him the error into which he had fallen, alarmed, nevertheless, with the acrid and unmannerly reply that my sister had tendered to him, hoping, yet that he would not be disdainful, or perpetrate aught prejudicial to our common interest.

"The long nights of the froward December never gave more pain to the lover who awaited satisfaction on the coming dawn, than this delay gave me disgust ; for it was in the niggardliness of the summer that by the new light I desired to go and see that light by which my visual orbs saw.

"Now, ere the stars had lost all their clarity, and being in doubt as to night itself or day, impelled by my ardour, with the opportunity, too, of sallying forth to feed my flocks, I left the hamlet, and with a motion more hasty than I was wont to employ, I reached the spot where I used to find Artidoro, whom I detected alone, and so, without further indication, save what my heart indited, I divined the evil which was in store for me.

"How oft, seeing he came not, did I long to beat the air with the cries of my beloved Artidoro, breathing, come, my adored one, I am the true Teolinda, who loves you more than she herself loves, and seeks you. Whilst fearing that others might hear my words, I kept silence. So after walking around the banks and the thicket near the gently flowing Henares, tired, I sat at the foot of a green willow, awaiting the wide expansion o'er the soil of Phœbus' rays, that by their clearness there should be nor bush, nor hollow, thicket, hut, nor cabin, which I had not sought out. Scarce

had the early light enabled eyes to distinguish colours, when
to my eyes appeared a white, dwarf elm straight before me,
on which I saw sundry letters engraven, and incontinently
did I recognise the handiwork of Artidoro there planted, and
so rising with precipitation to see their purport, my dear companions, there I read as follows :—

1. Shepherdess, in whom beauty
   In such excess is found,
   That thou art without parallel,
   In innate cruelty except
   My firmness and your fickleness,
   Have with a full hand sowed
   My promises on the sand,
   My hope too in the winds.

2. Ne'er could I have imagined
   There had been what I saw
   Between a sweet yes
   And a scornful, bitter, galling no.
   I had not been deceived
   Had I set in my good fortune,
   As in thy beauty,
   The eyes, which have beheld thee.

3. Yet by how much thy uncommon grace
   Promised, all joyful and harmonious,
   By so much disturb and disconcert
   My dire misfortune and entangled skein,
   Eyes have me bewildered
   Which once seemed with compassion quite replete.
   Oh, treacherous orbs, yet lovely,
   In what have they sinned who have looked on them ?

4. Say, cruel shepherdess,
   Who will not deceive
   Thy open, intelligent face,
   Thy words of honey ?
   Now by me appreciated,
   With less than thou effectest ;
   Days are gone in which you found me
   A captive and a victim, and deceived.

5. The letters I inscribe
   On this rough bark
   Will grow with greater strength,
   Than has my faith,
   Which you lodged in thy mouth,
   And in vain promises,
   Variable as sea and winds
   Though founded on immoveable vast rocks.

6. So terrible, and hardened,
   Like to a viper trodden under foot,
   Cruel equally and benignant,
   Lovely and false in the same measure, too ;
   What your cruelty orders
   I will accomplish without more ado,
   For ne'er was my desire ·
   In opposition to your will.

7. In exile will I die,
   That in contentment you may long survive.
   Yet see that love feels not
   The way you have treated me,
   For in the voluptuous dance,
   Though love interpose restraint,
   Its tendency is fixedness,
   And tolerates no change.

8. As in comeliness
   All other of your sex you do excel,
   I thought that in desire
   More constancy you had ;
   Now know I by my passion,
   Which nature loves to frame,
   An angel in your figure dwells,
   But in deportment worldliness.

9. Would'st learn whither I go,
   And the conclusion of my doleful life ?
   The blood shed by me
   Will you, where I am, transport ?
   And though no one cares
   For our union or our love,
   Thou wilt not the corpse refuse
   One sorrowful last farewell.

10. Hard indeed, wilt thou be,
    More impenetrable than a diamond, far,
    If my corpse and sepulture
    Will turn you not to pity
    In this unfortunate condition,
    A sweet parting will I tender,
    If I thee quit, abhorred in life,
    In death by thee I may lamented be.

" What words would suffice, shepherdesses, to convey to you the extreme pang which seized my heart when I clearly discerned that the verses I have just repeated were those of my beloved Artidoro? Still, no reason exists why I should be thus endeared to them, for they did not go the length of finishing my days, which from that hour I have held in abhorrence, so that nothing sweeter could arise than my destruction. The sighs I then emitted, the tears I shed, the pity I felt, were of such a composition, that no one would hear them without taking me for a possessed person. Finally, I remained so, that without consulting my honour, I proposed an abandonment of my country, to quit parents and dear brothers, and to leave to its own care my simple flock, and without giving heed to aught else but what conduced to my own necessities, that so one morn, embracing one thousand times the bark which the hands of Artidoro had engraved, I went away with a view to settle on those banks where I know Artidoro dwells, and to ascertain if he has been so intemperate and cruel to himself as to give effect to the verses he wrote. Should this be so, I promise you, sweet friends, that from this time, my desire and quickness to execute shall be no less to follow him in death, than it has been my will to love him during life. Woe is me! How can I believe that suspicion and act may not be consequent. Now nine days are passed since I touched on these banks, nor of him I love have I heard anything, and I pray heaven that when I do hear news it may not realise my forebodings.

" You have now, discreet shepherdesses, the lamentable result of my enamoured life. I have also informed you who I am and whom I seek, should you be cognizant of aught tributary to my content, withhold it not from me." With such tears did the love-smitten sheperdess accompany her

words, that scarce heart of steel had not sympathised.
Now Galatea and Florisa were of piteous temperaments,
and could not restrain a flux of tears, nor did they not try
ny soft and efficacious reasoning to console her, asking her
still to remain some time in their society, for it might happen in that lapse they should hear news of Artidoro—for
that heaven would never allow in youth such a delusion to
adhere to a so discreet shepherd as she had depicted him;
and it might well be that Artidoro had on reflection and
good counsel again gone to his own district and dear friends,
and it was probable that these hopes might be realised.
With these and analogous reasons the shepherdess yielded
to consolation, and rejoiced to dwell with them, thanking
them for their courtesy and their desire to procure her satisfaction.　At this season the serene night, hastening onward
through the heavens, the starry car gave note of approaching day, and the shepherdesses, desiring repose, arose and
passed through the fresh garden to their places of rest.
Scarce had the luminous orb of day dispersed with his
potent rays the thick mist, such as through the fresh
morning is diffused, when the three shepherdesses, deserting
their luxurious couches, went to commence their daily toil
of feeding the cattle, yet with far different thoughts walked
Galatea and Florisa, than those of Teolinda, whose gait
was sad to a marvel.　It occurred to Galatea, to see if she
could not divert her, and so solicited her to remove her
melancholy, to sing some verses to the accompaniment of
Florisa's instrument.　Thus replied Teolinda, " If in the deep
cause I have for grief, and the little cause I have to sing,
charming Galatea, I could find aught to diminish it, you
would assuredly pardon me did I decline your proposition;
but knowing from experience what my tongue avers that
my heart ratifies, though with sobs, yet will I fulfil your
behest, for how contrary soever it be to my wish, it will
realise yours."　Incontinently Florisa touched her wind instrument, and Teolinda sang the following sonnet :—

TEOLINDA.

1. I know to my sorrow whither approximates
　　The rough power of a recognised deceit,
　　And how love essays by my hurt,
　　Me life to give, which very fear denies.

2. My soul disjoins itself from flesh,
    Pursuing that which by unusual fate
    Binds me in pain, and in a size so vast,
    That good disturbs it, and grief mollifies.

3. If I do live, it is by faith in hope,
    Which feeble being, yet sustains itself,
    At once adhesive to the power of love.

4. Firm beginning, frail mutability,
    Bitter sum of a most sweet account,
    How will you terminate this my weary life ?

Scarce had ended Teolinda this canticle of love when the three females distinguished on the right by the side of the fresh vale, the sound of a pipe, of such sweet breath, that for a while all were suspended and stood fixed to hear and enjoy the rapture.

At a little distance, too, from the pipe was a slender rebeck, which kept time with grace and exactness, that the two shepherdess were held mute in admiration, imagining who could be the swains whose music so enchanted them, for from none of their acquaintances, save Elicio, could such power proceed. "At this season," said Teolinda, " if my ears betray me not, dear ladies, I conjecture that you have in your district those two very renowned hinds, Thirsis and Damon, natives of my country. At least Thirsis, who in the far-famed Compluto, a town founded on Henares' banks, was born ; and Damon, his intimate and faithful friend, born, unless my information be untrue, on the mountains of Leon, and educated in the well-known Mantua Carpentanea. Both supreme in general discretion, science, and commendable exercises, who not alone in our circuits are known, but far and wide enjoy estimation and respect. Think you not, gentle shepherdesses, that the ability of these two swains consists solely in a knowledge of the pastoral state. No— the very secrets of heaven and the undiscovered mysteries of earth they teach and dispute about ; and I am perplexed in thinking what cause should have moved them, for Thirsis to abandon the adored Phillis, and Damon the fair, the virtuous Amarillis. Both so beloved, that in our village or in the adjacent ones, no plain or wood, meadow, fount, or stream, which is not familiar with their warm, their honest loves." "Cease now, Teolinda," rejoined Florisa, "to praise these swains; it imports us more to listen to their strains, for in my idea there is no greater grace than the voice and instrument operating in accordance." "What will you say," again reiterated Teolinda, when you see how this excels the worth of poesy; the one is as if the renown of divine had been assigned, while the other savours more of humanity." Whilst in this position the shepherds saw how by the edge of the valley whence they passed, there emanated two shepherds of lively bearing and a notable cheerfulness, the age of each being nearly alike, and very well dressed in the pastoral costume, which gave to their figures a more *bizarre* appearance than what appertained to shepherds of the mountain. Each wore a well-cut pelt of white fine wool with lion and pard coloured border, colours congenial to shepherds. There hung from their shoulders broad two pouches, but not less handsome and decorated than the skins. They were crowned with green laurel and fresh ivy, with the tassels which fell therefrom lodged under the arm. No one was with them, and thus absorbed in their music on they came, and some time elapsed ere they detected the shepherdesses who were walking on the same banks, not a little admired for their grace and liveliness by the swains, who with voices in concert began and answered each other, singing the following canticles responsively :—

DAMON.

1. Oh Thirsis, who the body solitary,
    With a bold step, though forced, dost remove
    From that light with whom thou dost leave the soul.
    How is't in noise you do not dolorous grieve,
    Since thou hast so much reason to complain,
    Of the disturber harsh of thy repose !

THIRSIS.

2. Oh, Damon, should the wretched corpse divide
    Without the soul's half in division,
    Leaving the most exalted part of it,
    With what virtue or spirit shall be moved
    My tongue? which I for dead freely account,
    For with the soul existence doth remain.

Although a proof I see, I hear, I feel,
Yet am I a phantasma formed by love,
By hope alone myself I do sustain.

DAMON.

3. Oh, Thirsis, rash, how envied now in truth,
Is by me with just cause thy destiny,
To be exhausted by love's influence.
Absence alone can really thee disgust,
And still you hold fast the support of hope
Which consolation gives to the soul's distress.
Yet woe is me!—Wherever I proceed,
The cold, coy hand of fear still reaches me,
And of disdain the cruel spear, I ween,
Hold life for death, though more in vividness
It shows itself, shepherd.   Such is the torch
Which when it dies displays its light e'en more.
Nor with the time which doth so lightly flit,
Nor with the means which absence offers too,
Can my outwearied soul true comfort find.

THIRSIS.

4. The firm and chaste love never can decrease
In course of bitter absence.
By virtue, yea, of memory it grows.
So whether absence be or long, or short,
No remedy can the perfect lover see,
To give relief unto the amorous weight;
For memory doting on the object dear,
Which love in the mind infuses, represents
The cherished image stamped upon the sense,
And there in silence soft doth give account
Of its weal or its woe, as it appears
Impressed by love, or from its power exempt.
If you observe my soul emits no sighs,
The reason is that Phillis rules my breast,
Both calling me, and forcing me to sing.

DAMON.

5. If in the lovely face vexation aught
Thou would'st in Phillis see, when you parted
From the joy you held so contentedly,
I know, sage Thirsis, that so sorrowful,

Thou wouldest come afflicted, as I come,
Seeing far different from what thou hast seen.

THIRSIS.

6. Damon, with what I said, I'm entertained,
By absence moderating the extreme of ill;
Cheerfully moving, staying, on I go.
That which is born for a living precedent
The deathless beauty here upon the soil,
Worthy of marble, crown, temple or tower—
With its rare virtue and an honest zeal,
The covetous eyes quite blinds.
Mistrusting not a contrary event—
The close submission which doth not deny
My soul unto her soul, the lofty aim
Which rests and assuages in its worshipping.
Cognizance admitting of this love,
Phillis, its correspondence in pure faith
Banishes dolour and contentment draws.

DAMON.

7. Happy Thirsis, with good fortune Thirsis,
Which for protracted ages may you hold
In amorous taste, in peace, security.
I whom the short, implacable gates of fate
Have urged into a so uncertain plight,
In merit poor, rich in anxiety;—
Well, 'tis for him who dies, for being dead
From cruel Amarillis no more fears,
Nor the disorder of ungrateful love.
Oh more than heaven, lovelier than the sun,
For me more durable than the diamond,
To my discomfort quick, slowly to good—
What south wind, what northeaster, what east wind,
With keenness blew on you, that you ordained,
My step should fly, nor be before you found.
Die will I, shepherdess, in foreign land,
Since you do so appoint—condemned I,
To irons, death, to yoke and galling chains.

THIRSIS.

8. Since with such 'vantages has thee endowed
All piteous heaven, friend Damon,

And genius given so quick and elevated—
Moderate with it grief, dole moderate—
Reflecting well that not unceasingly
The sun doth burn us, or cold petrify.
I would remark that our stern destiny
Followeth not a path with even steps
To bring us calm repose.
Occasionally by circumstance unseen.
From satisfaction and glory removed,
It bears us to a thousand dainty ends.
Revolve, dear friend, the memory,
By virtuous acts, which some time love gave you
For pledges positive of victory,
And if 'tis possible, a pastime seek.
The mind distracting, so that may pass away
This disenamoured, angry, heavy time.

DAMON.

9. To chill which for a term quite scorches me ;
To fire which without term congeals me too ;
Who will a limit fix, shepherd, or rate ?
In vain is wearied, in vain overwatched,
Is the deserted one, who at will obtains
The power of cutting the strong web of love.
Where love aboundeth there good fortune fails.

Thus concluded the exquisite songs of the well-favoured
swains, but not to the taste of the ladies who listened ; they
indeed did not wish a so early termination, for their ears
were unaccustomed to such ravishment.

Now the two swains advanced towards the spot where
the ladies stood, to the alarm of Teolinda, who feared she
might be recognised by them, so she asked Galatea to retire
from the situation. This she did, and on went the shepherds, and in the transit Galatea heard what Thirsis said to
Damon.

" These banks, friend Damon, are those where the heavenly
Galatea feeds her flocks, and where the enamoured Elicio
brings his, thy very intimate friend, to whom good fortune
imparted such success as his loving, honest, chaste desires
merit.

" Some days are past since I am unacquainted where his

lot has directed him, but as I have heard say from the circumspect state of the discreet Galatea, for whom he flutters on the verge of death, I fear he would be rather querulous than satisfied."

"At this I should not be at all surprised," replied Damon, "for with such accomplishments, so rich and rare, as the heavens have endowed Galatea, yet is she a woman in whose fragile composition one finds not always that intelligence which she ought to have, and that which is requisite, not less than fortune is, to life.

"What I have heard relative to the amours of Elicio is, that he adores Galatea, without falling into extravagance, and that Galatea's discretion is also such that she gives no indication of preference for, or aversion to, Elicio. So the luckless wight proceeds from mischance to mischance, awaiting time and fortune, almost lost, which may extend or abridge his existence, yet is it more probable that a shortening of it will ensue rather than a sustentation." To this point did Galatea hear what concerned her and Elicio, and what the shepherds discoursed, from which she received no little satisfaction, ascertaining what fame had published, and that it all was inconsistent with undoubted propriety; from that juncture she resolved to give Elicio no cause to remark that fame and fact did not coalesce. Now-at this epoch the two distinguished swains, with unequal steps, slowly wended towards the village, desirous of being present at the marriage of the unfortunate shepherd Daranio, who was to be joined in wedlock with Silveria, of the lively eyes (ojos verdes), and that was one of the reasons they had left their flocks, and had gone to Galatea's village.

Now, when they were a little off the road, on the right of the path, an instrument struck up with sweetness, and Damon, stopping, inserted his arm into that of Thirsis, saying, "Stop, hearken a little, for if my auditory organs deceive me not, the sound which arouses them is from friend Elicio's rebeck, on whom nature has lavished so much grace and aptitude; and if you listen duly you will know if it is he who performs on the instrument."

"Believe not, my Damon," said Thirsis, "it is only now that I know truly the parts of Elicio, for time it is that fame hath confirmed me in it. Yet be silent awhile, and let us learn if he chaunts aught indicative of the condition of his life."

"Thou hast well said so," rejoined Damon, "but that we may the better hear, let us conceal ourselves in these boughs, that out of sight we may listen nearer."

This they accomplished, and arranged themselves so nicely that not a word either said or sung by Elicio but might be heard and recorded.

Elicio was in company with his tried friend, Erastro, from whom rarely he separated, as his conversation and taste were in unison with his own, and much of the day did they pass together, in singing and modulating their instruments.

At this moment Elicio struck his rebeck, and Erastro gave his pipe breath, when Elicio poured forth these verses:—

ELICIO.

1. Restored to my loving thoughts,
   With my grief satisfied—
   Hoping no further glory
   I follow what my memory pursues,
   For invariably in it is represented
   A freedom and exemption from love's wiles.

2. With the eyes of the soul it is impossible
   To see the placid countenance
   Of my enemy.
   Glory and honour as much as heaven creates,
   And those eyes of the body exist alone, in seeing her,
   Blind, for in her the sun is seen.

3. Oh, hard bondage, though bearable—
   Oh, heavy hand
   Of love, can you so
   Quit me—ungrateful, the good compromised
   To do me; when free you jeered me
   About yourself, your bow and quiver.

4. How much beauty, oh, how white a hand
   My tyrant is;
   How you laboured
   First to cast o'er my neck the noose.
   You had indeed been vanquished in the strife
   Had Galatea not been in the world.

5. She alone was the one who could
   Deal out the cruel blow,
   Heartless,
   And the free thought subdue,
   Which, at your will, if it surrendered not,
   It had been steel or marble.

6. What freedom can thy charter shew,
   Before a severe visage,
   More than Phœbus, beauteous,
   What excites, and what insures repose.
   Ah, face, which on earth
   Discloses what heaven conceals.

7. How can nature blend
   Such rigour and fierceness
   With so much comeliness,
   So much courage and a state so rough?
   But my fortune, consenting
   To my ruin, unites contraries.

8. It is to my brief lot easy
   To see with bitter death
   Sweet life joined,
   And grief to be where good nestles itself;
   Hence, amidst opposites, I see
   How hopes decline, but not so the desire.

No further sang the love-impressed swain, nor would Thirsis and Damon longer remain, but giving lively and unexpected proof they advanced towards Elicio, who on seeing them recognised his Damon, and with incredible alacrity sallied forth to receive him, saying—

"What fortune, judicious Damon, has enacted it that you honour these banks with thy presence? How long have they desired it?" "Good, and naught else, can it be," replied Damon, "since it has caused me to see thee, O Elicio, and it is a thing I desired as my love was towards you, and your protracted absence, and the friendship I bear you, obliges. But if, for any reason you can repeat what you have said, it is because you have here before you the famous Thirsis, glory and honour of Castilian soil."

When Elicio heard that it was really Thirsis, known to him by fame only, receiving him with all courtesy, he said, "In sweet accord is thy well-favoured countenance, renowned Thirsis, with what thy valour and sobriety in near and remote lands speaking fame announces. So to me, who have admired your writings, and have desired, and have been inclined to know and serve you; may you henceforward hold me to be, and treat me, as your well-tried friend." "Very well is it known what I gain thereby," answered Thirsis, "so that uselessly would fame diffuse the esteem in which you hold me, did I not acknowledge the honour you do me by desiring me to be in the catalogue of your friends. Yet between people so situated as words of compliment should be excused, so let us cease, and let us rather supply evidence of our free will."

"Mine will be ever to serve you," rejoined Elicio; "as you will see, O Thirsis, should fortune or time enable me to be of any use to you." "For what I now possess, which for naught else would I exchange, is such that I can scarce proffer even desire—enjoying as you do, yours in so exalted a position," said Damon, "whose standard I should consider it to be a futility to reduce. Hence, friend Elicio, speak no evil of your present state, for my assurance is, that when it is contrasted with mine, I should rather envy than pity it."

"It seems to me, Damon," said Elicio, "that some days ago you left these banks, but you knew nothing of what love has caused me to feel on them.

"If this be so, you need not know or have experience of the condition of Galatea, for if you did, you would convert into pity the envy you have of me."

"He who has investigated Amarillis' state, what novelty can he expect from that of Galatea?" answered Damon. "Should you stay on these banks as far extended as I desire, you, Damon, will know and see on them, and you will also hear on others too, how equally poised are her cruelty and gentleness, extremes which will end the life of one, whose misfortune it was to adore her."

"On our banks of Henares," said Thirsis, "now Galatea has more fame for beauty than cruelty; but above all there is no question as to her discretion, and if that, as it should be, is true, from discretion arises knowledge; hence esteem.

and that precludes all compromise, and this too awakens restlessness."

"Now, seeing, Elicio, how unequally she responded to your solicitations, you give the name of cruelty to what you should rather term circumspection. I am not then surprised that this is the proper state of unrequited suitors."

"Reason good would you have, O Thirsis," replied Elicio, "did my desires deflect from a course compatible with honesty and soberness; but if they are so measured, and such as courage and credit exact, to what end this disdain? Such bitter and unsavoury replies? What can conceal a face whose glory is to be seen? Oh, Thirsis! Thirsis!" rejoined Elicio, "how can you consider love in so exalted a state of content, and yet with a so subdued spirit you discourse of its effects? I cannot see how what you now say agrees with what you formerly sang, thus :—

> Woe, from what rich hopes do I descend
> To the most shrunken and poorest desire—

with the residue, which to this you annexed."

To this moment Erastro stood silent, observing what passed between the swains, wondering at the openness and bearing, with other evidences, which each gave of his discretion. Seeing, however, they were constrained to reason on love matters, as one versed in them, he broke silence and spoke—

"Well, I believe, discreet swains, that wide experience will have evinced that one continued state of enamoured hearts exists not, which, impelled by external agency, are obnoxious to accidents; and thus, you, famous Thirsis, should not be surprised at what Elicio has advanced, or he at your assertions, or take for a specimen what he says you once sang, much less what I know you sang when you harped on 'my wanness and my weakness.'

"By which you exposed the woful state in which you then were, for in brief space there travelled to our cabins the news of your contentment, solemnised in your numerous verses, which if memory serves, thus began—'The morn arises, and from its fruitful hand—' "

"It is obvious then what difference time effects, and in its revolution love alters its condition, one day smiling, the next in deep laments.

"But to be fully aware of this condition, there was no need of asperity, or the coy disdain of Galatea, to complete my subversion, for of her I hope nothing further than what she desires. Who awaits not success from an enamoured, yet well measured desire, such as that which you have shown, O shepherd," said Damon, "merits renown rather than despair. Yet is it a matter of importance what you pretend from Galatea. Now assure me, swain, does she thus yield to you, and is your desire within the fitting medium, so that you do not transcend the point?"

"You may well yield credence thereto, friend Damon," said Elicio, "for the integrity of Galatea gives no place for aught else to be desired or hoped. And yet is this so hard to obtain, that sometimes Erastro's hope slackens in its ardour, and on me a cold chill comes, so that for certain he holds it, yea, for an established fact, that sooner death shall ensue than the fulfilment of it.

"Seeing, however, there is no reason to greet honoured guests with the acerbity of our misery, let us here remain, and hence proceed to the hamlet, where you may rest from the heavy toil of the road, and with more ease. If it be agreeable, you may hearken to our unquietness."

All delighted to acquiesce in the wish of Elicio, who with Erastro, recollecting the flocks, there being yet a superflux of time, in the society of the two swains, talking on divers affairs, all of a loving proclivity, they wended towards the village.

The pastime of Erastro was to sing and play, hence as well for this as for the desire to know if the two swains were equally competent in music, he touched his instrument to incite them to follow his example, asking Elicio to sound his rebeck also, and then he began to sing—

ERASTRO.

1. Before the light of certain serene eyes
   Which to the sun gives light—light to the earth—
   My soul is all in flames, so I suspect
   O death, that quickly you will snatch your spoils.

2. With light rays bundles do adjust themselves,
   The rays which emanate from great Delos' lord;
   Such are the hairs which I accustomed am,
   The beauty to adore, with fennel blent.

3. Oh light perspicuous, clear rays of the sun,
   Before the sun itself, from you I hope,
   Only you would consent, Erastro, love.

4. But should in this heaven a niggard prove,
   Ere grief complete the doleful death I die,
   Dispose it so, O rays, that one ray slay.

This sonnet did not seem ill to the shepherds, or did Erastro's voice discontent them, and although it was not an exquisite voice, yet was it in harmony, and quickly Elicio, moved by Erastro's example, touched his pipe, to the sound of which this sonnet was sung—

ELICIO.

1. Woe to the lofty purpose which exists,
   In contemplations loving and intense,
   In opposition heaven, fire, wind, present,
   The water, earth itself, my enemies are.

2. Adverse are those from whom I should have fear,
   The emprise abandoning and good intent,
   Who can avert that which the violent
   Implacable destiny wills?   Can love contend?

3. The heaven upraised, love, wind and fire itself,
   The ocean vast, the earth, my enemies are—
   With violence each, combined with destiny,

4. Prevents my good, scatters, scorches quick
   My hope undoes, so that without its aid,
   To quit what is begun 's not possible.

When Elicio ended, Damon incontinently, to the echo of the same flute, woke into voice what follows :—

DAMON.

1. More ductile was I than soft wax itself,
   When on my soul the sweet face I impressed,
   Of Amarillis lovely, coy, and hard,
   Even as marble, or a savage beast.

2. Love me exalted to a lofty sphere,
 The highest of her goods, and fortune's height,
 I live in dread that sepulture alone
 My young presumption will annihilate

3. On hope love leaned, eternal in the breast,
 As on the elm the vine, I mounted up,
 His humour failed me, and the flight was stopped.

4. It is not from my eyes, from whose long use,
 Fortune knows well there no cessation is,
 From rendering tribute to face, breast or soil.

When Damon had finished, Thirsis began to recite this sonnet to the sound of the instruments of the three shepherds—

THIRSIS.

1. Clean through the medium of the threads of death,
 My faith was severed, and to such state am come,
 That I no envy have of highest place,
 Which can encircle fortunate human lot.

2. From only seeing you arises this,
 Phillis, oh, Phillis fair, whom destiny
 With rare and extreme essence has endowed
 To smiles grief turning, and to evil good.

3. How softened is a sentence's harsh rigour,
 If the condemned turns to the sovereign face—
 A law it is that nothing right distorts.

4. Thy dear enchanting presence all before,
 E'en death flies off, and evil self recedes,
 Life and advantages leaving in lieu.

At the conclusion of Thirsis' strain, the combined instruments of the swains elaborated most sweet music, conferring satisfaction on all who heard, and even within the dense branches a thousand painted warblers, with divine harmony, echoed the chorus.

A little distance had they gone, when they reached an ancient hermitage, which had its site on the side of a hillock, not so remote from the path but that a harp was heard, on which Erastro remarked, " Stay, swains, for methinks this day we shall hear what I have longed to hear of a long season, namely, the voice of a truly well-conditioned youth who is within the hermitage, and who some twelve or fourteen days only has come to dwell in it, and to pass a life too rigid for his years, and sundry times as I have been going by I have heard a harp twang, and accompanied by a voice so bland, that my desire has been awakened to hear it, but I have always arrived just as he finished ; yet in conversation with him have I made myself his friend, offering him all I could, and all I have ; never could I learn who he was, or what occasioned one so young to expose himself to so much solitude and a so confined state." What Erastro communicated relative to the youth and the hermit in his noviciate, awakened in the shepherds the same curiosity, and so they agreed to proceed to the hermitage, and, without being known, to listen to what he sang before any conversation ensued.

This doing, it succeeded so well, that they located themselves so as not to be seen or heard, and their ears were gladdened with the tones of the harp which was within, and the verses also.

1. Had it pleased heaven and fortune,
   Without being offended with me,
   To have been content to fix me in this state,
   In vain did air transmit my heavy groans.
   In vain even to the moon
   Is my thought raised.
   Oh, rigorous fate !
   Through what strange unwonted ways,
   My sweet joys
   Have come to settle into such extremes,
   That I am dying, yet existence dread.

2. I 'gainst myself burning with anger go,
   Seeing how I suffer.
   This breast is bursting ; to the wind I give
   This soul, which in the midst of heavy woe,
   From the heart withdraws
   The last remnants of breath.
   Now anew I feel,
   That hope assisteth to supply me strength—
   A feigned force for life.
   No pity from heaven,
   With length of life much suffering is ordained.

3. Of the dear friend, the sadly injured breast
    Mine melted,
    Taking charge of the hard enterprise.
    Oh, discreet feigning of madness !
    Oh, deed such as was ne'er seen !
    Oh, accident most tasteful ! bitter, yet.
    How liberal and large
    For good externe has love displayed itself.
    How covetous and replete
    For me, with both fidelity and fear ;
    But a firm friend doth bind us more and more.

4. Tributes unjust with just desires, too,
    At each step do we see,
    By the disdainful hand of fortune given ;
    And of thee, false love, of whom we know
    How thou rejoicest and tasteth
    That by which dying, constant lovers live
    A burning and a quick
    Flame is kindled on your pinions' light.
    The good and evil
    Arrows into dust resolve,
    Or to revert, themselves against to strike.

5. By what cause, with what fraud and subtlety
    By what a compass extraordinary,
    Of me entire possession hast thou ta'en ?
    And how in my piteous deep desire,
    Into my pure inwards,
    The sound will, false one, hast thou changed —
    Judgment will suffice
    The sight to bear in patience, perjured one,
    Between the free and safe.
    In treating of thy glories and thy wrongs,
    Upon the neck the chains harshly are felt.

6. Yet not of thee or me would there exist
    Reason for a complaint,
    For to thy fire it no resistance makes,
    Myself delivered up, I caused to blow
    The wind which slept
    With rage and violence for the event.
    Most righteous sentence

'Gainst me has given heaven, who now expire.
However, hope yet lives,
That from my luckless fate and fortunes ill,
A sepulture may not complete my woe.

7. Oh, my sweet friend ! oh, enemy how sweet !
Timbrio and Nisida the beautiful.
Happy united, yet unhappy are
What hard, unjust, inexorable star,
Enemy of my wrong,
What power unjust of fate implacable
Does us asunder keep ?
Oh, miserable, human, fragile lot,
How quick is changed
Into a sudden grief, a joy,
And darkest night follows the clearest day.

8. To changes great, and to the inconstancy
Of sublunary things,
Where is the bold one who would trust thereto ?
Time on its hasty wings its flight pursues,
Hope in the rear
Ariseth in the midst of smiles and wails,
And ere heaven sends forth
Its favour, sole contributing with zeal,
That which to holy heaven doth exalt
The soul on fire, undone by its own love,
And that which no less hurts than does advance.

9. I, my good Lord, as I can elevate
The one and other palm,
My eyes intent on the all sacred sky,
By which my soul doth hope
To see protracted grief turned into smiles.

With a sigh, piteous and profound, the retired youth
terminated his mournful ditty in the hermitage; and the
swains, perceiving that he did not advance, without further
delay collectively they entered, where they saw at the end,
sitting on a hard stone, a well-looking and a graceful youth,
somewhat between twenty to twenty-two years old, clad in
a rough coarse cloth, (tosco buriel), his feet unshod, and a
sharp rope around his body, which served him for string.
His head was leaning on one side, and his hand rested on

that portion of the tunic which covered his heart, while the other arm fell down loosely by his side; and as he made no movement when the shepherds entered, they clearly perceived that he was bewildered, as in truth it was so; for the depth of his sorrow had brought on that effect.

Towards him went Erastro, and uniting his arm to his, caused him to revert to himself, although so much disordered, and as if he had awakened from heavy sleep, which signs engendered in those who witnessed it no small grief, when Erastro said, "What is the matter, Sir, what oppresses thy exhausted breast? Fail not to say, for where are they who will refuse nothing to supply relief?"

"These are not the first offers," replied the adult, with a somewhat half-delirious voice, "that you have made me, nor would they be the last of which I should avail me if I could. But fortune has reduced me to such a state, that you can do nothing, or I satisfy you more than with desire. This can you take for the good you purpose me; and should you wish to know aught else, time, which nothing conceals, will reveal what I had rather you should not know."

"If you leave it to time to satisfy us," said Erastro, "that tribute will not suffice; for in spite of us time openly discloses the secrets of the heart."

Then the rest of the swains asked him to recount his misfortunes, particularly Thirsis, who added cogent reasons, and caused him to know that in this life there is no evil without a corresponding remedy, unless Death, the interposer, prevents. To these remarks he annexed others, while the pertinacious youth gave motion for a satisfying reply as to all they sought to know, and thus said on:—

"Since it had been better, gracious companion, to live what is left of life, and to have retired to a deeper solitude, yet not to prove obstinate to the wish you have announced, I make up my mind to state to you what it suffices to know, and how fickle fortune has brought me to the state you see. Yet, presuming on the lateness of the time, and remembering the multitude of my sorrows, it were possible that night would close ere my recital ended.

"It would be better to repair to the village, for even this night can I undertake the journey without inconvenience, which I had projected for the morrow, and this is imperative, as in your village I should be provided with all I require for my sustenance, and so by the way, as we may the better do it, I will inform you truly of my disasters."

Now this to all seemed reasonable, and so placing him in the centre with some deviousness of path they pursued their way to the village, and incontinently the afflicted hermit, with signs of woe, commenced the record of his realised sorrows.

"In the antique and famous city of Xeres, whose indwellers are favoured by Minerva and Mars, was born Timbrio, a cavalier of celebrity; and were I to recount his achievements and qualities, it would impose on me a heavy task.

"Suffice to know whether by the excess of his goodness, or by the influence of stars which caused me to gravitate towards him, I managed to make of him a particular friend by every human means; and, in this, heaven proved so favourable that those who knew us, almost forgetting the name of Timbrio, and that of Silerio, which is my name, they called us the two friends, whilst we so operating by our continual unanimity and good works justified the appellation.

"Subordinate to this lot did we two with incredible satisfaction pass our adult years, now in the chase, now in the city, honoured by Mars, up to that hour (for the many unlucky days (aciagos) which the enemy of time has made me to see) when it happened to my friend Timbrio to have a serious quarrel with a valiant cavalier, near to the city. The affair was brought to an issue, when the knight was touched in his honour, and so Timbrio was constrained to absent himself, to give time for the furious discord which had been kindled between the parents to cool, leaving a letter written to his enemy, stating that he should go to Milan or Naples in Italy, and that his enemy would them find him ready to give further satisfaction.

"From this period ceased the factions between the relatives of both parties, and a challenge ensued between Timbrio and Pransiles, the name of the offended knight, and the place of combat·was made known to Timbrio.

"My luckless fate ordained when this occurred that my own health failed, and I could scarce rise from my bed, so I was forced to forego the accompanying of my friend, who on taking leave of me with much reluctance, charged me that on the restoration of my health I should find him in Naples, quitting me with more anguish than I can repeat.

"At the end of a few days, (finding my desire to see him greater than my physical weakness to stay away) I set off; and that my journey should be accomplished more securely, and with despatch, chance offered to me the convenience of four galleys which in Cadiz lay ready for sailing, in all marine gear perfect. In one of these I embarked, and, the winds favouring, we discovered shortly the Catalon coast, and, having cast anchor in one of the ports, for I was sadly sick of and by the sea, I disembarked, being assured that certainly the vessel would not put out again that night, with only one servant—never believing that at midnight the sailors, or those commanding the galley, seeing the serenity of the sky, and that a prosperous gale had arisen, and not to lose the precious opportunity, at the second watch, would launch the vessel. So hauling up the anchor, they set the oars in motion on the quiet ocean, the sails were given to the favourable gales, and off they set with so much celerity that with all my endeavours to re-embark there was no time. Thus was I left to wander on the beach, and to feed on the annoyance of what had occurred, badly provided with necessaries which were indispensable to a continuance of my journey.

"Reflecting, however, that slight remedy remained, I resolved to return to Barcelona, a city large enough to supply what had failed me, the prices of articles corresponding with the Xeres and Seville markets.

"With these thoughts I awoke to put them into execution, and waited till day had advanced, and being on the point of leaving, I perceived a terrible earthly noise, and saw the populace making for the principal city gate, and on inquiring what it was, the reply was, 'Go, sir, to that corner, and the bellman will tell you all about it.'

"This did I, and the first thing that struck my eyes was a crucifix, and much people, a sign that some one sentenced to death was on the way, which the voice of the town-crier confirmed, exclaiming, that being a highway robber and a brigand, justice ordained that he should be hanged.

"As I advanced towards the supposed culprit, in a

twinkling I recognised my dear friend Timbrio, who onward came, his hands in fetters, a close garment to his neck, and eyes rivetted on a crucifix, which was before him, disputing with the priests who accompanied him, and alleging, by the name of that God in whose presence he should quickly be, whose effigy he bore before him, that never in his life had he committed an act for which he deserved public execution, and he supplicated all to petition the judge to give him time to prove his innocence.

" Only let me then consider what must have been my feelings at this dreadful spectacle. I must tell you, friends, that I was so astonished and beside myself, and my senses were so suspended, that I should have had the semblance of a statue of marble to any one who looked on me. But when the confused noise of the populace, the upraised voice of the criers, the piteous expressions of Timbrio, and the consolations of the priests and the true condition of my good friend had brought me out of my amazement, and my o'er-charged blood had given succour to my faint heart, and had awakened in it a desire to avenge the wrongs of my Timbrio, regardless of the imminent peril. Looking to Timbrio, if by any means I could liberate him, or follow him to the the grave, careless of life, I clutched my sword, and with supernatural fury I rushed into the centre of the mob and forced a way to Timbrio, who not knowing if these weapons were unsheathed for his good, with a mind perplexed in the extreme, looked on what took place, until I addressed him— ' Where is the vigour of thy valiant breast, O Timbrio! what are thy hopes? what seest thou? why does not this occasion succour you? Up! friend, and save thy life, while mine shall be your buckler and a defence against this injustice.' These my words, and Timbrio's recognition of me, were such, that fear fled, and with it the bonds and manacles were burst ; yet had been his courage of little avail, had not the clergy, moved by compassion, aided his desires, who seizing on him bodily, despite those who would hinder, made for a church hard by, leaving me in the midst of justices, who did their best to capture me, which eventually they did, for I could not resist alone the united force brought against me ; and with more offence than it seemed to me my crime deserved, they bore me off to the public prison, smitten with two wounds. My audacity, and enabling Timbrio to escape, augmented my crime, and the disgust of the judges, who weighing my excess, they adjudged that I was worthy of death, and so forthwith passed sentence, remanding execution to a subsequent day. This additional piece of bad news heard Timbrio in the church, and as I learned lately it gave him a severer shock than if his own death had been announced, and to disengage me from such an alternative, he volunteered to surrender himself again to justice. The priests, however, took counsel together, and thought that would not do, for it only swelled the evil, and was a step from one disgrace to another, for that he could not be taken that I should be released; that crime being committed, it was law that it should be punished.

" The reasons for persuading Timbrio not to surrender were not inconsiderable, yet he calmed his conscience by proposing one day to reciprocate the benefit, to discharge his obligation to me, or die in the attempt. All this I ascertained from a priest to whom I had to confess, and then I informed him that the best remedy for my wretched state was that he should secure his safety, and go with all despatch and impart the story to the viceroy of Barcelona, ere there was any further thought about capital punishment. I now learned why my friend Timbrio was involved in a penal verdict from the priest's mouth—for it came to pass that Timbrio prosecuting his way through the province of Catalonia, just as he entered on Perpignan, some brigands fell on him, whose head was a valorous Catalan captain, who to satisfy sundry enormities, as their savage wont is, when they are persons of mark, sally forth and work all the abomination they can, as well on the cultivation as on the farms—a very curse on Christianity itself, and worthy every reprobation. It fell out, that when the brigands were stripping Timbrio, the lord and master came up and enjoined that no personal injury should be inflicted on him; nay, seeing that he was a gentleman, they acted very courteously, soliciting his stay for the night, and with them in an adjacent place, and that the next day he should be provided with a pass of safety, which extended to the limits of the province. Now Timbrio could not reject this refinement, bound by so many obligations; so all went together, and they arrived at a little spot, and were received cheerfully by the people. But fortune, which had played Timbrio tricks, ordained that in the night a company of soldiers should drop on the brigands, and were so disposed that by a sort of *coup de main* they surprised and put them to the route; and as the chief escaped, they took and slew many, and captured Timbrio, whom they took to be a most famous member of the company, and of course such an inference was natural; for they did not imagine he was other than he appeared to be, and the evidence of others infused such malice into the breasts of the judges, that without further verification they sentenced him to death, and this had taken effect, had not kind heaven interposed and ordered that the galleys should sail, and I be left on land to remedy the evil before us. Thus, Timbrio remained in the church, I in prison, making arrangements to part that night for Barcelona. I trusted to arrest the fury of the enflamed judges from this great misfortune. Timbrio and I were liberated. But would to heaven that on me only had its fury fallen, so that it had been removed from that small and unlucky people, whose necks were exposed to the edge of a thousand barbarous swords.

"It would be about the middle of the night, a time dedicated to wicked deeds, and in which the over-worked world surrenders its tired limbs to nature's sweet restorer—balmy sleep, when unexpectedly a confused cry arose from the mob, —'To arms! to arms! the Turks are here.' The echo of such doleful screams, who doubts that female breasts would not quake, and even infuse fear in men's hearts? True it is, gentlemen, what I say, but in no time almost did the wretched soil begin to burn with so great fury that the very stones themselves supplied *pabulum* for a conflagration which involved all in ruin. Through the light of the tossing flames were distinguished, the scymitars flashing, and the white attire of the Turks, who, furnished with axes and hatchets of durable steel, beat down the house-doors, and rushing through them, carried off Christian spoils.

"What the wearied matron bore, what the tender child, who with worn out or feeble groans, the mother for the son, and the son for the mother asked; and some I know who with sacrilegious hand arrested the accomplishment of the

6

just desires of the chaste recently espoused virgin, and the
unhappy mate, before whose eyes of grief, perhaps, saw
gathered the fruit of what he unluckily trusted shortly to
enjoy.   Such was the turmoil, such the cries and *melée* of
divers voices, that fear predominated everywhere.   The
savage and bedevilled mob, seeing resistance to be feeble,
were emboldened to enter the holy fanes, and set their ex-
communicated hands on the holy relics, appropriating the
very gold which adorned them, then hurling them to the
ground with disgusting contempt.   Sanctity did not serve
the priest, or the convent the fire ; a hoary head was no
protection to age, or sprightliness to youth, to the child its
natural simplicity.   No—those unbelieving dogs exposed
all to one general sack ; who after burning the houses, spoil-
ing the temples, devirginating maidens, slaying defenders,
more tired than satisfied, when morning broke, without any
obstacle, returned to their vessels, and charged them with
the choicest plunder, leaving the place desolate and destitute of inhabitants; for the mass made off and retired to
the mountains and elsewhere in divisions.   Whose hands
could rest still, whose eyes dry at such a spectacle ? Woe—
woe, how full of miseries are our lives ! what a doleful story
have I recounted, and can Christian hearts rejoice ? and
some there were in prison who in the general misfortune
concealed their own hopes, for at the sound of going to the
defence of the people they burst the prison gates and became free, not caring to defend the oppressed, but to save
themselves, and among them I got my liberty also, so dearly
acquired.   Seeing now that none made head against the
enemy, not to come near them, or return to prison, forsak-
ing the forlorn populace, with no little grief at what I had
seen, and the pain my wounds caused me, I followed a man
who said to me that he would safely lead me to a monastery in
the mountain range, where I should be healed of my wounds
and protected also, if any further quest was made of me. Him
I followed, as I have stated, to ascertain with zeal the fate of
my friend Timbrio, who I found had escaped with some
wounds, and had taken some mountain route, different from
what I had chosen.   He stopped at the port of Rosas, and
there abode some days, trying to discover what had been
my fate. Hearing nothing for certain, he left in a vessel and
with a fortunate gale reached Naples.

"I reverted to Barcelona, and there procured what I needed. Recovering from my wounds, I prosecuted my voyage, and without any accident I got to Naples, where I soon found Timbrio unwell; and such was the joy that we mutually had, that I have not strength enough to appreciate it (encarecerosle). We mutually recounted our lives, comprising whatever had overtaken us. Still was this joy diluted in not finding my friend Timbrio, as I wished; in fact, his infirmity was so distressing and of so uncommon a nature, that had I not then reached him, I had just come in time for his obsequies, and not for delight in a personal visit. Having received from me all required information, and his eyes in tears, he said, 'Alas! friend Silerio, now I believe that heaven has o'erwhelmed me with disasters, exchanging health, each day I should be more bound to serve you.' These words touched my soul, but for courtesy's sake, so little applied. I was filled with astonishment. So not to weary you with minute particulars as to my answer, or his rejoinders, in fine, I reveal it, that the luckless Timbrio was deep in love with a distinguished lady of Naples, (whose parents were Spanish), but born in Naples. Her name was Nisida, and her physical perfections such that I am bold enough to aver, that nature concentrated in her all her attractive graces, and so sweetly were blended beauty and virtue, that what kindled one the other froze, and the desires which her gentility raised to an unwonted elevation, her marked propriety again brought down to earth. Hence poor Timbrio remained as destitute of hope as rich in thought; this impaired his health, and set him on the borders of death, without disclosing his passion, such fear and reverence had he for Nisida.

" Now, when I discovered his malady, and saw Nisida, considering the high quality of her parents, I resolved to surrender for his benefit land, life and fame, yea more, if more could be. So I devised a scheme more curious and *outré* than any yet known, and this was, to attire myself like a buffoon, and guitar in hand invade Nisida's house, which, as being one of first-rate quality, also entertained divers of the same type.

" This idea suited Timbrio, and he handed over to me the burden of the affair. Quickly I transformed myself, and in my new vestments I essayed my novel undertaking before Timbrio, who laughed heartily to see me in a buffoon's dress, and to observe if aptitude and habit corresponded, he said to me, considering he is a great magnate, and I but a freshman there, that I should address him in a few fugitive words.

"If I do not forget, and you, gentlemen, are not worn out with my tale, I will recite to you what I then sang for the first time."

All concurred, saying no greater content could they experience, than hearing minutely the detail of the business, and moreover subjoined that no fraction even should be omitted.

" Hence you will accord me this licence," said the Hermit, " that I fail not to inform you exactly as to how I began my undertaking of a fool ; yet was it with the accompanying verses which I sang to Timbrio, imagining him to be some grand mi-lordo, to whom they were addressed."

SILERIO.

1. From a prince, who on the ground
   Shapes his course to a just level,
   What can hope therefrom,
   Save works that are divine?

2. One sees not in the present age,
   Or did one in the past age see,
   A republic governed
   By a so prudent prince,
   From him who measures his zeal
   By a christian standard
   What can one hope therefrom
   But works divine?

3. Who acts for another's good
   And covets not more spoils,
   Mercy in his eyes,
   Justice in his bosom,
   The more of this soil there is
   The less there be in it of ill ;
   What can hope one therefrom
   If they be not works divine?

4. Your free fame
Which towers heavenwards,
Whereby you do retain a pious soul
Proof gives us, and clear evidence
It diverges not a hair
From being to heaven loyal ;
What can one hope therefrom,
But that they heaven's works be ?

5. Who with a christian breast
Always rigour retards,
Justice keeps him,
With clemency his right ;
Where'er the flight uplifts,
Nothing touches him ;
What can one hope therefrom
If they be not works of divine nature ?

These and such like things did I sing to Timbrio, in downright playfulness, making the briskness and the ductility of the body accommodate itself, so that there was no doubt as to acting the buffoon, and out of it I got so well, that I have obtained a city reputation, so that the name of buffoon became general, and they desired to see me at the house of Nisida's father, with which request I should fully have complied if too curiously I had not apprehended close questions.

Still I could proffer no excuse when, one banquet day, I could not be there, and came to detect more closely the just cause for Timbrio's suffering, and the cause which heaven supplied me, for taking away that content which ever should remain to us in life. Nisida, I saw, not to say more—for having once seen her, it sufficed—Oh, powerful force of love, how little do all our powers prevail ! Is it possible that in a twinkling, in a moment thou couldst break up all my fortifications and adjuncts of loyalty, and lay them in the dust ? Woe if the consideration of who I was should retard a little its succour, the friendship which I owed to Timbrio, the innate virtue of Nisida, and the degrading buffoon habit in which I was, all which was a hindrance to the new desire, and amorous too, which had taken root in me, had there not also arisen the hope of attaining that which is the support on which love walks, or reverts to the first principles of love. In a word, I beheld the beauty mentioned, and though it was of value to me to see her, I essayed to secure the friendship of her parents, and the whole household, through the medium of the office which I executed with all possible grace and discretion.

One day, a knight, one of the guests, begged me to sing something in praise of the lady's beauty, and it happened that my memory furnished some verses thrown off a little before, for a like occasion, and these were the words :—

SILERIO.

1. Nisida, in whom heaven
   Has shown itself so liberal,
   In giving you to us, and gave to earth
   An image, and has removed
   What the close veil concealed ;
   Had heaven only given you
   We readily apprehend
   What the possible pretends,
   To praise you who pretends.

2. Of this foreign beauty
   The sovereign perfection 'tis
   Which wafts us heavenwards ;
   As to human 'tis impossible,
   So to a divine tongue belongs its praise,
   And let it say, I know that it is right
   That to the soul which in itself doth dwell,
   That it should wonderful and lofty be.
   Should the all beauteous veil accorded be,
   More were it than the world or had, or has.

3. It took the rays of the sun,
   Of the sloping sky the brow,
   The light of beauteous eyes,
   More luminous than a star
   Which yields no light before them,
   As one can and is bold enough ;
   Of scarlet and of snow
   It robs the colours :
   And what are the most perfect of them eke
   Belongeth to thy cheeks.

> 4. Of marble and of coral
> Teeth and lips it formed ;
> Whence emanate a rich possession
> Of sayings acute and wise,
> A harmony celestial ;
> Of stubborn marble is framed
> The white and lovely breast.
> And of such works so left,
> By how much the pure clay improved is,
> By so much is high heaven satisfied.

With these and other songs which I sang, all were in raptures with me, especially the parents of Nisida, who offered me all I wanted, and requested me to visit them daily. So never imagining or discovering my aim, I succeeded in my first essay, which was to gain facile entrance to the house of Nisida, who was charmed with my easy deportment.

However, in a few days, and much conversation, and the amity which all extended to me in that mansion, were removed some of the shadows of fear, which I entertained as to breaking my object to Nisida, so I resolved to see how Timbrio's good fortune eventuated, as he awaited all from my zeal. But alas, I required medicine for my own wound rather than seeking safety for another ; for the liveliness, beauty, discretion and gravity of Nisida had wrought such effect in my breast, that its subtle influence had invaded it in a no less woeful assault than in that of Timbrio. So I leave to your discreet minds the task of imagining what a heart could do, which at once had to combat the duties of loyalty to a friend, and the invincible laws of Cupid—for if one oblige me not to deviate from what reason dictated, the other constrained what satisfaction alone would ratify.

These surprises and inward contests so harassed me, that without regarding the health of another, I began to doubt the stability of my own, and became so weak and wan, that it awakened a general compassion in all beholders, particularly in the parents of Nisida ; even the lady herself with pure and christian sympathy, asked me often whatever was the cause of my infirmity, suggesting that she herself would try to remedy it. " Woe," (said I within myself, if Nisida is so benevolent) " and with what ease, lovely Nisida, could your hand impart balm to the wound which your loveliness has made." Still I kept myself of so good mind, that though I knew my remedy for certain, yet did I hold it to be impossible and uncertain, so that I could not accept the prescription. Now these reflections quite upset my reason, and I could answer nothing to Nisida ; hence she and her sister Blanca (younger, yet by no means of inferior prudence or beauty) were astounded, and with a deep desire to learn the origin of my grief, beset me with importunities, that I should withhold nothing from their knowledge. Seeing how chance had furnished me with an occasion to effectuate that which until now my industry had failed to do, one day when the two damsels were quite alone, and who again reiterated their enquiries, I said to them—" Conclude not, ladies, that the silence I have hitherto observed in not disclosing to you the heavy grief, which you conceive I feel, had been the result of any indisposition to satisfy you, know then, that if my deplorable state still retains aught of good, it is the having cultivated your acquaintance, and as a servant, to obey you. The cause alone has been to imagine that, despite the discovery, it will only aggravate the grief, contemplating how far the remedy is still off. But as you forced me to satisfy you in this particular, learn, dear ladies, that in this very city dwells a knight, who is a Spaniard born, whom I call master, for shield and a friend the most generous, sober, and gentle soul that may be found, who is now away from his own beloved land on account of certain events, which impelled his settling here, believing that if in his own country he left foes, here, in a foreign soil, he should not fail of friends. His ideas have been so reversed, that one sole enemy he has unwittingly created, and to such extremity are matters come that if kind heaven aid him not, his woes and enmities will bring him to the grave. Knowing, as I do, the good attributes of Timbrio (the name of the gentle cavalier, whose history I tell, and I also know what the world will lose in his loss, and especially my own loss), I offer proofs of a sensibility which you have seen, and even these are inconsiderable if I count on the danger in which Timbrio is placed. Well I conjecture what you, dear ladies, would desire to know, which is, who is this enemy, who has involved the valiant cavalier you have just depicted, in such desperate straits. However, I knew that in mentioning him, you will not be surprised, save how, as yet, he is not consumed and dead. His enemy is Love—that general destroyer of our calms and successes. This relentless foe seized hold of his vitals ; for on his arrival here his eyes lighted on a lady of singular quality and beauty, yet so raised in society, and so virtuous, that the miserable patient has not dared to declare his passion.'

To this point I had attained when Nisida remarked, " Of a truth, Astor," for I then went by that appellation, " I have my doubts if this cavalier be so brave or discreet as you allege, since he has so easily abandoned himself to this newly-engendered disorder, and thus hopelessly has surrendered himself to despair. In my case, though I never yield to such amorous effects, still do I hold it for mere simplicity and debility in him who is so touched to discover his grief to him who is the main cause of it ; for what affront can ensue to her to show how fondly she is loved, or to him what greater evil, from a bitter and tasteless reply, than death itself, which he causes by concealment ? And would it not be better than holding a reputation for rigour to relax a little from right ? But suppose death should happen to a man so silent and sensitive as your friend, say would you call the lady cruel of whom he is enamoured ? Of a truth not. How can wounds be cured, of whose inveteracy nothing is known, or what obligation exists in any one to remedy evil which is not brought to light ? Now, let me assure you, Astor, that, from such acts as these, your friend deserves not the laudation which you have showered upon him."

These reasons once heard from Nisida's own mouth, quickly wished I to discover the inward secret of my breast ; but appreciating the goodness and plainness of her communication, I held back, and awaited a more solitary and proper conjuncture, and thus I answered—

" When man sees love cases, charming Nisida, with freedom, so much rashness ensues, not less than utter risibility, that they merit pity. Once let the imprisoned soul find itself in that subtle, amorous net, then arise sentiments so laboured and foreign to nature that memory is the treasurer and warder of the objects which the eyes have seen. The mind is occupied in scrutinising and sifting the worth of what is beloved, whilst will, memory and understanding engage in nothing else. So the eyes see as by a magnifying glass, enlarging all they view. If at all favoured, hope enlarges, if unlucky, in comes fear. This is what has occurred to Timbrio, whose lofty vision reached its object and lost it when attained, yet was love the cause of all. Who knows? it may so be. Thus vanishes hope in a moment, between two waters, as one is wont to say; if one should be forsaken of all, with the other would love fly.

"Hence originates the going between fear and daring in the heart of the afflicted lovers, which, without venturing to reveal it, gathers up itself, and aggravates the wound, and hopes, but from whom he knows not, the remedy he discerns to be so remote. Precisely thus found I Timbrio, although, at my intervention, he has addressed a note to her for whom he is dying, which he entrusted to me to deliver, and to learn if in it there existed anything unacceptable, that it might be amended. Thus I undertook the charge to place it in the hands of the lady, which I thought impossible, not because I would not venture on such an act, nay, I would even venture my own life to serve him, but that I had no fear opposition would arise."

"Let us look at it," said Nisida, "for I would gladly see how love-letters can be discreetly penned."

On the instant, out I drew, from my bosom, the very note, which was only a few days old, hoping Nisida would read it, and so the opportunity occurring, I showed it to her, and now from memory, for many perusals impressed it there, I will give you its very arguments :—

TIMBRIO TO NISIDA.—"I have resolved, beauteous lady, that my wretched end should inform you who I was, as it seemed to me more fitting that you should rather praise my silence in death than blame my boldness in life. For I deem it more appropriate to my soul to leave this world in your favour. In the other world love refuses not the reward of suffering ; hence I make known to you the condition into which your rare beauty has thrown me, which is such that the power of indicating it would not furnish a remedy. Since, for small matters, no one would dare to do violence to your extreme worth, from which, and from your intense liberality, I hope to restore a life to serve you, or reach death, whereby I can no further offend."

Nisida was very earnest in hearing the contents of the letter, and at its close said, " The lady to whom this note is addressed, has small cause to be affronted, unless out of pure pride she abandons herself to coyness, a disease which few ladies of this city escape. Yet Astor, with all this, you must not fail to give it to her, as I have remarked no greater evil can result from an answer than is the suffering of your friend ; and thereto, to incite you more, I wish to assure you that there is no lady so circumspect, and so mounted on a watch-tower (puesta en atalaya), to guard her own honour, whom it would much afflict to know and see that she was beloved.

" She then discerns that her presumption is not vain, which would be quite the contrary, if she found herself to be courted by no one."

My reply to this was, " All this I know in truth, dear lady, yet have I some apprehension about daring to give the note, for at least it would cost me something to deny doing so, whereby a not less evil would accrue also to me than to Timbrio."

" You desire not Astor," rejoined Nisida, " to ratify a sentence not proclaimed by the judge. Cheer up, this is a not so much to be dreaded battle on which you venture."
" Would to heaven, charming Nisida," I again said, " that I found myself so situated that with freer will I should offer my breast to the dangers and fury of a thousand opposed arms, than my hand to deliver the loving letter to one who might take offence at it, and so to throw on my shoulders a fault which another deserves to bear. Despite these inconveniences I would follow your counsel to me, for I await a time when fear may not possess my breast so much as now. In the meanwhile I beseech you to admit that you are the person for whom the note is intended, and that you will also furnish me with some reply to Timbrio, that with this subterfuge he may entertain himself a little, and that I may find precisely how to act, according to time and event."

" You would use a discreditable artifice," answered Nisida, " for suppose I, in a feigned name, gave a soft or scornful reply, see you not that time the interpreter of events will clear up the deceit, and that Timbrio will be more vexed with himself than satisfied? Yea, further, for having given no reply up to this moment to such notes, I would rather not do it feignedly, though he should know my acts are against myself. If you promise to tell me who the lady is, I will tell you what you may say to your friend, and so to leave him satisfied for the time being ; and should matters eventually turn out adversely, yet will no untruth be proved from that circumstance."

" This you do not order me to do, O Nisida, for I am reduced to no less a strait in announcing to you the lady's name than in delivering the note. Suffice it to know that it is expedient, or without doing hurt to you, to say that her beauty is such that I prize it above all living types."

" At this I am not surprised, for with men of your condition and dealing, flattery is a trade. Putting this on one side, for I would not you should lose the advantage of such a friend, I counsel you to tell him you went to give the letter to his lady, and that you have exchanged with her all the reasons, as with me, without any diminution, and as she perused your letter, and the spirit with which he inspired you to deliver it to your lady, thinking it was not addressed to her, and that though your courage could not go so far as to reveal all which you have known of her, that though she should learn that the note was really for her, that the deceit or the truth will not cause much annoyance.

" By this he will receive some solace in his trial, and having discovered your intentions towards his lady, you can announce to Timbrio her answer, since up to this point with which she is conversant, the fiction remains in force, and the truth of what would happen without any deception at all."

I was quite astonished at the subtle contrivance of Nisida, not without suspicion of the validity of my artifice, and so, saluting her hand for the consolatory advice, and leaving with her the success of the business, I made off to recount to Timbrio all the interview with Nisida, that I might awaken in him new hope, and sustain him too, and banish from his heart those clouds of fear, which up to the present time had darkened it ; and all this comfort was increased by

my promising him that my services were ever at his call;
so at any other time if he was in Nisida's company he could
play the card with the success which his thoughts deserved.
I forgot to add one thing, that during the interview with
Nisida and her sister, the cadet lady never uttered a syllable,
but manifested a strange silence, and I will say too, gentleman, if she was so mute, it was not for want of a discreet
or lively talk, for in these two ladies nature had gone very
far in every excellence, so that I know not if I should tell
you if it pleased me, that heaven had denied me the good
fortune of knowing them, especially Nisida, the head and
end of my misfortune; but what can one do? for what fate
ordains no human affairs can avert.

All my best wishes were for and towards Nisida, yet so
inoffensively towards Timbrio, that my exhausted tongue-
spoke only in favour of him, concealing always, with unusual discretion, my own pain to remedy his.

It occurred, however, that the comeliness of Nisida was
so sculptured on my soul from the first time I set eyes on
her, for I could not retain in my breast a so rich treasure
unconcealed,—that alone or in company, in passionate or
doleful canticles, I betrayed it under feigned appellations;
and one evening, not thinking that either Timbrio or anyone was listening, to relieve my wounded spirit, in a retired
apartment accompanied with a lute, I rehearsed these verses,
which having superinduced in me a sort of grave confusion,
I will repeat—and these are they :—

SILERIO.

1. What labyrinth is this wherein is closed
   My foolish and upraised fantasy?
   Who has exchanged my peace into fierce war,
   And all my joy into such deep sorrow?
   Oh, what fate dragged me earth to contemplate?
   The which my burial more fitly serves.
   Oh, who will reduce my flighty vagrant thoughts,
   To that same limit sanity exacts?

2. If with the bursting of my fragile breast,
   And the despoiling me of my sweet life,
   The heaven and the earth are satisfied.
   Of whom I kept the faith to Timbrio due,

Without resemblance of the savage act,
A homicide am I, beside myself;
But if I die, in that act quickly dies,
All amorous hope, and fire augments instead.

3. May gilded arrows come in showers and fall
From heaven, God-sent, and with insane rigour
Reach in directness to the sorrowing heart,
Shot with a cruel and relentless hand.
Though wounds have made all ashes and all dust,
My very inwards, what in truth I gain
In thus concealing her deep-seated wound,
Is rich compared to the requital.

4. Silence eterne on my too wearied tongue,
The law of sincere friendship will impose;
Whose unequalled virtue lessens quite
The pain which termination now expects.
Though it ne'er ends or e'en diminishes,
Honour and health will yet be what it was,
My purer faith firm, and yet more opposed,
Is like a rock within the angry sea.

5. From all the humour which these eyes distil,
And from the piteous office of the tongue,
From the undoubted good to anger due,
And from the will the solemn sacrifice,
Reaps the rewards sweet and the spoils too,
The friend renowned, good augury indicating
Heaven-self to my desire, which e'en pretends
Another's good, and 'gainst itself offends.

6. Assistance lend, O kind love, rise and guide
My humble mind, in this its hour of doubts;
And to the wished-for points give strength enough
To the soul and to the tongue beset with fears,
Which will be able, if its boldness rise,
Matters to effect most difficult.
Breaking misfortune, and the bond of fate,
Its greater virtue surely to attain.

So transported by these ceaseless imaginings there was a
cause why I should take no heed of the verses cited with a
voice so meek, or of the place where I was concealed, to

hinder Timbrio from hearing, which, when he heard, the same thought occurred to us both, that I was not free from love, and, if any, it was to the very Nisida, as he collected from the strain, and, though he conjectured right, that did not reach my wishes. On the contrary, hearing the opposite of what I thought he did, he determined to absent himself that same night, and go where he could not be found, that I might without inconvenience devote myself to the service of Nisida entirely.

This I ascertained from one of his pages, the warder of his secrets, who in much distress came to me, and said, "Learn, Señor Silerio, that Timbrio, your master and my friend, is trying to leave us, and to be off this night, not telling me where, only that I should supply him with I know not what money, and impart it to no one, particularly not to you. Now this idea supervened after hearing certain verses which you sang recently; and, according to the excesses which I saw, something like despair hovers over him ; and it appears to me that, ere I should furnish a remedy, or obey his order, I should advise you of it, that you might so interpose as to avert the baneful proposal." With a start I heard the page's story, and off I repaired to see Timbrio in his apartment, and, before I dared to enter, I stopped to see what he was about.

He was extended on his bed, with his mouth downwards, shedding a flux of tears, followed by heavy sighs ; and, with a low voice, and broken expressions, it seemed to me as if he uttered these words : "Take care, my faithful Silerio, to cull the fruit which by your toil and anxiety you deserve ; and conclude not that you are under any obligation to my friendship, so as to interfere with your desire, for I will restrain mine, though it bring me to life's extremity. As you freed me from it when you exposed your life, with so much love and zeal, to the peril of a thousand swords, it is no great thing if I recompense you in part for a work so noble, by yielding up the impediment which my presence causes. You may enjoy her on whom heaven has sealed and consigned all beauty, and love showered down satisfaction. One thing only weighs my spirits down, dear friend, which is that I must take leave of you in a bitter parting. Still you must admit that you are the cause of it."

Oh, Nisida, Nisida, how undoubted must be your beauty, that he who looks and loves must pay the penalty, and that is death itself.

Silerio saw her, and had he not left what I thought he would leave, I had lost much of the good opinion I entertain about him—but, since my fortune has so willed it, may heaven know that I, am not less the friend of Silerio than he is mine ; and, for verification of this fact, let Timbrio separate from his glory—banish himself from hls own contentment, become a wanderer in a foreign land far away from Silerio and Nisida, the two real moieties of his soul.

Then, with great precipitation, he arose from his couch, opened the door, and finding me there, he said, " What will you, friend, at this hour ? Something new, perhaps ?" " Much," said I ; " had it been less, it had not so embarrassed me."

Now, to weary you no longer, I came to such terms with him that I persuaded him, and made him to discern how fallacious was his judgment. Not that I was enamoured, for Nisida it was not, but her sister Blanca, who was my choice, and this I advanced so subtly that he credited it, and that greater probability should be given, my memory recalled some stanzas which I had previously thrown off to another lady, but of the identical patronymic ; and then I avowed that I had composed these verses for Nisida's sister, which, coming so opportune, though it may be alien to the story, I cannot pretermit, and they were as follows :—

SILERIO.

1. Oh, Blanca fair, to whom e'en snow doth yield !
    More frigid even than the candied frost—
    Conceive you cannot that my grief's so light,
    Thou should'st be careless to its remedy.
    Observe that if my ill nor melts nor moves
    Your souls conspire to my misfortune—
    My fate on me shall tnrn itself as dark,
    E'en as your name and beauty are so fair.

2. Blanca, in whose alabaster breast
    Love's sweet contentment nestles, closes up,
    Ere that my breast, bathed and dissolved in tears,
    To dust reverts and miserable soil,

> Shew that your breast in something is satisfied,
> As to the love and woe which girdles mine—
> To me a full requital that will be,
> Contributing my sufferings to allay.

3. Blanca, thou art for whom I would exchange
The finest Dukedom into solid gold,
And for so lofty a possession too,
Would I surrender loftiest estate.
Your amorous disdain abandon quite;
Contrive it so, O Blanca, that love shall
Make you my lot, if you true Blanca be.

4. Though I be found in poverty's hard gripe,
Of that sole fair one I should be possessed;
And were that you, I would not you exchange,
For all the riches of this nether world,
Should I myself in very self-return
From Juan de Espera en Dios, most blessed
Should I be, if I sought then, the three whites,
And thee, O Blanca, them amidst I found."

Silerio had pursued his story, had not the noise of some pipes and instruments of sweet breath stopped him, which sounded at his back, and turning his head, he observed about a dozen lively swains in lines, and in the centre a shepherd was posted, crowned with a honeysuckle garland, and divers flowers.

He bore a staff in his hand, and walked very deliberately, and the other shepherds to the same sounds, touching instruments, indicating an agreeable and unusual sympathy.

No sooner had Elicio caught sight of them but he recognised Daranio as the centre celebrity, and the rest to be neighbours who were invited to the wedding, to which also both Thirsis and Damon came to animate the betrothing, and so to honour the newly-engaged party till they reached the village. This, on observing how his advent had arrested Silerio's story, invited him to join them that evening in the village, where he should be treated with courtesy, and could complete the account of his commenced success. This Silerio promised, and at this season came a crowd of jocund swains, who recognising Elicio, and Daranio, and Thirsis, and Damon, his friends, received all with evidence of

unalloyed joy, and setting the music off again, and renewing
contentment, they pursued the beaten path ; and, as soon
as they reached the hamlet, that which struck on their ears
was the oaten pipe of the enamoured Lenio, and this gave
infinite pleasure to all, for they were aware of his forlorn
state.

Lenio saw and acknowledged them without any cessation
of his harmonious song, and thus singing towards them he
advanced :—

1. Very fortunate
   Full of satisfaction and joy
   By me will be held
   My dear company
   Though I so feel love's tyranny.

2. I will salute the earth
   Which presses on that, which from its thought,
   The false love banishes—
   And holds the breast exempt,
   From that relentless fury, that torment.

3. And I will still him happy style ;
   The rustic, the herdsman discreet,
   Who lives cautiously
   With the furniture of his humble cot.
   Turning a sour face on harsh froward love.

4. From such time the lambs
   Ere the season be full
   Shall become mothers.
   And in the roughest time he
   Pasture will find, and clearest water too.

5. Should love be angry,
   He can substitute coyness.
   I will remove his flock
   With my own,
   To the abundant pasture and clear rill.

6. And while incense
   From the holy ground mounts heavenwards,
   Methinks a just observer will say too,
   With pious and righteous zeal,
   That bended knees were prostrate on the earth.

7. Oh, all righteous heaven,
    Who art the protector of him who essays
    To do what thy will is,
    Await on the safety
    Of him who serving thee, doth love offend.

8. Let not this tyrant seize
    Spoils which are thy due;
    Rather with hand beneficent,
    And meritorious prizes,
    To the o'erwrought feelings vigour restore.

When Lenio had finished his song, he was courteously received by all the shepherds, who, when he heard the names of Damon and Thirsis, whom he knew by fame, was astonished at their presence, and said, " What endearments would suffice, though eloquence herself supplied all her aid to exalt and appreciate your worth, most renowned shepherds, if by chance the fooleries of love were not interwoven with your celebrated works?"

" Since you are sick of love, to all appearances, incurable, by estimating your rare discretion it pays your due, it is impossible for my homeliness not to blame your ideas."

" Were your ideas, discreet Lenio," replied Thirsis, " without the inklings of that vanity which characterizes you, you would see directly how clear were ours, and the more the glory because they bear the tincture of love, which by no subtlety or discretion can be concealed."

" Let us have no more of it," replied Lenio, " for I well see with such and so obstinate enemies that my arguments have small avail."

" Were they so," again said Elicio, " such friends to verity are all who stand here, that even laughter will not gainsay it, so you can note, Lenio, how you deviate, for not a soul approves your words, and even your intentions are doubted." " Then in truth," said Lenio, " will not your intentions save you, O Elicio, but murmur them to the air which you augment with your sighs, and those meadows which grow by the addition of your tears, and the lines you sang the other day, and which you wrote on the beeches of the wood. In them one will see in what it is you praise yourself, and how you me do blame."

Lenio had not left this challenge unanswered had he not perceived the beauteous Galatea to approach towards them, with those worthy shepherdesses Florisa and Teolinda, who, not to be recognised by Damon and Thirsis, had covered their alluring visages with white veils.

Up they came, and were greeted with all courtesy, especially by the two love-sick swains, Elicio and Erastro, who were excited with unwonted joy at the sight of Galatea, for Erastro could not dissemble ; and to prove it without ordering anything, indications were made to Elicio to awaken his pipe, to the sound of which, in sweet and in joyous accents, he broke forth :—

ERASTRO.

1. I view the lovely eyes
    Of that sun I so much admire ;
    If they go away,
    With them goes eke the soul ;
    Without them is no lustre,
    No hope to my soul ;
    Away from them,
    No light, no health, no freedom I desire.

2. Let him who can but look upon these orbs,
    It is not possible to praise them ;
    But he who them admires,
    For a spoil must life surrender.
    Them I saw, yea I saw them,
    And at each fresh view
    I give
    A new desire to the soul I concede.

3. Now no more to give have I,
    Or imagine more than I may give,
    If, for reward of my fidelity,
    Desire is not admitted.
    My ruin is assured
    If these eyes, whence good abounds
    In operation
    And not in good intention, fixed are.

4. Though this should last
    A thousand ages, as I wish

To me, so well discern I,
'Twould seem but a mere point.
Light-footed Time itself advances not
To alter my condition,
Whilst I behold
The beauty of that life for which I die.

5. In this vision reposes
My soul, and it finds ease,
And dwells in the living fire
Of its pure and beauteous light.
And love doth make so lofty a proof
With her, that in this flame
It recalls the sweet
Being, and as a phœnix it renews.

6. With my thoughts I arise,
Sweet glory seeking ;
In memory finally I discover
Content to be closed up.
There, there it stands, and there it hides itself ;
Not in command, not e'en in power,
Not in pomp,
In Lordship not, or riches of the earth.

Here terminated Erastro's song, and the passage to the village also.

Thirsis, Damon and Silerio repaired to the cot of Elicio, in order not to lose the occasion of hearing how the story of Silerio ended.

Those two admirable shepherdesses, Galatea and Florisa, having engaged themselves to be of the wedding party of Daranio on the next day, now left the swains. Many others remained with the betrothed ones, while they went home, and that self-same night Silerio, invited by his friend, Erastro, and out of desire, for it fatigued him to return to the hermitage, recounted the sequel of his narrative, of which in the following book there is record.

BOOK III.

Daranio's wedding preparations.—Continuance of the story of Silerio.
—Challenge sent by Pransiles to Timbrio by reason of an affront
offered in Xeres, relative to Nisida.—Lines written by Timbrio in
shape of a letter to Nisida before he left for the estate of the Duke of
Grasina, where the duel was to be fought,—Emotions of Nisida on
perusal of the poetic epistle.—Those who went to witness the duel,
with some account of the preliminaries.—Narrative arrested by the
voice of a complaining swain, singing between two trees.—Mireno,
the object of compassion.—His doleful strain.—Resumption of
Silerio's narrative.—Nisida swoons, and is adjudged to be dead.—
Departure of Timbrio for Naples.—Silerio follows, but does not find
Timbrio, who had quitted the city without signifying whither he
went.—End of the story of Silerio.—Resumption of the wedding
process for Daranio, dashed by the presence of the mournful Mireno,
who sighs for Silveria, the betrothed of Daranio.—His manifestations
of grief interrupted by certain who came to announce the espousals
of Daranio.—Mireno draws from his bosom a paper, to be delivered
to Silveria.—Elicio reads the effusion to the assembled clan of shepherds —Daranio's wedding.—Games at it.—Daranio's appearance and
a description of his attire with that of his bride, Silveria.—Conversation of Erastro and Elicio.—Lines sung by Lenio.—Sacrifice at the
fane where Daranio and Silveria were united.—Account of the banquet.—An eclogue recited by Orompo, Massilio, Crisio and Orfenio,
in which their especial loves were celebrated.—About the superiorities
of the contenders.—Dissertations on the tender passion, by Damon.
—Dancing resumed.—Introduction of three shepherds, Francenio,
Lauso, and Arsindo.—Answers and replies to riddles and glosses.—
Inspiriting verses by Arsindo.—Proposal to escort Galatea home,
which she declines.—Teolinda oppressed with affliction at the non-
appearance of Artidoro at the revels.—She passes the night with
Galatea and Florisa.

THE noisy rejoicings which, on occasion of the wedding of
Daranio, took place that night, did not hinder Elicio, Thirsis,
Damon, and Erastro from partially participating them, yet
were they not so disturbed that Silerio could not resume the
thread of his narrative, who, asking silence, when the company was settled, thus pursued the story :—

With the feigned verses of Blanca, which I told you I
recited to Timbrio, he rested satisfied that my sorrow did

not appertain to Nisida, but to my love for her sister ; and, thus assured, asking pardon for his false impression, he turned to a remedy, and forgetting my own, I did not neglect what reference to his. Some time elapsed, yet did not fortune, as I wished, open to me an opportunity to disclose to Nisida the truth of my cogitations, although she always asked me how my friend succeeded in his love matters, and if the lady was aware of them. To this I hinted that the fear of giving offence restrained me from advancing anything, at which Nisida was disconcerted, and called me recreant and bereft of discretion, adding that as I had deflected from manliness that either Timbrio did not feel the grief which I had announced, or that I was not the true friend I boasted to be.

All this induced me to discover myself the very first opportunity, which I did one day when alone with her, and she listened, with a subdued silence, to all I wanted to say. Then to the best of my ability I appraised the virtue of Timbrio, and the undoubted love he entertained for her, which was so powerful that it had moved me to undertake the mean office of buffoon only to find an occasion of imparting to her what I had already done, superadding other reasons which made Nisida credit the statement.

She did not wish to express by words that which by acts she could not conceal—indeed with gravity and a marked probity, she reproved my temerity, charged me with audacity, misrepresented my words, and shocked my confidence, yet not so that I was banished her presence, which was what I had most in apprehension. She wound up, however, by telling me that from this time forth it would be more profitable to rely on her sense of propriety, and not to mention any more about the disguise. This result closed the tragedy of my life, for I understood from her that Nisida would listen to the complaints of Timbrio.

What breast could contain the grief which was concentrated in mine, for the end of this desire was the all and the end all of my contentment. I now rejoiced at the good beginning I had made in behalf of Timbrio's remedy, and this joy greatly redounded to my grief, as it appeared to me, for in truth it was so, that seeing Nisida in another's power, my own fell off. Oh, strength, inexpressible of true friendship, where dost thou extend thyself, and to what hast thou brought me ! for I, forced by thy obligation, whetted the steel, by my own industry, which was to cut off my dear hopes, which dead in me revived in Timbrio, when he heard from me the nature of the interview. Yet she contrived all so warily with me and him, that she never gave indication of love for either of us, nor did she denote disdain, the fore-runner of a total abandonment of the cherished enterprise.

A notice having been forwarded to Timbrio from his old foe Pransiles, that knight whom he had affronted at Xeres, and desirous of satisfying his honour, a challenge was sent, notifying that a clear space and no favour was to be found on the property of the Duke of Gravina, allowing six months from thence to the day of combat.

The care of this advice did not interfere with what related to love ; on the contrary with my renewed solicitude and his services, Nisida acted so that she betrayed no coyness when she saw Timbrio, or when he visited her parents, pre-serving all that decorum which became her character.

The date of the proposed duel approximating, and Timbrio seeing it could not be put off, resolved to go, but ere he departed he wrote a letter to Nisida, comprising in it what many months back, and in many words, he had commenced. This very letter I carry in my memory, and to perfect my story I will not pretermit the occasion to recite it.

TIMBRIO TO NISIDA.

1. That health he sends to thee, who knows not health,
   Nisida, or expects future fruition,
   It it come not through your abundant hands.

2. The name abhorred of an importunate man,
   These lines, I fear, will duly light on me,
   Written in my blood, each severally.

3. Still the relentless fury of passion
   So much disturbs me that I cannot fly,
   Or break my amorous uneasiness.

4. Between a daring state and a cold fear,
   Resting on my true faith and on thy worth,
   Whilst you do this receive, I sad remain.

5. You thus addressing, I undo myself,
   If what I say you lightly entertain,
   And to disdain yourself surrender up.

6. Heaven veracious my true witness is,
   That thee I have adored from the moment
   I saw that face which is my enemy.

7. Sight and adoring are concomitant,
   For who could he be who does not adore
   Of a good angel the rare portraiture?

8. My soul, thy beauty to the world so rare,
   Looked on so curiously that it not desired
   The light of thy sweet countenance to stop.

9. There in thy soul is such a paradise
   Disclosing there such treasures of the mind,
   That they assurance of new glory yield.

10. With these rich pennons, swiftly up you mount
    To the welkin's height, and, being on the earth,
    The wise admire, the simple are surprised.

11. Happy that soul which doth contain so much,
    And not the less he, who, in truth for it,
    His own surrenders to the loving war.

12. In doubt am I as to my fatal star,
    Which wills I yield to what envelopeth
    A soul so beauteous, in a case so fine.

13. Oh lady, your condition me informs
    Of the sad disenchantment of my thought,
    And hope in me from fear defends me quite.

14. But on the faith of purpose honourable,
    Against distrust stubborn I lift my head,
    Taking new breath at the extremest gasp.

15. 'Tis always said hope love accompanies,
    ·Perhaps 'tis mere opinion, I've no hope,
    The power of love o'ertakes me not the less.

16. For thy benevolence I love, desire,
    Attracted by thy natural comeliness,
    Which was the net which love first stretched out.

17. With subtlety unwonted to attract
A free soul, careless of all love's device,
Into the loving knot and narrow bond.

18. Its orders and its tyranny love sustains,
Distinct in beauty, and distinct in breast,
But from impertinent fancy is exempt.

19. Yet looketh not at love's contracted noose,
Which in fine golden tresses doth appear,
Leaving the admirer quite unsatisfied.

20. Or on the breast which some call alabaster,
But that which passes not within the breast,
Or on the marble of the stranger's neck.

21. But to the hidden centre of the soul,
Observe, contemplating its purity,
With it assists, and to the meeting comes.

22. Beauties consisting in mortality
And frailty, too, suffice not mortal souls,
Moving from perfect light into the dark.

23. Peerless in virtue thou bearest the palm,
And of my cogitations all the spoils,
All baser feelings into calm are sunk.

24. On seas I plough, on sand itself I sow,
When the o'eruling force of fond desire,
More than to contemplation me condemns.

25. I see your loftiness and my lowliness,
And in extremes of such great difference,
Medium for hope is more than I possess.

26. They offer for this inconvenience
Numberless remedies, in multitude
As stars in heaven, people on the earth.

27. What suits the soul in me is conversant,
Better I know it, and the worse I reach—
Raised up by love which entertains the soul.

28. True, sweet Nisida, to the point I come,
By me desired with mortal anxiousness,
Where to complete my sufferings, I may.

29. The hostile arm in opposition raised,
    Awaits me, and the fierce and sharpened sword,
    Your rage, conspiring all against my life.

30. Thy stern will quickly shall avenged be
    For this my boldness and my vanity,
    By thee without just reason so despised.

31. Some other harder fact, some agony,
    Though it were more intolerable than death,
    My sorrowing fancy never could disturb.

32. If I desired, in my short bitter lot,
    To see thee satisfied with my desires,
    So may I see the contrary arise.

33. The path of my good narrow have I found,
    That of my evil broad and spacious,
    Of which my misadventure has been made.

34. For this goes cruel, and runs, hastening
    Death, fortified by thy dread scornfulness,
    To triumph o'er my much desired life.

35. For this my good is fairly vanquished,
    And by thy harshness, lady, persecuted,
    Whose object is to finish my short life.

36. Conducted to such sorrowful, frightful ends,
    My fate detains me, so that I apprehend
    The cruel and offended enemy.

37. Only to see the fire in which I burn,
    'Tis ice in the deep breast, and this is why
    That to the extreme circumstance I bow.

38. If on my side you do not show yourself,
    No living soul will dread my weak right hand,
    Though art and power do it accompany.

39. Should you assist me, what great Roman chief
    Or Greek commander in opposition would
    Be, for the attempt would it not futile prove?

40. In peril greater would I throw myself,
    From the fierce hands of death in contest fierce,
    Secure, his spoils would I swift snatch away.

41. 'Tis you alone can raise my wretched lot,
Above all human pomp, or throw it down
To the centre, where nought good enclosed is.

42. For if the power to sublimate it, too,
Love did possess, I would that fortune eke
It on the difficult summit would sustain.

43. Mounted to the heaven from the moon,
Discerned were the hopes which now repose
In that spot where no hopes are entertained.

44. So stand I thus which me doth satisfy,
Avoiding the evil of thy cruel scorn,
Whatever wretched consequence ensue.

45. Only to see that in your memory
I live. Remember, Nisida, mark too,
What ill you purpose I for good receive.

46. With greater ease truly could I recount
The ocean's waves, or grains on the white sand,
Or the bright stars illumining the sphere.

47. No pain, no grief, eke no anxiety,
To which the rigour of thy bitterness
Me, without thee offending, hast condemned.

48. Your worth you mete not 'gainst my humbleness,
Which, as regards the famous being here
On earth, some loftiness will ever bear.

49. Such as I am, I love, and dare to say
That I advance firmly, a lover true
To the extremest point that love attains.

50. 'Tis not for this the treatment I deserve,
An enemy's due—quite opposite meseems,
A just remuneration is my due.

51. Ill with such beauty sympathises such
Enormous cruelty, and badly sits
Ingratitude where valour flourishes.

52. Would you then ask, O Nisida! for an account
Of the soul I gave thee—where you threw it to,
Or how without it I myself support?

53. Be mistress of a heart accepted not,
    Then how can one give more than he desires?
    Here your presumption shows itself outright.

54. Bereft of soul I was from the first time
    I saw thee to my woe, and to my good,
    For all had evil been wert thou not seen.

55. Myself I give to my volition's rein,
    You govern me, for you alone I live,
    And your resistless power can yet do more.

56. In love's pure fire I habitation find,
    And yet undo myself.   From what phœnix
    By death of love do I sweet life receive?

57. By living faith, I ask and I inquire,
    Alone believest, Nisida, it is sure
    That living, scorch I in an amorous fire.

58. That after death you can, by potency,
    To life reduce me—in a moment's point,
    From furious ocean me restore to port.

59. That between you and me the juncture may
    Exist in wish and power, which is all one—
    Discrepance or deficiency without—
    And thus I cease my importunity.

I know not if the arguments of this letter, or those I had previously enforced on Nisida, assuring her of Timbrio's true love to her, or the unbroken services of Timbrio, or whether heaven had decreed it, moved the tender feelings of Nisida, but when she came to the end of the reading, she called me to her, and, with eyes full of tears, she said, "Oh, Silerio, Silerio, how I believe that at the cost of my health thou hast wished to purchase that of thy friend; may the fates who have dragged me to this point make your words true with the works of Timbrio; but if both have deceived me I will take vengeance from heaven, which I put for a testimony of the strength which desire has produced that no further concealment may exist. But, alas! what a light discharge is this for a fault so heavy.

"Rather would I die in silence, that my honour should survive, than by speaking what I willingly would speak. Bury it, and thus terminate existence."

These words of Nisida involved me in confusion, and the surprise more than all with which she spoke them ; so being desirous, by words, to urge her to declare herself without fear, it required no great persuasion ; for in fine she told me that not only did she love Timbrio, but actually adored him. That sentiment had ever remained concealed, had not the forced parting of Timbrio constrained her to disclose it.

How I remained, shepherds, after hearing Nisida's declaration, and her leaning towards Timbrio, you cannot enhance the position, and well it is that such a grief should be without appraisement. Not because it weighed me down to see Timbrio beloved, but to find that content with myself was impossible, for it was clear as day that without Nisida I could not live, so, as before narrated, the seeing her transferred to other hands was to alienate me from all comfort, and if fate yielded me aught in this state it was to reflect well on the welfare of my friend Timbrio, and this was the reason that my death and Nisida's declaration did not simultaneously occur.

I listened as best I could, and confirmed her in the integrity of Timbrio. She replied that she had no need of my assurances, for it so stood that I could not dissuade her, and all she required was, that I would interpose so with Timbrio that he should not come into hostile collision with his enemy.

I replied that it was not practicable so to do without a stain on his honour ; she was softened, and taking from her neck a precious relic, she gave it to me to bestow on Timbrio, ere he departed, as her special gift.

It was so arranged between the two, and she was cognisant that her parents intended going to see Timbrio's duel, and that they would take her and her sister also. But as her courage was not equal to being present at this untoward circumstance, that she should pretend illness, and should remain in a pleasure-house which her father should choose, some half league from the town where the combat was to take place, and there to meet good or bad fortune, as fate should dispense it to Timbrio.

She ordered me also, as well, to abridge the wish she had as to learn Timbrio's success, that I should bear a white coif with me, which she gave me, and if Timbrio had vanquished,

that I should tie it on my arm and return with the news,
but if he were defeated that then I should not tie it on, that
so from afar she might be sure whether satisfaction or the
end of her life was in store.

All she requested I promised to do ; so, taking the relics
and the coif, I quitted her in consummate sorrow and the
liveliest satisfaction also.

My small venture caused sorrow, while that of Timbrio
provoked joy. From me he learned what I bore from
Nisida, and was so gay with it, satisfied and proud, that the
danger of the battle which he awaited he set at nought, as
the fact of his being encouraged by his lady quite counter-
worked the idea of death.

For the moment I will pretermit the exaggerations which
Timbrio made to evince pleasure at what was due to my
care, but in reality they were so extravagant that while
treating of them he seemed beside himself.

Thus impelled and emboldened with good news, he commenced preparation for departure, taking with him, for
seconds, a Spanish and a Neapolitan knight. On the report
of this particular duel, much people of the kingdom went to
see it. The parents also of Nisida, taking Nisida and her
sister Blanca too ; and as it appertained to Timbrio to
choose the weapons, he wished to show no advantage
thereby, but that in reason only his right was founded, and
so he selected sword and dagger, and on them mainly to
rely.

A few days passed, when, at the appointed time, Nisida
and her father quitted Naples with divers others. Nisida
first arriving, she adverted to the arrangement concerted
between us, and that I should bear it in mind. But my
much taxed memory, which was encumbered with what
only disgusted me, not to alter my condition, quite forgot
the injunctions of Nisida, so that I thought I should destroy
myself, or consign me to the degraded state in which you
now find me.

The shepherds heard all this with patient attention, when
the thread of the story was interrupted by the voice of a
complaining swain, who was singing between two trees not
very remote from the dwelling-house where they were congregated, so that he was distinctly heard.

Now this voice soon imposed silence on Silerio, who did not proceed. In short, he bade the shepherds listen, for only a portion of his tale being untold, there was time enough left to finish it.

This had disconcerted (hicieronseles) Thirsis and Damon, had not Elicio said, " We shall lose nothing, shepherds, by attending to the unlucky Mireno, for it is he who sings, whom fortune has so reduced that I fear he abandons all content." " What has he to hope if to-morrow," said Erastro, " Daranio marries with the shepherdess Silveria, with whom he thought to marry? for to say truth the riches of Daranio has had more effect on the parents of Silveria than the ability of Mireno."

" Very true," replied Elicio, " but with Silveria, the will of which Mireno was cognisant, had more power than any treasure at all, and moreover Mireno is not so poor, though Silveria should unite with him that his necessities should be published abroad."

In consequence of these reasons, as eliminated by Elicio and Erastro, there grew a desire in the shepherds to listen to the song of Mireno, so Silerio was requested not to continue his theme; and all stopped to listen, and attentively heard. So that the shepherd aggrieved at the ingratitude of Silveria, seeing that her espousals were with Daranio, in rage and sorrow at the act, had rushed from the house with his rebeck only, and as a little meadow suited him by reason of its peculiar solitude, and which was adjacent to the village, and in the conviction that during a night so tranquil no one would hear him, he sat him down at a tree's base, and tuning up his instrument, gave voice to these words :—

MIRENO.

1. Oh heaven serene ! which with so many eyes
   Clearly beholdest such sweet amorous thefts,
   And in thy course alleviate or sadden
   The being who, in thy silence, his sad woes
   To him who causes them reveals—or whom
   You draw from such a state, offering no space—
   If by chance you are not deficient
   In benevolence towards me.
   For I by only speaking, satisfied am ;

And you know what I do—
Not much it is you listen to my say—
That my doleful voice
Will with its doleful soul·soar clean away.

2. Yea, my exhausted voice and my laments
Will little insult offer to the air ;
For I shall so reduced be at last,
That love which offers to the angry winds
My hopes, and in a truly foreign hand
Has lodged the good which I had merited—
The fruit shall be culled,
Which my loving cogitation sowed,
And with my weary tears bedewed be.
My hands unfortunate,
Which failed of merit,
The venture nullifying,
Which difficulties smooths and rectifies.

3. Now he who views his glory surely changed
Into a grief so bitter and perverse,
A road selecting for prospective good.
Why ends he not a life so contrary ?
Why breaks he not a purely vital chain,
Defying all the strength of destiny ?
By degrees a road
To the sweet circumstance of bitter death.
And thus the valiant and enfeebled arm
Suffers the embarrassment
Of life—or fortune thus exalts itself,
To know what satisfactory is to Love,
And grief effects what iron ought to do.

4. Certain my death is fixed, or possible
'Tis not he lives who entertains a hope
So dead, and from glory so far removed.
And yet I trust that love impossible
May make my death—that a false confidence
Shall lay a burden on my memory.
But what ? if, by the history
Of my goods passed away, it I possess.
And well I see that all are passed away,
And the grave cares

Which in their stead I hold,
A greater reason will this be,
Why from my goods and from my life I part.

5. Ah, sole and only good to my poor soul,
Sun which my tempest so serene hath made,
The end of worth which so desires itself !
Will it be possible that the day arrive,
In which I learn you have forgot me quite ?
Let love permit me that I witness it
Ere this be,
Ere thy white beauteous neck
By foreign arms closely encircled be,
Ere the golden
Or rather should I say tresses of gold,
Should be enriched by Daranio's clasp,
Simultaneous finish life and woe.

6. In truth, no one in merit have I found
Transcending you, yet faith is dead I see
Which in good works not manifests itself ;
If I should estimate life's rendering up
To certain woe, glory uncertain too,
I could expect a joyous festival.
In this 'tis not admitted
The cruel law which love adopts, the wish
A proverb is it ancient lovers among,
That love is works :
This for my evil I possess alone
The will to do.
Failing therein on what can I rely ?

7. Thinking on you that there would broken be
The law misused by avaricious love,
Shepherdess, your beauteous eyes would raise
To a soul subdued, which is thy prisoner,
So nice adjusted to your own request,
That knowing it, you would esteem it too.
I thought you would not exchange
A faith which evidence gave of so much worth—
For one who refines his desires (quilata)
With the vain successions (arreos)

Of wealth o'erweighed with care,
Yourself surrendered to the gold you have,
And me delivered to a ceaseless wail.

8. Oppressive poverty, the main instrument
Of the sad grief which desolates my soul,
Who praises thee, let him have thee in sight.
My shepherdess, thy face disturbs the eye ;
Love has thy bitterness put quite to rest,
His foot withdrawing not to encounter thee ;
Ill he co-operates with thee,
Who would pursue love's amorous intents.
Lofty aspirations down you drag
And sow change on change
In bosoms feminine and covetous.
You perfect ever
With love the worth of every personage.

9. All gold the sun, whose vigorous ray can blind
The acutest vision, if it baited is
With false appearance of a good profit.
To liberal hands there no denial is,
What a notorious proof can extricate
From a mild, beauteous and eager breast,
Right gold distorts
From pure intention and a faith sincere.
More than a lover's firmness
A diamond doth achieve.
Its durability is turned to wax,
How hard soever,
With it enacting all that it desires.

10. It quite o'erwhelms me, sweetest enemy,
That all thy many pure perfections
With niggard proofs you quite deformed have ;
Of gold yourself so much the friend you show,
That you have slighted all my passion,
And to oblivion all my cares have cast.
In fine, what hast thou married ?
Him hast thou wedded ; shepherdess, may heaven
Cause your election turn out as it wills.
And for my sufferings
Unjust, receive thou no due recompense

> What woe—may friendly heaven
> Virtue reward, and evil castigate.

So terminated Mireno's song, and with such indications of grief, that it created the same in all who heard it, especially in those who knew him and recognised his virtue, his lively disposition, and honorable bearing.

After advancing some remarks relative to the extraordinary state of the women, and in particular about Silveria's marriage, who, oblivious of Mireno's love and benevolence, had surrendered herself to the wealth of Daranio, all were desirous that Silerio should bring his story to a close : and silence being proclaimed, without any necessity solicited, he resumed, saying, The day of the terrible combat arriving, having left Nisida some half a league from the village in a garden, as previously concerted, the parents accepting the excuse of her indisposition, as I left her, it was understood at my return it should be notified by the signal of the coif, that is, if I carried it or not, which would denote the evil or unfavourable issue of Timbrio.

I returned to make the promise, though I grieve that I undertook the mission, so I fled from her, and her sister who remained with Nisida.

Having reached the locality of the duel, and the hour for beginning was come, the seconds passed through all the requisite preliminary ceremonies and warnings, and they placed the two knights on their proper ground in the lists, and at the sounding of a hoarse trumpet they attacked each other with so much dexterity that it caused a general admiration. But either love or reason, which is better, which favoured Timbrio, imparted to him such vigour, despite sundry wounds, in brief space gave him the advantage, so that holding his adversary by the feet, stricken and stained by blood, he besought him, if he would have his life spared, to surrender at once. But the unlucky Pransiles begged him to slay him, as it was easier and of less hurt to encounter a thousand deaths than to concur.

Yet the noble-minded Timbrio would not sacrifice his enemy, not even if he should confess to a surrender,—who only contented himself with saying and acknowledging that Timbrio was as good as himself, which Pransiles readily acknowledged, for by it he effected little, and without finding himself in such a strait, he might well say so.

All who heard of the passages between Timbrio and his enemy lauded him extremely. Scarce had I witnessed the good success of my friend, when with an incredible joy and speed I hurried off to divulge the news to Nisida. But woe again, the carelessness of then brought on me the care of now. Oh! memory, memory, why didst not thou contribute to what was most important? I believe a fatality existed in my affairs, and that the spring of that joy was the sum and the end of all my satisfaction.

To see Nisida I used all despatch, but I went without the preconcerted coif being attached to my arm. Nisida, who with augmented desire stood expecting and watching from one of the lofty corridors for my return, seeing me without the pre-arranged signal, concluded that a fatal disaster had overtaken Timbrio; this she thought, and she felt it so acutely that without more ado, all her spirits fled, and to earth she fell in such an unusual swoon that every one thought her dead. On my arrival, I found the entire house in commotion, and her sister manifesting inexpressible grief over Nisida's sweet body.

When I discerned this, and believing she was dead indeed, by this grief my own senses were stupefied, fearing that in such a condition I could say nothing or disclose even a bare thought, I sallied forth, and by degrees I conveyed to the luckless Timbrio the unhappy news. The intensity of my anxiety having deprived me of physical and mental power, my pace was not so rapid but that others had informed the parents of Nisida of the event, assuring them that an acute paroxysm had left her for dead.

Timbrio heard it, and he remained even as I did, or peradventure worse. I alone could say that when I came to the spot where I thought to find him, it was dark, I learned from one of the seconds how he had gone by post to Naples, with as much disgust as if he had been vanquished and even dishonoured.

What might be, I speedily inferred, so without delay I followed, and ere I had reached Naples, I learned for certain that Nisida was not dead. Her swoon had lasted for twenty-four hours, when she revived with sighs and tears.

With the assurance of this intelligence I consoled myself, and more contentedly I touched at Naples in hope of there seeing Timbrio ; yet was he not there, for the cavalier with whom he travelled, stated that on his arrival in Naples he again quitted it without imparting a word to any soul, and whither he went he knew not ; he conjectured that seeing him so sad and woe-begone, after the duel, that he had fallen on some desperate alternative. This renewed in me my stanched tears, and as if my evil fortune was not satisfied, it so adjusted itself that in a few days the parents of Nisida came to Naples, but without either of their daughters, who as ascertained, for so went current the fame that both had absented themselves in one night, going, however, to Naples without the privity of their parents.

In such confusion was I at this that I hardly knew how to act or speak, and in this woful plight I learned, but with uncertainty, how Timbrio had embarked for Spain in a large vessel which left the port of Gaeta ; and inferring there was truth in it, I quickly repaired to Spain, and in Xeres and other places in which I thought he would be, I searched, and that too without finding even a trace of him. Next I went to Toledo, where Nisida's parents dwelt, and all I could ever ascertain was that they had returned to Toledo without any news of their two daughters. Seeing myself thus separated from Timbrio, an alien from Nisida, I considered that though I might yet find them, it would be for their advantage, but my perdition. Wearied out and disenchanted of things appertaining to this world of woe, I resolved in spirit to turn to a better star and to pass what remains to me of life in the service of him who esteems our good desires, and gives to our works their just due.

" Hence I have adopted the habit you see, and elect to be the hermit I am, so that in a soft solitude I may contract my desires, and walk diligently to a better paradise ; for my evil actions have been many, and their stoppage is difficult, as some new transgression ever ensues ; and so, remembering what is past and gone, I may renew a right spirit within me.

" When I find myself in this state, with the harp which I chose for companion in my solitude, I try to alleviate the weight of my cares until it shall please heaven to remove me, and transport me hence, panting for a happier seat.

"And now, shepherds, you have had a true recital of my grief, and if the narrative has been tedious, it is because its details have not been so to me; all I ask is, that you will let me return to my hermitage, for though your company is very attractive, I am yet of opinion that nothing is so grateful as solitude, so you will learn the nature of my life, and the sufferings I undergo."

Silerio's story ended, but not so the tears which were its accompaniment. All the swains did their best to console him, especially Damon and Thirsis, whose objects were to give him courage as to his again seeing Timbrio with a renovated joy, for it was not possible but the sky would again become serene, whereby hope would arise, for no consent there was as to the false news of Nisida's death, and that some notice of Timbrio would follow long before despair could set in, and that, relatively to Nisida, a conjecture might be hazarded that to meet Timbrio she had gone in quest; and if fortune, by these unexpected straits had disjoined them that by some equally unwonted events a reunion would ensue. These reasons, and others equally cogent, were advanced, and they really brought consolation to him, but not so decidedly as to awaken a newness of life in him, or to make him persuaded that the life he had chosen was the most fitting and appropriate.

Most of the night had elapsed when the swains were in accord as to the necessity of repose, awaiting the day which was to witness the espousal of Daranio and Silveria.

Scarce had the beauteous Aurora quitted the uneasy couch of her jealous husband, when the company of swains arose, and each, according to his capacity, began the rejoicings; some to fetch in green boughs, for the adornment of the bridal door, while some with their instruments of sweet breath, paid tribute to the morn. Here was witnessed gaiety in its fulness; there awoke the harmonious rebeck, now the old fashioned psaltery, now the expert flute (cursados albogues).

Some with coloured ribands decorated the castanets for the much expected dance, some polished and furbished up the rustic furniture (aderegos) to indicate a predilection in the eyes of some much cherished shepherdess, so that throughout the village all went content at the prospect of pleasure and the festival.

To the mournful Mireno alone these preparations gave increase of woe, who, evacuating the village, not to sacrifice his glory, ascended a little hillock hard by the hamlet, and there adjusting himself at the foot of a beech tree, bald with dry antiquity, his hand upon his cheek, and his capouch fixed towards his eyes, which were rivetted on the ground, began inwardly to dwell on the wretched condition to which he was reduced, and without power sufficient to arrest it, he saw the very fruit of his wishes by others enjoyed. This sad fact made such an impression on him that his eye-drops were salt, which enforced tears from all who looked on. Now Damon and Thirsis, Elicio and Erastro arose, and approaching a window which looked towards the fields, the very object which met their eyes was the woe-begone Mireno, and noting his sad plight, they instinctively participated his sorrow; moved to compassion they were bent on his consolation, which they had effected, had not Elicio proposed to go alone to him, for he imagined that Mireno being his friend, and perhaps, on easier terms with him than with others, he would impart his sorrow to him. To this the swains agreed, and so Elicio went on his mission and found poor Mireno beside himself, so upset by grief, that he recognised him not, nor could he exchange a word.

Now when Elicio observed this he signalled to the other swains to advance; they dreading that some untoward accident had overtaken Mireno, for Elicio's cries were hasty, quickly went and saw the bewildered Mireno with eyes settled on the ground, and so motionless, that he might have been a statue, yet neither on the advent of Elicio nor indeed on the approach of any of the swains there congregated, did he turn from his stupefaction; but after a space, some mutterings issued from between his teeth to this purport. "Art thou Silveria, Silveria? if so, then am not I Mireno?" "We are neither of us ourselves. "It were as impossible for Mireno to be without Silveria, as the contrary. Yet who am I, son of dark affliction?" "Who art thou, unhappy one?" "Sure am I that I am not Mireno, for thou art not the much cherished Silveria, at least the Silveria you should be and what I once deemed you were."

Now he upturned his eyes, and seeing four shepherds environing him, and recognising Elicio to be one, he stood erect, but without abandoning his bitter sorrow, he threw his arms around his neck, adding, " Ah, my really true friend, now hast thou no occasion to envy my lot, when thou didst envy it, what time Silveria favoured me ; if, however, you once styled me fortunate, now is my condition changed—barter all the lively titles you then showered on me, whose bitterness now befits me more.   I call thee happy, Elicio, for the hope of being loved is your solace, and the dread of impending oblivion wounds thee not."

" In confusion am I cast," rejoined Elicio, " to see you hurled into such extremities about Silveria's acts, when I remember she has parents to whom obedience is imperative." " If she had the power of love within her, there had been no impediments in her parents as to the satisfaction of love's dues, hence I infer, O Elicio, that had she loved me, she did ill to marry, but if her love for me was all a fiction, worse did she to deceive me, and impose on me the disenchantment when I could not avail myself of it, save by transfering my life to her custody."   " Your life is not at an end, Mireno," said Elicio ; " the remedy yet exists, and it may be that a change in Silveria does not abide with her volition, but exists in the predominance of paternal authority. If you courted her so honorable for a bride, you may yet enjoy her acquaintance when married, circumstances being within the capacious sphere of propriety."

" You are little acquainted with Silveria, Elicio," again remarked Mireno, " if you think she would condescend to anything improper."   " Now your own reason condemns you," replied Elicio, " for if you, Mireno, know what Silveria has done, and there is no harm in it, then is there no error."   " If she has not done wrong," replied Mireno, " she has yet assuredly robbed me of the happy consequences which so raised my hopes ; in this I blame her, that she gave me no warning of this wrong, nay, when she discovered my apprehensions, with a strong asseveration she denounced them as phantasms or hideous dreams, and averred that she had never entertained thoughts of marriage with Daranio, nor would she marry, though her refusal involved her in endless disgrace with her parents ; and then, despite this repudiation, and her promise to me, to fail, and violate her faith in such a way as we have witnessed, where then is reason lodged ?　What can it endure ?"

And now renewed in himself was the grief of Mireno, and thus was also resuscitated the pity of the shepherds. At this juncture came up to them two youths, one a relative of Mireno, and the other Daranio's servant to call Elicio, Damon, Thirsis, and Erastro, and to announce the commencement of the espousals.

It grieved them to leave Mireno in solitude, although Mireno's relation did offer to remain with him, and even Mireno told Elicio that his wish was to retire, that he might not have before his eyes a daily witness of his own disgrace.

This determination found favour with Elicio, who charged him to apprise him of his place of retreat.　This Mireno promised, and drawing from his bosom a paper, he beseeched him, when the opportunity presented, to deliver it to Silveria. This done he disappeared from among the shepherds, with indications heavy of pure grief.

But Elicio, when separated from Mireno, curious to learn the contents of the paper—it was unsealed—and thinking it no treason to peruse, opened it, and inviting the whole clan of the shepherds to listen, he perceived that it contained the following verses :—

MIRENO TO SILVERIA.

1.　The shepherd who delivered has to thee
　　More than he possessed,
　　Oh shepherdess, now sends to thee
　　Less than he has left,
　　Which is this poor paper,
　　Whereby you will discern most clear
　　That faith which in thyself thou wilt not find,
　　And the grief that therein dwells.

2.　Peradventure it availeth little
　　To give you a contracted 'count of it.
　　Should faith not profit me,
　　Or my wretchedness you satisfy,

Think not my intention 'tis
For that you me abandon to complain,
Slowly arrive these complaints
Of my too early passion.

3. Time was when you would hear
The story of my grievances,
And if my eyes moisture distilled,
You could dry up the tears.
Then was Mireno,
He who was admired of thee—
But alas ! what transformation
Has time, good time effected ?

4. Should this deception endure
'Twould temper my disgust,
For bad taste superior is
To a notorious and a certain ill.
But then for whom is ordained
My terrible, evil progress,
Hast changed by this mutation
Good into false, inevitable pain ?

5. Thy flattering accents
And my too credulous ears
Gave me fictitious wealth ;
The ills which are really so,
The good which in appearance
My health increased,
But evils in verity
Redoubled have my woes.

6. Hereby I judge and discern it,
For a fact certain and notorious,
That love holds his glory
At the door of the lower regions,
And disdain conveys,
And oblivion in a moment
From glory to the torture
That which in loving not employs itself.

7. With such precipitation hast thou made
This transformation extraordinary,

That in the centre of an ill am I,
Nor can escape provisions,
For I imagined that but yesterday
It was when you me loved,
Or at least you so pretended,
A circumstance in itself credible.

8. And the agreeable sound
Of your savoury words
And loving reasons
Yet tinkle on my ears.
These beloved memories
Have passed to me more torment,
Since thy words the sighs
Awoke, and you know the direful results.

9. Was it thou that sworest
That thy days should end,
If thou lovedst not Mireno
'Bove all that mortal could?
Was it thou, Silveria,
Who made of me such a possession,
That being all thy evil,
Did estimate me, too, for all thy good?

10. Oh, what titles would I give thee
Of ungrateful, as thou meritest,
If you do me abhor,
Could I then thee abhor
Avail me I cannot
Of this means of thee abhorring;
For more I do esteem my love for thee,
Than thou hast done in quite forgetting me.

11. Woful groan to my song,
Has thy fierce hand imparted—
A winter to my spring,
And to my smile a bitter, bitter wail—
My kind and loving usage (gasajo) to mourning
    changed.
And from love's benignity
Turned into cruel thorns the flowers are
With poison in the fruit.

12. Thus wilt thou say this wounds me,
The having married thee,
And having thus forgotten
An honest, noble deed.
Extenuation would be allowed,
Were it not notorious
That in thy espousals,
Is the close certain of my sorrowing life.

13. But your approval was
An approval and yet just—
For with a so unjust reward,
Did pay the due my faith inviolable,
Which, seeing that an offer now is made,
To indicate the faith which it attains,
Your change nor alters it,
Nor does my evil fail.

14. Whoever comes this fully to understand,
Sure am I no alarm will take—
Seeing how that I am of the opposite sex,
And that, Silveria, thou a woman art—
Whence lightness
Hath a seat continual,
Whence in me my suffering,
Another nature is.

15. Thee wedded I now beheld,
Erewhile to be repented of—
For it is a recognised fact,
That to one thing thou art constant never;
Try cheerfully to bear
The yoke which on your own neck you have laid.
You may it detest,
But never can you disentangle it.

16. Yet wert thou so inhuman,
And of such essence mutable,
That what to-day you longed for,
To-morrow wilt in strict abhorrence hold.
Speaking of an extraordinary being,
By the world will you be identified,
Beauteous, yet variable,
All change, but yet with beauty strong endowed.

This composition of Mireno did not appear to the shepherds to be badly conceived, still the occasion for which the verses were thrown off, considering with what haste the change of Silveria had brought them to a juncture in which friends and country were forsaken, each feared that in the result of their own pretensions the same thing might ensue.

Having entered the village, and reaching the place where Daranio and Silveria were stationed, the feast was initiated, and that with so much joy, that the banks of the Tagus for many a day had not witnessed the like; Daranio being one of the richest shepherds of that division, and Silveria the handsomest shepherdess on the margin of the stream. All assisted at the wedding, or at least the best part of the females, and there was a very judicious union of the two sexes, and among those who signalised themselves by variety and aptitude in games were the mournful Orompo, the ardent Orfenio, the absent-minded Crisio, and the disenamoured Marsilio, all youths, and all open to love's sway, although disturbed by different passions, for the premature death of the much cherished Listea afflicted Orompo, while jealousy consumed Orfenio—he was in love with the attractive shepherdess of Eandra. The absent-minded Crisio was bewildered at finding himself separated from Claraura, a most discreet shepherdess, whom he considered as his own, and the desperate Marsilio by the aversion which for him was involved in the breast of Belisa.

All these were friends and inhabitants of the same village, so that the loves of each were well known to all, and in aggravating competition they found themselves, each enhancing the cause of his torment, each endeavouring as best he could that his grief should benefit another, holding it to be the *maximum* of glory to be harshly entreated, and each having so much wit, or, rather, so much suffering, that, signify what it might, it was the extremest that one could imagine. For these amicable controversies, were they famous and renowned on all Tagus' banks, and a desire existing in Thirsis and Damon to know them, and bring them there altogether, each gave the other a courteous reception, and, especially, all with astonishment looked on Thirsis and Damon, of such well-founded reputation, hitherto known to them only by report.

At this moment sallied forth the rich pastor Daranio, clad as a mountaineer, with a long robe in plaits at the collar, a vest of frieze, a green upper garment hollowed round the neck, his lower attire made of thin linen, azure-coloured buskins, round shoes, his girdle studded, with a cap quartered of the same colour as his vest. Not the less elegantly was dressed his spouse, Silveria, for she had on a petticoat with a lion-skinned body, bordered with white satin, a camiset for the breast, decorated with blue and green, a ruff sewed with yellow thread, and powdered with silver spots, the taste of Galatea and Florisa, who helped to put on her attire, also a cap of network, azure with a fringe of violet silk ; a shoe bedizened with gold, slippers uniform in size and symmetry, with rich corals and a ring of gold, and, above all, her own innate beauty, which surpassed all ornament whatsoever. Close behind forth sallied the incomparable Galatea, like the sun behind Aurora, and her beloved Florisa, with a cloud of beauteous maidens who came to honour the nuptials, among whom walked Teolinda, with all precaution, to avoid recognition by Damon and Thirsis ; and quickly the women following the swains at the voice of the musical instruments, wended towards the fane, where they found Elicio and Erastro, who fed their eyes on the seductive face of Galatea, who hoped their journey might be as extended as the peregrination of Ulysses, and, so content at seeing her was Erastro, that, addressing Elicio, he remarked, " What seest thou, shepherd, if thou seest not Galatea? How wilt thou be able to admire the sun's rays in her locks, heaven in her forehead, stars in her eyes, snow in her complexion, pomegranate in her cheeks, ruby in her lips, ivory in her teeth, crystal in her neck, and marble in her breast ?" " All this have I observed, O Erastro," answered Elicio, " yet not one of these treasures is the spring of my torment—but it is the asperity of her bearing, for were it as you know it to be, and you admit all this comeliness in Galatea, yet were they cause for our greater glory."

" Very true," said Erastro, " but were Galatea not so comely, you cannot deny she were not so desirable, and, without desire, no such pain would arise in our breasts, for in verity is this created by desire."

"I cannot deny, Erastro," said he, "but that all grief and weight of affliction whatever arise from the privation and loss of what we earnestly court, still I would tell you that the quality of love is much lessened, in my idea, for which I thought you loved Galatea; for if you only love her on account of her comeliness, that is a minor consideration, because there is no man, how rustic soever, who sees her but desires her, as beauty attracts and awakens warm desire.

"Hence this mere simple fact of desire is natural enough, and deserves no reward, if so by only desiring heaven we should claim a reward.

"Thus you observe how inverted all is, as truth points out to us; and presupposing that beauty and general comeliness are the chief attractions to desire and its fruition, the truly enamoured person should not set up such a condition of things as his last good and final hope. If beauty conducts him to this desire, he should love it solely for its own value, unless another motive impel him; this he can only style true and perfect love, which is worthy to be received and honoured; as we see the agent in all things rewards those who are not influenced by other motives, such as fear, suffering, or hope of glory, desiring it, loving it, serving it, solely for its being estimable in itself, and worthy to be loved. This is the test and greatest perfection comprised in love divine, and even in human love, when we desire no more than that what we love should be good, without defect of intelligence; for it does eventuate often that good and ill are confounded, or we love one and dislike the other, hence such a love in lieu of reward merits reproof.

"I should infer from all I have said, Erastro, that, if you desire and love only the mere physical beauty of Galatea with a view to enjoy it, and that your desire extends no further than fruition, increase of fame, health, life, and property, understand from me that your love is a nullity, and, if so, you ought not to receive requital." Erastro was desirous of replying to Elicio, and to give him to understand that he was not cognisant of the character of his love towards her, but the sound of the rebeck of the disenamoured Lenio, who wished to be one of the guests at Uranio's wedding, and to enliven the feasts with his strain, stopped him, so placing himself before the plighted pair,

when they had reached the fane, at the sound of Eugenio's
pipe, he sang these verses :—

LENIO.

1. Unknown, ungrateful love, thou tramplest out,
    Of gallant souls the very core of hearts,
    With vain imaginings, and shadows vain,
    A thousand passions pour'st on the free soul.
    If a divinity you would be estimated,
    Styled by a so exalted title, pardon not
    Him who delivered to the marriage tie,
    To a new knot desire would render up.

2. In conservation of the love sincere,
    And pure, of sacred marriage put thy strength,
    Your ensign on this holy plain unfold,
    Imparting strength, as to your state belongs,
    What lovely flower, delicious fruit awaits
    Him who for a slight toil forces himself
    To bear this yoke in a becoming way,
    For though a charge it is, that charge is light.

3. You may in truth, if you forget your deeds,
    And your uncomfortable condition,
    A happy wedding institute, and a couch,
    Where in the conjugal yoke two nestled are.
    Wrap thyself up within thy soul, thy breasts,
    Till life's impulsive course be quite run out,
    Let them go, and enjoy in mature hope,
    The charming, grateful, never-ending spring.

4. The pastoral cottages small abandon too ;
    His office let the liberal shepherd do ;
    Fly higher yet, although your flight be such,
    Its aspiration being a loftier point.
    O'erwatching and fatigue both futile are,
    While making of the soul a sacrifice.
    With better purpose you surrender may
    Yourself to Hymen's sweet conjunction.

5. Here can'st thou indicate the powerful
    Hand of thy marvellous coercive strength,
    Effecting so that the new tender spouse
    May love, and of her choice may be beloved.

From every low-born jealousy exempt,
Disturbing satisfaction and repose,
Or that the peevish and the coy disdain,
Of sweet and tasteful rest may them deprive.

6. But if, perfidious love, thou never heardst
The supplications from friends emanating.
May mine indeed be quite repudiated.
Thy evil-noted works, condition too,
To which the world is ample testimony
Enforce it so that from thy hand no hope
Or joy, content, or fortune can exist.

Astonished in truth were they who stood listening to Lenio, the disenchanted of love, and to mark with what humility he treated of such matters; styling him a divinity, and of a most potent agency, which was most unusual. However, having heard the verses with which the song closed, they could hardly resist smiling, for it seemed to them as if he threw temper into it, and, should he proceed further in his strain, he would deliver himself up to very love as he had before done. But time failed as the journey finished.

Now they reached the temple, and the priests having completed the accustomed sacrifices, Daranio and Silveria were bound in a close perpetual knot, yet not without the envy of many beholders, or the grief of those who coveted such a beauty as Silveria. But the grief which would have supervened in the luckless Mireno would have far surpassed all other, had he been present.

The wedded pair, returning from the temple with the same company which followed them there, went to the chosen spot in the village, where they found the banqueting tables set out, and here Daranio wished to make a public demonstration of his wealth, by giving an entertainment in a generous and sumptuous fête.

The spot was covered with boughs, looking like a beauteous greenhouse, branches being interwoven about the ceiling so closely that even the sun's rays could not transpierce to heat the fresh ground, which was also strewed with sword-like flags and rushes, and other kinds of flowers. Here, with a general satisfaction, was celebrated the banque.

to the multifarious sounds of pastoral pipes, yielding no
less gratification than those instruments of sweet stop
which are wont to be heard in palaces. But what gave
greater importance to the fête was, that on removing the
tables, and in the same place, with due despatch, they
erected a building where the four wise, yet much to be
pitied shepherds, Orompo, Marsilio, Crisio, and Orfenio, to
honour the wedding, and to satisfy the longing which
Thirsis and Damon had to hear them, desired to recite an
eclogue, which they collectively had composed by dint of
their mutual sorrows. A general seat accommodation being
arranged for the assembly of both sexes, after the rebeck of
Erastro, the lyre of Lenio and the other accompaniments
had lent to the company a peaceable and surprising silence.
The first who appeared in this humble theatre was the
sorrowful Orompo, vested in a black sheepskin jerkin, and a
shepherds' staff made of yellow box-wood, at the end of
which was a hideous figure of Death, crowned with leaves
of the mournful cypress, all ensigns of grief, which in him
predominated by reason of the premature decease of his
beloved Listea; and after that, with sad aspect, he had cast
his weeping eyes on all sides, with denotements of infinite
distress and bitterness of heart. Silence he broke with
these arguments of an analogous sorrow :—

OROMPO.

1. Start from the cavity of the care-worn breast,
   Ensanguined words with death co-mingled.
   And if deep sighs detain thee firm attached,
   Open and burst the wayward continents.
   The air impedes the inflammation
   Whose venom in your accents finds itself.
   Stand forth, and may the winds you carry off,
   Which me, with all I love, transported have.

2. Seeing them lost, but little wilt thou love.
   The lofty subject yet to us is fled,
   By which in perfect style and gravity,
   Of things exalted, you discoursed have
   Noted in time, and duly recognised
   For sweet and joyful, and of savoury taste,

Still woful now, bitter and dolorous,
By heaven and earth wilt thou retained be.

3. Yet though you rise, in trepidation words
By which you may impart, all have I felt.
My cruel torture quite unequal is
By any lively painting to be made.
But yet, alas ! lacks me the how and when
My grief's excesses or defects to note.
That which my tongue unable is to do
My eyes supply with drops continual.

4. Oh, death, which shortens, cuts away the thread
Of endless human pleasurable hopes.
The mountains slope in an eye's twinkling,
And equal make Henares and the Nile.
Why temperest not, O traitor, thou thy mode
Which cruel is, and why, to my despite,
Hast plunged in my pure and softened breast
The fury and the edge of cruel steel ?

5. In what offended thee, false one, the years
So tender and so youthful of that lamb ?
With her thyself, why showest thou so fierce ?
By it my wounds much more augmented are ;
Oh enemy mine, yet friendly to deceit,
From me who seek thee you absent and hide,
And will that reasons and accounts be joined
With him, who dreads too much your mighty ills.

6. In ripened years thy very unjust law
Its strength augmented well may indicate.
Do not discharge the intolerable wound
'Gainst him whose life slender enjoyment has ;
To this thy sickle all directed is,
Which neither bends to treaty nor to prayer.
With rigour thus the tender flower is lopped,
Like to the reeds so knotted and robust.

7. When from the earth, Listea, you removed
Your essence, value, force and liveliness,
Your anger, your commands and potency
In this sole triumph did you notify.
By her removal, also, hast thou ta'en

The grace, behaviour, beauty, meekness all.
  The best of the world, and in her sepulture
Goodness and perfection buried lie.

8. Bereft of her in darkness had been bound,
My feverish life, which so extended is,
To my crushed body insupportable.
To the truly miserable, life is but death.
I have no hope in fortune or in fate ;
Nor time itself—e'en heaven is hopeless too—
Or any one to take sweet counsel of,
Or good to hope in so superfluous ill.

9. Oh ye who feel how sharp a thing is grief,
Come and take counsel from my during ills ;
Seeing its force, its metal, earnestness,
Your ills will show greatly inferior.
Where are ye now, ye lively shepherds all ?
Crisio, Marsilio, and Orfenio what ?
Why come ye not justly acknowledging
My injuries to be greater than your own ?

10. Who is that mortal who both looks and breaks
Through the cross-windings of this very path ?
Doubtless Marsilio, who love's prisoner is—
The cause Belisa, whom he celebrates,
Him the fierce water-snake gnaws and corrodes,
And fierce disdain his breast and soul invades.
His life in torture without calm is passed,
A fate as black as is my own dark fate.

11. He thinks his soul, and that which presses him,
Has a much deeper grief than my mischance ;
Into this thicket well it were I went,
And hid myself to find if he complained.
But woe, the pain which ne'er abandons me,
Madness it is to think his equals it.
The path then open and the way close up,
Which good approximates, and the bad cuts off.

MARSILIO.

1. Steps, which to that of the grave
Transport me gradually.
Your dreary sloth I am constrained to blame.

Follow so sweet a lot.
In this bitter path
Is my good, and in that of your despatch.
Lo the hardness
Of my enemy,
In the angered bosom,
To my advantage adverse.
In its integrity stands what is wont.
Let us elude, if possible it be,
Its bitter rigour terrible to feel.

2. To what sequestered clime,
To what region of doubt,
Wend I to dwell, which can me guarantee
From the woe which o'erbears me
From sorrowful and sure anxiety?
No end can be until I ended am;
Remain I cannot, or change me
To the sandy Lybia,
Or to the habitation wherein dwells
The sanguinary, pale-faced Scythian.
A short point my grief assuages;
My content consists not
In making changes of a dwelling place.

3. Here and there reaches me
Rigorous disdain.
From my incomparable shepherdess,
Save love or hope,
A happy end
Would promise me in this contention.
Belisa, light of day,
Of our age the glory,
If with thee avail
The supplications of a constant friend,
Temper the enraged fury of thy hand;
And this, my fire,
In thy breast, may it all the frost dissolve.

4. Yet deaf to lamentation,
More implacable and more cruel far
Than to the wearied mariner the voice
Of lawless winds

Which the wild ocean rages and disturbs ;
The last ill threatening to mortal life.
Marble, diamond, steel,
Alpine rock impenetrable.
Holm oak, antique and stout,
King of the forest trees, which never bends
Its lofty boughs to the north gale, which drives
All soft is and sweet,
Compared to rigours which thy soul contains.

5. My hard, my bitter fate,
My stars inexorable,
My will to all consenting,
Hold me as one condemned.
Belisa, beauteous, but ungrateful too,
To serve thee and to love eternally,
Although thy pretty forehead,
With too severe a frown,
And thy eyes serene,
A thousand cares announce.
Of my soul mistress wilt thou be,
While on this earth,
A corporal veil mortality enclose.

6. Can aught equal
The woe which me torments ?
Can woe in this world more disdainful be ?
One and the other emanate
From all human belongings,
And yet without it, live I a quick death.
In scorn I quicken
My faith, and there it kindles
With a congealed frost.
See what dotage,
And grief outworn, which sorely me offends.
And it will equal
The ill I would rather to advantage turn.

7. But who is he who moves
The complicated boughs
Of this round-headed myrtle and green seat ?

OROMPO.

A shepherd who dares,
On reasons well based,
In the pure truth of his anguish,
Show that the sentiment
Of his augmented grief
Does thine exceed.
However you may estimate it,
You raise it and exalt.

MARSILIO.

In such a shuffle, conqueror wilt thou be,
Orompo, faithful friend ;
And of the fact thyself will witness be.
If of my solicitudes,
If of my mad woe,
The smallest part thou knowest,
Thy strife will cease,
Orompo.　Sing, plainly,
That thou in joke do suffer, I in fact.

OROMPO.

Chimeras make
Of thy extravagant woe ;
It pales before mine,
Which existence ends.
From this deception thee I hope to draw,
Manifesting openly
That thine a shadow is, mine a proved ill.
But the sonorous voice
Of Crisio I hear, which sounds
A goodly shepherd, who in this concurs.
To him now let us listen,
For his exhausting suffering,
No less than thine, tends him to aggrandise.

MARSILIO.

To-day time proffers me
Coincidence and place
Whereby I may show
To both and all of us.
From what alone my misadventure springs.

OROMPO.

Await awhile, Marsilio,
The voice of Crisio, and his lamented theme.

CRISIO.

1. Oh, hard, importunate ! oh, absence drear !
How far from knowing thee should that one be
Who equal thought your force and violence
To the invisible power of grim death.
Judgment pronouncing with severest rule,
What more can in his boundary be done ?
From the knot solve, with recent ligature,
Which soul to body tightly doth attach.

2. Stiff scimitar to greater ills thyself
Extend ; the spirit parting in two moieties.
Oh, miracles of love, naught understood,
Which neither art nor science e'er can reach ;
Half thyself leave with him who understands.
There is my soul, and hither drag the part
Most fragile ; evil more susceptible
Than absence is a thousand times from life.

3. Absent am I from those seductive eyes,
Which once assuaged the tortures of my soul,
Eyes, life of him who truly them did see,
Of phantasy's existence destitute.
To see and think he merited their orbs
Is madness, alienation, nothing else.
Unlucky, once I saw them, and now see,
And with insane desire myself destroy.

4. I see disunion, reasonably I desire
(To terminate the misery of my days)
Old friendship to divide, supporting bonds
To soul and body of prodigious love,
Which from the flesh is so emancipated,
That with celerity and extreme flight
'Twill turn again those eyes, to revisit
Which are a rest and glory to my rage.

5. Rage is the payment and the recompense
Which love concedeth to the absent man ;

Wherein is writ the evil and the offence
That in love's doings felt and inclosed are;
In its defence is no discretion,
Nor a firm will in upraised hardihood.
Itself avails to moderate the pain
And fury violent of this torture sad.

6. Violent is the rigour of this grief,
Strictly united with duration,
Which first the sterling patience subdues,
And then falls in existence, wretched course.
Deaths, wrong ways, jealousies, inclemencies
Of the enraged breast, condition variable,
Not so torment or heavier damage make,
Than this affliction whose name dread implies.

7. 'Twere dread indeed, though a so cruel grief
Such mortal griefs could not originate;
Though all are weak, yet all I cannot die,
Absent from life, and all that's dear to it.
Cease now my downcast, melancholy strain,
Which to a company, so discreet and rare
As here I witness, 'twould be juster far
On seeing it more relishing taste to evince

OROMPO.

Good Crisio, your presence heralds joy,
At a time coming, when with ease we may
Our ancient difference duly rectify.

CRISIO.

If it's your wish, Orompo, let us commence,
For as a judge of our contention,
Marsilio we hold in rectitude.

MARSILIO.

Proof do you give, a recognised show
Of error, in which absorbed, you are dragged
By this notorious vain opinion;
For your desire to mine preferred be
Your griefs, which the minutest are among,
Much more bewailed than they are recognised:
But as both heaven and earth, united, see

How infinitely less your grievance is
Than those anxieties which oppress my breast,
The very humblest which my breast contains,
I trust I shall show to your competence
Precisely what my genius slow can prove;
To you the judgment I will now submit,
Declare if my distress not greater is
Than is the rigour of an absence long.
Oh, bitter apprehension of a death,
Of which ye both incautiously complain,
Hardly and briefly wailing both your lot.

OROMPO.

Content am I, Marsilio, with this,
And reason good have I in this respect,
From triumphs which o'er torments do ensue.

CRISIO.

Though in exaggeration's art I fail,
When I my sorrows publish you will see
How yours aside in justice you should set.

MARSILIO.

What absence reaches to the obstinacy
Of my rare shepherdess, though obdurate
Yet must of beauty be pre-eminent.

OROMPO.

Oh, in how good time arrives and joins
Orfenio, do'st observe? be ye but still,
And you will hear him his misfortunes weigh;
Jealousy of his torture is the cause.
Jealousy, sword, divers disturbers are
Of his love's peace and satisfaction.

CRISIO.

Attentive be and listen to his plaints.

ORFENIO.

Oh, light obscure which ever you pursue
To my confounded, sorrowing fantasy;
Troublesome darkness, in frigidity,

You my contentment and my light pursue.
When will your endless rigour mitigate?
Oh, cruel monster, harpy horrible—
Upsetting my delight, what gain?
Or what advantage me abandoning?
But if the state in which thou art arrayed
Extends so far, that at my life it aims,
Which gave thee thine, and thee engendered,
No wonder that of me thou really art,
And of life's essence cruel homicide.

OROMPO.

If in the delicious mead
Orfenio to thee is cheerful as before,
The fortunate time,
Come, you a day will pass
In our distressful company,
With the sorrowing, the sorrowful,
Observe you will how they do acquiesce.
Come—here is repulsed
By the limpid brook,
Of rising Phœbus the o'erpowering ray.
Come—and the accustomed means
Raise, and defend yourself as was your wont
From Crisio and Marsilio,
Pretending severally
To prove his ill alone to be an ill.
I alone in this case
Will you and them oppose,
As further ills I suffer,
I could enhance them well,
Yet never show the largest part of them.

ORFENIO.

Not to the palate is it savoury,
So to the lamb insatiable
The grass—nor joyous
Health restored
To him who really gave it up for lost.
So is it tasteful in me clear to shew
For the contention, which is imminent,

That the piercing grief
Which the heart endures
Above the level does enlarge itself,
Its continents o'erflowing.
Be silent as to thy great supreme ill,
Orompo; Crisio conceals his grief,
Marsilio is mute.
Nor death, scorn, nor absence
With jealousy bear competition ;
But, if heaven will,
This day I bring my contest to the test,
Commence who may,
And proofs to others give
Of his deep grief, with head debased, or tongue
No elegance exists
Or mode of giving the foundation
And principal support
Of a true narrative,
But has its seat in undisguised truth.

CRISIO.

Pastor, I feel that they much arrogance
In this sad struggling of our passions,
Infinite proofs of madness will disclose.

ORFENIO.

Temper the sprightliness, or in season shew it
In anguish does the pastime thee involve,
Time's resolution the soul mitigates,
And of such sufferings no account does make.

CRISIO.

My torment's so fierce and unusual,
In truth I trust that you will even say
That my distress has no comparison.

MARSILIO.

E'en from the cradle luckless have I been.

OROMPO.

I think ere life accorded to me was
That deep misfortune marked me for her own.

ORFENIO.

In me misfortune has quite drained herself.

CRISIO.

Your grief's a by-word, as compared with mine.

MARSILIO.

Opposed to the intensity of my extreme ill,
The damage a glory is, which works you ill.

OROMPO.

This tangled skein will show itself more clear,
When to the light my heaviness is exposed,
None now extols his own particular woe,
But I with mine my narrative commenced.

My hopes that were
Sown in good fashion,
Promised sweet fruit,
And when they were ready to yield it
Heaven turned them into woe.
Behold that marvellous flower
In infinite ways desirous
To impart to me a rich lot,
And at that very juncture death
Invidiously cut it down.

That labourer am I,
Who, by the unceasing toil
Of his extended work,
The bitter fruit of grief
Destiny concedes to him.
E'en the hope is withdrawn
Of any advantageous novelty.
For covered is with the earth
The heaven, wherein enclosed is
Confidence in his welfare.

If to the close I touch,
And as for satisfaction and glory,
I live in black despair;
That I greatly suffer
A certain and notorious thing it is.
Let hope assure us that

In our distress extreme
A happy exit soon will supervene :
But woe to him
Who in the sepulchre is sure enclosed.

MARSILIO.

I, whom the moisture from my eyes
Have ever felt flowing,
In place, whence have arisen
A thousand thorns and brambles,
My heart transpiercing.
Wretched am I,
Never to have shown
My visage dry one moment,
Nor leaf, nor flower, nor fruit
Have I collected from my ceaseless toil.

Should I any evidence discern
Of any the least benefit,
It would assuage my breast,
Though no completion followed,
Satisfaction will remain at last ;
For if I but saw what awaited
My truly enamoured constancy,
Which is so distasteful to some,
My ice would be kindled,
And on my fire, frost would imposed be.

But if the labour is futile
Of my sighs and wailings,
To my inhuman grief
What can be equalled ?
What thy grief arranges
Is, that the deadly cause it is,
Orompo, of this, thy mournfulness.
The greater my integrity,
The greater suffering is superinduced.

CRISIO

I, retaining in season
The fruit which is due
To my invariable passion,

A sudden occasion
Prevents my enjoying it,
Well may I, all others beyond,
Be styled unhappy,
Since to suffering I shall come,
For perish wholly I cannot
Where I have left my soul.

The good which death takes away
There is no power to recall,
And it turns itself to ease,
And as to a good heart and strong,
Why, time is used to soften it.
But in absence one is concerned
About a strange accident,
The shadow of good, without
Jealousy, death, scorn ;
This, and much more, does the absent dread.

When the fulfilment is delayed
Of near approaching hope,
The torture more effective is ;
And there the suffering reaches
Where nothing else can touch,
In unequal anxieties
The remedy for ills
Truly is to hope no remedy.
But destitute of these means are
The mortal ills of absence.

ORFENIO.

The fruit which was sown
By my endless toil
To the ripe time arriving,
Was with prosperous destiny
To my power delivered,
And scarce could I touch
The end, so incomparable,
That when I came to ascertain
The cause of that joy,
'Twas only woe to me.

I bear the fruit in hand,
And this fatigues me quite;
For in my inhuman lot,
In the red ear,
A cruel worm corrodes it.
I detest what I love;
I die for that I live.
I conjure up and paint
An intricate labyrinth
Whence is no hope of flight.

Death I seek in my ill,
Which is absent from my grief;
In verity I do deceive myself,
Absent and present
My mighty evil doth itself expand.
No hope reaching so far
As to be a balm to my strong woe,
Neither to remain nor go;
Impossible to remove me 'tis
From cruel, living death.

OROMPO.

It is no recognised error
To allege that the ill-wrought by death
By wide extension,
Somewhat satisfies
If it removes hope,
What then to grief can be administered?

If of a defunct glory
Living memory exists not
Disturbing satisfaction,
It is known to all
No hope there is to retain it;
Grief is in part assuaged by its very loss.

But if memory exists,
The memory of a good achieved,
More lively and burning
Than that I possess,
What doubt but that same evil
With more than other miseries is full?

MARSILIO.

If to a poor wanderer
It should chance to him on a byeway path,
To fly ere
The day's close,
The wished-for lodging in vain haste procured.

Doubtless he would abide
By fear bewildered, which presents to him
The dark and silent night,
Unless dawn arrives,
Or heaven to his fortunes
Yield not her pure and serene light again.

I am he who travels
A fortunate habitation safe to reach,
And when most near,
On repose meditating,
That fugitive shade
Flies my hoped good, while grief my senses scares.

CRISIO.

That flowing river, deep and impetuous,
Is wont the passenger to intercept,
The wind, snow and frost
Smooth the country keeps,
And the resting-place beyond
Show as if 'twere a moderate distance off.

Thus my contentment hinders
This painful absence in its prolixity,
Which never itself disposes
My grief to mitigate.
Almost before my eyes
I see what will my molestation cure.

Contemplating my misfortunes,
My remedy so close, this pinches me,
Them greater making,
For by some mysterious cause
The nearer good approximates
The further flies it off from my sure grasp.

ORFENIO.

It showed me at sight
A place of entertainment rich in good –
In the conquest I triumphed,
But when serener grown,
Dark fate to me exhibited itself,
A vile exchange to black obscurity.

There where consists
The good of lovers who are truly loved,
There my woe works ;
There we blended see
The whips and scorns,
Where every good accustomed is to be.

This habitation within
Am I, making no effort to escape—
Based for my grief,
On such a mighty wall,
I think it humiliates
All who love it and see, and combat too.

OROMPO.

Or ere the sun its fiery course shall end
Its proper medium, wending through the sky,
Having the zodiac's signs fully traversed,
The lesser portion of our wonted wail
Declare we can what ailment it affects—
Ere goodly speech its flight direct should take.
Crisio, you say that he who absent lives,
Dies—I then am dead, for my poor life
To death delivered is, inclement fate.
And thou Marsilio do affirm that lost
Thou hast all good and profitable hope,
And that fierce scorn has been thy murderer.
Orfenio, you reiterate that the lance
Sharpened by jealousy has thee transfixed,
Smiting the breast not only, but the soul ;
But how the one the other doth exceed,
Appeareth not ; grief sole exaggerates,
Thinking one woe the other doth transcend.
But for our melancholy contention,

With sorrowful arguments everywhere abounds,
The banks of Tagus' deep exulting stream.
Yet not the less is grief diminished,
Quite opposite the treating of the wound
To larger suffering the martyr condemns,
How much the organ of our speech can say.
The sorrowing thoughts can meditate how much,
On the occasion grief to renovate.
Let arguments acute fall to the ground,
No woe there is, but sore fatigues and pains,
Or any good to countervail distress—
Sufficient evil hath he who hath life,
In a contracted sepulchre immured,
Keeping himself in bitter solitude.
Unlucky he who without fortune's smile,
The suffering of jealousy undergoes,
With whom nor strength, nor meekness can avail.
Who in the rigour of absence prolonged,
Passes his very miserable days,
Leaning alone on patience weakest reed.
Nor less feels he in rigid constancy
When most he burns for a scornful shepherdess
Whose heart is hard with tendencies all frost.

CRISIO.

That which Orompo asks let us now do.
Our flocks again into the fold let's bring;
Time moving on towards that necessity.
And when to the accustomed spot we are
Duly arrived, and the bright sun declines,
His torch concealing in the verdant mead,
With bitter tone and lamentable wail
To sounds of our well-tuned instruments,
That sorrow chant which sore oppresses us.

MARSILIO.

Oh, Crisio, in your accents let's begin—
Which to Clauraura's hearing will arrive,
Softly subduing e'en the winds themselves,
As each one in his grief is mollified.

CRISIO.

He to whom absence gives
His bitter chalice for a draught,
No ill fears,
And hopes no good—
In this bitter grief,
No woe but what is registered.
Fear of self-oblivion ;
Jealous at another's presence,
Who would come this to prove,
Speedily will learn to know
That there is no ill to be greatly feared,
Much less of good in confidence to hope.

OROMPO.

See if its evil is that presses me,
More than a recognised death—
For life conjures up complaints
Which even death doth leave.
When death withdrew
My glory and content,
Me to insure a torment worse,
It left me life—
Evil care and good recedes
With flight so light,
That life complaints doth conjure up,
Which even death doth leave.

MARSILIO.

In my terrible anguish
For very rage fail,
Tears in my eyes,
For sighing breath itself.
Scorn and ingratitude
Me in such rigour hold
That I hope, and death invoke
Being to life and good superior,
We can arrest it but little.
Hence in my anger fail
Tears in my eyes,
For sighing breath itself.

ORFENIO.

Jealousy in truth may do,
What I had rather do,
If jealousy were love,
And love jealousy.
By this exchange certainly we should gain
Of good and glory so much,
That victory and the palm
Would quickly bear the enamoured one quite off.
But even should be in such wise
Jealousy in my favour,
If love were jealousy,
Alone I would be love.

With this last song of the jealous Orfenio, the worthy pastors terminated their eclogues, satisfying by their discretion all who had listened to them, especially Damon and Thirsis, who received much satisfaction from the display, to whom it appeared that the reasons and arguments were of a more pastoral character, than what the shepherd had proposed. But a contention arising amongst the bystanders, which of the four shepherds had alleged most in favour of his claim; finally the opinion which the discreet Damon gave was accepted, saying, that he agreed that amidst all the disgust and aversions which were inseparable from love, nothing so disturbed the enamoured breast as the incurable rage of jealousy, that the loss of Orompo was no equivalent to that, or the absence of Crisio, or the distrust of Marsilio. The cause, he added, is that it was futile to attempt to attain what was not within possibility's sphere, or could time itself repay the object of search, or wear down the desire to reach it; for that to him who was set on a hope to touch the impossible, it was obvious the more his longing predominated by it, by so much was he deficient in a right understanding; therefore I aver, that the suffering of Orompo is but a compassionate sorrow for what is lost and gone; and having lost it so, that recovery was impossible, that ceasing his grief, was his only remedy; for that human reason was not always uniform, that it ceased to feel a loss which was irrecoverable, and that virtually it evinced evidences of its emotions in tender tears, ardent sighs, and piteous words, under the sentence that he whose feelings were not obnoxious to the consequences, partook rather of the nature of an animal than an intelligent essence.

Finally the current of time superseded grief, reason assuaged it, and the succession of events tended to obliterate it from the tablet of the memory. All this is the reverse in absence, as Crisio pointed out in his strains, that as hope in the absent man is so blended with desire, that the delay of the return awakens evil; for naught else intercepts fruition, save an arm of the sea, or remoteness; that which is the principal thing, is the wish of the beloved one, which gives annoyance to his predilection, things much less than a little water or earth, impeding his felicity and glory. To these are annexed the fear of oblivion, variableness in the human heart, and while absence lasts undoubtedly there abounds harshness and bitterness, all hurtful to the feelings of the unlucky absent individual. Still a remedy is nigh, which consists in a return, and hence some alleviation to the torment; but should absence follow and cut off all hope of revisiting the desired object, that very impossibility supplies a remedy as sure as death itself. Now this is the grief to which Marsilio is obnoxious, for it is identical with that I suffer, and so I enhance it beyond all others, still I will not fail to avow what reason indicates before that to which passion incites.

I do confess that it is a very grief to love without reciprocity, yet would it be a greater ill to love and be spurned. If we direct new aspirants in love by what reason and experience teach, we shall find that all initiations are difficult, and that in love there is no exception, rather the principle is reinforced, so that for a young lover to complain of the stubbornness of a beloved one exceeds due bounds, for love being by nature voluntary and not enforced, I should not complain if my proffered love were not returned, or should I appropriate the possession by an assurance that an obligation exists to be loved, because I am in that predicament; for presuming that the party beloved should not by law or courtesy be ungrateful towards the one who is devoted, yet no necessity enjoins that an exact conformity should exist. Were this so, an infinite tribe of lovers would presume on importunity, which they would consider a right ; and since love holds knowledge for a parent, it may be that I found not in myself that which is an important element in my beloved one, moving and inclining her to evince her love to me. Hence she is not bound to love me, though I might adore her, finding in her that of which I myself am destitute. These are reasons good why a spurned love ought not to complain of his mistress, but of his misfortune. Who does not recognise in him the attributes which can move a lady to reciprocate love? So should he by protracted services, with seductive arguments, and with importunity, joined to the exercise of grace and virtues, infinite as men may undergo, obliterate and amend in himself the faults which nature made. Such is the chief expedient, and this I aver, that it is impossible but that one may be loved who by honest means tries to secure the goodwill of his lady, and as the evil of scorn has its remedy, let us console Marsilio, and extend our pity to the luckless, yet zealous Orfenio, in whose disgrace is comprised as much as love can perpetrate. Oh, ye jealous perturbators of a tranquil, amorous peace ! jealousy, weapon against the stoutest hopes. I know not what he can know of lineages who made you a child of love. Quite the reverse are you, for love would cease so to be, if he were parent of such an offspring. Oh, jealousy, hypocritical and treacherous rogue, why is such account made of you in the world, seeing if there arise a scintilla of love, in any breast, you would incontinently be mixed up with it, changing its colour, and trying to usurp its sovereignty and its sway. Hence it arises that as there is such a union with love, for by your results, you would give to understand that you are not love itself, so you would try to let the ignorant know that you are of the sons born of a mean suspicion, generated of a vile and wretched fear, nurtured at the bosom of imaginations false, growing by a low envy, and sustained by mischief and untruths.

And because we see the desolation which this accursed disease of jealousy causes in the hearts of lovers, being one of the jealous, let us peaceably be among the jealous in love, for it is impossible, I add, but it should be a traitor, astute, turbulent, mischievous, prejudiced, and of a low education. So wide does this jealous passion extend itself, that it gains such sway over him who loves much that he even cherishes ill to his rival.

The jealous man wishes that for him alone the object of his choice should be attractive, but to the world the contrary. Wishes, too, that she may have no eyes to see but what he likes, or auditory nerves to hear, or tongue to speak ; that she should be retiring, tasteless, proud and ill-conditioned. Sometimes he desires, impregnated with a fiend's fury, that his mistress should die, and the end all be there. Such emotions awaken jealousy in lovers' breasts, quite opposite to those graces which pure and simple love multiplies in true and courteous lovers, for in their hearts are concentrated discretion, courage, liberality, politeness, and what is laudable in a nation's eyes. The potency of this fierce poison is such, that no antidote counteracts it, or counsel that avails, or friend which aids, or extenuation which pleads,—all this is heaped up in the jealous breast, aye, and more. Whatsoever shadow may frighten it, foolery disturb, or false or true suspicion may undo it. And to this misfortune may we one more add, that even extenuation deceives us. Now there being no other cure for jealousy but excuse, and this inadmissible by the poor patients, it ensues that the infirmity is remediless, and should take precedence of all other ills. My own opinion is that Orfenio is a martyr, but not the less a lover, for jealousy is little conversant with love, but much in opportune curiosity. If these be tokens of love, it is as a calenture in an infirm system, which, by its seizure, is a sign of life, but life weak and illy constituted,—so jealousy is a proof of little self-confidence. Let this be a truth, then, and let the really enamoured man show it, who, without touching on the darkness of jealousy, lights upon fear's shades, yet' not so conversant does he with them become, but that the sun of his content is darkened, nor can he separate himself from them so as to be careless of an anxious and fearful march. Should this discriminate apprehension fail in a lover, I should stamp him as one imbued with pride and vainly confident ; for one of our running proverbs hath it, " Who would love well, let him fear." So is it reasonable that a lover should have fear, seeing what he loves is exquisite, or to him so it appears, though in the eyes of her he loves this may not be the conviction. Love, then, procreates in another what it can, and yet advances to disturb its own. He fears, and let fear the truly enamoured times change, and those new occasions which to his damage may present themselves, that with brevity the fruition of his happy estate may not end; but this apprehension should be kept so close, that no tongue should reveal it, or eyes give evidence of what it means. Now a quite contrary effect does this fear work in the breasts of jealous souls, who nurture in them new hopes to increase love if possible, or to procure, with all solicitude, that the eyes of the beloved one see not aught unworthy praise, evincing, at once, generosity, urbanity, neatness, propriety and good manners; and by how much this virtuous dread merits praise, by so much do the jealous stigmatise it.

Here the renowned Damon was silenced, and divers opinions of the listeners followed in the wake, yet were all satisfied with that truth which had been delivered with so much plainness. Replies, however, had ensued, had the pastors, Orompo, Crisio, Marsilio, and Orfenio been present at the meeting, who, tired of reciting eclogues, had gone to their friend Daranio. All being united, they wished to resume the dances, when they witnessed to enter through the locality, three very decent looking shepherds, whose identities were soon known; the gentle Francenio, the liberal Lauso, and the ancient Arsindo, who advanced into the centre of the bystanders with a graceful garland of green laurel in his hands, and traversing the pleasure-ground, stopped just where Thirsis, Damon, Elicio, and Erastro, and the foremost shepherds were, whom they saluted with appropriate words, and in return received due courtesy, particularly Lauso from Damon, an old and tried friend.

On the lull of these courtesies, Arsindo, fixing his eyes on Damon and on Thirsis, he uttered these sentiments:—
"The renown of your wisdom, whose circulation moves far and wide, discreet and liberal shepherds, is such that I, and other pastors, request you to be judges in an amicable contest which has arisen between two of our

party; and it is that after the feast, Francenio and Lauso were present, and held sweet discourse with some ladies of rare beauty, and so to while away the heavy-footed day without *ennui*, among sundry diversions they instituted that of questions."

It came to pass that one of the pastors had to propose, and he desired that the shepherdess by his side, and whose right hand he grasped, should be treasurer of his soul's secrets, because her renown for discretion and amiability was denied by none.

Approaching within his hearing, she said to him, "In flight hope vanishes."

This shepherdess, without further respite, proceeded, each saying openly what one to the other had in secret whispered. Now the shepherdess followed out the proposition by saying, " Retain it with ardour."

The acuteness of the answer was applauded by the bystanders, but he who honoured it the most was the pastor Lauso, and not less pertinent did it appear to Francenio. Each severally perceiving that the question and answer were measured, offered to expound them, and each having so done, each tried that his interpretation should excel the other, and to confirm this, they solicited me to be the judge. But as I was aware that your presence delighted our banks, I counselled them to apply to you, to whose unusual science and perspicacity questions of great validity could be confided.

Having acquiesced in my view—and I took to myself the trouble of forming this garland, for an adequate reward— shepherds, you will see whose is the best gloss.

Arsindo was silent, and awaited the reply of the shepherds, which was the good opinion he entertained of them, and he offered to be a dispassionate judge in this honourable rivalry. Quite assured of this, Francenio quickly turned round to repeat his verses and to declare his gloss, which was this—

In flight hope vanishes,
Retain it with ardour.

THE GLOSS.

  1. When I think myself to save
    In my love's faith,

> Quickly are found wanting
> The errors of desert.
> In the superfluity of grief,
> Extinct is confidence,
> And life pulsation wants ;
> So one discerns by my uneven gait,
> By apprehension persecuted,
> In flight doth vanish hope.

> 2. Fly, and with you take
> All relish of my suffering,
> Still leaving, for my greater chastisement,
> Of my chain the keys
> In power of my enemy ;
> For far removed is it, that methinks
> 'Twill soon invisible be.
> And in its lightness plainly I discern
> That I nor can, nor is it possible
> With ardour it to hold.

When Francenio had repeated his gloss, then began Lauso his gloss, saying—

> 1. At the identical moment you I saw,
> How beautiful I found you.
> Quickly hope came and fear,
> And by them were abashed,
> Producing verily
> Confidence weak
> With an unmanly fear.
> Not finding you beside me,
> In flight hope vanishes.

> 2. Although it quits me, and doth disappear
> With extraordinary rapidity,
> Miraculously will you see
> That it will end my life ;
> But of my love's faith there shall be no end.
> Yet to carry off the trophy
> Of a lover, without profit,
> I neither wish, nor could I
> With ardour it retain.

At the conclusion of Lauso's gloss, Arsindo spoke :—
" You see here, famous Damon and Thirsis, the recognised

cause about which the shepherds' rivalry arose. It remains now for you to assign the garland to whomsoever may deserve it. Lauso and Francenio are such friends, and your award so just, that they will hold for equity the judgment you have pronounced."

"Do you not understand, Arsindo," replied Thirsis, "that with extreme quickness, although our wits were of the quality you conjecture, that you should not pass a verdict, if there be any discrepance in these sagacious glosses. What I can advance about them, I fearing no contradiction from Damon, is that all are apposite, and that the garland justly belongs to the shepherdess who gave rise to this curious yet laudable strife ; and if you are content therewith, honour us further with your company at the nuptials of our friend Daranio, with your captivating songs delighting us, sanctioning all by your personal presence."

This sentiment of Thirsis was approved by all, and the two pastors being agreed, they volunteered to carry out the suggestions of Thirsis. But the males and females of the party who knew Lauso, were amazed to see how disengaged he was, and yet involved in the net of love. Soon they perceived, by the yellow tinge on his countenance, and the mute state of his tongue, and in the conflict he held with Francenio, that his volition was not quite so exempt as hitherto, and he was shrouded in his own imaginings as to who that shepherdess could be who had so completely gained his heart.

Some thought it the discreet Belisa, some the gay Leandra, and others fixed on the incomparable Arminda, inducing them to think that this was the usual habit which Lauso had of visiting the cabins of the shepherdesses, and that each of them was framed to subdue by gracefulness, moral worth, and attractiveness, other hearts free as that of Lauso. Some days elapsed in certifying this doubt, for the love-stricken pastor, to himself, scarce trusted the secret of his own passion.

This concluded, the youth of either sex the dance resumed, and the rural instruments struck up becoming music.

When the golden sun hastened his course towards the west, the concert of voices finished, and all resolved to conduct the betrothed to their home.

The time-honoured Arsindo, to achieve what Thirsis had promised, in that space which stretched from the pleasure-grounds to the house of Daranio, to the rebeck's sound, played by Erastro, he poured forth these inspiriting verses :—

ARSINDO.

1. May kind heaven indications give
   Of content and rejoicings,
   On this well-omened day.
   On every section of the soil be celebrated
   This cheerful wedding
   With universal joy.
   May this day plaint and woe converted be
   Into a sweet and an harmonious song,
   And in the stead of woe
   To thousands delight come,
   All weariness of spirit banishing.

2. May all felicity in profusion fall
   Such an espoused pair between
   For matrimony born.
   Let the elm tree offer pears,
   And cherries the holm ;
   Yea, the flourishing myrtle cherries large,
   In the crags even may pears be found,
   And lentils yielding grapes.
   The carobe tree apples supply,
   And without apprehension of fierce wolves
   May apricots to magnitude expand.

3. May barren ewes
   Goodly twins produce,
   Doubling the flock ;
   May the busy bees
   Within the furrows of the threshing floors
   Honey's substance in excess produce,
   May they in perpetuity enjoy
   The seed in field and town,
   In time precise, in season garnered,
   No insect in their vines,
   Or cockle weed enter their precious wheat.

4. In twins may they exult,
   The progeny of peace and heavenly **lov.**,
   As much as they desire ;
   And in time's fulness
   May one physician be
   The other spiritual pastor of the spot.
   Pre-eminent may they be
   In opulence and worth.
   If this shall be, and they be gentlemen,
   If not, may they go bail
   For sharp-practising collectors.

5. May they live longer than old Sarah did,
   In good health's daily confirmation,
   The doctor ever disappointing eke
   No woe incur
   From the ill-sorted marriage of a girl,
   Or son a gambler be ;
   And when the pair shall come
   To touch antique Methuselah's long years,
   Go hence, divested of perdition's fear,
   Closing their end in sure felicity.

With the greatest satisfaction were heard these rustic lines of Arsindo, who had amplified them had they not reached Daranio's house, who, inviting all who came with him, stayed there. It happened however, that Galatea and Florisa, lest Teolinda should be recognised by Thirsis and Damon, would not remain at the banquet of the betrothed ones.

Both Elicio and Erastro earnestly desired to escort Galatea as far as her house, but she would by no means consent, so they made up their minds to continue with their associates, and the females, tired of dancing, went away.

But Teolinda was more oppressed than ever, because she found not Artidoro present at the sanctimonious rites of Daranio's marriage, where so many swains had assisted.

With this mournful feeling she passed that night in the company of Galatea and Florisa, and freely passed it, when what on the next day happened the next book will disclose.

BOOK IV.

The ardour of Teolinda to go in quest of Artidoro.—Is accompanied on her way by Galatea and Florisa.—Four men observed on horseback, and others on foot, with hawks, dogs, and attendants.—Two shepherds emerge from a thicket.—Some shepherdesses in masks.—One, divesting herself of her hood, is discovered by Teolinda to be Rosaura.—With her comes Grisaldo, whom Rosaura addresses, charging him with perfidy.—Grisaldo's defence, who announces his projected marriage with Leopersia.—Rosaura attempts her own life, but is restrained by Grisaldo.—Scene which followed.—Teolinda exclaims that the visage seen was that of her sister Leonarda, and a mutual embrace ensued.—The sisters mutually requested the stories of their lives.—Narrative of Rosaura.—The voice of the shepherd Lauso recognised.—His song indicative of his love for Silena.—Disguises of Teolinda, Leonarda, and Rosaura.—Silerio asks permission to return to his hermitage.—The shepherds reach the font, and there encounter three cavaliers and two ladies.—The cavaliers wish to remove on finding the shepherds offer to yield their places to them for their siesta.—The two ladies unmask.—Conversation about court and rural manners, between Darintho and Damon, which ends in the recitation of verses said to be Lauso's song.—Lenio's harsh remarks about love, in a diatribe, which provoked observations from Erastro.—A rejoinder by Lenio.—Arrival of Aurelio, father of Galatea; also Galatea and Florisa, with Rosaura, Teolinda, and Leonarda, in disguises.—Lenio descants in opposition to Thirsis, on love, as a theme morally and physiologically.—The oral treatise ends in some appropriate verses by the disenamoured Lenio.—Thirsis prosecutes the affecting argument with some prolixity, yet to the edification of the listeners, who, in response, rounded his metaphysical reasonings with half a dozen stanzas.—All agree he had the best of the argument, but his desponding opponent, Elicio, adds a summary.—Proposition to retire.—Nisida's name is announced.—Disclosures made as to identities, and sundry colloquial interchanges.—Darintho, on hearing about Silerio, takes horse, and Timbrio overtakes him.—Reunion of the females.—Nisida recounts the friendship of Timbrio and Silerio.—Sudden appearance, at the fountain, of a virgin of fifteen years old, asking for a remedy for a love which related to her brother and a shepherdess, whom he had pathetically addressed without avail.—Mistaken identity by Leonarda and Teolinda, as to their lovers.—Explanations thereon.—Resemblance of Galercio to Artidoro.—Maurisa takes leave of Rosaura and Galatea.—Parting of the females and shepherds, some towards Silerio's hermitage.—To the sound of Florisa's rebeck Elicio pours forth a canticle.

WITH ardent desire did the beauteous Teolinda await the coming day, to take leave of Galatea and Florisa, and so to finish her quest after the cherished Artidoro throughout the banks of the Tagus, with a view to terminate her days in a sorrowful and bitter solitude, if she heard no further news of the beloved shepherd. Now was come the desired hour, when Sol began to diffuse his rays over the world, when she arose, and with eyes bedewed with tears, she solicited of the shepherdesses favour to prosecute her intents, who most reasonably induced her to stay yet some days with them, Galatea offering to send men belonging to her father to seek for Artidoro on Tagus' margin, where it was hoped he would be found.

Teolinda acquiesced, but she did not wish to do all they required, for having shewn by words to the best of her power, what she knew, the obligations in which she found herself for the rest of her life to carry out the works received from them, and so embracing them with tenderness, begged they would only detain her one single hour. Galatea and Florisa, observing how vainly they laboured to keep her back, charged her that whatever success, good, or ill, might eventuate in this amorous enterprise, she would announce it to them, which would be received with satisfaction, if fortunate, and with sorrow if the contrary. Teolinda volunteered herself to be the medium through which the good news should transpire, but if ill news her life would suffer, and so this would be apology enough for default of communication. With this Teolinda's promise, both Galatea and Florisa were content, and they agreed to accompany her a space beyond the locality. So taking their staves and fortifying the wallet of Teolinda with sundry provision for a troublesome journey, forth they sallied from the village just when the beams of the sun most directly, and with their utmost force encountered the ground. Having been her companions for about half a league, just as they purposed returning they observed to pass at a break, a little distance off, four men on horseback, and some on foot, whom they soon recognised for hunters by their attire, their hawks, and dogs; and stopping to see if they knew them, they marked how had emerged from some dense thickets, which were adjacent to the break, two shepherdesses of graceful mien. They had their visages enveloped in white linen, and one of the ladies uplifting her voice, asked the foresters to stop, which they did. Hence both ladies, nearing one of them, who seemed the principal by his figure and position, they seized the reins of the steed, and stood thus discoursing with him awhile, without the three other shepherdesses hearing what passed, by reason of the distance which prevented.

Only they saw that a short distance off, the cavalier dismounted, and having, as one could judge, ordered those who were with him to return, leaving one boy only with the horse, linked his hand in those of the women, and gradually entered with them into a thicket which lay near. This being witnessed by Galatea, Florisa, and Teolinda, they resolved to see if they could discover whoever were the masked shepherdesses and the cavalier who accompanied them, so they agreed to compass one part of the wood and see if they could so arrange themselves that they might satisfy their curiosity. This done, as they thought, they intercepted the cavalier and the ladies; so Galatea, seeing between the boughs what was going on, she observed that by twisting to the right they might secrete themselves in the densest part of the wood, and quickly by the same route they followed the cavalier and his fair companions, who seemed to be within the thicket, in the centre of a narrow meadow, which was environed by numberless brambles, and there they stopped.

Galatea and her friends approached so close that, quite unobserved, they heard and saw all the parties did—who, casting about to learn if they could be seen of any, and in this conviction one disencumbered herself of her hood, and in a moment she was recognised by Teolinda, and coming within hearing of Galatea, she said in the lowest possible whisper,—" A most extraordinary adventure is this, for if I have not lost all remembrance from the pain I suffer, doubtless that shepherdess who removed the hood from her person is the beauteous Rosaura, daughter of Roselio, lord of a village contiguous to ours; nor can I conceive what motive has induced her to expose herself so, quit her locality, and thus do what is so injurious to her reputation. But unlucky me," added Teolinda, "for that cavalier, who is with her, is Grisaldo, eldest born of the rich Laurentio, who possesses two whole villages hard by." "You utter a truth, Teolinda," replied Galatea, "I know her. But hold your peace, soon we shall be certified as to the cause of her coming." With this she quieted Teolinda, and earnestly watched what Rosaura did, who, approaching the cavalier, a man of some thirty years old, with a faltering voice, thus began :—"Here we are, deceitful cavalier, where I shall be able to take the long attended vengeance of your infidelity and neglect. But though I might avail me of the moment which might cost you a life, that would little repay me for the injury you have done me. Look you here, unknown Grisaldo, unknown, though I recognize you ; see one who has disguised herself to seek you, and who never abandoned that hope. Reflect, ungrateful and variable man, that what in your house and amidst your servants could not move her, now for your sake travels from valley to valley, from mountain's brow to mountain's brow, with such solicitude, seeking your person." To all these arguments, which the lovely Rosaura used, the cavalier listened with eyes rivetted to the soil, making some strokes on the ground with the point of his hunting-knife, which he held in his hand. Yet Rosaura not satisfied with what passed, she pursued the discourse with similar words. "Say now, know you by chance, do you know, Grisaldo, that I am that being who lately wiped thy tears, stifled thy sighs, consoled thy pains, and beyond all I am her who gave credence to your words ! Or peradventure dost thou understand that thou wert he to whom all oaths seemed nugatory, which assured me of the truth whereby you deceived me ? Art thou by chance that Grisaldo, whose boundless tears softened the hardness of my honest heart ? Thou art—yes, I see you ; and I am— yes, I know myself. But if you be Grisaldo, as I believe, and I be Rosaura, as you imagine, fulfil your promise to me, and I will offer that promise which I never denied you. I am told you are to marry Leopersia, Marcelio's daughter ; so much to your taste, that you selected her. If this news has caused me anguish, you can divine why I have done

11—2

this, it is to prevent its accomplishment ; and if you can act honourably I leave it to your conscience. What answer make you, oh mortal enemy of my rest? Perhaps you grant it, though silence indicates its justice. Raise your eyes and drop them on those who for her woe beholds them —raise them up, and look on whom you deceive, whom you abandon, whom you forget. You will see that you deceive, if you reflect, her who is all truth to you. You will abandon her who has abandoned her honour to follow you. You will forget her who never let you slip from her memory. Consider, Grisaldo, that in nobleness I am behind you in nothing, and in fortune I am equal, I surpass you in generosity of soul and in faith's holy firmness. Fulfil what you avowed if you can appreciate yourself as a gentleman, or disregard not yourself as a Christian. See, now, unless you respond to what you owe me, I will besiege heaven that it may chastise you—fire, that it may consume you—that air may fail you—water drown, and earth abhor you—and my relatives take vengeance on you. Look you, if you fail in the obligation you owe me, you will find in me a ceaseless tormenter of your comforts, whilst I breathe vital air—ay, even after life will I scare your recreant soul with frequent shadows, and with fearful visions will I worry your deluding eyes ; remember I ask no more than is my due, and your profit is in yielding it, for by denial you are a certain loser ; speak, now, and undeceive me, what is the cause of offence ?" Here the lovely lady ceased, and awhile awaited Grisaldo's answer, who, raising his face, which hitherto was downward, inflamed with the vengeance denounced by Rosaura, with softened voice thus replied—

"Should I desire to deny, O Rosaura, that I am not a debtor in more than you recapitulate, I should deny that the sun's light is clear, or aver that fire is frost, and that air is hard. Hence I admit my debt, and am forced to pay it. Still I cannot settle it as you desire, for my father's injunctions have prohibited that, and your stern disdain has added an impossibility to it. I would only call yourself as witness, who know how oft, and with what effusion of tears I solicited you to accept me for your husband, you being assured that I would fulfil all the promises, and yet, you, for your own conceptions, or else to acquiesce in

—Artandro's vain promises, would never conform to this suggestion; rather day by day would you entertain me, and elicit proofs of my constancy, so as to be certified as to my entire devotion to you. You know very well, Rosaura, the desire my father had to put me in a certain position, and his very haste to do it—alluring me with rich and honourable unions, and how I framed infinite excuses to evade it, requiring of you not to retard what was agreeable to me, and what you desired, so that one day I conveyed to you the fact that my father wished me to marry Leopersia, while you, on hearing her name, in a downright fury requested me not so much as to speak to you again, and that I might marry Leopersia, or anybody else that suited my inclinations. You know very well how often I persuaded you to desist from those mad ravings, that I was yours, and not the suitor of Leopersia, that you would not admit my excuses or give ear to my complaints, nay persisting in your unaccountable obstinacy, and in favouring the suit of Artandro, you hinted that it would give you joy never to see me more. On this hint I acted; yet, not to break through your orders, and to fulfil those of my father, I determined to betroth myself to Leopersia, so that to-morrow I shall espouse her according to the concurrent wishes of our parents. Hence you must observe, Rosaura, how I am exculpated from your charge, and how late has been the recognition of your unreasonableness towards me. But that you may not judge me for the future to be as ungrateful as your imagination has painted me, see if I can anyhow satisfy your wish. If I cannot marry you, I will proffer you my property, life, and honour." Whilst Grisaldo spoke these words, the lovely Rosaura rivetted her eyes on his face, shedding tears copiously, which indicated the depth of her grief. When she remarked that Grisaldo ceased to speak, giving a profound and dolorous sigh, she said to him, 'As you, Grisaldo, in your early time, have had no experience of the many accidents incident to love, I am not surprised, but a little disdain on my part justifies the liberty of declaring it. Should you, however, know that these jealous fears are but incentives which cause love to deviate, you would clearly discern that my fears about Leopersia were redundant. But as you treated my affairs so cavalierly, on the slightest occasion, you disclosed the little love you entertained for me, and of course confirmed my true suspicions, and so it is that you announce to me your marriage to-morrow morning with Leopersia; but I avow that ere you lead her to the chamber you must conduct me to the tomb,—if you are not so cruel as to refuse that to a corpse, over whose departed soul you were absolute lord; and since you clearly know and see that she who lost her honour for you, and put all in jeopardy, will also lose her existence. This identical sharp dagger which now I draw, shall realise my desperate yet honourable purpose, and it will be a testimony of the savageness which your recreant breast incloses."

This finished, she drew from her breast a naked dagger, and with despatch was directing it through her heart, had not Grisaldo held her arm, and the disguised shepherdess, her associate, had not pressed forward to close with her. Some time elapsed ere Grisaldo and the shepherdess could wrest the dagger from her hands, who said to Grisaldo: "Let me, traitor, accomplish the tragedy of my life at once, for by your disdain you would make me take proof of death." "This shall you not do on my account," rejoined Grisaldo, "for I would that my father rather failed of his word relative to Leopersia, than that I should be wanting in aught honourable to you. Calm your breasts, Rosaura, for on my honour I desire naught else but your satisfaction." With these comforting assurances of Grisaldo, Rosaura awakened from her mortal sorrow to a new life, yet without ceasing to grieve, she bent her knees before Grisaldo, asking his hands as a token of the favour he had shown her. Grisaldo did the same, and encircling her neck with his arms, both stood unable to give utterance to their feelings, yet both drowned in tears.

The disguised shepherdess witnessing the happy issue, exhausted by the fatigue she had encountered in rescuing the fatal dagger from Rosaura, and fearing no longer her disguise, removed it, discovering a face so like to Teolinda, that both Galatea and Florisa were surprised. Still, Teolinda it was, who without dissimulation, uplifted her voice, saying, "O heavens, and who do I see? Is not this my own sister Leonarda, the perturbator of my repose? the same in truth." And without further delay, she sallied forth, and with her Galatea and Florisa. When the other shepherdess saw Teolinda, in a moment was the recognition, and with open arms both embraced, wondering how they could have mutually met in such a place, such a season, and under such a conjuncture.

Grisaldo and Rosaura seeing what Leonarda did with Teolinda, and how they had been discovered by the shepherdesses Galatea and Florisa, with no small shame at the condition, arose, and cleansing themselves with tears, with dissimulation and good breeding received the shepherdesses, who were incontinently recognised by Grisaldo. But the discreet Galatea, to convert into a security the uncomfortableness which perhaps at sight of her the two enamoured shepherds had experienced, with that grace with which she could say things, addressed them—"Let not our advent here annoy you, venturesome Grisaldo and Rosaura, for it will only contribute to augment your satisfaction. Our expedition has ordained that we should see you, where no thoughts are concealed, and since heaven has conducted it to a so fortunate end, in satisfaction calm your breasts and pardon our audacity." "Never has thy presence, my pretty Galatea," replied Grisaldo, "failed to give satisfaction everywhere; this being a recognised verity, that we rather stand in obligation to you, than incur any discomfort at your arrival among us." With these also other reasons were interchanged, very different from what followed between Leonardo and Teolinda, who, after mutual embraces with tender expressions, mixed with tears of love, mutually requested the story of their lives, all beholders in admiration as they stood, for such was their semblances that they appeared the same, save in one particular; and were it not for the apparel of Teolinda, which differed from that of Leonarda, doubtless not even Galatea and Florisa had distinguished them; and then it was they saw how it came to pass that Artidoro had been deceived in taking Leonarda for Teolinda.

Now Florisa remarked that the sun had run its midday course, and that it would be expedient to seek a shade for defence, or return to the village at least, for the opportunity of feeding their sheep having gone, it was not good to re-

main in the meadow, and said to Teolinda and Leonarda,
"There will be ample time, shepherdesses, with more convenience to satisfy our wants, and to give a more extended
account of our reflectons, so that it will be politic for us to
select a spot where we may pass the heat which threatens
us, or go to the cool font at the outlet of the valley just
behind us, or else reverting to the village where Leonarda
will be accommodated, as you, Teolinda, from Galatea and
myself are informed.　And if to you, shepherdesses, I make
this proposition, it is not that I am forgetful of Grisaldo
and Rosaura, but because it seems to me that I cannot, in
consideration of his valour and merit, offer less than his
desire."　"So long as I have life, I will never fail in this,"
replied Grisaldo, "to do, shepherdess, that which contributes
to your service, for we should never pay with less these
wishes; yet as it appears to me just to do what you propose
and to remember that you are not ignorant of what has
passed between Rosaura and myself, I will detain you, or
myself, in referring thereto.　I only request you will be
pleased to take Rosaura in your company to the village,
whilst I effect in mine certain preliminaries to realise what
both our hearts covet, and to the end that Rosaura may be
free from suspicion, and rely on the faith of my word, with
due consideration, and you witnesses of the same, I give
her my hand as her veritable husband."　This finished, he
extended his hand, and took that of the lovely Rosaura,
while she was beside herself at what Grisaldo did, so that
words were intercepted; leaving her hand in his, after a
brief interval she spake: "Love has brought me to this
point.　Oh, Grisaldo, mine! and for this I shall rest under
perpetual obligation to you—and since you have desired
this correspondence, beyond my merit, I will do my part,
which is to re-transfer to you my soul in recompense for
the favour, and may heaven also reimburse you for this act
of spontaneity on your part."　"No more of that," interposed here Galatea, "no more of that, gentlemen, for affairs
glide on so justly, that it leaves no further space for superfluous compliments. What remains is, to solicit kind heaven
to conduct to a happy issue these beginnings, and may you
in celestial felicity enjoy your loves.　And in reference to
what you say, Grisaldo, let Rosaura come to our village, and

by thus conferring on us this kindness you will accede to our wishes." "Most willingly I will accompany you," said Rosaura, "for I know not what will charm me more than by assuring you that the absence of Grisaldo will be indemnified in your presence."

"Now," said Florisa, "the village is some way off, the sun is directly on us, and our delay is remarked. You, Grisaldo, can go and do what you desire; you will find Rosaura in Galatea's cottage, and a shepherdess, with the two others who may scarce be called two." "As you like it," said Grisaldo, and touching Rosaura's hand, all left the wood, in the understanding that some day Grisaldo should send a shepherd from the many in his father's service, to advise Rosaura of what she had done; and that having sent the shepherd without observation he might converse with Galatea or Florisa, and convey the orders most expedient. This arrangement seemed most suitable, and so sallying forth from the wood, Grisaldo awaited his servant and horse, and embracing again Rosaura, and taking leave of the ladies, he was accompanied with tears from Rosaura's eyes, and this continued until she lost sight of him. As the shepherdesses were now alone, Teolinda soon went off with Leonarda to learn the cause of her coming.

Rosaura recounted to Galatea and Florisa the reason which induced her to assume a shepherdess attire, and to come out seeking Grisaldo, saying, "It would not cause you astonishment, my charming daughters of the wood, to see me thus, if you did but appreciate the potency of love, which not only suggests a change of habit, but even change of will and soul, and I had utterly lost my lover had not this alternative been adopted."

"You shall know, my dears, that being in the village of Leonarda, the lord of which is my own father, that Grisaldo came there to spend some days in the solitary occupation of the chase, and as my father and hers are friends, he courteously offered him the hospitalities of the place. This he did, and the advent of Grisaldo to my home was for the purpose of carrying me from it, and though this cost my shame something, I will aver that the sight, conversation, and valour of Grisaldo impressed my heart so deeply, that not knowing how, in the few days of his visit, my liberty

was entirely gone, for to him I wholly surrendered myself. Yet was this not so unreservedly but that I first
satisfied myself of the acquiescence of Grisaldo, by many
unmistakable tokens. Fully informed as to this fact, and
how advantageous it would be to me to have him for a
suitor, I conformed to his desires, while I realised my own,
and so with the participation of a young female of the household, Grisaldo I met frequently in an adjacent portion of
the house, without anything further than a mere interview,
he giving me his word, which this very day in your presence
he has reiterated. My heavy fate ordained, that in the very
conjuncture that I was in the fruition of joy, there came to
see my father a very valorous Arragonese cavalier, named
Artandro, who overpowered by my beauty (if any I possess)
made overtures to me of marriage without my father's sanc-
tion. But Grisaldo had so worked his proposal, and I
evincing more rigidity than was necessary, entertained him
so adroitly to the end my father should recede from pressing
my marriage, and that Grisaldo might solicit me for a bride.
But he would not consent to this, for he knew that his
father's wish was to unite him to the rich and attractive
Leopersia, with whose fame for wealth and loveliness you
are cognizant.

"This came to my knowledge, and I assumed a feigned
jealousy, solely to test his faith, and was indeed so careless, or rather so very simple, that presuming I held him
fast, I began to coquet with Artandro, which, being
observed by Grisaldo, he indicated how much he suffered
by such a demeanour, and even advertised me that if I
was indifferent as to his pledge to me, it would be indispensable in him to agree to the wish of his parents.

"To these remonstrances and advices I answered naught,
replete with pride and arrogance, secure in the net which
my beauty had thrown over Grisaldo's soul, which was not
so easily severed, or that any other rival beauty could
break. My undue confidence, however, came to a failure,
as Grisaldo soon evinced, who, wearied with my foolish and
coy disdains, had no alternative but to desert me, and obey
his parents' will. Yet scarce had he left the village, and I
found myself alone, than I recognised my fatal error, and
with so much earnestness did Grisaldo's absence oppress me,

and jealousy of Leopersia, that the desertion of the one
and the jealousy about the other almost annihilated me.
Reflecting still, that if my remedy was delayed I must
surrender my life to my vexation, hence I determined to lose
a little, that is in honour, to gain much, that is Grisaldo,
so framing an excuse to my father to go and see my aunt,
who was an inhabitant of an adjoining village, out I sallied
from my father's house, accompanied by his servants, and
arriving at my aunt's dwelling, I disclosed to her the whole
affair, and I requested her to invest me in the suit in which
I accosted Grisaldo, adding that if I did not return,
that the project had proved abortive. She conceded on
condition I would take Leonarda with me, as one in whom
she reposed much affiance, so sending through her to our
village, and supplying me with the said attire, and adverting
to the business which both had to enact, we took leave of
her, now just eight days ago, and there being six days since
we reached Grisaldo's village, never once did we have an
opportunity to speak to him alone till this morning, when
I knew he was on a hunting expedition. I awaited him
where he stopped, and all has happened to which you were
witnesses, with which good luck I am so content, as it
accords with my earnest desires. Now ladies, you have the
story of my life, and if its recital has caused *ennui*, throw
the blame on your curiosity to hear it, and on me too for com-
plying with your solicitation." "Quite the reverse," replied
Florisa, " we are involved in obligations to you, though we are
ever in a desire to serve you, your debtors we remain."
" No, it is I," rejoined Rosaura, " and I will repay you to
the extent of my strength. Now relinquishing this, turn
your orbs, shepherdesses, and behold those of Teolinda and
Leonarda submerged in tears, which, by sympathy, will
extort water from yours."

Galatea and Florisa turned round to observe, and the
truth of the fact was obvious. The cause of the weeping
in the two sisters was, that after Leonarda had told her
sister what Rosaura had informed Galatea and Florisa, she
said, " You will know, sister, that as you quitted our village,
it was inferred that the shepherd Artidoro had carried you
off, for he disappeared, also, on that identical day, without
taking leave of a soul. I fortified my parents in this sup-

position, by recounting to him what had passed with Artidoro in the wood, whereupon his suspicion augmented, and
my father resolved to go in quest of you and Artidoro,
and effectively to put it into operation, if in a pair of days
no shepherd should come to our hamlet, that when he was
seen, all should take him for Artidoro. Now news coming
to my father that your ravisher was near, out he went, with
certain legal authorities, who asked him if he knew about
you, and whither he had carried you. This shepherd
denied, with an oath, ever having seen you, and declared
his utter ignorance of the questions put. Not a little surprise overtook all who heard this positive denial, as he had
sojourned in the village now ten days, and had conversed
with and even danced with you frequently, and no manner
of doubt existed as to Artidoro's culpability, and so without
admitting exculpation, or even listening to a word, off they
hustled him to prison, where he stayed several days
without a syllable said to him. When he was ordered to
confess, he swore he knew nothing of you, and had only
been once in your company in the said village, and that
they would look, and this he repeated, that the Artidoro
for whom he was suspected might not be his relative, and
that an entire error had arisen, he being mistaken for
Artidoro—that his name was Galercio, son of Briseno, and
was born in Grisaldo's village. Such proofs followed this
assurance, that it was admitted he was not Artidoro ; on
which a sudden astonishment fell on all, that such a likeness
should prevail between the parties.

" What was announced relative to Galercio, induced me to
go and see the captured man, and such was its results, that
I remained without my object, yet I encountered what gave
me satisfaction, though I failed of seeing Galercio. Yet the
worst of it was, my dear, that off he went from the village
without knowing that with him away went my liberty also,
for I had no place to disclose it to him ; so judge of my distress, until Rosaura's aunt sent for me, for a few days, to accompany Rosaura, whereby a fresh joy supervened to know that
we should go again to Galercio's village, and that there I
might inform him of his debt to me. My venture has
been so abridged, that after four days' stay here, I have not
seen him, despite of inquiries, and I learn he is with his
flock in the country.

"I have also asked for Artidoro, and they say he has not been in these parts for some time. Not to quit Rosaura, I have had no time to seek Galercio, who might furnish news about Artidoro. This is exactly what has happened to me and more, that you have seen with Grisaldo. O, sister, since you quitted the village, Teolinda was struck with astonishment at what her sister had recited, but when she came to learn that in Artidoro's own village nothing was known of him, there was no repression of tears, though certain relief was at hand, in the belief that Galercio had news of his brother, and so a firm resolution possessed her to run after Galercio wheresoever he might be found; so Leonarda having stated, with the utmost brevity, all her accidents whilst in chase of Artidoro, with a fresh embrace she returned where the other shepherdesses were, who stood a little off the road to defend themselves from the heat of the sun." On her arrival Teolinda repeated to them all her sister had said, and the success of her amours, with the apparent identity of Galercio and Artidoro, which caused no little surprise. Then said Galatea, "Whoever remarks the extraordinary similitude between you, Teolinda, and your sister, will have reason good for wonder, though he sees others, yet none comparable to you." "Little doubt is there," replied Leonarda, "save that that which exists between Artidoro and Galercio is such which if it exceeds not ours, it falls little short of it." "Heaven may desire," said Florisa, "that as we all resemble each other, so we may appear in the transaction, and that fortune may favour us, and all the world envy our contentment as it admires our general likeness." To these remarks Teolinda had replied, had not a voice intercepted, which they heard from between the trees, and all stopping to catch the sound, they soon recognised that of the shepherd Lauso, from which Galatea and Florisa received inward satisfaction, desiring to know of whom Lauso was enamoured, and they thought what the shepherd sang would elucidate that point, so without further locomotion, they listened to the strain. The swain was resting on the foot of a green willow, in company only with his own meditations and a small rebeck, from whose sound started these words —

LAUSO.

Should I declare the value of my thought,
The good possessed to evil might convert,
So the good felt is not to be disclosed.
   Within myself is my desire confined,
   My tongue refusing to give utterance,
   Placing its trophy in a silence strict.
May artifice here stop, may art surcease
To exaggerate a taste, which in a soul
With generous hand love knows surely to diffuse.
   Suffice to say that in a pleasing calm
   He passed the amorous sea, in confidence
   Of honest triumph and a victorious palm.
Of the cause ignorant, the sufferer knows,
Which is a good beyond all measurements,
Alone reserved for the pure souls' content.
New life I feel, entire existence new,
A name recover from the soil entire,
Itself illustrious and to fame well known.
   May the pure purpose and the amorous zeal
   Enclosed within my deep enamoured breast,
   Exalt me straight to heaven's highest step.
In thee, Silena, hope and affiance is.
Silena, glory of my inward thought,
The north star to direct my freest will.
I hope your mind, in power without compare,
Readily will lead you to confess
That faith exceeds in merit all things else.
   Oh, shepherdess! I trust you will extend,
   After experience has made you conversant,
   A chartered liberty to a true man's breast.
What good does not your presence guarantee?
What ills avert? and who bereft of it
Will suffer absence for a moment's space?
Oh beauteous even more than beauty's self!
Discreeter far than e'en discretion,
Sun to my eyes, my polar star at sea.
   Not her who in the famous isle of Crete,
   Carried off by the false and beauteous bull;
   To thy own loveliness can be paragoned.
Nor her who in her garments grains of gold

A full shower felt, whose influence
The virgin treasure wholly overpowered.
   Nor her who with a fierce uplifted arm,
   In the chaste blood of her own chastest breast,
   In purity the dagger sharp did stain.
Not her who moved to fury and despite
The Grecian hearts against the Trojan hosts,
For whose undoing Ilion was undone.
   Nor her who caused the Latin squadrons move
   With a hot fury 'gainst old Teucer's race,
   In Juno's self stirred deadly hatred up.
Not even her whose fame truly consists
In its entirety, and the trophy which
Her virtues recognized will ever guard.
   Who Sicchæus bewailed of her, I speak
   As does the Mantuan Tityrus record,
   Of a vain longing and unequal wish.
Nothing of all that beauty boasts in past
Ages, nor present superadded too,
Nor aught expected in the time to come,
   Can reach or overpass my shepherdess
   In valour, wisdom, or in beauty's grace,
   Which merit may superior excellence.
Thrice happy he who in pure confidence
With thee shall be, Silena, much beloved,
Nor bitterness of jealousy e'er taste.
   Love, me who to such altitude has raised,
   Do never with a heavy hand depress
   To the obscurity of oblivion dark;
   Ever my master, but no tyrant be.

The shepherd sang no more, nor could the shepherdesses
come to a knowledge of what he desired by what they
heard, except the declaration of the name of his lady, Silena,
a name unknown to them. And as they imagined that Lauso
had traversed many parts of Spain and even Asia, and all
Europe, that it must be some foreign shepherdess who
had listened to his love; but reflecting that only a brief
time ago they witnessed him glorying in his liberty, and
even railing at those who were affected by love, doubtless they believed, that, under a feigned name, some un-

known shepherdess was designated, who was lady of his thoughts, so, without satisfaction as to their suspicions, they moved towards the village, leaving the shepherd where they found him. They had not progressed very far when they encountered several shepherds, their acquaintances, for there were Thirsis, Damon, Elicio, Erastro, Arsindo, Francenio, Crisio, Orompo, Daranio, Orfenio, and Marsilio, with all the foremost shepherds of the vicinity, and among them the disenamoured Lenio, with the melancholy Silerio, all of whom had sallied forth for a *siesta* at the stone fountain, in a shade where the thick boughs and green trees indicated defence against heat.

Before the shepherds arrived, Teolinda, Leonarda, and Rosaura had taken care to envelope themselves in a white covering, that neither Damon nor Thirsis might recognise them. The shepherds arrived, making due salutations to the tender sex, inviting them to participate in the *siesta*. Galatea, however, excused herself, alleging that the shepherdesses of the wood who accompanied her were obliged to return to the village..

Thereupon she took leave, yet carrying with her the souls of Elicio and Erastro, and even the concealed shepherdesses the desire to know them, as many as there were.

So they went to the village, and the men to the cool fountain; but, ere they reached the spot, Silerio took his leave, asking permission to return to his hermitage, and though Thirsis, Damon, Elicio, and Erastro begged of him to pass the day with them, they could not obtain with him, so he embraced all, and went his way, charging and requesting Erastro not to fail to visit him whenever he passed by his hermitage. This Erastro promised; so, threading his path in one continued weariness of spirit, he returned hermitage-wise—quitting them in grief at the narrowness of life he had self-selected in the greenness of his years. This feeling was also participated by those who knew the quality and integrity of his person.

The shepherds having attained the font, there they encountered three cavaliers, and two young ladies on the road, somewhat weary, yet attracted by the amenity of the place, who thought it best to deflect from the road, and here to get through the oppressive hours of *siesta*.

Some attendants were with them, indicating they were people of quality. The shepherds were desirous, as soon as they met them, to surrender the unoccupied place to them. One of the cavaliers, the chief, noting that out of courtesy the shepherds yielded their places, wished to move to another spot, and said to them, " If by chance your intent, courteous shepherds, was to pass the *siesta* in this delicious spot, do not let us disturb you, but give us the pleasure of your company, to augment our satisfaction by your addition, for your urbanity argues no less, and as the locality is capable of accommodating many, you will create discontent in me and my ladies, if you do not acquiesce in that which, in my name and theirs, I respectfully solicit."

" Now to do, my lord, what you desire," replied Elicio, " we concur, but it extends no further than pursuing a conversation to beguile the weary hours of the *siesta*, and though our object were different, we would strain it to what you ask." " I am your obliged," answered the cavalier, " and, to ratify the same, know, shepherds, that, around this fresh spring, where with things which the ladies have brought for refreshment, you may provoke thirst, and assuage it also in the clear sources which it offers." This they all did, obliged by such politeness.

Up to this time the ladies' faces were fenced with rich masks, and, seeing how the shepherds remained, they discovered themselves beauties of the first water, extorting admiration from all beholders, for it seemed to them, excluding Galatea, that no such beauties abounded.

In fine, both the ladies were of equal lustre; the one, who seemed something the elder, had pre-eminence over her who was smaller in stature, in actual liveliness. Now, all being seated, and comfortably, too, the other cavalier, who had uttered nothing, spake. When I stop to consider, agreeable shepherds, the advantage which your pastoral and humble carriage hath over the haughty bearing of a courtier, I cannot but pity myself, and be really jealous of your deportment."

" Why do you utter this sentiment, friend Darintho ?" said another of the cavaliers. He replied, " because I note with what curiosity you, and I, and those of your fraternity, seek to adorn their persons, sustain their bodies, swell their wealth, and how little reverts to us therefrom, but purple, and gold, and fine linen. Our very faces are stained with the results of ill-digested food, eaten at inappropriate hours, as costly as ill-digested. Nothing adorns us, or polishes us, or do they improve our appearance in the eyes of lookers-on. Now, how different is what we observe in the exterior of those who follow field exercises. Your experience, then, in what is before you, brings you to consider with what simple diet they are sustained, so diametrically opposed to our surfeits. Just look at the healthy dye of the cheeks, which promises health, and the broken pallor of ours, and how well befits their robust and supple limbs a pelisse of white wool, a leopard-coloured head-dress, and buskins of any colour. With these advantages they must appear more attractive to the females than our fancy-dressed courtiers to domesticated ladies. Who would speak, then, of the simplicity of their lives, the evenness of their state, and the integrity of their loves? No more I will say than my ignorance may suggest that I would willingly exchange my mode of life for theirs." "In debt are the swains," said Elicio, "to you for your good opinion, "but I must admit that in rustic life there are as many slips and toils as in a courtier's life." I must also agree," replied Darintho, "that war abounds on the earth in our lives; yet in the pastoral state there is less of it, because the occasions alter and temper the spirit." "Though I should conform to your opinion, Darintho," said Damon, "there is a shepherd friend of mine, ycleped Lauso, who passed part of his days as a courtier, and even some in cruel battle, who finally returned to a rustic life, and e'en before that he evinced a desire thereto, as a song shews which he composed, and sent to the famous Larsilio, a man of deep court experience. This I committed to memory, and would recite to you, if I thought you would not grudge the time, or grow weary by hearing it."

"No pleasure will be greater to us than the hearing of it, discreet Damon," replied Darintho, calling out his name, which he heard from the other shepherds his friends; "so I request individually that you recite to us Lauso's song, and you retain it in my memory, and so it must be meritorious."

Now Damon began to repent of what he had advanced, and tried to evade the promise, but there was such a volley from both sexes that his excuse went for nothing. So a little composed, with a grace and docility, he made an essay.

DAMON.

1. The vain imagination of our mind,
Swayed by a thousand contrary winds,
On every side in hasty course impelled—
Human condition feeble, suffering,
In downward pleasures is most occupied;
No repose finding where it seeks it most.
A false world promising cheerful delights,
A syren's voice scarcely attended to
Delights exchanges into sheer disgusts.
Confusion, chaos, all I see and read.
The careful, courteous act, joined to desire
Has placed the pen in my too tired hand.

2. I wish, my Lord, that it indeed would reach
As far as my desire; contracted flight
Of my too thick, and badly pointed pen,
That soon as may it should be occupied
In raising to the summit of its flight
Your goodness and your virtues, excellent.
Who is there would presume upon his back
Such charge to throw, new-born Atlas except?
With strength sufficient heaven and its weights to bear,
And be constrained to ask additional aid
Changing the burden to Alcides' arms—
And though with bends and transpiration too
This labour for relief I well approve.

3. Yet to my power is this impossible;
Useless desire I proffer for a proof
Of what shuts up in me judicious thought—
See now, perhaps, if it be feasible
The discontented and weak hand to move,
And by enigma some content to shew;
So weak I feel, my strength must be quite forced,
Your ears apply to hear deep-seated groans
From a disdainful, over-anguished breast
 Gainst which fire, air, the sea, and e'en the earth,
Make war continual—in conspiracy—

12—2

To my misfortune, clenching and closing in
Till my ill-luck transfer me to the grave.

4. If 'twere not so, an easy thing it were,
A passage through the realms of taste to extend,
Bringing a thousand things to memory,
Painting the mountain, river, and the bank.
Nor love, fate, fortune, chance, or casualty,
Can to the swain his perfect glory yield;
Time triumphs, too, o'er this sweet history
Leaving the smallest shadow in its stead,
Which now alarms and terrifies
The cogitation which is spent on it,
A state inherent in all human lot.
Quickly our taste into disgust is turned,
And nothing will be which in many years
With true taste can ere be realised.

5. Turn or revolve on high, or low descend
To the profound abyss thoughts' vanity.
From Tile to Bathro rush in a moment's space,
This will certify how much more's the toil.
At last escaping from his very self,
Lodged in a sphere, or in the eternal pit.
Oh very many times fortunate is
The simple herdsman who with sheepcote poor
Lives more content and in more sweet repose
Than Crassus rich or Midas covetous.
In such life strong, pastoral, simple, sound,
Misery, falseness, courtly acts forgets.

6. In winter's rigour, stiffening everything,
At the robust oak's undecayed trunk,
Warmed and consumed by Vulcan's element,
There lodged in peace he wisely ponders on
The treatment of his flocks, determining
Not to expose an intricate account;
And when the shrunken, sterile, hardened cold
Makes him to fly, and Delos' mighty Lord
The air burns up, and soil; on the bank
Of a river seated, planted with willows, elms,
In rustic concert giving his voice play,

Sounding his pipe, from time to time we see
The stream suspended his soft strain to hear.

7. The visage grave there little him annoys,
Of a favoured man, which demonstrates in shew
Power to command, where no obedience flows.
No haughty exaggeration with sweet voice
Of flatterer false, one who in absence brief,
Changes opinion, factious criminal;
Nor peevish scornfulness does him upset
Of subtle secretary, or honoured height
Of golden key, or divers princes bond.
From his meek flock no space appreciable
Does he depart, because the fury of Mars
Wrathfully rages loud from side to side,
Ruled by such art, his follower scarce afraid.

8. With paces few his footsteps he brings back
From hilly mountain to the peaceful plain,
From the fresh fountain to clear river's stream,
Only to see the lands divisible.
Old Ocean's moving mighty territory
He ploughs with senseless, antiquated rage;
No sprightliness awakens him to know
How that a monarch deemed invincible
Dwells near his village, though his good requires it,
Little distaste in missing him, receives.
Not like the ambitious intermeddler, who
With senses lost, goes without favour, or
Intimacy, in that he ne'er tinged his sword,
Or lance in Moorish or in Turkish gore.

9. No alteration colour or face knows,
For colour changes, countenance changes too,
Of master whom he serves, owning no Lord,
Who him constraineth with a tongue so dumb,
Clicia pursuing towards her gilded lover,
The sweet or bitter taste which comes to him;
Then you will not perceive what painfulness,
The fear of carelessness, a nothingness
In the ungrateful breast, the Lord's right
Blots from his service, and the sentence passed,
Of a brief farewell too.

There is no apparent evidence
Other than what a sterling breast contains,
For rustic wit,
A courtier's falseness never can o'ertake.

10. Who in contempt such life as this will hold?
Or will not say that this is life indeed,
Which leads the soul to true serenity?
Who holds the courtier in no respect,
Makes known his goodness such to him who asks
That he aspires to good, the ill declines—
Oh life whose taste, in solitude terminates—
Oh pastoral humility, higher than highest
Sceptre, most exalted, and sublime.
Delicious flowers, shady groves, clear streams,
Who, for brief space ye in fruition have;
May ills like mine never disturb their ease.
Go, little song, and soon be recognised
Your superfluities and miscarriages—
But if your power remain, quickly announce
With humble countenance made strait to prayer—
My Lord, your pardon; what impels me here,
To you and your request I did confide.

"This, gentlemen, is Lauso's song," said Damon, on finishing it, "which was as celebrated by Larsileo, as well received by those who witnessed it at that time" (vieron). "With reason may you say," replied Darintho, "for the truth and the artfulness of it is worthy condign praise." "These melodies are to my liking," remarked at this juncture disenamoured Lenio, "and not those which frequently reach my ears replete with indefinite amorous conceits, so ill-disposed and intricate, that I could swear there are some, which, however discreet he is who hears, never touch him, or understands them himself, even the very author. Others there be, which no less fatigue by entanglements in giving praise to Cupid, in exaggerating his power, his valour, wonder, and miracles, making him lord above and lord below, ascribing to him infinite attributes of potency, lordship, and sway, and what annoys me most is that when they speak of love, they understand I know not what, a certain Cupid, whose nominal signification implies, who he is, a mere sensuous entity, vain, and meriting blame to the utmost." The disenamoured Lenio spoke, and then ceased his diatribe on love, but as the bystanders knew his state, they did not stop at his reasons, while Erastro said to him, "Peradventure you think, Lenio, you are ever talking to the simple Erastro, who cannot contradict your opinions, or reply to your arguments? But I must advertise you that it will be more politic to observe silence, or touch on other matter, than to calumniate love, and if you do not like that, the discretion and skill of Thirsis and Damon should illuminate the darkness in which you are, and point out to you clearly what they understand, and what you should mean also by love and its appurtenances."

"Of what will they inform me of which I am ignorant?" said Lenio, "or what can I reply to them which they know not?" "This is vanity, Lenio," replied Elicio, "and in it you evince your deviation from love's truth, and how you proceed rather to the north of your predilections, and not by what you ought, which is truth and experience."

"Contrariwise, by the proof I entertain of love's doings," rejoined Lenio, "I am as opposed as I seem, and I shall ever continue in that mind." "On what is your reason founded?" said Thirsis. "In what, O shepherd?" said also Lenio; "by effects, I judge of evil causes." "What, then, are these evil causes in your estimation?" rejoined Thirsis. "Well, if you listen, I will state them to you," said Lenio; "yet I would choose my discourse did not fatigue the ease of the company who had rather hold conversation on more agreeable topics." "Nothing will suit us better," said Darintho, "than hearing a discourse on this very subject, especially where opinions are so well sustained. For my part, if the shepherds oppose not, I beseech you, Lenio, to enjoin silence ere the dissertation on love begins." "Willingly will I do that," retorted Lenio, "for I am fortified in the opinion I have, relative to love, and to blame even those whose convictions are opposite."

"Begin now, O Lenio," said Damon, "that you may no longer stand obstinately in opinion, and let my companion, Thirsis, announce his own." At the very juncture when Lenio was on the point of launching his tirade against love, there came to the fountain the venerable Aurelio, father of Galatea, with some companions; likewise came Galatea and

Florisa, with three disguised females, Rosaura, Teolinda, and Leonarda, whom they met at the entry of the village, and from whom they learned that a bevy of shepherds were at the fountain of pebbles, and, at their request, caused them to turn round, as the said shepherdesses of the woods trusted they would not be recognised by any one. All arose to receive Aurelio and the shepherdess who sat with the other ladies, while Aurelio and his party joined the swains.

But when the ladies took note of Galatea's comeliness, their surprise was such they could scarce withdraw their eyes. Not the less did Galatea admire their beauty, particularly that of the eldest. Some exchanges of courtesy ensued, which ceased on learning what the discreet Thirsis and the disenamoured Lenio intended; at which the venerable Aurelio rejoiced greatly, for he was quite alive to the business, and to hear the dispute, and to witness the skill of Lenio; so, without further ado, Lenio, sitting on the trunk of a maimed elm, with voice at first almost inaudible, then sonorous, thus gave vent:

LENIO.—" I already divine, valorous and discreet company, how your judgments will condemn me for a temerarious man, since in the little wit and minute experience incident to a rustic life, in which I have been brought up, I wish to run a tilt with the famous Thirsis, whose education in celebrated academies, and whose well grounded knowledge indicates an assurance to me that I cannot be victor in the contention. Still I entertain a certain affiance that natural parts sustained by experience may discover new paths, which may compensate for years of knowledge, hence this day I am emboldened to reveal in public what has induced me to be the declared enemy of love, and so I have merited the *sobriquet* of a disenamoured person, and though nought save your orders had prevailed on me to move, yet that may not be an adequate excuse; the more so, as I have little to glory in, should my attempt be abortive, yet fame will announce that I had courage enough to enter the lists with my antagonist, Thirsis. So with this concession, with no other ally than pure reason, to it I turn, and supplicate that she grant me such vigour in words and arguments, that reason may indicate publicly also how great a foe she is to love.

"Love is, then, as I have heard from my predecessors, a

desire of beauty ; and this definition, given it among many others, has its intrinsic value. Yet if you do concede to me that love is the desire of beauty, you must also concede that there must be reciprocity between the lover and the loved ; and because beauty is twofold, corporeal and incorporeal, love, which corporeal beauty holds for its ultimate end, cannot be good, and of this I am the enemy.

" Now corporeal beauty is subdivisible also into two parts, dead corpses and living ones ; love may entertain a corporeal beauty which is good. Let us contemplate corporeal beauty in either sex of youths, which consists in recognised symmetry, making one perfect whole, constituting a body fashioned in uniformity of members, and in complexion. The other beauty of corporeality is not animate, consisting in pictures, statues, edifices, with which beauty man may be in love, without sensual love, or blame. Incorporeal beauty likewise diverges into two parts, the virtues and attributes of the soul, and that love which adheres to virtue, must be good, and not the less so, what oscillates towards science and all analogous agreeable studies.

" Hence, as there exists two kinds of beauty, provoking love within us, it is a consequence that in loving one, the other is good or evil, for if beauty is appreciable by the eyes of the understanding, clear and unprejudiced—and beauty corporeal is judged by a fleshly power as compared with the incorporeal, it is disturbed and dark. And how comes it that bodily sight is quicker to survey corporeal beauty, which delights it, than the eyes of intelligence to consider that incorporeal but absent beauty which glorifies it. It follows then, that mankind more commonly oscillates towards a failing, mortal beauty, which destroys them, than the invisible spiritual beauty which ennobles them ?

" Now, from this love or corporeal predilection, arises, and will arise desolation of cities, ruin of states, loss of empires, death of friends, but if this does not happen, what greater ills ensue ? heavy torments, fires, jealousies, sufferings ? What deaths can mortal wisdom conceive, compared to what a miserable lover suffers ? and the cause of this is, that as all the happiness of the lover consists in the fruition of what he loves, and that same is not within the compass of possession, or any way attains to his wishes, it engenders in him sighs, tears, complaints, and general disturbance.   It is obvious then that the beauty of which I reason cannot be had in perfection, for man cannot completely enjoy what is external to him, and not his own.   Now externalities are subordinate to the will of what is styled fortune and chance, and not in our own arbitrement, hence it follows that where love is, grief exists also ; and who would this deny, would also deny that light is bright, and fire burns.   But because it may happen with greater facility in the recognition of the bitterness which love incloses, discoursing with passions of the mind, certain truths must appear.   These mental passions, as you know well, worthy auditory, are partible into four generalities, and no more.   Desire ardently, rejoice much, dread of future ills, grief at present calamities ; these passions, like contrary currents, which upset the soul's equanimity, are styled perturbations, and of these the foremost is love, for that is only another appellation for desire—hence desire is the source and font of our passions, from which issue streams.   So that it occurs, whenever aught inflames the heart, there is a ready motion to follow and seek it, often involving us in numberless inordinate sequences.   This very incentive induces a brother to solicit from a relative illegal embraces, the mother-in-law the same from the son-in-law, and, worse than all, even parents to obtain favours from their offspring.   Such tendencies suggest thoughts which conduce to dangerous results.

" Nor does it avail that we oppose obstacles by reason, for while we clearly see the turpitude, yet we do not secede ; and not satisfied alone is love in keeping us on the quick, that it is indubitably the *primum mobile* of all our passions. So from the parent desire flows all derivatives, which in minds prone to love are infinite, and though all converge to a point generally, objects are so diverse, and the fortune of lovers so various, that each has its peculiar attraction. Some there be, who to realise all their hopes, stake all on one die, and what difficulties and disappointments do not eventuate ! How often do they catch falls, what thorns make their feet to bleed, losing force and breath in the vain hope of success.

" Others, again, really do possess what they desire, and wish no further, save keeping their wealth, and on this concentrate their thoughts, consuming time and labour—in joy, wretched—in opulence, poor—in good chance, unfortunate.

"Others, although wanting possession, turn to them, using protestations, promises, conditions, tears, and in the sad conclusion, put a period to their lives. On the first dawn of these desires no such troubles appear ; love pointing out a deceitful path for entrance, in appearance broad and ample, which gradually is circumscribed, that there is no way for advance or retreat. So that loves, so beguiled by false smiles, with a turn of the eyes, by fictitious terms which engender a false and feeble hope in the breast, march behind, impelled by desire, and then at short intervals finding all remedy for care intercepted, and the road to the wish impeded, finish with moist eyes, a visage discomposed and wan, and the auditory nerves fatigued with complaints insufferable, and worse is behind, if these alternatives attain no desired end, swift they change their policy, and try to effect through evil ways what was not practicable to good ones.

"Hence are born hatred, anger, decease of friend and foe. By this we discern at every advance how delicate and tender women enact extravagant and temerarious deeds, whose every thought is the fertile parent of fear.

"Now we view holy conjugalities bathed in gore—now we see the sorrowing spouse—now the incautious and unguarded husband. The last stage of this eventful history is that brother betrays brother, father son, and all things change to their confounding contraries. This is cause of enmities, tramples on respect, traverses the laws, forgets obligations, and seduces those who are affined and kin. By this it is clear in what misery lovers are involved ; in fine we know the force of the incentive, and nothing urges us to the point proposed like the spur of love, so that neither joy nor content exceed the due bounds like a lover's passion to reach his *ultimatum*. This is admitted, for what person will acknowledge due judgment, save the lover, who reaches the summit of felicity, if he but touch his mistress's hand, or a jewel, a rapid inversion of the eyes, and such *addenda* of so small consideration as a dispossessed lover hopes. Yet not for these realised goods, so pursued by lovers, do we say they are fortunate and happy. No content hath he which has not its drawbacks, and alloys, with which love attacks him, so that no amorous glory reaches him, but pain is its substitute. So fearful is the lover's joy, that it superinduces alienation of mind, turning wisdom into fatuity. Now they make their strength and will and means to gravitate towards the ideal of their minds, disregarding aught else, so that property, and honour and life are involved in one continuous ruin. Finally, in exchange, they constitute themselves slaves of endless anguish, their own very enemies. Now how, when it happens in mid career of taste, the cold iron of the heavy lance of jealousy touches them? Then the heaven is obscured, the air in tumult, and the elements are confounded. No source of satisfaction, because there can be no termination to their wishes. Here plays about ceaseless fear, desperation too, sharp suspicion, variety of ideas, solicitude without profit, false smile, grief in its truth ushered in with strange and rude concomitants, which affright and consume. The very accident of love annoys, he sees, he laughs, he turns, revolves, is dumb, and then uses utterance, and finally all grace which was instrumental in seeking for good, converts to the torture of the jealous lover.

"And who knows not if an adequate venture does not advance his loving principles, and with rapidity does not conduce to a beneficent end ; how costly are to the lover all other expedients which the unlucky one adopts to follow out his intents ? What tears are shed, what sighs are scattered, what letters written, how many insomnious nights, what and how adverse are his thoughts, what suspicions harass him, what dread overawes him. Similar to Tantalus, whose martyrdom lies between fruit and water ; so is the woe-begone lover interposed between fear and hope. The services of a lover who lacks favour are the vessels of Danaus' daughter, exhausted without profit, and they never can realise even a minute portion of their object.

"There is an eagle which consumes Titius' bowels, as jealousy gnaws those of a jealous individual. Stone too, there is, which overweights Sisiphus' shoulders, as love bears down the cogitations of the enamoured. The wheel, too, of Ixion, which wounds at each revolution, revolving more frequently than the varied ideas of timorous lovers.

" We have too, Minos and Radamantus who punish vindictively the luckless condemned souls, like to love, avenging itself on the enamoured breast, still subordinate to the insufferable injunction. Are there not cruel Megæras, maddened Tisiphone, vengeful Alectos, who as frightfully beset the soul as these furies do ? whose desire is that they should recognise him for lord, and bow to him as vassals, who allege in extenuation of their fooleries, and aver, or at least will so do, that this instinct which rouses and impels the enamoured one to love a stranger more than his own proper life, is a divinity, known as Cupid. So, urged by his divine power, they can do naught else but follow in the wake of what he wills.

" He moved them to say this, and to invest with the name of divinity this desire, whose supernatural effects are discerned in those in love. Doubtless it appears that it is supernatural to see a lover at once confident and timorous, burn afar from his beloved one, and free in her presence—dumb, yet speaking—a speaker, yet inarticulate. Singular to pursue who flies me, praise who blames me, utter a voice to one who listens not, to serve ingratitude, hope beyond hope, or do aught else how virtuous soever.

" O bitter, sweet, venomous medicine for unsound lovers, sorrowful joy, flower of love, you indicate no fruit whatever, save tardy repentance. These are the effects of this would be God, these his deeds and works of wonders. Should we but see these in a painting, representing a vain God, how futile would they not be ? Him they do paint as a child, naked, winged, with bandaged eyes, bow and arrows well in hand, to let us know amidst other things that once in love we convert from the simple condition of a child of predilection, which is blind in pretensions, light in thought, cruel in operation, naked and divested of the riches of the mind. They say too, that between his arrows he conceals one of lead, and one of gold, for different effects, that of lead creates hatred in the breast it touches—that of gold increase of love where it strikes to advise us that one metal is desirable, and the lead to be abhorred ; one indicative of wealth, the other of poverty. For this occasion not gratis do poets sing of Atalanta o'ercome by three beauteous apples of gold, and of the lovely Danae impregnated by a golden shower, and of the pious Eneas descending into the low regions with a branch of gold in his hand. In fine, gold and the donative is one of the most powerful shafts which love holds—wherewith the most hearts he subdues. Quite contrary from that of lead, a low, depreciated metal, like penury, which begets rather hate and abhorrence, than the smallest benevolence.

"Hence, if my already quoted reasons suffice not to explain all I conceive to be evil in perfidious love, just turn to some examples true and passed, and we shall both see that no one with understanding eyes reaches the truth I follow.

"Let us observe now, who but this love was it that caused Lot to break his chaste intent, and perpetrate familiar violence? This very incentive caused David, the chosen servant, to become a homicide and a commandment breaker. The same forced the too lively Amon to commit an act of turpitude, and put the head of the strong Sampson into the false folds of Dalilah ; so losing his virtue, all lost their protection, and at last he and many lost their lives. This power moved Herod's tongue to promise to the dancing girl John Baptist's head. This created doubt as to the salvation of the wisest and richest of kings, aye, even the most of men. This brought low the strength of Alcides' arms, accustomed to wield the heavy club, to set in motion a diminutive spindle, and turn to female employments. It was this that made the love-stricken Medea disperse through air the tender limbs of her kindred; this cut Progne's tongue, with Aracne and Hippolitus, defamed Pasiphae, subverted Troy, and murdered Egisthus. This caused to cease the newly attempted works of rising Carthage, and her earlier queen to transpierce her chaste breast with the sharp weapon. This again lodged in the hands of the renowned and beautiful Sophonisba the vase of deadly poison, by which life was terminated. Did not Turnus die for the same cause, and Tarquin's kingdom, was it not wrested from him, as was the power from Mark Antony, with the life and honour of his cherished one? Did not this cause the delivery of Spain over to Algerine barbarism, solicited to take revenge for the outrageous love of Don Roderic?

"But why do I think that night will envelope us, ere I cease proffering to our memories these sad examples, the exploits achieved by love, and which love still enacts ; I wish no further to advance, but to give place for reply to my antagonist Thirsis, begging first, worthies, that a song may not offend, which for some time I have made to spite my enemies, and which if memory fails me not, runs in this strain :—

1. Of fear, disdainful both of frost and heat,
   The arrows and eke the bow of tyrant love ;
   To his dishonour do I lift my strain—
   Who has to dread a child in darkness bound,
   Of various predilections and warped mind,
   Though damage threatens, and its consequence ?
   When to true canticles I lift my voice,
   Which justly derogates from love's potency,
   With truth so raised, manner and form combined,
   That his malevolence is clear to all,
   The ill announcing which love close conceals.

2. Love is a fuel which consumes the soul.
   I freeze who freezes—arrows which ope the breast,
   Which from its cunning, disregarded lives
   A troubled sea with no prospective calm,
   Minister of anger, parent of despite,
   Of the disguised friend the enemy ;
   Giver of little good, and ill heaped-up,
   Affable, flattering tyrant, cruel, fierce,
   The enchantress Circe, who transforms us all
   To divers monsters, without that human aid,
   To our relief by any means may come,
   Though reason bright could succcur us in need.

3. Yoke that humiliates the stiffest neck,
   White, whence proceed desires which induce
   The blandest case, bereft of reason born,
   A net deceitful of attractive hair,
   Covering and seizing in base, ugly acts
   Those of the world involved in its folds ;
   Savoury evil to all sentients—
   Poison concealed, that gilded medicine,
   Ray which once touching, burns and cleaves right through,
   The angry arm which treason self offends.

The executioner of captive thought,
From flattery sweet its false intents defend.

4. Evil which pleases in those rudiments, when
The sight rejoices in the object seen,
Such as when beauteous heaven itself displays.
By how much more this admiration is,
By so much pines openly and concealed,
The heart, endued with extreme suffering.
Dumb talker too, a talker who grows dumb.
Discretion which distracts, total ruin
Of life the best arranged, joyful and free,
A shadowy good, converted into ill,
Flight which uplifts us to the heavenly spheres—
That falling, grief should live, and feeling die.

5. Invisible thief, who at destruction aims,
Stealing the best part of our property,
Taking our souls from us at every step—
Lightness o'ertaking that which it pursues,
A mere enigma understood of none,
A life existing in a lengthened trance,
A chosen warfare, whence perchance ensues,
A truce of short duration, cherished ill,
A pregnancy which all abortion is,
A weakness ever to the soul affixed,
A coward who daringly thrusts himself on ills,
Debtor denying the debt he ever owes.

6. Enclosed labyrinth, where is nestled
A cruel animal, who himself sustains
On human hearts untimely rendered up,
A snare which circumvents the very life,
A lord who of his stewards asks account
Of deeds and words, and his intentions too.
Covetousness with infinite pretence,
A worm which maketh substance rich and poor,
Dwelling in narrow space, and then expires.
Seek ever that which no one knows to seek,
A cloud which darkens sensibilities,
A knife that wounds ; 'tis love, pursue, if good.

With this song ended his reasonings the disenamoured Lenio, and with it and him, all present stood in admiration, particularly the cavaliers, as it seemed to them that what Lenio had said savoured of more account than befals to pastoral wit, and with commotion they awaited the reply of Thirsis, each persuading himself that he would soon have the advantage of Lenio, both by his experience and age and maturer studies, and this also assured them, because they did not want the opinions of the love-renouncing Lenio to prevail.

True, however, is it, that the sorrowing Teolinda, the love-stricken Leonardo, the handsome Rosaura, and e'en the female who accompanied Darintho, clearly discerned in the discourse of Lenio an infinity of love's successes, especially when he came on the particulars of sighs and tears, and at what a heavy rate love's satisfaction was purchased.

The beauteous Galatea and the discreet Florisa stood alone out of this affair, because to this moment love had never obtained with them, so they both stood attentive to catch all the sharpness of the shepherd's dispute, without letting the effects of love interfere with their volition. But Thirsis, anxious to test the opinion of the disenamoured, without solicitation, and being assured of the concurrence of the bystanders, opposing himself to Lenio, with a sweet and elevated tone, made his effort.

THIRSIS—" If the keenness of your wit, O shepherd, lost to love, did me assure that with ease one might reach the truth, from which you are so far strayed ; rather than set myself to the labour of opposition, I should leave matters as they stand for a sufficient castigation.

" But because of the blame you have engrafted on love, the good principles you entertain for reducing it to a better condition, I do not wish by my silence to give rise to scandal in those who hear us, or to love so decried, or to you pertinacious and vain-glorious—so befriended by love, to whom I appeal. I think, briefly to show to you how different are the effects of it from what you have advanced. Talking merely on love as you understand it, and adopting your definition, which is a desire of beauty, defining what is beauty, and then disparaging all the effects of love as detected in truly enamoured breasts, and reinforcing it with a chain of disastrous events which you ascribe to love.

"Though the definition you have put forth be the commonest entertained, yet is it not so quite as obnoxious to no opposition; for love and desire are two different matters, for all we love we do not necessarily covet, or contrariwise. Reason is obvious in all things possessing it, so we cannot aver justly, that is desire, only that we love—as he who enjoys health, will not say he desires health, only that he loves it. He who has children, says not he desires them, but that he is fond of them; neither of the things we desire can we say that we love them, as the death of enemies, which we may desire, but it is different from love. Hence, these passions may be said to vary considerably. Very true is it, that love is the parent of desire, and amidst other definitions this may go for one. Love is the first alteration we perceive in the mind, as evinced by the appetite which first moves and then attracts us towards it, delighting and appeasing. Now this delectation engenders motion in the soul, styled desire, and in its working desire is the motion of appetite towards the beloved object—a wish to obtain what it possesses, its object, which is the real good. As there be divers kinds of desires, and love is one which awaits and contemplates the beautiful, yet for a definition and division of love, we divide it into three parts, viz., honest, useful, and delectable love. Now these same divisions are again partible into love and desire according to volition, for honest love respects heavenly things, eternal and divine. Useful love is conversant with earth, joyful yet obnoxious to decay as wealth, command, and lordships. Delectable love relates to the sensuous and agreeable, as bodies animated, as you have admitted, Lenio.

" Now of whatsoever sort love be, no vituperative tongue should lavish its slander; for honest love is, was, and will be clean, simple, pure and celestial, alone dwelling in the Creator, whose attribute it is. Productive love being natural, must not be condemned; nor yet the delectable, for being more natural than productive.

"That these kinds of love are natural in us, experience proves; for as soon as our daring first father transgressed the Divine commandment, from being lord he was degraded to servant, and went into bondage. Soon did he feel the misery into which he had fallen, and the wretched dependence of his estate; then took he leaves to cover him, and he laboured and perspired over the broken earth to support him, that he might live as commodiously as he could, and besides this (obeying his God in this better than in other things) he became parent of children, for the perpetuation and joy of the human race. Now since through disobedience death entered him and through him on all his posterity, so we are heirs to his passions and affections precisely as we inherit his nature. He having essayed to remedy his wants and poverty, so we turn towards the rectification of ours, whence is derived to us our tendency to things useful for this state of life, and the nearer we approach them, the more certain is our cure. So our desire is to perpetuate our species, and corporal beauty is an incentive to desire, as a means to conduce to a favourable end.

"Now delectable love, so led without intermixture with accidents, is more worthy praise than blame, and this is the very kind of love you, O Lenio, held for your enemy. You neither understand nor know it, for you have never seen it alone, and in its own shape, but even attended by pernicious desires too warm and ill-assorted. Now this is no fault of love, which abstractedly is good, and evil only from contingencies, as we observe it falls out in some full stream which draws its source from a liquid, pellucid font, it continues to diffuse clear and fresh supplies; yet if it recedes too far from its origin, its sweet and crystalline waters convert to turbid and bitter, from the many impure affluents which merge therein.

"So this *primum mobile*, love and desire, as you term it, cannot emanate save from an untainted spring. Here is the recognition of beauty, which once admitted, must produce love—which has such a strong hold over us, that its potency alone was a reason for ancient philosophers (blind and devoid of the light of faith to conduct them), embued with natural reason and attracted by beauty, as in the starry firmament, and in the machine and rotundity of the earth, to contemplate; wonderstruck with its much symmetry and beauty, tracing it by their understanding, and so by steps mounting to first principles, and the cause of causes, and they discerned that there was but one beginning without a beginning.

" Yet what much excited astonishment and reflection was the sight of man, so constructed, so perfect, and beautiful, that he was styled a world of himself ; this is truth, that in all works framed by the great Overruler, Nature, nothing is of such perfection, or discloses greater grandeur in the Framer. For in the figure and composition of man we mark all beauties which through other essences are diffused ; hence arise love, and this appearing in the countenance shining bright, directly we light on a fair face, a love first is evoked and attracts.

" Whereby it follows, as women have this advantage over men, we are chiefly devoted to them ; we solicit them and obey, as a being in whom beauty resides, most congenial to our predilections. Now, our Maker and Preserver, noting it to be an instinct in our souls to be in one continual motion and desire, that it should not rest solely in God as in its own centre, willed that we should not give free rein to the desiring of perishable and futile things, without interfering either with free will, set on these properties a vigilant sentinel, to advise men of the dangers which would oppose, and enemies who would persecute him,—this was reason which corrects and restrains our inordinate tendencies ; and seeing too that human beauty would draw with it our affections and inclinations, not to abstract from us the desire itself, thought right to temper and correct it, by the ordinance of the holy yoke of marriage, under whose protection both sexes might carry out lawful intents.

" Seeing these two remedies are lodged there by the divine hand, we must moderate all that excess in natural love, which you undertake to blame, Lenio, which love of itself is so good, so that, if it failed us, we and this globe would end together.

" In this identical love under consideration, are indicated all virtues, for love is temperance, and both the united pair religiously should contribute to that end. It is a fortress, for the lover might suffer any adversity for the beloved. It is justice, for both mutually concur in what is lawful. It is prudence, for love is adorned with all wisdom whatsoever."

" Now I ask you, Lenio, you who aver that love is the cause of the ruin of empires, destruction of cities, deaths of friends, of perpetrated sacrileges, framer of treason, transgressor of laws. I repeat it, that you will tell me, what extant good soever, may not be abused? Philosophy is under a ban, because it reveals to us our faults, and many philosophers have been evil men—they burn the works of heroic poets, because their verses reprehend man's vices— they blame medicine because poison kills—eloquence they pronounce to be useless, because arrogance may make the worse appear the better cause—no arms should be forged, because robbers and homicides use them—nor should houses be built, because they may topple o'er their owner's heads. Even the use of fruit should be interdicted, because diseases issue therefrom—and no one should procreate issue, because Ædipus, impelled by a cruel fury, slew his father, and Orestes plunged the iron into his mother's bosom.

"Even fire may be in the category of evils, for it burns houses, and may consume cities. Water again may be disdained, for once a cataclysm surprised the nether world. The elements, for they may be diverted from good to bad uses—so all good is convertible into evil, and disastrous consequences ensue if they drop into the hands of those irrational beings who know not how to employ them. That ancient Carthage, rival of imperial Rome, warlike Numantia, well-constructed Corinth, haughty Thebes, learned Athens, and Jerusalem, the Lord's city, which were all overcome and rendered desolate. Say we therefore that love was at the root of all this? Thus those who speak ill of love, from habit, should apply it to themselves, for love's gifts, if used with moderation, are worthy all praise. A becoming moderation is laudable in all things, as excess is to be blamed. If we do not observe the rule of not too much, the wise man will have the imputation of a fool, and the just one of a man of iniquity.

"The ancient Chremes, in the tragedy, was of opinion that the blending of wine and water is good, so love becomes profitable if diluted, a result which does not happen to the intemperate. The generation of rational animals and brutes would be nothing, if there were no procession from love, and if they failed on the earth it would be desolate and bare. The ancients readily believed love to be the work of the Gods, a gift for the care, comfort, and preservation of humanity.

"Coming now to that which you, Lenio, call the sorrowful and strange effects which love produces in the enamoured breast, holding them in incessant tears, deep sighs, desperate thoughts, without any repose even for an hour; we see by chance what is desirable in this life, whose attainment costs no fatigue and effort, and by how much is the value of a thing, by so much we have to suffer, and suffer we do. For desire presupposes want of the desired, and the mind becomes excited to attain it. Now, if all human desires could be satisfied without reaching entirely all they covet, or have participation in it, or be interested in pursuing it, how much so is it to reach that which cannot satisfy or content desire save from itself, it suffers, it waits, it fears, and hopes?

"Who desires lordships, rule, honours, wealth, and perceives he cannot reach the wished-for goal, when he reaches one especial point, is partly satisfied, for the hope which fails him as to ascending higher, causes him to rest where and best he can. All which is contrary in love, for it recognises no other pay or satisfaction, save love, and that alone is the only true recompense. Hence it is impossible that the lover rest content, till he knows without doubt he is beloved, the signals of love's signs having been made manifest, so he esteems a favour a revolution of the eyes, the merest pledge from his beloved one, even the semblance of a smile, a word, or a joke, which he takes for something truthful, as *indices* which denote the indemnity to be desired, and all indications which are opposite to this, cause in the lover lamentation and anguish, without moderation in his grief, for he cannot remain in contentment, though favourable fortune and assuaging love should make concessions; and, as it may be a feat of great difficulty to reduce an adverse will to one that is not so, and to join two different souls in one indissoluble knot and closeness, so that one only thought should exist, one consentaneous act, it is not much to attain a so lofty enterprise; suffering more than for any other thing, since after the attainment it satisfies and spreads joy over all things which one can desire in this life.

"Not every time are tears with reason shed, or the sighs of the enamoured scattered; for if all these sighs and tears shew that there is no response to the wish as it should be, with the repayment it requires, due consideration should first be given, whence fancy is exalted, and if it be exalted more than is judicious, it is small wonder that these new Icaruses fall consumed into the slough of misery. But for this love is not to be blamed, it is downright fatuity. I therefore do not deny, but affirm that the desire of reaching what we love of necessity causes woe, by reason of the very infirmity it presupposes, as intimation has already been made. Yet I say that on attaining it, is great satisfaction, like as to a weary man repose, to an invalid, health.

"Hereto I confess, if lovers mark, as in antiquity, with white stones and black, their fortunate or evil days, the evil would surely exceed. Yet do I know, too, that the equality of one white stone would override a vast congeries of black ones.

"And in verification of this we see lovers find here no repentance, yet, on the contrary, should any one premise to free them from their amorous infirmity, they eject him like an enemy, for suffering is sweet to them. Hence, O lovers, let no fear stop you from offering yourselves to love what seems most difficult, or complain, or repent if to your height you have raised low things, for love equalises the humble and sublime, the more and the less; so, with proper measure, he adjusts these various states of lovers, when with pure affection grace enters the breast. Bend not to dangers, for such is the glory, that it sweeps away all sentiment of grief. And as with ancient captains and emperors in compensation for fatigues, triumphs were ordained equivalent to their victories, so lovers reserve a multitude of pleasures and contentments; and as to some a glorious reception causes oblivion of inconveniences and past annoyances, so to the lovers from the beloved fearful dreams, uncertain rest, nights of insomniousness, unquiet days are converted into joy and gladness ineffable.

"So, Lenio, if from sorrowful effects you condemn love, you should absolve it from its more agreeable results.

"As to the interpretation of the figure of Cupid, I make bold to say you are deceived there, as in all other your tirades against love. To paint him a child, blind, naked, with arrows and a bow, signifies naught else but that a lover should be like a child in his innocence, pure and simple, and blind to all but to one sole object, to whom he may unreservedly deliver himself., Naked he should appear, as owning nothing but what he loves; wings, too, that in his lightness he may fly where orders point. Paint him with arrows, because the lover's wound should be deep and secret, and that cause discovers the wound which alone can remedy it. Love strikes with two arrows, both working differently, which doth mean that in perfect love there is no medium in desire, and no desire in a single point, but that the lover surrenders himself wholly, without coyness or coolness. This love, Lenio, was that which destroyed the Trojans, and aggrandised the Greeks—made Carthage to sink, and Rome to rise—wrested from Tarquin his kingdom, and brought the republic again to liberty : and, though I could adduce here countless examples as opposed to what I said relative to the good effects of love, I will not dwell here, for they are notorious to all. I must, however, solicit you to credit all I have advanced, and that your patience stop to hear one of my songs, which I intend should be a rival to yours. So, if for it, and what I have said, you still persist in obstinacy to love, and are still averse to accept the truths which I have announced, if time admits, or in any way you choose or indicate, I will undertake to satisfy all replies and arguments, which, in opposition to mine, you please to start, so, for the present, be attentive, and listen.

1. Let from the pure, enamoured breast arise
   The voice sonorous, and in accent sweet,
   Of love the wonders recapitulate ;
   So, in content and satisfaction,
   The freer and unfettered thought may rest
   In full perception, only hearing them.
   Do thou, sweet love, who can them all relate,
   Shouldst thou my tongue require, such grace concede,
   That with the palm of taste and glory, stand ;
   Say who thou art, if that thou aidest me,
   As I do trust, in quick flight we shall see
   Your virtues and my own to heaven ascend.

2. Love is the principle of all our good,
   The means by which we reach, and do enjoy
   The happiest end to which we do aspire ;

Master of all other sciences,
A fire, which, though the bosom be of ice,
The flames of virtue clear enkindleth;
Strengthens the weak, and tramples on the strong;
The root whence grows the well-conditioned plant,
Translating us to heaven, with fruit, sating
The soul, with goodness, valour, honest zeal,
Of matchless taste, rejoicing heaven and earth.

3. Courteous, gallant, wise, and judicious,
Lively and liberal, mild and potent, too,
Whose sight is keen, although your eyes be blind,
Veracious guardian of all respect,
Captain who in the wars had triumphed,
Expecting honour only for his spoils;
A flower which grows brambles and thorns between
Both life and soul adorning, enemy
Of fear, and friend to everduring hope;
The guest which most delights when he returns,
Instrument of honourable wealth,
In whom we see to thrive,
The honoured ivy on the honoured brow.

4. A natural instinct which induces us,
To such an altitude our thought to raise,
That human sight can scarce attain thereto;
A ladder by whose steps the bold man mounts
To the sweet region of a holy heaven;
A mount whose top delightful is, and plain;
Facility levelling the intricate;
A north star guiding sanity on the vexed
Ocean, solace to the sad fantasy;
A godfather who no presence requires,
A Pharos which does not conceal itself,
Or port discover in the whirlwind's height.

5. A painter who depicts our very souls,
In shadows meek, and colours well subdued,
Now mortal, now a beauty deathless quite,
A sun which every cloudy thing slips through,
A joy to him whose griefs are tasteful, too,
A mirror in which nature self is seen
Free, in which freedom a just medium is;

Spirit of fire, blindest, illuminating,
Of fear and hatred the sole remedy;
An Argus, quite impervious to sleep,
Through ears, of some feigned God, counsel to reach.

6. Army, of an armed infantry,
Trampling down a thousand difficulties,
Ever retaining the victorious palm,
Adverting place whence joy assistance brings,
A visage which no wholesome truth conceals,
Clearly denoting what is in the soul.
From whence the hurricane a sweet calm is,
In time expecting to restrain its force.
Refreshment opportune, curing complete,
The scorned mortal, when he comes, do die.
Love's life, in verity, is glory, taste,
Sweet consolation, follow quick, pursue.

The conclusion of the reasoning and the song of Thirsis, was a plea for confirming anew in all the opinion of his discretion, save in the love lacking Lenio, who did not think that the reply satisfied the understanding enough to divert him from his original view.

This seemed manifest, for he wanted to reply again to Thirsis, if the praises which were dispensed to both by Darintho and his companions, and all the present shepherds, had not deterred him, for, taking his hand, the friend of Darintho, he said—" Now I know that the power and wisdom of love is co-extensive with the earth, and that it is refined and purified in pastoral breasts, as we have heard from the love-bereft Lenio and the discreet Thirsis, whose reasons and arguments appear more ingenious among those educated in halls and in literature than among those whose nativity and culture is amidst village cabins. Yet should I not so much be astonished, if that was the opinion of him who said that the knowledge of our souls is to agree in what they know, presupposing all are educated. But when I perceive I ought to follow another opinion better than that which affirms that our souls are nothing else than a mere blank, containing no impressions, I could not choose but wonder how that has been possible, for in the company of sheep, in the solitude of fields, we can learn sciences, which even learned universities would not dispute. If I do not wish to persuade myself to what I first stated, that love is of universal extension, and communicates to all, raises the fallen, advises the simple, and perfects those who are advanced in knowledge."

"If you will know, sir," replied at this time Elicio, "how that the education of the renowned Thirsis has not been confined to trees and flowers, as you imagine, but in the royal courts and recognised schools, you would not wonder at what he said, but at what he did not say, and though Lenio, disenchanted of love, in his humility has confessed that the rusticity of his life can promise slender fruits of wit, yet I assure you that he did not melt down the marrow of his youth in goat keeping, on the hills, but on the banks of the fluent Tormes, in laudable studies and judicious conversational exchanges.

"So that if the dialogue which these two have sustained be more than a mere pastoral exercise, contemplate them as they were, and not as now they are, and the more so, because you will find shepherds on our banks who would fill you with wonder if you heard them, even as these have done. For on them feed their flocks, the famous and renowned Tranio, Siratro, Filardo, Silvano, Lisardo, and the two Matuntos—father and son—one for the lyre, the other in poesy over all excelling; and to end all, turn your eyes and recognise Damon, whom you now have, where your desire may stop, if desire consists in discretion and wisdom."

The cavalier sought to reply to Elicio, when one of the accompanying ladies said to the other—"It seems to me, Nisida, that as the sun sinks, it were better for us to retire, if we have to go to where they say your father is." This was scarce pronounced by the lady, when Darintho and his friend looked at her evincing regret that they had exchanged names.

Now, when Elicio heard Nisida's name, it occurred to him to ask if it were the same Nisida, of whom the anchorite Silerio had recounted so much, and the identical thought struck Thirsis, Damon and Erastro. But Elicio, to make sure of his suspicions, said—" A short time ago, friend Darintho, I, and those now with me, heard the name of Nisida, as this lady has done, but accompanied with more tears and adverted to with more surprise."

" However," replied Darintho, " is there a shepherdess on these banks styled Nisida ?"

" No," said Elicio, " but her, of whom I speak, was here born, and was brought up in the sequestered parts of the famous Sebeto." " What is that you say, swain ?" replied the other gentleman. " What you hear, and what you shall hear," said Elicio, " if you assure me in the suspicions I have." " Say now," said the cavalier, " what would satisfy you." Again Elicio spoke :—" Peradventure, sir, your real name is Timbrio ?" " That is what I do not deny," said he, " for my name is Timbrio, and this I would conceal until a more opportune occasion, but the wish I have to know is why you suspect that to be my name, and this induces me to withhold nothing you desire to be informed of." " Nei-ther will you deny," said Elicio, " that the lady who is with you is styled Nisida, and as far as I can conjecture, the other is her sister, ycleped Blanca." " You have made a good hit," replied Timbrio ; " still I have refused you nothing as to your inquiries, so do you tell me what inducement you had to ask me."

" She is so good, and will be so much to your taste," said Elicio, " as you will see shortly."

All those who knew not what the anchorite Silerio, had recounted to Elicio, Thirsis, Damon, and Erastro, stood con-fused on hearing what had ensued between Timbrio and Elicio. " Yet," said Damon, turning towards Elicio, " you do not delay the good news which you can communicate to Timbrio." " And even I," said Erastro, " I will not with-hold telling to the wretched Silerio, the discovery." " Heavens, all holy, and what do I hear !" said Timbrio, " whatever do you say, shepherd ? Is it by chance that the Silerio you have mentioned is my true friend, the moiety of my life, one whom I would desire to see before all other things ? Relieve me from this doubt, quick, and so may grow your flocks and herds, that all other shepherds may be jea-lous." " Trouble yourself not so much, Timbrio," said Damon, " for the Silerio, of whom Erastro speaks, is the identical one you speak of, and is one who would know more of your life, to sustain his own ; for since you quitted Naples,

as our story goes, he has suffered so much from your absence
that the pain, combined with other losses, of which he informed us, has reduced him to the condition, that in a diminutive hermitage, a short league hence, he passed the most
straitened life one can imagine, with a resolution there to
await his end, as the success of your life cannot be satisfactory."

"Of a truth we know this, Thirsis, Elicio, Erastro, and I ;
for he has recounted to us your mutual friendship with all
the antecedents and sequences, till fortune, by such extraordinary accidents, divided you, to make him dwell in so
singular a solitude, enough to awaken wonder." "May I
see it, and reach my last hour," said Timbrio, "and so I
beseech you, illustrious hinds, by that courtesy which dwells
in your breasts, that you will tell me where is this hermitage
in which Silerio dwells." "Where he may die, you will
better say," replied Erastro, "for he will live from henceforth on the news of your advent ; and since you so much
desire his wish, and your own, arise and let us go, ere the
sun interposes. I will set you with Silerio, but on the
condition that on the way you will recite to us what befel
you since you quitted Naples, that in all things all here
present may take our fill."

"Of me you ask a very slight reward," replied Timbrio,
" for so large an offering, for I do not say I can recount all
this, but only that which of my knowledge you require and
more." So turning to the females who were with him, he
said to them—" Since on this favourable occasion, beloved
and my lady Nisida, the presupposition has been broken
which extorted from us our real names, with the delight
which the goodness elicits, I beseech you not to detain us,
but that we go incontinently to visit Silerio, to whom you
and I are indebted for our lives, and the placidity we now
enjoy."

"It is excusable that you solicit me to do what I inwardly
desire, and what so profits me in the doing of it. Let us
be off now, for every moment's delay in seeing him, counts
for an age."

The same said the other lady, viz., her sister Blanca, the
same Silerio had spoken about, and with so much satisfaction. Darintho, alone, at the news of Silerio, adjusted him-

self so that his lips moved not, but with a strange silence rose and ordered a servant to lead a horse where he should come ; so, without taking any leave, he ascended the animal, and turning the reins, at drawn out steps left all behind him. When Timbrio saw this, he mounted another horse and pursued Darintho till he overtook him, and laying hands on the reins, made him stop, and held converse with him for a while, and then Timbrio rejoined the swains, while Darintho moved on, sending to exculpate himself with Timbrio for quitting them without saying adieu.

At this juncture Galatea, Rosaura, Teolinda, Leonarda, and Florisa joined the two beauties, Nisida and Blanca. The discreet Nisida in brief words recounted to them the great friendship which existed between Timbrio and Silerio, with the consequents which ensued. But on the return of Timbrio all would prosecute their route towards Silerio's hermitage, and just then appeared at the fountain a charming young shepherdess, of some fifteen years of age, with her scrip on her shoulders, and crook in hand, who when she saw such agreeable society, her eyes in tears, she said to them : "If by hazard there be among you, gentlemen, one who takes cognizance of the strange effects and results of love, and tears and sighs can soften the breast, let him assist, if possible, to remedy and restrict such tears and sighs, as never before emanated from eyes and heart. Help me, then, O swains, in what I beseech, and you will see by my experience, that my words are veracious." Thus saying she turned aside, and the company present followed her. Now the shepherdess, observing that they followed, with hastening step took refuge between some trees adjoining the font, and had not far advanced, when, turning round to those behind her, she said—" You see, gentlemen, the cause of my tears, for that swain there is my brother, who for that shepherdess, before whom he is on his knees, he will leave his life in cruel hands."

They directed their eyes where the shepherdess indicated, and remarked that at a willow's foot a shepherdess was leaning, vested like a huntress, with a rich quiver pending from her side, and a bent bow in her hands, with hair ruddy and handsome, coiled in with a garland.

The shepherd was beside her, on his knees, with a rope

depending from his throat, and knife, unsheathed, in his right hand, and with the left he held fast to some white lawn which the lady bore around her. She displayed a frown on her face, and disgust, that the swain should forcibly detain her. But when she noted that she was watched, with considerable earnestness she tried to disengage herself from the swain's hand, who, with a plenitude of tears and endearing words beseeched her to let him give token of the sufferings he was undergoing on her account. The lady, however, disdainful and angry, disentangled herself from him just as the other shepherds reached them, who heard the man address her in this plaintive language :—

"Oh, ungrateful and heartless Gelasia, with what justice hast thou reaped the renown of cruelty ; turn, hard hearted one, turn those eyes to look on him, who, on looking towards thee, experiences more woe than imagination can body forth. Why, why fly one who follows you? Why not deign to look on him your servant? Why dread him who is your adorer? Oh, my most unreasonable enemy, hard as the raised-up crag, passionate as a wounded snake, deaf as dumb wood, coy as a rustic, rough as a wild beast, fierce as a tiger, a tiger which battens on my bowels! can it be that my tears will not soften you? my sighs awaken no pity? my services not move you? Yes, possible it will be, for my brief and luckless fate wills it so and it will be possible too, that you wish not to tighten the noose which is appended to my neck, or direct the knife through the core of that heart which adores you. Turn, shepherdess, turn and finish the tragedy of my woful existence, for with so much ease you can tie the knot to my throat, or stain this weapon in my breast."

These and other recapitulations of reasons uttered the wo-begone swain, attended with such sighs and tears that compassion seized the bystanders. Yet this did not cause the female to deflect from her course without wishing even to cast back her eyes on the sufferer, who stood fixed to receive this consolation, which awakened surprise in all who witnessed the wrath of the fair one ; and her conduct bore resemblance to the cruelty of Lenio's mistress.

Thus he with the venerable Arsindo, advanced to make interrogations, finding it prudent to turn round and listen to the complaints of the enamoured shepherd, though without any intention of interference. Yet nothing would alter her resolve; she even requested them not to consider her uncourteous in her disobedience, for her fixed intention was to abide a mortal enemy to love, and to all supplicants, however urgent; for one of her chief reasons was that she had devoted herself to the exercise of the chaste Diana, annexing thereto reasons why she could not acquiesce; so Arsindo thought it judicious to quit her and return, which also did the love-abandoned Lenio, who on observing that the nymph was as hostile to love as she seemed to be, and that the circumstances bore analogy to his own, he resolved to set on foot inquiries as to who she was, and to pursue her for a brief time, and thus he also declared himself to be the sworn enemy of love, and to all its adherents, asking her, since there was such a conformity of opinion between them, not to let his company be tiresome, for that he would not obtrude it more than she pleased.

The shepherdess was charmed to know his view of the subject, and granted him companionship to the village, which was some two leagues from that of Lenio. Now Lenio took leave of Arsindo, begging him to exculpate him to their friends, and announce the reason why he accompanied the shepherdess; so, without more ado, he and Gelasia hastened their pace and shortly disappeared. When Arsindo reverted to what had passed with the female, he found all the other swains had joined to console the love-affected shepherd, and that of two of the disguised shepherdesses, one had fainted in the folds of the lovely Galatea, and the other was embracing the attractive Rosaura, whose face was also shrouded from sight.

Teolinda was with Galatea, and the other, her sister, Leonarda, who, on sight of the despairing swain, whom they found with Gelasia, a sort of jealous and enamoured fainting fit pervaded their hearts, for Leonarda believed that the shepherd was her cherished Galercio, and Teolinda found it for a truth to be her beloved Artidoro, and so the twain witnessing him persecuted and lost by the heartless Gelasia, they sympathetically joined their sentiments, so that the result was that one, fainting, fell into the folds of the vest of Galatea, and the other fainted in the arms of Rosaura.

Now Leonardo's spirit soon returned, and she said to Rosaura, "Woe is me! dear friend; now I believe that all the passages to my cure fortune retains, for the will of Galercio is so remote from mine, as we can divine by the words which that shepherd announced to the love-indifferent Gelasia; for I would have you to know, my dear, that he it is who had despoiled me of my freedom, and who will eventually end my days."

Astounded at what Leonarda said was Rosaura, and more so when Teolinda recovered from her sorrow, she and Galatea called her, and so uniting with Florisa and Leonarda, Teolinda declared that the shepherd was her adored Artidoro. This word was scarce emitted, when her sister interposed by remarking that she was deceived, but that it was Galercio, her brother. "Oh, traitoress Leonarda!" rejoined Teolinda, "it is not sufficient that you have separated me from my own; and now I have found him, you would say he is yours? Now undeceive yourself, for by this act I declare you to be no sister of mine, but a pronounced foe."

"Of a verity you are in error, sister," again replied Leonarda, "and no wonder, for into thy mistake fell all the village, believing this swain to be no other than Artidoro, until they clearly perceived he was his brother Galercio, whose resemblance is such, that you and I are not more alike, and if so, their similitude surpasses ours."

"I cannot credit this," rejoined Teolinda; "for though we are so, these miracles appear rarely in nature. So I would have you to know that in that experience which invests itself with certainty, I cannot cease from believing that the swain I saw, was Artidoro. Should aught interpose a doubt, it does not relate to Artidoro, with whose identity I am conversant, or through fear that any chance may force me to forget him."

"Console yourselves, shepherdesses, then," said Rosaura, "for soon will I cause you to emerge from this dubiety," and so quitting them, advanced where the shepherd stood, giving account of the strange state of Gelasia, and of the injuries she exercised toward him.

At his side the shepherd detained the lovely young shepherdess, whose brother she said she was, to whom Rosaura called, and separating with her, she importuned her, and beseeched her to say what was her brother's name, and that he seemed to be some other person. To this the shepherdess replied that his name was Galercio, and that Artidoro was another person, yet so alike that with difficulty they were identified, save by certain signs on their vests or voice, in which some difference existed. He asked, also, what Artidoro had done. The lady replied, that he betook himself to the mountains somewhat distant, superintending the pasture of Grisaldo's flock with a herd of his own goats, and that he did not desire to enter the hamlet, or hold converse with anyone since he had come from Henares' banks, and he subjoined other such particulars that Rosaura was satisfied he was not Artidoro, but Galercio, as Leonarda had stated, and the shepherdess said from whom they ascertained that she was styled Maurisa; so moving her with him towards the spot where Galatea and the other females stood, again in the presence of Teolinda and Leonarda recounted all she knew from Artidoro and Galercio, so that Teolinda was comforted and Leonarda discontent, seeing how indifferent was Galercio as to her interests. In the confabulations held by the swains, it fell out that Leonarda called by her name the disguised Rosaura, and Maurisa catching it, said, " If I do not greatly err, lady, on your account has been my advent here, and that of my sister." "How so?" said Rosaura. " I will tell you, if you will let me speak with you alone," said the shepherdess. "Willingly," rejoined Rosaura, and pairing off with the shepherdesses, thus spoke—

" Without doubt, graceful lady, that to you and the shepherdess Galatea, my brother and I came with a message from our friend Grisaldo." " Just so it should be," replied Rosaura ; and calling Galatea, both gave ear to what Maurisa communicated from Grisaldo, which was to inform them how that in a pair of days he would come with two of his friends to take her to her aunt's house, where privately they might celebrate the nuptials, and jointly on that day from Grisaldo he gave to Galatea some rich golden jewels, as in thankfulness for the hospitality shown to Rosaura. Rosaura and Galatea thanked Maurisa for the good intelligence, and in compensation for it the discreet Galatea wished to divide with her the present which Grisaldo had sent, but Maurisa declined receiving it. So now they turned again to the extraordinary physical resemblance between Galercio and Artidoro.

During the whole time which was spent in talking between Galatea and Rosaura, and Maurisa, Teolinda and Leonarda entertained themselves in looking at Galercio, for the eyes of Teolinda feasted on Galercio's face, which did so resemble that of Artidoro, that there was no withdrawing the gaze ; and as those of the love-stricken Leonarda knew at what they looked, so was it impossible to withdraw them.

Now the swains had consoled Galercio, though from the woe he had experienced, he held all counsel vain and redundant, still all turned to the detriment of Leonarda.

Rosaura and Galatea seeing the swains verging towards them, took leave of Maurisa, telling her to say to Grisaldo, that Rosaura was staying with Galatea.

Maurisa took her leave of them, and calling her brother, privately informed him of what had taken place with Rosaura and Galatea, and then with all courtesy bid adieu to the ladies and the swains, and turned their backs on the hamlet did she and her brother. But the love-smitten sisters, Teolinda and Leonarda, who saw in the departure of Galercio that the light of their eyes was quenched, and their life of lives, too, both made off to Rosaura and Galatea, and asked permission to follow Galercio, Teolinda proffering for excuse that Galercio would tell her where Artidoro dwelt, and Leonarda, that it was possible that the will of Galercio might alter, seeing the obligation in which he stood.

The shepherdesses consented, but with the condition that ere Galatea had requested aught of Teolinda, that she should treat of her good or disadvantage.

Teolinda turning to renew the promise, and again taking leave, pursued the road which Galercio and Maurisa had taken. They took the same route, though a different way ; Timbrio, Thirsis, Damon, Orompo, Crisio, Marsilio, and Orfenio diverged to the hermitage of Silerio, with those two charming sisters Nisida and Blanca, having first taken affectionate leave of the venerable Aurelio and of Galatea, Rosaura, and Florisa, as well as Elicio and Erastro, who would not continue with Galatea, while Aurelio offered,

that on their attaining the hamlet he would go incontinently
with Elicio and Erastro, to seek Silerio's hermitage, and that
he would take something to satisfy the inconvenience, which
to entertain lovingly such guests Silerio would strive.

With this understanding they divided, and missing a
leavetaking of old Arsindo, they saw without bidding farewell to anyone that he deviated from the road which Galercio and Maurisa and the disguised ladies took, whereat they
marvelled; and noting how the sun hastened to enter the
western portals they would delay no longer, in hopes of
reaching the hamlet ere the shades of night overtook them.
Seeing then Elicio and Erastro before the lady of their
thoughts, to shew what they could not hide, and to alleviate
the toil of the road, and to fulfil the command of Florisa,
who ordered them on their reaching the hamlets, that they
should give voice to something to the sound of Florisa's
rebeck, Elicio began to sing and Erastro to reply :—

ELICIO.

1. Who would the greatest loveliness behold,
   The most complete the earth has witnessed,
   Fire and the crucible, by which is purged
   The whitest chastity and purest zeal
   All that which valour can, being and gravity,
   A heaven newly graven on the earth,
   Blended in loftiness and courtesy,
   Come and behold my shepherdess's charms.

ERASTRO.

2. Come and behold my shepherdess's charms,
   Who would recount to nations far remote
   What's seen by another sun, conferring light
   More clear than what from orient beams is shed.
   He may allege that fire engenders frost,
   And burns the soul which it doth seem to touch,
   By the quick rays of eyes so beauteous,
   That having seen them, naught is left to see.

ELICIO.

3. That having seen them, naught is left to see.
   This do well know these wearied eyes indeed ;
   Eyes, which for my destruction were so bright,
   Occasion principal of my distress.

I looked on them, and felt how that they burnt
My inward soul, the spoils surrendering
With all their potency to the fierce, rash flame,
Which all at once consumes, chills, casts, and calls.

ERASTRO.

4. Which all at once consumes, chills, casts, and calls,
This sweet enemy of my renown—
Of whose illustrious existence can
Fame constitute a strange yet faithful history.
Only those orbs whence love can shower down
Grace infinite as man can undergo,
Giving materials that shall upwards raise,
To heaven the pen which has a grovelling flight.

ELICIO.

5. To heaven the pen which has a grovelling flight,
If to the loftiest sphere you would raise yourself,
Sing of the courteousness and holy zeal
Of this Phœnix incomparable, sole and prime—
Our age's glory, honour of the soil,
Pride of clear Tagus and her verdant banks ;
Unequalled discretion, beauty rare,
Wherein kind nature magnifies herself.

ERASTRO.

6. Wherein kind nature magnifies herself,
Whence thought and art have equalised themselves,
Whence valour and politeness blended are,
Which were diffused as different properties,
So that humility with greatness may
Alone the same parts duly occupy,
Where love retains its nest and refuge too ;
That lovely mortal has my enemy been.

ELICIO.

7. That lovely mortal has my enemy been,
Who loves and could, and in a moment knew,
To hold me fast by the most subtle hair ;
The free abounding thoughtfulness I had.
And though to the tight snare I surrendered,
I feel a glory in my prisoner state—

My feet and neck to chains abandoning,
Declaring bitter pains to be most sweet.

ERASTRO.

8. Declaring bitter pains to be most sweet,
The tired brief existence, I pass through,
Of a sorrowful soul, sustained with difficulty
The body, too, lost in inanity.
Fortune with hands o'erflowing offered me
A perfect faith comprised in briefest hope.
What taste, what glory, or what good presents,
Whence hope decreases, and true faith augments.

ELICIO.

9. Whence hope decreases, and true faith augments-
The high intent discloses itself, and shows
From the robust thought of the enamoured,
Whose consolation is in purest love.
It lives assured of an indemnity,
Which wholly satisfies the longing soul.

ERASTRO.

10. The miserable love-sick, whom infirmity
Subjects and worries, in contentment bides
When the fierce torture him oppresses more—
Or any light alleviation comes.
But when a lukewarm suffering circumvents,
He calls on safety, seeking it entire.
After this guise the deep affected breast
Of him who loves dissolved in sorrow's pangs
Avows that good consists in suffering,
And the serene light of those eyes, to which
The remnant of his life he freely gives,
Admiring them with feigned or certain proof.
The more love quickly guides, and them repeals,
The more demands than e'er he asked before.

ELICIO.

11. The golden sun sits now behind the hill,
Erastro, us inviting to repose,
And the black night with stealthy steps comes on.

ERASTRO.

12. Near is the hamlet, and I am much fatigued.

ELICIO.

13. Let us upon the song silence impose.

They who heard Elicio and Erastro agreed (bien tomáran porpartido) that they should extend the journey to enjoy more the agreeable song of the two love-invested shepherds. But night was closing in, and their nearness to the village obliged a cessation, and that Aurelio, Galatea, Rosaura, and Florisa, should go home. Elicio and Erastro did the same, but with an intention to go immediately where Thirsis and Damon and the other shepherds were, and so it was arranged between them and Galatea's father, that they only waited till the silver moon should dislodge the obscurity of the night, and as she displayed her charming phasis they all went to seek Aurelio, and unitedly met at the turn leading to the hermitage; and what happened the next book will reveal.

BOOK V.

Solicitation to Timbrio to recount his story, which was further stopped by a shepherd's voice emanating from some trees, and recognised for Lauso.—His song.—He goes with Damon to the hermitage.—Lauso, at the instance of Damon, renews his song.—Followed by another to his mistress Silena.—Reach the hermitage without finding Silerio, but he shortly poured forth some genial poetry.—At the hermitage Nisida chants, awakening admiration.—Tumult in Silerio's breast, which Damon tries to repress by some feeling lines, and Timbrio adds an appendix.—Timbrio and Silerio interchange mutual solace. —Recapitulation of Timbrio's story, with thoughts by him in rhyme. —Prosecution of the sad narrative, disaster and shipwreck.—Concluding accidents and passages of his life, and the swains rejoice at the events being so favourable.—Timbrio discloses to Silerio Blanca's love for him, and that Darintho had been his rival.—Lauso reiterates his strain.—Aurelio addresses Timbrio.—Notice of Darintho's love malady.—Unexpected sighs from a pair of shepherds, who prove to be Elicio and Erastro.—Explanation of their situation. Exchanges between Damon and Elicio; the latter was to ask Galatea if she heartily acquiesced in the *parti* proposed for her by her father.— They meet eight shepherds with javelins, and a swain riding on a mare.—Faces all muffled.—Galatea sings to the dulcet pipe of Florisa, which confirmed in Damon the praises which had been accorded to Galatea.—The fact of her father betrothing her to Lusitano against her will.—Her moralising on free choice.—Damon's solace to her with Elicio's remarks on the projected union.—The master swains fall violently on Damon and Elicio; then on horseback advance; one seizes Rosaura, and seats her on the saddle, crying out that Artandro had abducted Rosaura by reason of her treachery.—Assault on the shepherds.—Grief of Galatea on the catastrophe, who with her companions go to the village, and there they heard some touching verses, outflowings of Erastro's heart, followed by reflections on love in a rhapsodical strain.—Galatea's colloquy.—Florisa recounts the abduction by Artandro.—Congratulations about betrothals, and Timbrio ends a sonnet which he had begun when he was recognised by Silerio.—At the conclusion Nisida annexed some captivating lines, and Blanca's voice swelled the numbers.—The enamoured Lauso again appears furiously traversing the briars in a grove.—Conversational interchanges with the shepherds, and Lauso bursts forth into song, evincing a change of love, temperament and conviction, on which Thirsis gratulates him, and they all pass on their road.— Meet Arsindo and Maurisa, Galercio's sister, who springs forward to embrace Galatea.—Addressed by Arsindo about the disenchanted Lenio.—Lauso replies, and Maurisa speaks at some length in explanation about Rosaura's abduction.—A cornet's sound awakens attention, and two venerable swains are seen, and between them a priest, recognised for Telesio.—Other swains arrive. — Aurelio addresses Telesio, who replies, signifying why he had convoked them, which was to render homage to the memory of Meliso, and to propitiate his manes.—Advancing towards the village they encounter Lenio, who indicating great disorder of mind, vented it in a strain of some length. —Upon his recognition of Thirsis he threw himself at his feet, and addressed him.—The latter rejoins in consolatory remarks.—Lenio adverts to the insensibleness of Gelasia.—The company wend towards the village.—They all unite to go to the valley of cypresses to celebrate the rites due to Meliso, where they hoped to find Timbrio, Silerio, Nisida and Blanca.

So excessive was the desire which the enamoured Timbrio and the two graceful sisters Nisida and Blanca entertained to reach Silerio's hermitage, that the lightness of their steps, which was remarkable, did not coincide with their volition ; and to know this, neither Thirsis nor Damon troubled Timbrio to fulfil his promise to recount all that had fallen out on the road since he quitted Silerio ; nevertheless, animated with the desire to know it, they had ventured on inquiry, had not, at that precise moment, a shepherd's voice fallen on their ears, which emanated from one singing amidst some verdant trees by the side of the road, which quickly—by the sound of a no well-measured voice in the singer—was recognised by Damon, the friend, for that of the pastor Lauso, who, to the sound of his rebeck, was reciting some verses. So being a well-known pastor, and the change which had come over his opinions being current, all stopped to learn what Lauso was singing, and the purport of it was this :—

LAUSO.

1. Who my free thought
       Came to subject ?
       Who can, with a soft cement,
       Without a venture, build
       The lofty tower, exposed to the blast ?
       Who to my freedom me restored hath
       In the fruition of security ?
       Satisfied with my life,

Who opened and burst my breast,
And from my free will stole ?

2. Where is the fancy
Of my condition coy ?
Where is the soul which I once called mine,
And the heart where
Abiding not where it was wont to abide ?
But where do I all exist ?
Whence come I and where go ?
Fortunately myself I yet do know.
I may be what I was,
Yet never have been who I truly am.

3. A straitened account I require,
No verification asked,
For doubtless am I to such point arrived,
That what in myself I find
Is but a shadow of what I have been.
No understanding do I understand,
Nor am I worth an estimation
In this confusion blind.
Certain my perdition is,
And on perdition only meditate.

4. Of my diligence the force,
And fierce consenting love
In such condition hold me,
That present time I only do adore,
The past bewailing.
In this myself die, I see,
And live in the past time.
In this my death adore,
And the past, my fate
Which I can ne'er attain.

5. In this extraordinary agony,
The feelings entertained go but for dumb,
Seeing that love defies,
And I am cast in midst of the fierce fire.
Cold water I abhor
Were it not for my eyes,
Which fire augments and spoils
In this amorous forge.

> I wish not or seek water,
> Or from annoyance supplicate relief.

> 6. Begin would all my good,
>   My ills would finish all,
>   If fate should so ordain,
>   That my sincere trust in life,
>   Silenca would assure,
>   Sighs assure it.
>   My eyes do thoroughly me inform
>   Me weeping in this truth.
>   Pen, tongue, will
>   In this inflexible reason me confirm.

The hasty Timbrio nor could nor would wait for the shepherd Lauso to pursue his strain, because he asked the pastors to show him the way to the hermitage if they wished to stop, and gave proofs of advancing onwards, and so all followed, and passed so near to where the love-stricken Lauso was, that he needs must perceive it, and came out to meet them as he did, in whose company all were delighted, particularly Damon, his fast friend, with whom he went all the way to the hermitage, discoursing on the divers accidents which had befallen them since their mutual separation, which was when the valorous and re-nowned pastor Astraliano had quitted the Cisalpine shepherds to go and bring home those of the famous Hermano, who had revolted from the true religion. And finally, they came to reduce their reasonings to the treating of the lover of Lauso, Damon asking him pressingly to say who that shepherdess was who, with so much facility of free will, had caused a surrender, and when he could not extort this from Lauso, he asked, with considerable earnestness, that at least he would say in what state she was, whether in fear or hope, if ingratitude oppressed him, or if the woe was jealousy.

To all this Lauso gave satisfactory replies, recounting many things which had passed with the shepherdess, and among the rest, he said that finding himself one day jealous and out of grace, he was driven to desperation, and to give some evidence redounding to the damage of her person, as well as credit and honour; but all this was rectified by a few words with her, and on her assurance that what he heard of her was false. This was ratified by the donation of a ring, the prelude to a better intelligence, and the favour was solemnised by a sonnet which obtained the estimation of all. Damon then asked Lauso to communicate it, so without further evasions he recited the following verses :—

LAUSO.

1. Pledge rich and fortunate, which now adorns
   The precious marble with the purest snow.
   Pledge of decease, and shadow most obscure,
   Which to new life and light has me restored.
   Thou hast exchanged the heaven of thy good
   With the deep hell of my miscarriage,
   That in a peace secure and sweet may live
   The hope which in me you have now revived.

2. What thou hast cost me knowest thou sweet pledge?
   My soul! and yet I rest not satisfied,
   For I surrender more than I receive.
   What, though the world your valour understands,
   Knowest thou my soul enclose thee in my breast,
   You will perceive how without soul I live.

Lauso finished his sonnet, and Damon turned to ask if he had written anything besides to his shepherdess he would recite it, for he knew what a delight there was in hearing his verses.

To this Lauso answered, "It shall be so, Damon, for having been your master in these things, and the wish you entertain to recognise what in me you approved, makes you desirous of hearing them; but be what it may, I can deny you nothing in my power. Hence I reassert that in these very days when I walked jealous, yet safe, I forwarded these lines to my lady shepherdess :—

LAUSO TO SILENA.

1. In a simplicity so notorious
   Of a sound purpose, child,
   Love guides the hand,
   And the intention doth your loveliness.
   Love and thy beauty,
   Silena, on this occasion

Will judge discreetly,
That which to madness surely doth induce.

2. The one impels me, and the other moves,
That I adore thee, and I thee address ;
And as in these two strives
My faith, emboldened also is my hand ;
And though in this grave fault
Your vigour threatens me
My faith, your charms and love
Will me exculpate from all error's charge.

3. But with such a prop
(Since a fault is ascribed)
Well may I good allege,
Which in my evil hath originated,
Which very good as I perceive it is,
Silena, is naught else,
Than that in pain exists
Some extraordinary suffering.

4. And yet do I little appreciate
This good of my endurance long drawn out,
Which had it not been,
Misfortune me to madness had impelled.
My feelings being in unanimity,
All have induced me to avouch
That though I expire
In suffering, yet in prudence I may die.

5. Still all well pondered
Impatiently will endure it·
In amorous suffering,
The jealous rejected lover,
Who in the evil of annoyance
All good upsets.
To a hope defunct adhering, standing
The enemy before my face.

6. May you, oh shepherdess ! a thousand years
The blessing of your thought strictly enjoy,
Which I wish not contentedly
May purchased be with any harm to you.

Follow thy longings, lady dear,
Since it to you so palatable seems,
While I, for any good extraneous,
Will think not of bewailing.

7. For it would be a levity pronounced,
My soul to abandon to another soul
Which holds for glory and a palm, likewise
Utter surrender of a liberty.
But woe, what wisheth fortune?
What love, which too therein comprised is
That cannot of the knife the neck
Elude? the deadly wound inflicting.

8. Clearly enough discern I that I move
Towards whomsoever me condemns,
And when upon divergence I do think
The more I stand the firmer fixed am I.
What nets, what snares possess
Your lovely eyes, Silena!
The which the more I fly
The surer keep me fast and hold me long.

9. Oh eyes, from which I strongly do suspect
That if of you I am seen,
The more anxiety hath its increase
Wisdom diminishing.
That your sight is feigned
With me is very truth,
For they repay my will
With pledges much abhorred

10. What dread, and also what suspicions
Pursue my cogitations,
And what contradiction do I feel
In my most secret loves?
Quit me, sharp memory;
Forget me.   Do not remember me
Of any good externe, for you do lose
Thereby your proper glory.

11. With bonds so many fully strengthening
The love in thy breast dwelling,

Silena, that, to my vexation,
You my ills confirm.
Oh, perfidious, cruel love !
What law of thine condemns me ?
Should I my soul to dear Silena give,
Myself denying my petition.

12. No more, Silena, do I touch
At all points this contention.
The least of them would
Me lifeless or mad leave.
Advance no further pen,
For you have made her feel
That I can not reduce
To space contracted such a sum of woe.

In proportion as Lauso was detained by reciting these lines, and in lauding the unusual loveliness, discretion, comeliness and virtue of his lady shepherdess, it made light the road to himself and Damon, and time escaped without impediment until they reached Silerio's hermitage, into which neither Timbrio, Nisida, nor Blanca would make entry for fear of disconcerting him on the unexpected advent.

Still did fate ordain it other, for Thirsis and Damon receding a little to observe what Silerio was about, they found the hermitage open and not a soul within, and were confused as to the whereabouts of Silerio at this time of night, when on their ears struck the sound of his harp, whereby they inferred that he was not far off, and so advancing to find him, guided by the instrumental music and the clarity of the moon, they detected him sitting on the trunk of an olive tree, only with his harp, which he touched so sweetly that, not to interrupt the sound, they would not proceed towards him, when they heard these words, which he commenced singing :—

SILERIO.

1. Light flying hours of light flying time,
Of idleness and weariness the causes are,
If ye have not conspired to my hurt,
Do now appear and finish up my days.

2. If now you me consume, quite opportune
   'Twill be when all my woes are at their full.
   See that they lessen if ye heavy are
   On me, that evil cease, time given to thee.

3. I do not ask you come with savoury sweets,
   For you will find nor road, nor path, nor step
   Me to bring back to that which I have lost.

4. Hours to any other fortunate
   That sweet one only of translation hence,
   That of my death alone do I exact.

When the shepherds had heard all that Silerio had sung, without perceiving them, they turned round to meet the rest, who came with a view to Timbrio's doing what now you shall hear; which was, that having spoken to him about the manner in which they had found Silerio, and the place where he was, Thirsis asked him that without anyone making him to understand, they should advance gradually towards him whether he saw them or not; for though the night was bright, no one could be recognised, and that they would arrange it so that Nisida or he should chant something, and all this he did to support the pleasure which Silerio would receive from their arrival. Timbrio with this was satisfied, and speaking to Nisida came into her very presence, and when it seemed to Thirsis that they approached so near that they could be heard by Silerio, he signified to Nisida that she should begin, who, at the sound of the rebeck of the jealous Orfenio, went off in this strain :—

NISIDA.

1. Though the good in reality I possess
   Is such that satisfies the longing soul,
   The crowd divides it and undoes it quite.
   That other good I saw not, or can see.
   That love and fortune are scarce
   To my existence foes.
   Evil they me dispense for a measure,
   Evil interminable and without rate.

2. In the amorous state,
   Though meriting it above,

As singly pleasure comes
As evil is accompanied,
All ills united onward motion have,
Without the smallest separation,
But goods to finish quite misfortune,
Divided infinite are found to be.

3. That which costs if it reach,
Of love, contentment some,
The sufferings declare
Love and hope ;
One glory costs a thousand anguish pains,
As one contentment doth a thousand woes.
Those eyes this truth know well,
And eke my wearied memory.

4. Which hath remembrance continual
Of him who can improve them,
But to find them is found
No path, no road.
Oh, sweet friend of him
Whom you discovered for his own so much !
And also when for thine he found himself,
So much am I of him.

5. With thy presence sure they will improve
Our unpremeditated chance,
And never may into misfortune lapse
Thy absence wide yet coy.
To a vast evil it provoketh me,
Memory which reminds me
How thou wert mad while I remained discreet,
Yet thou discreet wert, and I mad indeed.

6. I had for fortune good,
That you yourself would me endow.
Not so much was gained in the gain
As loss was in the loss.
The moiety of my soul in faith wert thou,
A mean whereby my soul
Can reach the joy
Which thy dear absence holds for very woe.

If the extreme grace with which the lovely Nisida sang

15

created admiration in those with whom she went, what cause should there be in the bosom of Silerio that without any loss he noted and acutely listened to all the circumstances of the song. And as he retained in his soul so deeply the voice of Nisida, scarce did his ear drink in her accents than he felt a tumult rise so as to be suspended and alienated from himself, and to be feelingly alive to what he heard ; and though it truly seemed to him that it was Nisida's voice, his hopes of seeing her were so remote, and in such a place too, that he could not realise a suspicion.

In this plight came all to the spot where he stood, and on Thirsis saluting, he said to him, " You left so well affected, friend Silerio, with your state and conversation, that Damon and I, attracted by experience, and all this company too by its fame, abandoning the road we took, come we to seek the hermitage, and not finding you we should have remained without the realization of our desire, had not the sound of thy harp and thy exquisite music emboldened us to come hither."

" Better by far had it been that you had not found me, for in me you will not find aught save occasions which move to woe, for what I endure in my mind time takes care to resuscitate, and not only with a memory of ills, but the shades of the present time, and so to the end, for nothing else can my misfortune hope, but feigned good and certain fears the reasonings of Silerio engendered sorrow in all his acquaintance, especially in Timbrio, Nisida and Blanca, who were so devotedly attached to him, and had desired to impart that feeling to him, had it not interfered with the injunction of Thirsis, who caused them all to seat themselves on the verdure, so that the rays of the brilliant moon, making incidence on the faces of Nisida and Blanca, they should not be recognised by Silerio. When Damon had imparted some words of counsel to Silerio, that all the precious time should not be involved in sorrowfulness, and to give a commencement to what Silerio should finish, he asked him to tune up his harp, on the sound of which Damon himself poured forth this canticle :—

DAMON.

1. If the sharp fury of the raging sea
    Should for a time in madness vexed persist,

'Twere difficult to find one launch his weak
Boat on the billows of the tumid flood.

2. No constancy exists in any state
Both good and ill, into each other blend.
If missing good, with evil still, the world
Would turn to its confounding contrary.

3. Night turn day, and heat convert to cold;
Flower into fruit consecutively turn,
The like producing from its contraries.

4. Subjection into lordship change itself;
Pleasure turn grief, and glory melt in air.
From such varieties hath nature charms.

Damon now ceased, and gave indications to Timbrio that he would follow, who, to the music of Silerio's harp, a sonnet began, which he had composed in the heat of his early loves, a song as equally known to Silerio as to Timbrio :—

TIMBRIO.

Firm hope I hold in deep foundations,
Though the fierce winds blow contrary and rude,
Yet from the cements no enforcement is,
Such valour, faith, and fate predominate.

Timbrio could not finish the already commenced sonnet, for when Silerio heard his voice and recognising him, and without reference to aught else, rose up from his seat and went to embrace the neck of Timbrio with signs of extraordinary contentment and surprise, so that without uttering a syllable he was so transported, that he remained without resolution. This imbued with such grief the minds of the bystanders, that they were afraid of some accident, and condemned the craft of Thirsis for very evil. The extreme of sorrow appeared in the beauteous Blanca, as the person who tenderly loved him. Quickly came up Nisida and her sister to remedy the swoon of Silerio, who in brief time returned to himself, uttering these words :—" Oh, potent heaven ! is it possible that whom I see present is my true friend Timbrio ? Is it Timbrio I hear ? and him I see ? if so, my chance does not jeer at me, or my eyes deceive." " No, chance does not jeer you, or your eyes deceive, my

cherished friend," replied Timbrio, "for I am he who was
nothing without you, and one who had been nothing had
not heaven permitted me to find you. Let your tears
cease, friend Silerio, if for me they have been shed, for now
I am present ; I arrest mine since I see you here before me,
styling myself the most fortunate of living men, since my
misadventures and adversities have brought on such a satisfaction that my soul rejoices in the possession of Nisida,
and my eyes in your presence." From these expressions of
Timbrio, Silerio understood that the person of whom he had
sung, and who was there bodily, was Nisida, and this assurance was ratified when she herself said, " What is this,
Silerio mine? What solitude, what dress is this, which
throw out such marks of your dissatisfaction? What false
suspicions, what deceits have brought you to such extremities, so that both Timbrio and I were involved in woe all
our days, absent from you who have informed us?" " These
were deceptions, beauteous Nisida," replied Silerio; " the
more for being such shall they be retained in my memory
while it lasts." The best part of the time did Blanca grasp
Silerio's hand, fixing, attentively, her eyes on his face,
shedding tears, too, which denoted the grief and joy of her
heart. Tedious were it to recount the words of love and
contentment which Silerio, Timbrio, Nisida and Blanca
interchanged ; so tender and of such a quality, that all the
shepherds who heard them found their eyes bathed in wet
drops of joy. Silerio recounted in brief the motive he had for
retiring to the hermitage, with a view there to expire, for into
it could no news enter, and all he said was an occasion for
resuscitating in Timbrio's breast the love and friendship he
entertained for Silerio, and in that of Blanca a friendliness
to misery, and as Silerio finished the narrative of what had
accrued after his quitting Naples, he beseeched Timbrio to
follow his example, for this he ardently desired, and that it
should not be suspected, by the bystanding shepherds, that all
they should know the intensity of their amity or its consequence.

Timbrio was delighted to fulfil the request of Silerio, and
the shepherds even more, who desired the same thing ;—
from what Thirsis had recounted all were conversant with
the loves of Timbrio and Nisida, and all that which the
same Thirsis had heard from Silerio.

Sitting therefore down, as we have observed, on the verdant mead, with extraordinary attention they awaited the statement of Timbrio, who thus spoke :—

"Since fortune was so favourable and yet so adverse, which left me vanquished by my enemy, and overcame me by the surprise of the false news of Nisida's death, in the grief you can understand, I incontinently left for Naples, and there being confirmed in the luckless fate of Nisida— not to see the house of her father, where I had seen her, and because the streets, windows, and other parts, where I was wont to see her, should not revive in me continually the memory of my previous good fortune ; and not knowing which road to turn, and my free will disregarding my better judgment, I sallied forth from the city and in two days' time I reached the fort of Gaieta, where I found a vessel whose sails were spread for Spain. In it I embarked, only to fly the hateful land where heaven had left me. But scarce had the band of sailors weighed their anchors, and unfurled their sails and put out to sea, when an unexpected and sudden storm arose, and a squally wind possessed the sails with such fury that the foresail snapped, and the mizen mast was rent from top to base. The ready mariners flew to the rescue, and with considerable difficulty they struck the sails by reason of the increase of the tempest, and the sea began to change, whilst the sky gave note of a permanent and fearful result.

"Return to the port was difficult, for it was a northwester which blew, and with such fury, too, that it was necessary to put the foresail to the mainmast, and to slacken, as they say, in the stern, and to let the wind carry us whither it would. Thus the vessel borne by its fury began running over the inflated sea with such lightness, that in the two days of the northwester, we ran through all the isles on the right without finding harbour, passing in sight of them, so that neither Stromboli would harbour us nor Lipari receive us, nor Cimbalo, Lampadosa, or Pantalaria would be of any use, and so close did we touch on Barbary, that we discerned the overthrown ramparts of Goleta, and the very ruins of Carthage were before us.

"No small fear invaded the tenants of the ship, dreading that if the wind should augment it would be imperative on them to land on a hostile soil.

"When we were most apprehensive of this, the better fate which hovered over us, or the heavens which heard our vows and promises, ordained that the northwest wind should change into a middling gale so reinforced, and which fell in the quarter of the southwest, that in two more days we reverted to the Gaieta port whence we had parted, with so much comfort from all, that many diverged to fulfil pilgrimages and promises on account of the danger they had escaped. Here the vessel put in port for four days to refit, and then set out on her way in a sea calm and wind propitious, passing in sight the pretty shores of Genoa, replete with well-ordered gardens, white houses, and shining pinnacles, which stricken by the sun's rays, became fervid, and would scarce bear a steadfast gaze.

"All these things might cause happiness to those who saw them from the ship, as well as those who witnessed them in the ship, save me, to whom it was a new motive for heaviness. The only abatement of *ennui* which I experienced, was bewailing my woes, by chanting them, or rather deploring them to the sounds of a lute belonging to one of the mariners, and one night I well remember, and well it is to remember it, for then my day began to shoot forth, the sea calm, and the winds quiet, the sails bound to the masts, and the seamen in the *dolce far niente* state, diffused over the ship, and the helmsman asleep for the indubitableness of the calm, which the aspect of the sky assured us. In the midst of this silence and my imaginings, for my griefs interdicted sleep, seated on the forecastle, I seized the lute and dashed into some verses, which I shall repeat, for they denote from what extremity of sorrow, and from what a right of woe I passed to a sudden joy, and what I then sang, if my memory abides by me, was what follows :—

TIMBRIO.

1. Now that the wind is hushed,
   And the sloping sea is calm,
   No rest is there for my torment.
   The soul stirs with the voice
   For very sentiment
   To recount my woes,

Demonstrating where they do all exist
In force—signals are supplied
By the soul and the heart,
Of living anxious mortalities.

2. In flight doth love exalt me,
For one and the other grief,
Till me it lodges in high heaven's vault.
And now that death and love
Have hurled me to the soil,
Love and death ordain
A death, and such love too,
As in my Nisida they also caused,
From my good and her ill,
Eternal fame acquiring.

3. With a new voice and terrible,
To-day e'en more, and in a fearful sound
I will make fame as credible
As love is potent,
And death insuperable.
Satisfied with its strength,
'Twill quit the world—we can aver
What deeds both have achieved,
What life death took.
Such love my breast conceals in its recess.

4. More I believe, too, since I am not come
To die, or be bereft of mind,
With the sore pains which I endured have,
Or that death can little do,
Or I no suffering have.
For should I have suffered
According to my strong augmented pains
Pursuing me, wherefore I should desire,
Though I in fact a thousand lives possessed,
A hundred thousand times to die outright.

5. My victory most exalted,
Was celebrated by the termination
Of a most illustrious life,
Which in the present or the past
Age, was ever known, nor is it yet

From it I raised for spoils
Grief in the heart's core,
A thousand tears in my eyes,
Confusion in my soul,
And in the firm breast an annoyance.

6. Oh, cruel hand of an enemy,
Would you but finish me there,
Thee I should recognise for a friend in need.
For if you killed me you would sure avert
The anxieties of my fatigue prolonged.
Oh what bitter abatement
Did my victory bring down.
For I shall pay as I perceive,
The solitary pleasure of a single day,
With ages infinite from torture's whip.

7. Thou boundless main, who listened to my complaint,
Thou Heaven, which so ordained it hath,
Love for whom I such lamentation prove.
Death which has my good thus carried off,
And my ruin finished too.
Thou Sea, my corpse receive;
Thou Heaven, collect my soul;
Thou Love, write with fame
That Death the palm bore off
Of this life, which existence does not claim.

8. Neglect not me to succour
Sea, Heaven, Love and Death,
Finish thy work by finishing me too.
Which will be the better lot,
And which, I hope, and you cannot concede;
For if the main not drowns,
Nor heaven collect my disembodied parts,
And love endureth by necessity,
And I suspect no death;
I know not where it is that I shall stop.

"I remember when I reached these last verses, which I have recited, when I could advance no further, interrupted by the infinite sighs and sobs which I ejected from my overladen breast, pressed by the memory of my misadventures, from whose pure feeling I actually lost my sensation in a paroxysm, which left me in an unconscious state ; but when the bitter accident had overpassed, I opened my wearied eyes, and found myself with my head enveloped in the folds of a female vested in pilgrim's attire, and at my side stood another lady clothed similarly, and both tenderly surrendered up to tears.

" When I perceived how I was situated, confusion surprised me, and I doubted if it were in sleep I saw it, for, certainly, no women had ever crossed the vessel since my entrance into it. From this confusion, however, did the lovely Nisida shake me, who also was there standing, and was that very pilgrim, and she said to me, ' Timbrio, my very worthy and approved good friend, what false images and what luckless accidents have ever produced events to bring us together; and that I and my sister may give a brief account, as we should do in honour, and without detecting any inconvenience in the fact that we have quitted our beloved parents, and our accustomed clothes, with a view to seek you, and to undeceive you as to my presumed death, which might precipitate yours.'

" When I heard these reasonings, I no longer inferred that I was in a dream, and I thought some vision was present to my senses, and that the perpetual idea that Nisida was not away, was the cause that this vision presented itself to my eyes. I made her a thousand questions, and to all an entire satisfaction ensued, which assuaged the understanding, and assured me of the personal presence of Nisida and Blanca. But when the very truth was revealed to me, the joy of it was such that I nearly lost my life, of such a weight had my grief been. Then I learned from Nisida how the error and neglect which you, O Silerio, produced in making signals with a head-dress, was the cause, that, believing some evil accident had overtaken me, there succeeded to it a certain paroxysm and fainting, so that all thought death had ensued, as I thought, and you, Silerio, believed it, too. He related, how, after the return to himself, that he knew the truth of my victory, in addition to my sudden forced parting, and your absence, the news of which induced a credit that death had supervened. But, as at the last they did not remove her, they arranged with her and her sister, by means of an attendant who was with them, that, disguising themselves in pilgrim's attire, they might, unknown to their parents, get off that night, which brought them to Gaieta, and then return to Naples.

"It was at the crisis when the ship in which I had embarked, after its repair from the results of the tornado, stood ready for sailing, and these ladies saying to the captain that they wished to pass over into Spain to reach Gallicia, an arrangement was made, and they went aboard with the idea of seeking me at Xeres, where they thought to find me, or ascertain something of me; and all the time they were afloat, some four days, they did not move from the cabin which the captain had assigned them in the stern, until, hearing me sing the verses of which I have made mention, and recognising me in my voice and what I had enunciated, out they came, as I have described, and inaugurated the event of the discovery with joyous tears; there we stood, each wondering at the other, without knowing in what terms to aggrandise our unexpected delight, which had gone on augmenting, and had continued until now, if concerning thee, friend Silerio, we had been certified of news. Yet, as there is no pleasure without alloy, which leaves a void in the breast, your absence not only failed us, but we were destitute even of news of you. The clearness of the night, and the cool and satisfying breeze, (which then began to operate favourably on the sails) a calm ocean, and unincumbered sky, all united, and helped to solemnise the joy of our hearts.

"But fortune, fickle ever, on whose permanence is no reliance, jealous of an accident, was set on upsetting, it in the most effectual way, had not time, and certain events anticipated.

"It fell out, that, at the time when the wind lifted up her voice, that the anxious mariners hoisted up the sails, and, with a pleasant unanimity, awaited a prosperous passage.

"One of them, seated at the prow, discovered, by the moon's assistance, that four rowing boats, on a wide and extended range, with celerity and certainty were nearing our vessel. These he detected to be adversaries, and, at the top of his throat began crying, 'To arms, to arms, some

Turkish boats are seen.' This cry and sudden noise created such a concussion in the vessel, that, not knowing how to counterwork the inevitable danger, one watched only the other; while the captain, who was not unused to such sights, going to the prow, soon measured the bigness of the boats, what they were, and added to the number seen by the sailor yet two more, and decided on their being galley-slaves, from whom there was much to fear.

"Still dissembling all he could, he ordered his artillery to be arranged, and to assault the adversary, playing on them as much as they could. Soon all came to expect close quarters, and, to each his post assigned, they awaited the arrival of the foe.

"Who can describe to you, friend, the anguish I endured, my contentment so rapidly invaded, and so likely to be annihilated. But when I saw Nisida and Blanca look about, and say nothing, overwhelmed by the noise and vociferation which abounded in the vessel, and, seeing that, I asked them in what cabin they would be stowed away, they prayed to heaven to be delivered from the hand of the enemy. This scene confounds the imagination when memory reverts to it. Their extorted tears, and the fortitude I exerted to repress my own, held me so fast that I was almost oblivious as to what I ought to do, who I was, and to what necessity the danger pushed me. Finally, I did prevail on the ladies, panic-struck, to retire, and, closing them in their retreat, I saw what the captain intended, by whose providential arrangement sufficient was done, and giving orders to Darintho, that same who left us to-day, to mount the prow-guard, and me to take command of the stern, he, with sundry sailors and passengers, were diffused through the body of the vessel. The foes were not laggards; the sea became calm, and this was our perdition. The opponents dared not board us, for, the weather slackening, they deemed it more politic to await for day to invest the ship; this they did, and, on day-dawn, though we had counted them, we discerned fifteen gross vessels to encompass us, and this went far to invest us with the dread of inevitable destruction.

"However great the disparity, neither was the captain nor his companions terrified, and awaited the attack; when

morn arose, they threw from the captain's ship a little bark
into the sea, and sent a renegade to demand unconditional
surrender, for he saw he could not fight so many, and the
best ships, too, and being threatened by Arnaut Nami, his
general, who shot at the vessel which touched the ship's
yard, and to this the renegade added threats, trying to persuade our captain to yield; but this he would not do so
readily, and told the renegade, if he would not quit the
ship, he should be fairly sunk.

"Arnaut heard this reply, and quickly put his ship in
order, and sent such .effective balls on our ship, both
furiously and promptly, that it awakened wonder and
noise, too.

"Our vessel followed suit, so that one of the others, which
fought at the stern, went to the bottom, for it was hit by a
ball between wind and water, so that the sea soon absorbed it.

"The Turks remarking this, they hastened the combat,
and in four hours they boarded us four times, and retired,
too, with infinite damage, we suffering also. But, that I
may not weary you with recapitulation, I will remark, that,
after a battle of sixteen hours, the captain and many in our
vessel having fallen, at the close of nine assaults, they finally
invaded us. Though I should wish it, I could not appreciate the woe which touched my heart, when I found out
that my beloved pledges, whom I now view before me, had
fallen into the hands of those merciless hangmen; and so,
impelled by the anger which this fear and reflection had in
me caused, all unarmed, I threw myself into the midst of
the barbarian swords, anxious to die by their blades, ere
I saw what I expected. But my idea was reversed, for
three lusty Turks grappled with me, and I struggling with
them, we all tripped up together at the door of the cabin
where Nisida and Blanca were lodged, and the violence of
the concussion burst open the door, which disclosed the
very treasure there concealed. The enemies were covetous
of them, so that one seized Nisida, and the other Blanca;
and when I found myself liberated from the grasp of two
of them, I soon got the third down at my feet, trusting to
serve the other two likewise, had not they, duly apprised of
the danger, abandoned their hold of the ladies, and, with

two mighty blows, they knocked me to the ground. This
Nisida saw, and, casting herself on my wounded body, with
a lamentable supplication, begged the Turks to desist. At
this crisis, attracted by the cries and screams of Blanca and
Nisida, up came Arnaut, the Admiral, and, being instructed
as to what had occurred, he transported Nisida and Blanca
to his galley, and, at the instance of Nisida, he ordered that
I should also be carried thither, since I was not quite dead.
Thus, without feeling, they bore me to the enemy's galley,
where I was restored with despatch, for Nisida had informed the captain that I was a man of mark, and would
pay a handsome ransom, with a view to awaken covetousness in the large amount derivable therefrom. It fell
out, that my wounds cured, I recovered my intellect, and,
letting my eyes stray on all sides, I knew that I was in the
power of my enemies, and in a foe's vessel, too. Nothing,
however, recalled me sooner to my senses, than seeing
Nisida and Blanca at the stern, sitting at the feet of this
dog of a commander, weeping profusely, indicating the deep
pressure of grief within. Not the dread of terrible death,
which I expected when you, my worthy Silerio, delivered
me from it in Catalonia; not the false rumour of the death
of Nisida, which I firmly believed; not the pain of my
mortal wound, or any whatsoever affliction, caused me, nor
could cause more suffering than what I experienced on witnessing Nisida and Blanca in the power of this disbelieving
barbarian, whose honour and virtue were within his scope.
Such, and of so deep an operation was this sentiment in my
soul, that my senses fluctuated again, and to take away
hope and life from the surgeon who had healed me, so that,
believing I was defunct, he stopped in the midst of the
cure, assuring all that I had breathed my last.

"The two ladies, apprised of this, let them say if they are
so bold, what I alone can say, that after learning they
were both removed, dragged by their auburn hair, and their
very faces scratched, and no one to help them, they
arrived where I lay in a swoon, and set up such a piteous lament that the very breasts of the barbarians were
softened.

"With the tears of Nisida which bedewed my cheeks, or
by reason of the cold and festering wounds which extorted

pain, I again recovered my mind, sufficient to appreciate my misadventure.

"I will pretermit the dolorous, yet amorous interchanges which passed between Nisida and myself, not to aggravate the present recital; nor would I dilate on the dreadful circumstances which she stated had passed with the commander, who, subdued by her charms, a thousand promises, a thousand presents, a thousand threats, proffered for her eventual surrender; but she, being as coy as virtuous, managed to stave off the hateful, unmastered importunities of the corsair. Yet as the daily presence of Nisida stimulated in him the more ardent desires, one doubtless had feared, as I did, that throwing away supplications and substituting violence, Nisida's honour might be lost, or else her very life; which, from her gentleness, might be expected.

"Now fortune, tired at dropping us down into the humblest state of misery, made us to understand what her well-known instability meant, through a medium which put us into a condition to ask of heaven to keep us even in our unfortunate state instead of losing our lives in the swollen billows of the angry main, which (at the close of two days of our captivity, and when on the direct course for Barbary) moved by a furious gale (xaloque) began to swell mountains high, and to distress the armed corsair band so violently, that the rowers, unable to use their oars, lashed them fast (afremillaron), and had recourse to the mainsail, and let all drive as might be, and thus increased the tempest, which in the space of half an hour scattered and severed the squadron, so that no one could carry out the captain's orders for following. In a brief space there was a general disunion, as I said, and our vessel stood alone, and was the most in danger of all.

"It now began to let in water at its sides, so that all the cabins at the stern, prow and midship, were inundated, and the water rose from the centre to the knee (rodilla). In addition, night supervened, and, as in all analogous cases, fear was augmented, so that a new storm was ushered in with the intense obscurity, and thus all were bereft of remedy.

"You would desire, gentlemen, to know nothing further but that these very Turks requested the Christians to ply the oars, and even to invoke their saints and Saviour to shield them from this misfortune. Now this was not done in vain, for moved by these effectual, fervent prayers the winds dropped, but not before their fury and rage had so far increased, that at day-break the watch alone indicated time, and the misdirected bark found herself on Catalonia's coasts, so near land, and without means of avoiding being stranded, that it was expedient to hoist a little sail, and to drive into a narrow place, so that the love of life made even slavery sweet to the Turks, from which they saw no escape.

" Scarce was the bark aground, when people of all sorts assisted on the beach, whose dress and dialect announced them for Catalonians, for the coast was in Catalonia, and e'en in that identical spot, dear Silerio, where, at the risk of thy life, you preserved mine.

" Who now could over-estimate the joy of those Christians, who, from the heavy and retarding weight of captivity saw their necks free and without restraint, and the prayers and solicitations of the Turks, a little ere while free, themselves become slaves, entreating that they should not be maltreated by those same Christians, who might harbour revenge for the offences of the Turks, dragging them from their home, as you, Silerio, well know.

" The fear they entertained did not so soon disperse, for the mob, rushing into the galley which lay entrenched on the sands, they murdered the corsairs *sans* remorse, that few escaped, and were it not that covetousness for rapine blinded them, every Turk had suffered death.

" Finally, on the surviving Turks and Christian captives which there assembled, was a regular sack made, and had not my garments been blood-stained I believe I had also perished. Darinto, who likewise came, assisted in looking for Nisida and Blanca, and took care that I should be transported ashore for my ultimate cure.

" When I got out and knew again the locality, and ruminated on the peril which had kept me in on every side, grief supervened, caused by the fear that I might not be recognised, and even chastised for no demerit of mine. So I asked Darintho that without delay we should be off for Barcelona, instructing him wherefore. This was not practicable, for my wounds were so heavy that I could not stir for some days without visits from a surgeon.

" In the meanwhile Darintho went to Barcelona, and providing the needful, returned, and finding me convalescent, we both hastened off for Toledo city, to learn of Nisida's relations if they knew aught of her parents, to whom we had written the accidents of our lives, begging pardon for our past infirmities, and all the satisfaction and woe of this variety of events which thy absence, O Silerio, has both increased and diminished.

" Now since kind heaven has furnished succour to us, and abated our woes, nought remains but condign thanks, and you, Silerio, will throw off the sorrowful past in the joyous present, and will not fail to give to it that which some time now exists without it, as you will find out when more alone, and hold further communication.

" Many things yet remain behind to relate, which have befallen me in the detail of my peregrination, but I pass them over temporarily not to incur the imputation of prolixity from these shepherds, who have been the instrument of my delight.

" This then, friend Silerio, and worthy swains, is the accident of my life. Mark now through what I have passed and do pass, so that without exaggeration I may predicate of myself that I am a man perplexed in the extreme.

" With these latest words, the joyful Timbrio wound up his story, and all present rejoiced at the happy issue which followed his labours, the satisfaction of Silerio being imparted to all the rest. Turning, however, to embrace Timbrio, impelled by the desire to know who the person was that on his account lived so dissatisfied, asking permission of the shepherds, he retired with Timbrio aside, and ascertained from him that the beauteous Blanca, sister of Nisida, was her who more than herself loved him, from the very moment she learned who he was and the courageousness of his character, and that she never, not to transgress honesty of purpose, had desired to discover this sentiment save to her sister, by whose means she hoped to be honoured in the completion of his wishes. Timbrio also told him how the cavalier Darintho, who had come with him, and of whom he had made mention in the previous conversation, and transported by her charms, had become so deeply enamoured, that he solicited her hand for a spouse from her sister Nisida, who undeceived him by saying that Blanca could in no wise consent; and Darintho, exasperated at this, believed it to be by reason of his want of energy that they rejected him, and so to withdraw him from this suspicion, made Nisida tell him how engaged in affection Blanca was towards Silerio; yet this did not quite upset Darintho, nor did he slacken his purpose, for he knew that as from you, Silerio, he could get no news, he imagined that the services he thought to render to Blanca and time would divert her from her original intention; and with this idea he could never quit us, until yesterday, hearing certain news of your life from the shepherds, and knowing the satisfaction with which Blanca had received it, and holding it to be impossible, as Silerio had appeared, that Darintho could attain his wishes, without taking leave of anyone, with signs of the heaviest grief, he severed himself from all. Added to this, Timbrio advised his friend to be satisfied if Blanca should take him, he choosing her and accepting her for a spouse, for he knew her, and was not ignorant of her surpassing virtues, cherishing the delight which the two would entertain in being united to the two sisters. Silerio thereto answered that time should be given to ponder on the act, though he knew that in the end it was impossible not to do what he ordered.

"Now the dazzling Aurora began to indicate approach, and the constellations by degrees hid their diminishing light. At this very point of time there touched their ears the voice of the love-stricken Lauso, who, as his friend Damon knew that that very night they had to pass in the hermitage of Silerio, was glad to be his companion, and to be with the other swains also. And his peculiar pleasure and pastime was singing, to the sounds of his own rebeck, the favourable or unprosperous successes of his loves: rising from his state, and invited by the solitude of the spot, and the tasteful harmony of the airy warblers, who began to salute and inaugurate the dewy morn with their combined music, in a low strain he extemporised these verses:—

LAUSO.

1. To the most noble part the sight did rise
   Of which imagination is susceptible.
   Whence valour I admire—admire the art
   Which loftiest understanding can suspend. '

16

Would you demand in truth which part that was,
That yoke imposed on an exempted neck?
He who delivered me, my spoils who took,
Mine eyes, Silena, are, and your eyes too!

2. Thine eyes, indeed, whose very light serene,
   Conducts me heavenward sans impediment.
   Devoid of all obscurity that light,
   The certain evidence of light divine.
   For it the fire, the yoke and heavy chain
   Which me disintegrates, weighs down, distracts
   The comfort and refreshment, the glory and palm
   To the soul—and life which to thee soul has given.

3. Ocular beams, the essence of my soul,
   End and conclusion of my whole desire;
   Eyes which e'en soften the day's darkest hour,
   For which I see, if I can boast of sight
   In your bright radiance, both my joy and pain,
   Has love implanted. There I contemplate
   And read the sweet, true, bitter history
   Of a sure hell and glory insecure.

4. In blind obscurity I tottered when
   Your radiance failed me. Oh, those eyes of fire,
   Hither and thither, starless, wandering,
   Sharp thorns between and brambles round about.
   But instantly, on slight impression,
   To my soul came the influence divine.
   Of your clear orbs I clearly saw the path
   Of fortune open in directest line.

5. I saw you may be, and will be, the eyes
   Serene to raise me, and may raise me too,
   To that small band numerical of good
   Which me to signalise the purpose is.
   This may you do sans alienation,
   With slight agreement about looking on.
   The greatest pleasure of the enamoured one
   In admiration and admiring dwells.

6. If this be truth, Silena, who has been,
   Nor is nor shall be, with just confidence
   As I love thee, nor shall be so beloved,

Unless love aid him and adventure too ?
The glory of your view I well deserve
For faith inviolate ; but it madness is
To think of really, truly meriting that
Which scarce is had in contemplation."

The song and the wayfaring ended at the same point, the love imbued Lauso, who of all those who were with Silerio, was lovingly received, augmenting, by his presence, the joy which all participated, by reason of the great success of the labours of Silerio, and as Damon was recounting appeared the venerable Aurelio, who, with some other of the swains, carried some presents for regaling the congregated party, according to promise the day before he left them. Thirsis and Damon were astonished to see him arrive without Elicio and Erastro, and the more so when they came to understand the cause of their leaving.

Aurelio came, and then contentment had abounded generally, had he not said, dispensing his reason to Timbrio, " If you value yourself, as it is reasonable you should, valorous Timbrio, on being a true friend to him who is your true friend, now is your time to show it, in assisting to remedy Darintho, who not far from here remains so sorrowful and vexed, and so adverse to admit consolation for his sufferings that some, as I told him, were not so to be considered. Elicio, Erastro and I found him some two hours ago in the midst of that mountain which lies on the right, his horse reined up to a pine tree, and he on the ground, his mouth downwards, heaving tender and doleful sighs, emitting words occasionally, and cursing his misadventure, at the report of which we accosted him, and by the moon's rays, yet with difficulty we recognised him, and importuned him to acquaint us with the cause of his woe. He told us, and now we know how slight the remedy is.

" Yet have Elicio and Erastro remained with him, and now I came to inform you how his thoughts are fixed. It is obvious too, that in you lies the remedy, by deeds or words."

" Words will be all good, Aurelio," replied Timbrio, "that I can spend on it, if he will not avail himself of the opportunity for being undeceived, and make up his mind till time

and absence produce their wonted effects; but because I do
not correspond to what his friendship obliges me, tell me,
Aurelio, where you left him, that I may incontinently go
there."

"I will accompany you," answered Aurelio; and quickly
arose all the swains to accompany Timbrio, to know the
cause of Darintho's malady, leaving Silerio with Nisida and
Blanca, and that with such satisfaction to them all, that
nothing was said."

On the road towards where Aurelio had left Darintho,
Timbrio gave account to those who journeyed with him, of
the nature of Darintho's malady, and the general hopeless-
ness of cure.   Since the beauteous Blanca, on whose account
he so suffered, was become the cherished object of Silerio,
stating himself that he had to use all his forced industry to
bring Silerio to the position which Blanca solicited, requesting all to aid and advance his intention, for in leaving Darintho, he desired that all should require of Silerio that he
should receive Blanca as his lawful spouse.   This the swains
offered to do, and during the talk Aurelio believed that
Elicio, Darintho and Erastro would be present; but they
found no one though they walked about and moved a great
party from a little wood which was there, which disquieted
them all.

Now, as they were standing there they heard a most dolorous sigh, which infused terror in them, and created a desire
to learn whence it came, on which event succeeded another
sigh not less mournful than the past, and wending towards
the spot whence the sigh arose, they saw, not afar off, at the
foot of a well-grown walnut tree two shepherds, one seated
on the green sward, and the other on the soil, extended, his
head lying on the other's knees.   The sitting one had his
head in inclination, shedding tears, and looking attentively
towards him on whose knees he was, and so, both their
colours fading, no one could recognise either; but on a closer
approach they detected in the two swains Elicio and Erastro,
—Elicio the depressed one, and Erastro the doleful.   Great
was the wonder and sorrow caused in all by the woeful
countenances of the two wretched shepherds, from his being
his great friend, and in ignorance, too, of the cause of their
deplorable state.   But he in whom the wonder most

abounded was Aurelio, from seeing he had just left them in company of Darintho, with signs of pleasure and contentment, as if he had not been the cause of all his misadventure.

Seeing now, Erastro, that the swains approached to him, Elicio quaked, saying to them, " Return to yourself, wretched swain ! rise and seek a spot in solitude to bewail your ills, for I think to do the same before life's close ;" and so saying, he embraced the head of Elicio with his two hands, and raising him from his knees, got him up on the ground, ere the shepherd was aware ; and Erastro rising too, he turned as if going away, but Thirsis and Damon, and the bystanders stopped him. Damon came where Elicio stood, and taking him in his arms, forced him back to proper consciousness. Elicio opened his eyes, and knowing all who there stood, held converse. Yet his tongue moved, and, forced by grief, could impart nothing which could assign cause for it, and though he was questioned by all the swains, he replied no otherwise than that he knew no more of himself save that talking with Erastro a fainting fit came on. So said Erastro ; hence the swains ceased further inquiry as to his condition, but solicited him to return with them to the hermitage of Silerio, and so off they took him to the hamlet or to the cottage ; but it was not possible that it should end here, except that they let him return to the hamlet.

Noting, however, that this was his desire, they did not oppose him ; contrariwise they offered to attend him, but he would have no companion, or would take one had not the pertinacity of his friend Damon overcome him, and so they went off together, Damon agreeing with Thirsis that they should see each other that night in the hamlet or cottage of Elicio, in order to return to his. Aurelio and Timbrio asked Erastro for Darintho, who replied to them that when Aurelio had separated from them, the fit overtook Elicio, and while he was succouring him, Darintho left in all haste, and that they had seen no more of him.

Now Timbrio seeing this, and his companions too, that Darintho was not to be found, resolved on returning to the hermitage to inquire of Silerio, if he would accept the fair Blanca for his wife ; and so resolved they did return, save Erastro, who wished to follow his friend Elicio. Thus, taking leave of them, and accompanied only with his rebeck, he went the very road which Elicio had taken, who a little before had deflected from the path which Damon and the rest took, tears in eyes and with evidence of unusual grief began to say—"Well, I know, discreet Damon, that your experience in love is such, that no wonder will start up in you at my narration, which so strange is, that on the strength of my opinion I hold you for one of the most disastrous of mankind, in matters of love."

Damon, who desired nothing more than to ascertain the cause of the depression and sorrow, assured him that nothing would be new to him when treating of the evils to which love is heir, and so Elicio with this assurance, pursued his discourse. "Now, you are not ignorant, Damon, how my good luck, for so I shall ever style it, though it costs me my life. I repeat then, that my good luck willed, as heaven and these banks know that I loved—what say I, loved?—that I adored the incomparable Galatea with as chaste a love as she merited. Verily will I confess to you, my friend, that in all the time that she knew of my desire, has she given me any reciprocity, but only such general warrant as a chaste and well regulated mind might proffer. Now, some years ago, my hopes buoyed up by an honest loving correspondence, I have drifted on in thoughts so joyous and satisfied, that I accounted myself the most fortunate shepherd that ever fed flocks, content alone but to see Galatea, and to observe that she did not abhor me quite, and that no other swain could flatter himself that she ever looked upon him, and this fed my longing and held my thoughts so firm, that I was jealous of no one. Confirming me in this truth, the opinion which the virtue of Galatea implanted in me, is such that no boldness has effect. Against this good, which love conferred on me at so little cost; against this glory so harmlessly indulged in by Galatea; against this preference so justly in accordance with my desire, an irrevocable sentence has this day been passed, which quite completes the good, the glory finishes, the preference changes, and finally concludes the tragedy of my inauspicious existence. For you shall know, Damon, that this very morn, coming with Aurelio, Galatea's father, to find out Silerio's hermitage, he told me *en route* that Galatea was to marry the shepherd Lusitano, whose occupation was to feed very many flocks on the banks of the soft-flowing Lima. He asked me if I would tell him what I thought; for from the friendship he entertained of me, and from my general judgment, he trusted to be well counselled. What I replied was, that it seemed to me a novelty that he should be deprived of his lovely daughter, banishing her to remote places, and that if he had taken and fed her on the riches of a stranger shepherd, that he should consider that he was not so much in want of them, and that he would not find to live in his territory other than rich persons, and that no one of the more opulent who inhabit the banks of the Tagus, would presume it to be otherwise than fortunate to obtain Galatea for a wife. These reasons were considered tenable by the venerable Aurelio, for he resolved, saying the chief among the shepherds (rabadan de los aperos) had ordered it, and he it was who had arranged it, and it could not be annulled. I then asked him in what spirit Galatea had received the news of the banishment? He told me that she has willingly complied, and that her desire was to coalesce in his desire as an obedient child. This I learned from Aurelio, and this is the cause of my anguish, and will be my death. For to see Galatea in the power of a rival, and out of my sight too, nothing but my end can ensue."

The enamoured Elicio ended his discourse, and tears were the sequel, and in such a flux, too, that the heart of his friend Damon being melted, he could not but accompany him in his tears, yet in a brief space he began with all his power to console Elicio, although words ended only in words, and nothing else was sequent to them.

However, they were unanimous that Elicio should speak to Galatea, and ascertain from her if it were of her unbiassed will that she should consent to the *parti* which her father had chosen for her; and if that were not the case, he offered to emancipate her by force, for that he was capable of it.

All this seemed to Elicio what Damon said, and he resolved on going to Galatea to get her declaration, and learn what was concealed in her breast, and so changing the road which they left from the cabin they pursued the village road, and coming to a crossway where four paths diverged, on one of them they saw some eight shepherds, all with javelins (azagayos) in their hands, except one, who rode on a very handsome mare, clad in a purple great coat, and the rest on foot, and all their faces were muffled in cloth.

Damon and Elicio stopped until the shepherds had passed; this was very near them, so courteously inclining their heads salutation followed, but never a word.   Most surprised were the twain, to see the unusual appearance of the eight shepherds, and they stood still to observe the road they took, and saw it was towards the village, though not exactly the one to which they purposed going.

Damon remarked to Elicio that they should follow them, but he would not, saying that on the road he had elected to take, near a fountain hard by, he was wont to see Galatea with other shepherdesses of the locality, and he would go and see too if in that spot she could now be found.

Damon acquiesced in Elicio's suggestion, and said he would be guided by him; and fate would have it as he conjectured, for not far in advance they were greeted by the pipe of Florisa, with the accompaniment of the dulcet voice of Galatea, which so enraptured the swains who heard it, that they were enchanted.   Henceforth Damon knew verily how much truth there was in all who had praised Galatea's accomplishments, and who was now in company with Rosaura and Florisa, and the lovely new-married Silveria and a pair of shepherdesses from the same hamlet.   Now, although Galatea saw the swains approaching, yet did she not cease her strain, but rather evinced an inward satisfaction in their hearing it, for to it they gave undivided attention.   What was sung is contained in the accompanying stanzas :—

GALATEA.

1. Towards whom shall I turn my moistened eyes,
   In this woe which besets me ?
   If good from me depart,
   The more distress approaches
   To a hard evil me condemns,
   The plague which me expels.
   If my own native land does this effect,
   What good can then a foreign land do me ?

2. Oh, just obedience get bitter too,
   Which I surrender for accomplishment,

All tending to confirm
The sentence of my death.
For I am bounded in such littleness,
That I should hold it for advantage great,
If life did fail me quite,
Or if at least I were bereft of tongue.

3. Brief hours, and weary
Were those of my content ;
Those of my torture endless,
Confused more, and more oppressive too.
My liberty I enjoyed
In my more moderate season ;
But subjection
Traverses my jealóus liberty.

4. Behold and see if the fierce fight it is
Which fancy doth awake,
If at the termination of his strife
Desire must entertain, yet not desire.
Oh government fastidious,
Which in respect of dear humanity
I cross the hands,
And bow the neck in flexibility.

5. What must I take leave
Of viewing golden Tagus,
Who with my flocks will stay
How sorrowfully I depart
To these sombre trees,
These narrow meads of green.
No more will they be seen
By these my sorrowing eyes.

6. Parent austere to me what doest thou ?
See what thing wisdom is,
If you deprive me of my existence,
To satisfy thyself,
Should my sigh naught avail
My insignificance to you disclose.
What my tongue cannot
Do my eyes indicate in mournfulness.

7. Though sorrowful should picture me
   The point of my departure,
   Sweet glory lost,
   The bitter sepulture besides
   The visage that cannot know merriment—
   No recognised husband,
   The toilsome road,
   And stepmother old and offensive too.

8. And infinite inconveniences
   All set in 'gainst me blank.
   The extraordinary predilections
   Of his parents and the spouse;
   Yet all these alarms,
   Which my lot evidently prefigureth,
   Will close in death,
   Which is the finishing stroke, the end all here.

Galatea sang no more, for tears coursing down her innocent alabaster cheeks, impeded utterance, and put an end to
the satisfaction of all who heard; for soon all well knew
what had hitherto been but confusion as to the projected
union of Galatea with the good swain Lusitano, and how
averse from it she was. But the tears and sighs which induced most affliction were from Elicio, who offered his life
for a remedy, if remedy could therein be found; but availing himself of his discretion, and his face dissembling the
utter grief which his soul felt, he and Damon moved to the
spot where the swains were congregated, whom they courteously saluted, and this was by them not less courteously reciprocated.

Galatea quickly asked Damon for her father, and he replied that he remained in the hermitage of Silerio, with
Timbrio and Nisida, and those who had accompanied them,
and so they proffered a story about the acquaintance of
Silerio and Timbrio, and of the amours of Darintho and
Blanca, Nisida's sister, with all the accompaniments which
had occurred to Timbrio in his love affairs.

To which Galatea replied—" Happy Timbrio, and happy
Nisida, for in such felicity have all your anxieties ended, so
that you may consign to oblivion all antecedent disasters.

They will contribute to augment your glory, for sure it is that the memory of past afflictions swells the satisfaction of all present joys. But woe to the luckless soul which has to close with a lost good, and with apprehension of imminent evil, not seeing nor finding remedy, nor medium for averting the threatened mischance; griefs in a degree fatiguing are commensurate with dread."

"True enough is it, beauteous Galatea," said Damon, " that there is no doubt that a sudden and unexpected grief which arrives does not worry so much, though it o'erleaps us, as that which with much time threatens and withholds all roads for remedy; yet do I aver it, Galatea, that heaven assigns not ills so extreme that all remedy is denied also— especially when at first it lets us not see them, for it would give place to reason, if we exercise ourselves, and be engaged in softening down or deflecting coming misfortunes, and often it is satisfied to annoy us with a semblance of fear, in that ever the same ill reaching us, and if it should come, the end is not yet—none should despair of cure." "Of this I entertain no question," replied Galatea, "if evils were so light which we dread or suffer, as to leave free and unembarrassed the discourse of reason; for well, you know, Damon, when the evil is so large as to deserve that name, the first thing to do is to benumb our sensations, and annihilate the power of free will, letting our virtue droop so low as not to be upheld, though hope should solicit it." "I do not know, Galatea," answered Damon, how in your youthful years you can have such experience in woes, or how, with your discretion, you can give any indication of them."

"Would to heaven," rejoined Galatea, "it were in my power to gainsay your assertion; I should thereby enjoy two things—remain in the good estimation you have of me, and not feel the suffering which so much experience elicits."

To this moment stood Elicio dumb, but unable further to endure the betrayal of grief in Galatea, he said to her—"If you imagine, by chance, incomparable Galatea, that the misadventure which menaces you can be averted anyhow by the will which you know I have to serve you, I would you should declare it to me. But if you will not, in compliance with a paternal injunction, grant me permission to oppose any one who would try to remove from these banks the treasure of your beauty, which is native here ; and know you not, shepherdess, that my presumption is such, that I can and will accomplish in works what I here threaten by words, as the love I bear you, for the great undertaking gives me breath. I disavow reverses, and so I intrust it to reason purely and to the consideration of all the swains whose flocks browze on these banks, who will not agree that they be snatched off, and that the light of their eyes be quenched, in your removal with the discretion which admires, and the beauty which animates them to a thousand honorable rivalries.

"Thus, charming Galatea, by the reason I have summoned, and by that of adoration, this offer I propose, which should induce you to disclose to me your will, that I may oppose you in nothing. Now, considering that thy goodness and incomparable honesty should move you to reply before seeking your father, I do not wish, my shepherdess, that you should declare it to me without my undertaking to do what I should do, always having your honour in view, and that you mean the same thing."

Galatea was about replying to Elicio, and to denote her acquiescence, when the sudden advent of the eight masked swains hindered, the same which Damon and Elicio saw. They all stopped where the ladies were, and, without talking, six of them with incredible speed violently fell on Damon and Elicio, holding them so fast that escape was hopeless.

In the meanwhile the other two (one came on horseback) advanced towards Rosaura, crying out that Damon and Elicio were secure ; yet, without allowing her any defence, one of the swains took her in his arms, and lodged her on the mare, handing her over to the man who removed his disguise, and turned to the company, saying—"Are you not amazed, good friends, at the apparent unreasonableness of these acts, for the force of love, and the ingratitude of this lady justifies it ? I ask pardon, though nothing further is in my hands ; and if in these districts should come (I expect he will) the well known Grisaldo, tell him how Artandro abducted Rosaura, as he would bear her deceits no longer, and if love and injury should induce him to revenge, tell him that Aragon is my country, and where I dwell." Rosaura had fainted in the saddle, and the other swains not wishing to desert Elicio or Damon until Artandro gave his orders; these being freed, took out their knives, and assaulted the seven shepherds, who put hands on what they carried in their breasts, their javelins, telling them how useless the effort would be. "Much less will Artandro gain," replied Elicio, "despite of his treason." "You do not style that treason?" replied one of the others, "for this lady has promised faithfully her hand to Artandro, and now to carry out the mutability of a woman, she denies it, and delivering herself to Grisaldo, has done a crying ill, and which cannot be overlooked by our friend, Artandro. So comfort yourselves, and hold us in better opinion, for this service as our master exculpates us." So, adding no more, round they turned, mistrusting the sorry appearance of Elicio and Damon, who remained in such disgust at not being able to neutralise that force, and so incompetent to take vengeance that they knew not what they said nor what they did. But the excesses of grief on the part of Galatea and Florisa to see Rosaura abducted in that way, were such that the very life of Elicio was endangered, for drawing out his sling, and Damon doing the same, they ran incessantly after Artandro, and at a distance, with skill and vigour, they began hurling stones, so that the pursued turned round and made defence. With all this it had succeeded ill with the two bold swains, had not Artandro ordered his people to advance and stop, just as they reached a thick ascent, adjacent to the road side, so that the stones directed against them were warded off by the trees. They had followed on, had they not seen that Galatea and Florisa and the other two ladies were advancing quickly towards them; so they stopped, giving way to the annoyance which excited them, and to the desired revenge which they pretended.

Advancing to receive Galatea, she said to them—"Moderate your rage, accomplished swains, since to the advantage of our foes, it cannot equal your diligence, though it had been such as the courage of your souls has evinced." "Remarking your discontent, Galatea," said Elicio, "I believe I should impart such strength to mine that those uncourteous swains will not praise themselves for their deeds against us, for in my luck is contained no holding what I desire." "The lover which Artandro has," said Galatea, "was he who moved them to this impropriety, and so with me in part he is exculpated ;" and then consecutively she recounted Rosaura's story, and how she was awaiting Grisaldo to receive him for husband, which might have come to the knowledge of Artandro, and that the rage of jealousy had moved him to enact that which they had witnessed."

"If it is so, as you aver, discreet Galatea," said Damon, " by the carelessness of Grisaldo, and the boldness of Artandro, and the variable temperament of Rosaura, I fear a great deal of woe and difference may arise." " This would be," answered Galatea, " when Artando should reside in Castille, but if he should enclose himself in Aragon, which is his country, Grisaldo would remain only with a desire of vengeance." " Is there no one to advise him of this affront?" said Elicio. " Yes," said Florisa, " for I tell you that ere nightfall he shall have notice of it." " Were that so," replied Damon, " he would (cobrar su prenda) fulfil his pledge ere he reached Aragon, for a breast once inflamed with love is not idle." " I do not think that will be Grisaldo's case," said Florisa, " for should not time nor opportunity fail him, I adjure you, Galatea, that we return to the village, for I would inform Grisaldo of the ill which has befallen him."

"Let us do as you will, my dear," answered Galatea, " and I will furnish you with a shepherd to communicate the news." Hence they desired to take leave of Damon and Elicio, unless they positively wished to accompany them, and as she wended village-wise on their right they heard the rebeck of Erastro, which was readily recognised, who was following his friend Elicio. They stopped to listen, and with touching sorrow they heard the following verses :—

ERASTRO.

1. Through rugged paths I am still following out
  The doubtful end of all my phantasy,
  Ever in covered night, obscured and cold,
  The strength consuming of my precious life.

2. And while I see my end, do not pretend
  From the restricted path to deviate,
  Which, in the faith of an unequalled faith,
  I understand, oppose extended fears.

3. Faith is the light which indicates the port
   Secure from danger, and alone is that
   Which to my journey promises success.

4. More than the medium which uncertain is,
   More than the sacred radiance of my star,
   Doth love encumber, and heaven outrage me.

With a deep sigh closed the enamoured strain of the woful swain, and thinking that no one heard him, he loosened his voice for like reasons—" Love, whose power, without effect on my mind, was the cause why my thoughts were so engaged, since you did me so much good, you do not wish to show yourself now, and do me the evil which you threaten. Your instable condition is worse than fortune. Look, sir, how obedient I have been to your laws, and swift to follow your orders, and how my will has been subservient to yours ; repay me that obedience by doing that which is so essential you should do ; never allow these our banks to be deprived of that beauty which endued is with fresh verdure, giving beauty to the lowly plants and upgrowing trees. Do not consent that from Tagus' stream the pledge be ravished which so enriches it, which is source of its fame, greater than the lands of gold concealed in its bosom. Take not from these shepherd-frequented mountains the light of their eyes, the glory of their meditations, inciting them to infinite honourable and truly virtuous enterprises. Well, consider if from these to other soils the dear Galatea be transported, that you spoil the banks of your undoubted sovereignty, for you use it on account of Galatea, and if that fails, hold it for a fact that you will no longer here be recognised, and all the dwellers therein would repudiate their allegiance, and proffer not the accustomed tribute. Mind, I supplicate you, it is in accordance with reason, that you would go deprived of it, if you do not hear my prayer, for what law, or doing, or what reason agrees that the beauty which we engender, the discretion which finds its source in these woods and hamlets, the grace accorded to this especial region, now we would cull the honest fruit of our riches, be carried off to strange lands for the fruition of others ? Heaven, all piteous, does not wish to inflict on us so notable an evil. O verdant meads which indulged us with her sight !

O odoriferous flowers touched by her feet, replete with every fragrance ! O, plants, and trees of this delicious grove ! do all you can, irrespective of nature, move heaven to grant all we supplicate."

Thus poured forth the swain, shedding tears so much, that Galatea could not refrain, or any of her companions, indicating a sentiment analogous to that produced by the sight of death.

At this juncture of time Erastro came up, and was graciously received by them, who, on observing that Galatea had been a partner in tears, without withdrawing his eyes, stood fixed in admiration for a spell, when he remarked, "Now know I, Galatea, truly that no son of man escapes the blows of mutable fortune, since you, whom by particular privilege, I thought were exempt, I now see are assailed with them; hence I am assured that by one stroke it has pleased heaven to afflict all who know you, and who acknowledge your peculiar virtue. Still do I entertain hope that her rigour will not be so far extended as to protract further misfortune to the prejudice of your contentment." " Even for this very reason," replied Galatea, " am I less secure in my mishap, for I have discovered it in what I desired, yet it does not consist with that honesty which I so much prize, and that implicit obedience due to my parents; so I ask you, Erastro, not to give me occasion to renew my sentiment, nor that you nor any other treat of this affair, which awakens in my mind the nauseousness which I dread ; hence, swains all, I beseech you, let me proceed to the village, for Grisaldo being notified, he awaits his time to be satisfied for the offence committed by Artandro." Erastro was ignorant of the success of Artandro. However, the lady shepherdess, Florisa, in few recounted all, at which Erastro was surprised, thinking that Artandro must be a man of might, who had exposed himself to such an issue.

The swains wished to perform what Galatea ordered ; if then they could not discover all the company of cavaliers, swains, and shepherdesses, who, the previous night had been to Silerio's hermitage, who, in token of great satisfaction, came to the village, taking with them Silerio in a different temper and bearing than hitherto, for he had quitted the hermit character, and became the joyful *fiancé*, as it was with

the beauteous Blanca with equal content and satisfaction to
them both, and his good friends, Timbrio and Nisida, who
had persuaded it, bringing with this wedding all miseries to
a close, and tranquillity to the thoughts which disturbed him,
for Nisida.   So with the rejoicings to which such success
gave rise, all came with indications of it, with music, and
modest, yet ardent songs, from which they ceased when they
recognised Galatea, and those her attendants, all being
greeted with excess of politeness.   Galatea giving to Silerio
the congratulation at his success, and to the elegant Blanca
that of her betrothal.   This did also the shepherds,
Damon, Elicio, and Erastro, who were very warm friends of
Silerio.

When the gratulations ceased, they agreed to prosecute
their road to the hamlet, and for diversion Thirsis besought
Timbrio to end the sonnet which he had began, when he
was recognised by Silerio.   Timbrio offered no apology, but
at the sound of the flute of the zealous Orfenio, with a rare
and sweet voice he sang, and finished his strain which was
as follows :—

TIMBRIO.

1. So well established are my utmost hopes,
   How keen soever blows the subtle wind,
   From the fast moorings shall they ne'er detach;
   Only such faith, force, virtue, reacheth home.

2. So far I yield to a consenting change
   In my firm mind and ever during thought,
   As to accomplish in my rack the end
   Of life, rather than undo confidence.

3. If in love's contest vacillation should
   O'ertake the enamoured breast, it not deserves
   The sweet and tranquil peace of that same love.

4. For this my love which faith doth aggrandize,
   Charybdis rages, Scilla threateneth,
   To the sea falls an offering to love.

The swains thought much of Timbrio's sonnet as well as
the grace of the performance, and it emboldened them to
solicit something more of him ; but he excused himself by

saying that his friend Silerio would answer for him in this particular, as he had done in sundry dangerous contingencies.

Now Silerio could not refuse what his friend suggested; so, delighted to see such a happy state of things, at the sound of Orfenio's flute, he sang—

SILERIO.

1. To heaven be thanks, since I escaped have
   The perils of this much uncertain sea,
   And at the chosen favorable port
   Without due cognizance arrived am.

2. Let us well gather in the sails of care,
   Put in repair the open battered bark,
   The vows fulfil death staring in the face,
   And promises made to the wrathful sea.

3. I kiss the soil, the sky do reverence,
   A lot embracing fully ameliorated,
   Proclaiming happy fatal destiny.

4. To the new chain incomparably mild,
   With new intent and amorous desire
   My wounded neck with cheerfulness I bend.

Silerio ended, and then solicited Nisida to be kind enough to charm those localities with her song, who, looking towards her beloved Timbrio, with her eyes asked permission to give effect to Silerio's solicitation, and he, acquiescing in appearance, the lady, without further delay, but with unusual grace, when the flute of Orfenio had ceased, to the sound of the pipe of Orompo, gave utterance to the words—

NISIDA.

1. Setting at naught the opinion of him who swears,
   That never love did true contentment feel,
   Whence flows the bitterness of acknowledged **pangs,**
   Despite the good which to the luck is joined.

2. I know that good it is, that 'tis ill luck
   I know full well its clear effects, and feel
   That by how much the thought is damaging
   To love's ill attribute, the more's confirmed.

3. Not to see me in power of bitter death,
   By reason of the ill-translated news,
   Or given up to barbarous corsair's hands.

4. Was bitter pain or grief so ponderous,
   That I not know it, and submit to proof
   The sweetest pleasure of a joyful life.

Galatea and Florisa stood amazed at the rapturous voice of the beauteous Nisida, which as it appeared to them that in chaunting about Timbrio and those of his party, they had taken a hand, they wished not that her sister should remain without so doing also ; hence, without much importunity, and with no less grace than Nisida, notifying to Orfenio to give life to his flute, at the sound of which she sang in this strain :—

BLANCA.

1. He who on Libya's sandy desert finds
   Himself, or on far Scythia, bound in cold
   Myself sometimes by fear of frost assailed,
   The warmth of fire ever renovates.

2. Much more the hope which grief alleviates,
   By either extreme thoroughly disguised,
   Found life preserved in its power, now
   By strength supported, now both cool and weak.

3. And though the flame of love should so remain,
   The long expected spring returns in time,
   At the conclusion of the winter's cold.

4. Thus, in sole and fortunate point of time,
   I taste the sweet fruit long awaiting it,
   With proofs extended of a faith sincere.

Both the voice and the words which Blanca sang did not less satisfy the swains than all those who heard, and as they wished to give proofs that all the ability lay not in these polite cavaliers, and simultaneously moved by one sentiment, Orompo, Crisio, Orfenio, and Marsilio began tuning their instruments, when a noise behind them made them to turn their heads, which a certain swain had caused, who with a sort of fury was traversing the briars of a verdant grove, and he

17—2

was recognised by all for the enamoured Lauso, at which
Thirsis was astonished, for the night before he had taken
leave of him, saying that he was bound on a business which
contributed towards finishing his wearisomeness, and making
his joy to dawn ; and so saying no more, he went off with
another swain, his friend, and he knew not what had happened to him, now that he travelled at such speed.

What Thirsis said induced him to wish to call Lauso, and
so called out for him to come. But noting he did not hear,
and that he attained a rising ground, he advanced with all
alacrity, and at the top of the other hillock he turned again
to call louder, which as Lauso heard and recognising the
party calling, he could not but turn, and nearing Damon he
embraced him with signs of extravagant satisfaction, and
this surprised Damon too, and so he said, " What is this,
friend Lauso? Have you accomplished all your wishes,
and is all done since yesterday with so much docility?"
" Much greater is the good I bear, true friend Damon," replied Lauso, "for the cause which seems death and desperation to them, has secured me both hope and life ; and this
has been a disdain and an undeceiving, accompanied by a precise coy lightness, which I have observed in my shepherdess,
which has restored me to my primitive condition already.
Swain, my belaboured neck feels not the heavy amorous
yoke, in my thoughts already is slackened the heavy and
retarding machinery, which dragged me along exhausted
with vanity. Now shall I turn again to the last conversation
of my friends. Now will the green herbs re-appear, and the
sweet smelling flowers of these calm, tranquil plains. My
sighs will have a truce, bail to my tears and rest to my
annoyances. For you will consider, Damon, if this is cause
enough for rejoicing and playfulness." " Yes, it is, Lauso,"
replied Damon ; " yet I fear that so sudden a joy is awakened,
that I doubt its duration, and my experience is that a liberty
begotten of disdain melts like smoke, and lively intention
quickly turns to follow its fancies. So that, good Lauso,
may it please heaven that your satisfaction be firmer, that
what I imagine, and that you may enjoy the liberty which
you preach, which would not only gratify me in what
I owe to your friendship, but discover an unaccustomed
miracle in your amorous intents." " Damon," answered

Lauso, "I now feel my liberty, and am master of my own will, and that your wish should be satisfied in the truth of my assertion, see what you desire should be in confirmation of it. Did you wish me to absent myself? Do you wish that I should not visit again the cottages which you surmise have been cause of my past woes and present joys? I will do aught to satisfy it." "The upshot of all is that you should be content," answered Damon, "and I will see you are so when in half a dozen days you see yourself in the same mind. For the moment, I desire nothing further of you, but that you relinquish the road you go, and will join me in going where the swains and females await us, and as for the joy you boast, that you solemnise it by an entertainment with a song until we reach the village." Lauso was agreeable to do what Damon suggested, so he returned with him whilst Thirsis made signs to Damon, that he should return. So without further politeness, Lauso said, " I come not for less than feasts and contentment, for if you listen with attention, let Marsilio sound his flute, and prepare to hear that which I never thought my tongue would have occasion to say or even my imagination to conceive." All the swains replied that it would give them greater pleasure to listen. And so, directly Marsilio with a desire to listen, touched his instrument, at the sound of which, Lauso commenced a song, in the following manner :—

LAUSO.

1. With bended knees on the receiving soil,
   And hands in posture of humility,
   And heart replete with ardour passionate,
   I thee adore ; holy disdain, in which
   Are writ the causes of delicious feasts,
   By me enjoyed in peaceful, virtuous times.
   Thou, from the rigour of sharp poison's tooth,
   Which closely compasseth the ills of love,
   The surest and the readiest medicine wert ;
   Thou, my destruction, turned me into good.
   Thy war to peace—a treasure infinite—
   Not once, but countless times, I thee adore.

2. For thee the radiance of my now wearied eyes,
   For so long time disturbed, and almost gone,

To the first being is turned which it retained—
For thee I turn the plunder to enjoy,
Which from my life and my volition
The antique tyranny of love did raise
For thee the night of error into day,
Of serene reason is changed, where reason was
In a slave's keeping, with a peaceful course.
Discreet, being now my mistress, me conducts
Where good Eterne developes more and more.

3. Me hast thou shown disdain, how fraudulent,
   How false and feign'd have ever been the signs
   Of love which you have pointed out to me,
   And that the amorous words which fed the ear,
   Which from itself the soul did alienate,
   Forcing itself to falsehood and contempt.
   The dainty soft sight of those eyes alone,
   Was that my early spring should sudden change
   Into a winter's harshness, when the clear
   Deception should stand forth, but truly thou,
   Oh, sweet disdain has found true remedy.

4. Disdain, whose office is the sharpened spur,
   Guiding the thought upon the rugged road,
   To the desired, amorous enterprise.
   In me condition and effect are change,
   That I for thee did separate from intent,
   Myself, running behind with speed unseen.
   And though the cruel, during love does not
   Cease from afflicting evil; yet will I
   Extend anew the snare to compass me.
   And, more to offend expose my breast to shots,
   Alone disdain, alone cans't thou avert
   His arrows, and deftly destroy his nets.

5. My love was ne'er so feeble, artless though,
   That one disdain could trample it to earth,
   It had required a hundred thousand fold.
   Just so without enduring long the stroke,
   The pine comes to the earth, on which it rolls
   By virtue of the last effective blow.
   Heavy disdain—of severe countenance,
   Founded in alienation from true love,

And in small estimation of a lot,
Foreign, to see it sweet has been the sight.
To hear and handle it, and with what joy
Hast thou been in conjunction with the soul,
Which thou down casts, madness accomplishing.

6. My madness you accomplish, and lend hand
To wisdom, wit, disdain, raising itself,
Shaking from off itself the heavy sleep;
That with a better and more sound intent,
New greatness and new praises, I may sing
Of others—if a grateful master is found.
From poison hast extorted all its force
With which ungrateful love my virtue pressed
Has numbed, and with thy ardent virtue hast
In me brought back new life and management.
And now I understand that I am he,
Can fear appreciate, without dread can hope.

Lauso sang no more; though what he had sung sufficed to impress admiration on all present, and as all knew that the day before he was enamoured and content so to be, it was a cause of wonder to all to observe how he had changed. This being well pondered, his friend Thirsis said to him, "I know not if I should gratulate you, friend Lauso, on the good attained so briefly, for I surmise you are not so firm as you suppose; yet I rejoice that you enjoy in so short a space the satisfaction which accrues to an attained liberty; yet it might be, that knowing how to appreciate it, although you revert to your broken chains and snares, you might employ more force to break them, attracted by the sweetness and delight which a free mind enjoys, with a calm, impartial will." "Do you entertain no dread, wise Thirsis?" replied Lauso, "that no new wile will induce me to settle my limbs in the amorous stocks, nor do you hold me to be of so much levity and so fanciful that it has not cost me something to put myself in the position I am; a thousand suspicions, infinite fulfilled promises made to heaven, that I might again turn to the lost light, and then in it I see how little before I saw, so I will strive to keep it in the best way I shall be able." "Nothing will be so good," said Thirsis, "as not returning to see what you have left behind; for

you will lose, if you turn, the liberty which has cost you so
much, and you will remain, as did that incautious lover,
with new cause for incessant grief, and hold for certain this,
friend Lauso, that there is no enamoured breast in the
world which disdain and qualified arrogance do not make
to slacken in eagerness, and even to secede from ill-adjusted
thoughts, and it makes me give credence to this truth, which
is to know what Silena is, though you have never told me, and
to know also her changeable character, her quickened im-
pulses, and the plainness, to give it no other appellation,
of her desires—things, which not to moderate and disguise
them with the unequalled beauty with which nature has
endowed her, yet which the world would have in aversion."

" You say truth," replied Lauso, " for doubtless her singular personal charms, and the semblance of the incomparable
integrity in which she arrays herself, are qualities for which
she is not only sought, but adored by those who behold her.
And thus no one should wonder that my free will had
yielded to such powerful contraries ; it is just that one
should be surprised how I escaped from them ; for since I
rise from her hands so illtreated, the will vitiated, the mind
bewildered, the memory in decadence, yet I seem to triumph
in the fray."

The two shepherds did not prosecute further their discourse, for they discerned, by the very road that they travelled, coming a beauteous shepherdess, and a little aside of
her a swain, who was soon recognised for the ancient Arsindo,
and the lady as the sister of Galercio, by name Maurisa—
who, being known by Galatea and Florisa, they understood
that with some message of Grisaldo for Rosaura, she had
come ; and as they advanced both to receive her, Maurisa
sprang forward to embrace Galatea, while the old Arsindo
saluted the swains and embraced his friend Lauso, who was
standing with earnest interest to know that which Arsindo
had done since they spoke to him who had gone in pursuit
of Maurisa.   And seeing him now return with her, he began
quickly to lose with her and the others all the credit which
his snowy locks had acquired for him, and even had finished in
losing, had not they which came not known by experience
how far the potency of love extended, and so in those who
blamed him, he found the extenuation of his error.

It seemed that Arsindo divining just what the swains conjectured of him, as if in satisfaction and extenuation of his care, said to them : " Hear, swains, one of the most extraordinary amorous events, which for many years on these banks or on any other has been seen. I well believe that you know, and we know all, the famous shepherd Lenio, whose disenamoured state acquired for him the *sobriquet* of the disenamoured—who, not many days, from speaking evil of love, was bold enough to come into rivalry with the famous Thirsis, now present; that same man, I assert, who could scarce wag his tongue save to libel love, and who with very vehemence reprehended those who were depressed by love's griefs.

" Now this openly declared foe to love, has come to such a decision, that I know for certain he considers not in love any one who may pursue it eagerly; nor does he hold him vassal to any who may persecute it; for it has made him in love with the disenchanted Gelasia, that cruel shepherdess, who to the brother of the same, hinting to Maurisa, in what condition he was, him he found the other day as you saw, with a rope at his neck to finish with his hands of cruelty his short and uncomfortable days. I say, in fine, swains, let the disenchanted Lenio die for the stony-hearted Gelasia, for her filling the air with sighs, and the soil with tears; and what is even worse, it appears to me that love has desired to avenge himself on the refractory heart of Lenio, surrendering it to the most unaccommodating and coy lady ever seen; knowing him, how he tries in all he says and does to reconcile himself with love; and for the very end for which he blamed love, now he exalts and honours it, and yet with all this neither does love move to favour him, nor Gelasia feel disposed to remedy it, as these very eyes can testify.

Only a brief time ago, coming in company with this lady, we found him at the pebble-font, extended on the ground, his face covered with a cold sweat, and his breast panting with extraordinary speed. I advanced to him, and I took him up, and bathed his visage in the fountain's stream, which recovered his lost spirits, and I asked him the reason of his woe, which, without any hesitation, he declared in tender expressions, how the lady was the cause, and this, too, without any sympathy from her. He magnified the cruelty of Gelasia, and the loves between them, and the suspicion which he entertained that love had drawn him on to take vengeance of the wrongs love had done him. I consoled him the best I could, and leaving him free of the paroxysm, I came, attended by this lady, to seek you, Lauso, for aid, and that you would return to our cottages, for it is now ten days since we set out, and we think our flocks will miss us more than we shall miss them.

"I know not, Arsindo, if I should reply," answered Lauso, "that for mere compliment you ask us to return to the cottages, having as much to do in other cottages, as absence from home for some days has shown. But setting aside what more may be said, for better convenience, may I ask if what Lenio says is true, for if it be so, I will affirm that love has enacted greater miracles in two days than in all his life besides,—namely, reducing and enslaving the hard heart of Lenio, and setting at liberty mine, which was subject to love."

"See to what you say," interposed then Orompo, "friend Lauso, for if love holds you captive, as you have indicated, how does the same love liberate you as you declare?"

"Would you understand me, Orompo," said Lauso, "you will discern that in nothing do I contradict myself, for I say, or would rather say, that the love which reigned and still reigns in the breast of that party, whom I so much desired, as it wends a different way from mine, since all is love, the effect which it has had in me is to land me in liberty and Lenio in bondage, and this, Orompo, you do but count as other miracles." This saying, he reverted his eyes towards the veteran Arsindo, and with them he said that about which the tongue was silent, for all understood that the third miracle on which one could count, was seeing the white locks of Arsindo enamoured of the few and green years of Maurisa, who, all this time, was standing talking apart with Galatea and Florisa, saying to them how another day Grisaldo would be in the village in peasant's costume, and that there he thought of espousing Rosaura clandestinely, for in public he could not, by reason that the parents of Leopersia, with whom his father purposed marrying her, had learned that Grisaldo wished to be off the promise, and in no way did they like that such an affront should be offered.   Yet with all this Grisaldo was resolved to correspond with all that was due to Rosaura rather than encounter the obligations due to his father.

"All I aver, ladies," continued Maurisa, "my relative Galercio told me I might communicate, who came to you with this messuage.   But this cruel Gelasia, whose charms have ravished the soul of my unfortunate brother, was the reason why he could not come to make this communication, for to follow her he ceased to pursue the road which he was going, trusting in me as my sister.   Now you have heard, ladies, at what I am come.   Where is Rosaura to allege it ? Or do you say so, for the strait in which my brother is, will not admit of my remaining longer."

When the lady had so said, Galatea stood meditating as to the cutting reply she thought of administering, and the woful news which came to the hearing of the wretched Grisaldo.   Yet, seeing there was no excuse for abstaining, and it was worse to detain her, immediately she recounted all that had happened to Rosaura, and how Artandro had abducted her, at which Maurisa was deeply surprised, and instantly desired to turn round and advise Grisaldo, if Galatea had not detained her, asking her what the two ladies had done that they had gone with Galercio and her. To this Maurisa replied, "I could recount to you things about them, Galatea, which would throw you into greater astonishment than even I have been as to what has befallen Rosaura, but time fails me.   I only say that the person styled Leonarda has been betrothed to my brother Artidoro by the most subtle artifice one has ever seen, and that Teolinda is fluttering on death's domains, or else will lose her intellect, the sight of Galercio alone supporting her.   Since what has happened to my brother Artidoro, she does not separate at all from his company, a thing as troublesome and annoying to Galercio as is the company of the cruel Gelasia sweet and attractive.   The method of how all this came to pass I will relate to you more at leisure when next we meet, for there will be no reason that by my delay the remedy be stopped which Grisaldo can have in his misfortune, and apply all diligence to amend it ; because it was only this morning that Artandro abducted Rosaura, and cannot be so very far from these shores, as to remove all hope of Grisaldo's recovering her, and the more so if I hasten (aguijo) as I think."

All seemed well to Galatea that Maurisa said, and so did not wish to detain her. She only requested her to return and see her as quickly as possible, to recount the success of Teolinda, and what had been done in Rosaura's case. The shepherdess promised it, and so without further detention, taking leave of those near, returned to the hamlet, giving satisfaction to all in the prodigality of beauty and gracefulness. But he who most felt her parting was the veteran Arsindo, who, not to indicate his desires too obviously, remained alone without Maurisa, but environed by thoughts. The shepherdesses, however, remained suspended as to what they heard relative to Teolinda, and were very anxious to learn the event, and standing thus inclined, they heard the clear sound of a cornet on the left hand, and turning their eyes they discovered, on a hillock, two venerable-looking swains, and between them an old priest, whom they soon recognised as the veteran Telesio: and one of the swains having again sounded the cornet, all the three came down from the rising ground, and went towards a spot adjacent, which mounting, they returned to give the instrument breath, at the sound of which many swains began to move from different parts to arrive where they might see what Telesio wanted, for by that signal he was wont to convoke the swains of that bank, when he would communicate something promising, or inform them of the decease of some shepherd of note thereby, or else remind them of some solemn day of festival, or melancholy obsequies. Then Aurelio and all the hinds that came, knowing the habit and condition of Telesio, approached where he stood, and when they all reached the spot, they united. Now when Telesio saw so much people, and knew how influential all were, descending from the hillock, he went to receive them with respect and courtesy, and so was equally well received of them.

Aurelio, going up to Telesio, said to him, "Recount to us, honourable and venerable Telesio, if in courtesy you will, what new motive induces you to join the swains of these meadows? Is it by chance the joyous festivities or lugubrious funeral rites? Would you point out to us something to improve our lives? Tell us, Telesio, what your will ordains, since you know that our wills will not rise up against what your will desires."

"May heaven repay you, shepherds," replied Telesio, "the sincerity of your intents, for all conforms to what contributes to your advantage. But to satisfy the desire you have to know what I would, I wish you to hold in remembrance the valour and reputation of the famous, and in merit surpassing shepherd Melisso, whose melancholy obsequies we renew, and we shall do so annually as long as shepherds dwell hereabouts, so that there be no omission of what is due to the courage and virtue of Melisso. At least I can dare say as far as I am concerned, and while my life is spared, I will never cease paying, seasonably, the respect due to the capacity, courtesy and true virtue of the incomparable Melisso, and so I now advise you that to-morrow is the anniversary of his death, by which we have lost so much in the person of the prudent shepherd Melisso, so I request you that to-morrow, at break of day, you will all congregate in the cypress valley, where lies the sepulchre of the honoured ashes of Melisso, that we there, with sorrowful plaints and pious sacrifices, may try to alleviate the pain, if any, of that much-enduring soul which has abandoned us to solitude. This saying, and with the tender concern which the memory of Melisso's death had caused, his venerable eyes were filled with drops, and it was not the less so with all those who attended, who, with one accord, offered to assist another day where Telesio should assign, and likewise did Timbrio and Silerio, Nisida and Blanca appear not to relinquish the solemn occasion, hence in union with so many celebrated swains, they also joined. Therewith they took leave of Telesio, and returned to pursue their projected path villagewards. However, they were not far from the appointed place, when they met, point blank, the disenamoured shepherd Lenio, with a visage so wan and distressing, that admiration seized all, and so transported was he in idea, and so absent, that he almost touched the company without perceiving it, in fact he bore off to the left, and had not proceeded far, when he threw himself down at the basis of a green willow, and giving a sigh so piteous

and profound, he upraised his hand, and placing it on the
collar of his pelisse, he heaved again deeply, and tore his
garments to pieces, and immediately he detached the
shepherd's pouch from his side, and drawing therefrom a
polished instrument, with great attention and calmness
began to tune it, and at the close of a brief space, with a
melancholy and pre-arranged voice, began singing so that he
constrained all who had seen him to stay and listen to the
end of his ditty, which was as follows :—

LENIO.

1. Sweet love, indeed I do repent me now
   Of my defiance past.
   This day do I confess, and feel at heart,
   It was on folly
   That its cement was proudly elevated.
   Now the rebellious neck erected is,
   Humbly I lower it, and reduce it eke
   To yoke of thy obedience
   The potency already know
   Of thy far-outspread virtue.

2. I know that thou can'st perpetrate what thou wilt,
   And that you will what is impossible.
   I know you indicate well who thou art,
   E'en in thy terrible condition.
   In thy pleasures, in thy pains ;
   And well I know that he I am
   Who your good evilly have taken ;
   Your deceit for candour,
   Thy assurance for deceit,
   And for endearments your profound disdain.

3. These things well known
   Have now discovered
   In the inward recesses of my heart
   That you the door were
   Where our life solace finds.
   You the whirlwind implacable,
   The soul tormenting,
   Turn into serene calm.
   You are the joy and light of the pure soul,
   The very food which it in health sustains.

4. Since, then, do I this judge and this confess,
   Though late I come to it,
   Moderate thy vigour and excess;
   Love, and from the bended neck and knees,
   Lighten somewhat the onus.
   On the already vanquished enemy
   No castigation need inflicted be;
   And as he does who doth himself protect,
   By so much more as he doth here offend,
   He seeks to be thy friend.

5. From obstinacy I emancipate
   Myself in which my malice placed me;
   And being in disgrace
   Unto your justice I appeal
   Before the face of grace,
   So that if to my slender virtue's power
   The favour tries me not
   Of your recognised grace,
   Quickly shall I abandon my poor life,
   To the grasp of grief resigned.

6. The hands of Gelasia have me lodged
   In such extreme of agony,
   That if there be defiance in it yet,
   My grief and my defiance,
   I know that all will soon end fatally.
   Oh, hard-hearted Gelasia! coy,
   Heartless, inaccessible and proud,
   Why, then, desire, oh lady say!
   That the heart which thee adores
   Should in such tortures for an hour be plunged?

Little was it that Lenio sang, but the wailings were
not so, for he had remained there dissolved in tears had
not the other shepherds assisted to console him.

But when he saw them advancing, and he recognised
Thirsis among them, without more hesitation up he rose,
and went to project himself at his feet, embracing closely
his knees, and, without letting a tear drop, said to him,
"Now you can, illustrious swain, seize vengeance for the
audacity which I took in competing with you, defending
the unjust cause which my ignorance propounded. Now, I

say, you may raise your arm, and with some sharp knife transfix this heart, which contains so much simplicity as not to recognise love to be universal sovereign of the world. But of one fact I would advertise you, that if you would take just revenge of my error, that you leave me with the life which I sustain, which is such that there is no death comparable to it."

Thirsis had now arose from the soil towards the bewildered Lenio, and holding him in his arms, with discreet and loving expressions essayed to console him, saying, "The great fault which exists in faults, friend Lenio, is obstinacy in them, for it is the condition of devils never to repent of faults committed, and thus one of the principal motives which impels us to pardon offences is to observe repentance in the offender, and the more so when pardon dwells in the hands of him who is perfectly disinterested, his noble state draws and forces him to do justice, remaining more rich and content with the pardon than with vengeance, as we daily see in those great exemplars, and kings, who arrogate to themselves more glory in pardoning than in exacting retribution; and since you, oh, Lenio, confess your error, and admit the o'erpowering quality of love, and recognise love to be king of kings, by reason of this new admission and solid repentance you may dwell in confidence and live safely, and be assured that a soft and generous love will bring you again to a tranquil and amorous state, and if now he punishes you with the pains you have experienced, do all, that you may know him, and that in future you may appreciate him duly."

To these ratiocinations others equally pertinent added Elicio, and the rest of the swains, whereby it seemed as if Lenio was quite appeased.

And directly he had stated how that he was dying for love of the insensible lady Gelasia, exaggerating her coy and unusual deportments, and how free and exempt she was from all effects of love, enhancing also the insufferable torture which for her the kind and gentle shepherd, Galercio, suffered, of which she took so little notice, that a thousand times he had been in the jaws of black despair.

But after a while they had reasoned on these facts, they turned as if to prosecute their path, taking Lenio with them, and without further adventure they reached the village, joining in the band Elicio, Damon, Erastro, Lauso, and Arsindo.

With Daranio there went Crisio, Orfenio, Marsilio, and Orompo. Florisa and the rest of the females accompanied Galatea and her father, Aurelio, it having been previously arranged that on the morrow at break of day they should unite to go to the valley of the cypresses, as Thelesio had enjoined them to celebrate the funeral rites due to Meliso.

At which, as before announced, they desired to find Timbrio, Silesio, Nisida, and Blanca, who lodged with the venerable Aurelio that very night.

BOOK VI.

Silesio, to the sound of his cornet, has a rural gathering, to assist at the funeral rites of Meliso.—Marsilio is exhorted to take courage respecting Belisa.—The holy valley is entered, and its description.—Sepulchre of shepherds, and particularly that of Meliso.—Address of Telesio, after which he orders the consecrated fire to be kindled, and walks round the pyre, diffusing incense, apostrophising Meliso, and reiterating orisons.—Address of praise, and exhortation to virtue.—Reunion of instruments.—Thirsis, Damon, Elicio, and Lauso interchange mournful stanzas in protracted lines.—An appeal from Telesio.—The women seek a certain section of the valley, and with them six of the eldest swains.—Nocturnal repast, and the visitors remain during night around Meliso's tomb.—A mass of fire appears, which Telesio approaches to discover the cause of the phenomenon.—In the centre arises a graceful nymph.—Her vesture.—The vision opens its arms on both sides, and delivers an address, in which she adverts to the lofty origin of poesy.—Declares herself to be the goddess of song, Calliope, and particularises the poets to whom she has been especial patroness.—Finally she seizes a harp, at whose sounds the heavens cleared up, and a novel splendour illumined the earth.—She sings the deeds of all illustrious Spanish bards, with some specifications to the extent of one hundred and ten stanzas of eight lines each.—At the close, the burning element, whose flames had diverged, reunited, and the nymph disappeared in the awful blaze.—Telesio descants on the immortality of the soul, and the good which lives after we are interred. — Exhorts the multitude to return to their homes, treasuring the memory of what the muse had inculcated.—Adjourn to the streamlet of Palms.—On the suggestion of Aurelio, Erastro awakened his rebeck, and Arsindo his pipe, and lending a hand to Elicio, he ventured on a dithyrambic ode, which was followed by Marsilio, in an equally impassioned mood.—This fired up Erastro who added to the harmony.—Crisio's love state impels him to give vent to his feelings.—Damon and Lauso, bringing up the rear, so that in broken air trembling, the wild music floats.—Galatea's voice could not be suppressed, and the general chorus was completed by the exquisite singing of Nisida and Belisa.—Meeting at the palms.—Aurelio proposes efforts of wit, riddles, conundrums, &c., himself giving the example.—The rest followed, and there is as much wit displayed in propounding as unravelling riddles.—A sudden sound is heard on Tagus' banks, and two swains are seen to hold down a young shepherd, who attempted suicide by drowning ; it was

Galercio, brother of Artidoro.—Teolinda addresses Galatea.—A piece of paper falls from the bosom of the suicide, which was placed on a tree to dry.—Gelasia's cruelty was the cause of the sad attempt.—She sings some verses with marked apathy.—Lenio also recites verses.—Galatea inquires about Artidoro, on which some explanation ensues.—Teolinda melts in tears.—Songs of Galercio to Gelasia.—Interlocution of Thirsis and Elicio.—Galatea disconcerted at her friend's farewell.—Letter of Galatea to Elicio, and his reply, which was entrusted to Maurisa.—Swains propose addressing Galatea's father about the forced marriage of his daughter.—Elicio's song.—In the morning Elicio receives his friends.—They agree, if Aurelio did not consent to revoke his decree respecting Galatea's marriage, that they would use violence to counterwork it, for they could not tolerate that she should be wedded to a stranger.

SCARCELY had the rays of the golden Phœbus began to display themselves on the lowest line of our horizon when the ancient and venerable Telesio caused the inhabitants of the hamlet to hear the melancholy sound of his cornet; a signal which moved all who heard it to quit the repose of their pastoral couches, and assist at what Tilesio requested.

But the first who gave effect to it were Elicio, Aurelio, Daranio, and all the shepherds there congregated of both sexes, not omitting the lovely Nisida and Blanca, and the venturesome Timbrio and Silerio, with divers other cheerful country inhabitants, who joined them to the number of thirty. Among the which went the incomparable Galatea, new miracle of beauty, and the late espoused Silveria, who was accompanied by the fair and disdainful Belisa, for whom the shepherd Marsilio suffered such amorous and mental anguish. Belisa had come on a visit to Silveria, to give her a greeting on her new state, and she hoped to find herself assisting in the celebrated obsequies which she trusted the many and famous shepherds would celebrate. All, however, sallied forth from the hamlet, where they found Telesio, with other shepherds, their friends, clothed so that they looked as if some melancholy business was on foot. Immediately, Telesio ordered, with the purest intentions, and the most subdued thought, that on that day should be celebrated solemn sacrifices, that all the swains should join the cortège, but separated from the females, and it was so; so that the few were content, and the more satisfied, especially the passionate Marsilio, who caught a view of the love-repudiating

Belisa, at whose sight he was so bewildered and beside himself that his friends Orompo, Crisio, and Orfenio noted it,
and, seeing him thus, approached him, and Orompo said to
him, "Courage, friend Marsilio, courage, and give no reason
by your faintheartedness to reveal your want of valour;
know you, as if heaven, moved to compassion at your woe,
has conducted to these banks the shepherdess Belisa for
your relief?" "Quite the opposite, it is to overthrow me,
as I believe," said Marsilio, "she is arrived here, and this
is fear enough. But I will do what you suggest, if, peradventure, in this hard trial, there dwell with me more
reason than feeling." With this Marsilio recovered his
serenity, and the shepherds and the women, each assuming
their own order, as Telesio had commanded, began to enter
the valley of the cypresses, guarding a singular silence, until
Timbrio, astonished at seeing the freshness and loveliness of
the pellucid Tagus, on whose banks they walked, turning
to Elicio, who was at his side, said to him, "Not a little
wonder does it cause me to note the incomparable beauty
of these fresh banks, and reasonably, too, for he who has
seen, as I have, the spaciousness of the renowned Betis,
and those which clothe and adorn the famous Ebro, and the
well-known Pisuerga; and in remote lands has passed the
sacred Tiber's shores, and the amenity of the Po, celebrated
for the fall of that temerarious youth, to say nothing of
having traversed the fresh borders of the peaceful-running
Lebetus, reason good why wonder should move me to see
other spots."

"You deflect not so far from the straight road in your
remark, as I think, prudent Timbrio," replied Elicio, "that
you see not with eyes the reason of your opinion, for in
verity you may believe that the amenity and freshness of the
river's banks give a notorious and recognised advantage to
all you have cited, though we should annex thereto those of
the far separated Xanthus, the memorable Anfriso, and the
enamoured Alpheus. For experience ratifies the fact, that,
in almost line direct on the greater part of these river-sides
there is a shining climate, and, with an extensive area and
brightness, it seems to invite to a rejoicing of the heart,
however averse to it. Now, if this be true, and that the
constellations and sun are supported from the nether waters,

I positively give credence to the idea that this river is instrumental in creating the beauty which environs it, as I shall believe that God, who, for a like reason dwells in the heavens, in this section has also made his habitation the earth which embraces it, vested in an infinity of verdure, seems to create festivals, and to delight in the possession of a donative so rare and delectable, and the golden stream, as if in exchange in the embraces of it, sweetly intertwining itself, fashions a thousand entries and outgoings, which, to him who admires, surcharge the soul with pleasure ineffable; whence it occurs, that, though the eyes turn and return countless times to view, yet new joy is ever found, and wonders without end. Turn now your orbs, valorous Timbrio, and mark how hamlets and rich cottages embellish these banks, which seem established for them.

"Here we observe, in each season of the year, that the laughing spring unites with the lovely Venus, in short and amorous garment, and Zephyr, the companion, with Flora, mother of all, beyond diffusing, with liberal hand various and odoriferous flowers; and mark what the industry of the dwellers has done, that nature married to art, constitutes a sort of turn, a third nature, to which as yet no name is assigned. With its well-cultivated gardens, before which even the Hesperides, and those of Alcinous, ('which one day bloomed, and fruitful were the next') should be silent. The dense woods, the peaceful olive, laurels green, and myrtles rounded like to cups. Its fertile pastures, cheerful vales, and well-clothed hillocks, founts and rivulets, which these banks can boast, I need add no more, but that, if the Elysian plains are extant, here they must be.

"What shall I subjoin of the mechanism of those lofty wheels which in endless revolution draw the liquid element from the profound waters, and humectate the arable, which is disjoined from the pasture land?

"And, above all, let us add to this the bevies of fair shepherdesses which in this vicinity do dwell. For whose testimony, segregating what experience teaches, and what you, O Timbrio, who are an indweller here, and hast seen, it suffices to adduce that shepherdess whom you see here."

And, so saying, he made signals with his crook to Galatea; and, adding no more, he left Timbrio to discern the

prudence and language which he had employed in praise of
Tagus' banks, and the fascinations of Galatea.

So, in reply, as no one could gainsay the remarks, in
these and others he beguiled the weariness of the way, until they caught sight of the cypress valley, where they
observed to sally forth as many more shepherds, and their
female train, as were in their own band.

All coming together, and with subdued pace, they began
their entry to the holy valley, whose site was so unspeakably
lovely, that even to them, accustomed to its view, it engendered new taste, and novel wonder. There arose on one
side of the far-famed Tagus' banks in four different and opposed quarters four green and pasture-clothed spots, as
walls and fortifications to this enchanting vale, which lay in
the centre, an approach to which by four ways was made,
which same hillocks stretched out so, that they formed four
huge and pasture-provided ways, constituting a wall on all
sides of lofty and countless cypresses, so beautifully arranged, that their boughs interwoven so did grow that none
dared traverse the other, or project at all.

In the closely-occupied space between the cypresses appeared roses and sweet jessamines, blended as are in the
well-protected vineyards, the thorny brambles, and the
prickly briars. At intervals from these fertile accesses
through the green and slender grass are seen brooks of clear
and salubrious water, which owe their origin to the niches
in the hills. At the termination of these paths is a narrow
round spot, which the rising ground and the cypresses form,
in whose centre stands an artificial fountain, fabricated of
white but precious marble, and so artfully constructed that
the rarities of the renowned Tivoli, and the grandeurs of
ancient Sicily can scarce hold comparison. With the water
of this marvellous fountain are moistened and sustained the
fresh flowrets of this delicious locality, and what superadds
to the site worthy estimation and reverence, is its being
appropriated to the sensitive palates of simple lambs and
gentle sheep, and all kinds of herds, serving as warders and
treasurers, of the honoured remains of some celebrated shepherds, which, by the general decree of their survivors all
round these banks, is assigned to them as a worthy place of
sepulture.

So there are seen between many and various trees which grow at the back of the cypresses, in the place and distance, into the skirts of the hillock, some graves, some of jasper, some of wrought marble, and on white stones are visible the inscriptions of those interred within.

But what exceeds all other beauty, and is more patent to the eye, is the monument of the shepherd Meliso, aside from the rest, adjacent to a narrow spot of polished and dark stones, and made of white and well-chiselled alabaster. At the very time that Telesio caught this, turning his eyes towards his agreeable company, in a subdued tone and plaintive accent, spoke—

"You here see, worthy swains, prudent and graceful shepherdesses. Here I repeat it; you see the mournful sepulture where rest the honoured bones of Meliso, once renowned—the honour and glory of our shores. Let us now lift up our hearts in humility to heaven, and with pure purpose, much tears and deep sighs, intone the holy hymns and devout prayers, and beseech it to receive, in the starry mansion, the blessed soul of him who lies here." So saying, he advanced towards a cypress, and cutting off some boughs he made a sorrowful garland wherewith to encircle his time-honoured brows, making signs to the others to follow his example. This moved all the rest, and they crowned themselves with melancholy boughs, and, led by Telesio, reached the cemetery, in which place the first thing done by him was to bend on their knees and salute the dull, cold marble. This did they all, and so softened were they at his memory, that their tears bedewed the stone as they kissed it.

This ended, Telesio ordered the consecrated fire to be kindled, and in a brief time they heaped up hearths in which the cypress only was consumed, while the venerable Telesio, with grave and quiet steps, walked round the pyre, precipitating into the burning flames a quantity of sacred and sweet-smelling incense. At each act he uttered a short and holy orison to pray for the departed soul of Meliso; at the close, he lifted up his tremulous voice, while all the bystanders, in a mournful accent, responded amen at three different times, at whose lamentable emission all the neighbouring hillocks and separated valleys re-echoed, while the boughs of the lofty cypresses, and the many trees which grew in the valley, smitten with a gentle breeze which blew, made and issued forth a dumb yet most lugubrious whisper, as if in sign, or that they really participated in the mournful sacrifice.

Thrice did Telesio circumambulate the sepulchre, and thrice did he reiterate the piteous prayers, and nine times was amen repeated.

This ceremony over, the aged Telesio leaned against a cypress, very lofty, which grew at the head of Meliso's grave, and revolving his orbs on either side, caused the congregation to be attentive to what he wished to deliver, and so incontinently raising his voice as much as his mature age would allow, with astonishing fluency began praising the virtues of Meliso, the integrity of his blameless life, the loftiness of his genius, the entireness of his mind, and the graceful gravity of his conversation, with the superiority of his poetry, and, above all, the care and solicitude he had for the strict sustentation of his own religious views, annexing thereto an infinity of virtues which were well known to all who heard him, and that he should be loved of all, were it for these virtues alone, if he were among the quick, and should now, as departed, be equally reverenced.

The old man ended his discourse by adding, " If Meliso's goodness reaches this acme, famous swains, and so I try to give condign praise, the lowness of my understanding, and the weak and slender force occasioned by my accumulated years, intercept my voice and breath, ere this sun, which illumines us, you should witness it bathed in the mighty ocean, before I would cease my discourse; but as my decayed age will not allow it, supply my failings, and show yourselves gracious to the cold ashes of Meliso, celebrating them in death, as love directs us in life to do. And as all this appertains to all, it falls especially on the two famous individuals Thirsis and Damon as well known to him and his associates, and fast friends. So to the utmost of my power, I beseech you answer this debt, supplying and singing, with the most subdued and sonorous voice, what I have omitted by reason of my vocal infirmity."

Telesio said no more, nor was it necessary for the swains to do what he enjoined ; so without adding more, Thirsis took out his dulcimer, and made signal to Damon that he would do so likewise, while Elicio and Lauso accompanied them, and all those swains who had instruments of sweet stop with them. Soon they got up a sorrowful and not unacceptable music, which, while it regaled the auditory nerves, moved their hearts to give signs of sorrow with tears to correspond. United to this was the dulcet harmony of the painted sparrow, which crossed the mid-way air, and some sobs which the women, already subdued to the reasoning of Telesio, and with what the swains had done, beating from time to time their beauteous busts, and so it was that this concord of sweet sounds in sorrowful music, with the melancholy harmony of the goldfinches, larks and nightingales, and the bitterness of deep groans, formed, in all, a strange and afflictive concert which no tongue can enhance. In a brief space, the instruments ceasing, were heard only the four, which belonged to Thirsis, Damon, Elicio and Lauso, who, approaching the tomb of Meliso, located themselves at the four sides, a signal whence all present should understand that they wished to sing something. Hence there was a calm and wondrous silence, and incontinently the far-renowned Thirsis, with a due elevation of voice, sorrowful yet sonorous, assisting Elicio, Damon and Lauso, began to sing in the following manner :—

THIRSIS.
1. What is the just occasion of complaint,
   Not only ours, but of the soil entire ?
   Shepherds, tune up the sorrowful canticle.

DAMON.
2. The air invading, even to the clouds,
   Are doleful sighs, fashioned and struck off,
   Just pity and just sorrowing between.

ELICIO.
3. With tender moisture ever shall be bathed
   My lids, so long as memory endure,
   Meliso, of thy much renowned feats.

LAUSO.
4. Meliso, worthy of immortal fame,
   Worthy in holy heaven to enjoy
   Cheerful existence and deathless renown.

THIRSIS.

5. Whilst to the greatness I upraise myself,
To sing his deeds, as I do think we ought,
Shepherds, tune up your sorrowful canticle.

DAMON.

6. How I, Meliso, may due recompense give
To your pure friendship with outpoured tears,
With holy orisons, and incense sweet.

ELICIO.

7. Thy death to grief truly converted has
Our sweet passed joys, reducing their effect
To one entire and tender sentiment.

LAUSO.

8. Those days renowned, void of obscurity,
Wherein the world his presence did enjoy,
To cold and miserable nights are turned.

THIRSIS.

9. Oh death, who, with such hasty violence
Such a life hast to little earth reduced,
What object does thy diligence not reach?

DAMON.

10. Oh death, since thou the bitter blow dealt forth,
Which from the earth our mainstay did eject,
No herb or meadow, or sweet flower is seen.

ELICIO.

11. Of this ills' memory I repress
The good; if any to my feelings should arise,
And with fresh bitterness I wound myself.

LAUSO.

12. Whenever a lost good itself restores,
And evil, without seeking is not found?
When quietude exists in mortal noise?

THIRSIS.

13. When from the furious close of fiery fight,
Existence triumphs, and against all time
Itself opposes, armour against or mail.

DAMON.

14. Our life's a dream, a pastime, evident
 A vain enchantment, which does disappear
 When a more firm one hath appeared in time.

ELICIO.

15. A day, which in mid course obscures itself,
 Succeeding to which is black night, covered in
 With shades, which fear the darkness aggravates.

LAUSO.

16. But you, famed swain, in the adventurous
 Hour, have traversed this wild ocean stream
 Unto the marvellous region of delight.

THIRSIS.

17. After that in the sheepfold of Venice
 You causes and demands determinedst
 Of the great shepherd of the Spanish soil.

DAMON.

18. With courage afterwards you suffered too,
 The accelerated stroke of fortune's blow,
 Which hit Italia, and sad Spain likewise.

ELICIO.

19. And when in calmness you reposed yourself
 Alone with the nine ladies, so much time
 You found yourself in sweet retirement.

LAUSO.

20. Without that the fierce Eastern arms themselves
 Or that the Gallic fury should disturb
 Your elevated but yet peaceful mind.

THIRSIS.

21. Then heaven desired that you should surprise
 The cold hand of a very wrathful death,
 And by your life our treasure snatch away.

DAMON.

22. Then did your fate remain ameliorated,
 To ours remained a sorrowful, bitter wail,
 In a perpetual condemnation.

ELICIO.

23. The sacred virgin beauteous quire then saw
    The native dwellers on Parnassus' top,
    Tearing their hair of gold, with deep laments.

LAUSO.

24. The wretched circumstance moved to tears
    The rival great of the blind infant boy,
    Who then to scatter radiance was bereft.

THIRSIS.

25. Not arms among, or in the midst of fire,
    Did the sad Trojans so afflict themselves,
    At the deception of the astute Greek
    Whom they bewailed, and oft reiterated ;
    The shepherds all honoured Meliso's name,
    And of his lamentable end they heard.

DAMON.

26. Not flowers of various essences and hues
    Adorned their brows, nor did they pour the song
    With voices sweet, in canticles of love ;
    With boughs of cypress sad they crowned themselves,
    On repetition's very bitter wail
    Songs they intoned, replete with melancholy.

ELICIO.

27. Thus I to-day break forth in bitterness,
    And memory's sharpness now renews itself,
    Shepherds, break forth in lamentable strains,
    For the sad case which urges us to grief
    Is such, that hard as diamond, is the breast
    That cannot wail at such commotion.

LAUSO.

28. The breast's due hardihood, the constant soul
    Which through adversities was always found
    In this good swain, a thousand tongues may sing ;
    How 'gainst disdain continually he bore up,
    Which the indignant Phillis' breast had caused,
    All found him firm as rock against the waves.

THIRSIS.

29. Let us reiterate the theme he sang,
   That in the memory of the world may dwell
   Proofs of his genius, noble, elevated.

DAMON.

30. Diffused o'er lands of divers latitudes,
   May fame's loud trumpet his good name proclaim
   In quick succession, borne on rapid wings.

ELICIO.

31. And from his chaste and amorous desires
   May wanton breasts a bright example take,
   And stimulate a lesser passion on.

LAUSO.

32. Meliso, venturous, who, in despite
   Of fortune's infinite oppugnancy,
   Joyful and satisfied, in being dwells.

THIRSIS.

33. A little wearies thee, and importunes
   The mortal humbleness which you have left
   Of changes fuller than the circled moon.

DAMON.

34. Had changed humility for firm loftiness,
   Or ill for good, for dissolution, life,
   And such security you hoped and feared.

ELICIO.

Who seems as fallen from this mortal state,
And to the end lives well, transplants himself,
As thou, Meliso, to the florid heights.
Whence there is more than one immortal throat,
The voice despatching which true glory sounds,
Glory repeats, sweet glory sings again.
Whence the clear torch, serene in loveliness,
Displays itself; in whose sight we enjoy
And view great glory in perfection.
My voice, though feeble, to your praise aspires,

And all the more desire is increased,
By so much fear withholds it, Meliso;
That him I now contemplate and survey
With understanding, raised by thy sacred
Character 'bove human ornament,
My very mind its powers feels repressed,
Alone I stop, my eyelids to raise up,
The lips to gather of the admired one.

LAUSO.

By thy departure in sorrowful wail you leave
All who rejoiced in thy good presence; while
Evil approaches, because you are gone.

THIRSIS.

In thy sound wisdom duly schooled were
The rustic shepherds, and in precise point
With genius new and right discretion dwelt.
But that forced point was touched in verity,
Whence you departed, and where we remain
Is little genius, and a heart defunct.
That bitter memory we have celebrated,
We, who in life have thee so much desired,
As now in death we deeply thee bewail,
For this at sound of woe so much confused,
Drawing continuously new inhalations,
Shepherds, tune up the woful, solemn chant,
Conduct us where hard sentiment conducts,
Tears which are shed, and sighs intensely drawn,
Wherewith the hasty winds we may augment;
I charge you mildly, little can I exact,
But you must feel that now, by so much less,
My tongue, chained down, can duly all relate.
But since the sun absents himself, and sheds
Upon the earth a covering mantle dark,
Until the expected morn shall rise again
Shepherds, cease not the melancholy strain.

Thirsis who had begun the doleful elegy, was the same who
ended it, and for a considerable time all who heard it were
immersed in tears. Just at this time the venerable Telesio

said to them, " since we have achieved in part, gallant and polished shepherds, the obligation which we hold towards the fortunate Meliso, stay, I beseech you, now, your tender tears, and give some surcease to your doleful sighs, for we cannot recover by sighs nor tears what we deplore, and since human sentiment cannot cease to evince itself in adverse circumstances, yet should we temper the excess of such casualties with that reason which attends on discretion ; and although tears and sighs be the indications of the love we entertain for the person we deplore, more profit attends the souls, for whom these tears are shed with pious sacrifices and devout prayers, which for them we raise, than if the ocean's stream were distilled in tears. So to give some solace to our out-wearied bodies, it will be well if abandoning that which remains for the coming time, now we visit our scrips, and effect what nature impels." This said, he commanded that all the lady shepherdesses should repair to a section of the valley, towards the burial spot of Meliso, leaving with them six of the most ancient shepherds, and the rest having a little strayed went to another part, and immediately with what they held in their wallets, and with water from the clear fountain, they satisfied the cravings of hunger, finishing when night, stamping with the same hue all things beneath the sphere, and the shining moon developed her beauteous face in all her integrity more than when her rosy brother communicates his rays. But in a brief space the wind rising, there were evidences of dark clouds which somewhat encumbered the chaste goddess, forming shadows on the earth, signals whence some swains who were standing by, masters in rustic astrology, expected a coming whirl-wind, yet did all stop in awaiting no longer the grey and serene night, and in resting themselves on the fresh herb, surrendering themselves to a sweet and settled repose ; this did all, save those to whom the task of sentinels was assigned for guarding the females, and some torches which flamed around the burial place of Meliso.

Already the tranquil silence had extended itself over all that consecrated valley, and already had the lazy Morpheus with his leaden rod touched the temples and the eyelids of all around ; at the time that, in their circuit of the pole, a large portion of the wandering stars had gone their course, indicating the period of the nights, at the very juncture from the tomb of Meliso there arose a vast and wonderful fire, luminous and clear, so that in a twinkling the dark valley was enveloped in such a blaze of light, as if the very golden orb of day had disclosed himself; on account of which unexpected marvel the swains who were around the tomb, and all awake, fell dismayed on the ground, dazzled blind with the radiation of the transparent flame; which worked a contrary effect on the sleepers, for, smitten by its rays, it drove off the weighty sleep, and though with difficulty the sleepers oped their eyes, and observing the extraordinary result of the fact, they remained confounded and in admiration, they some on foot, some reclining, and some on their knees, watched with surprise and terror the clear element of fire. All this observed by Telesio, in a moment enveloping himself in the sacred vestments, in company of Elicio, Thirsis, Damon, Lauso, and the other spirited swains, by degrees began to approach the fire with a view that by certain permitted exorcisms they might negative the effects of the elements, or learn whence proceeded the frightful vision which had appeared. No sooner had they advanced towards the burning flames than they observed a division into two parts, in the midst of which appeared a very beauteous and graceful nymph, which involved them in greater wonder than the lively fire. She shewed herself to be vested in a rich and thin woof of silver, drawn up and gathered together so that the half of her legs were disclosed, adorned with sandals, or so neatly shod, gilt and replete with enlacements of ribbons of diverse colours, which, slightly elevated by a cool zephyr, expanded itself. Over her shoulders she carried long and auburn hair, such as eyes scarce saw, and over the hair a garland fabricated of verdant laurel. Her right hand was engaged with a long branch of the yellow, victorious palm, and the left hand held a green and peaceful olive. With these ornaments she looked so beautiful and so much to be admired, that all who saw her, quite hung upon her in such a way that casting off the first fear, with secure steps they environed the fire, in the full conviction that in the presence of such a vision no injury could accrue. Thus, standing in transports on sight of her, the fair nymph opened her arms on both sides, and caused the flames to diverge, and so to disclose her person that she was seen of all, and immediately elevating her serene visage, with a grace and extreme gravity she spoke in the following terms:—

"For the consequences which my unexpected vision has caused in your hearts, discreet and agreeable company, you may consider that it is not in virtue of evil spirits that this my figure is patent to you, for one of the reasons is to enable where to determine between a good and bad vision, which is known by the effects produced on the mind, because the good, though it may cause admiration and surprise, yet are these properties blended with an agreeable disturbance, which by degrees assuages and satisfies; quite contrary is the emotion caused by a perverse vision, which bounds up, is discontent, induces dread, and never assures. This verity will experience clear up when you really know me, and I may tell you who I am, and the motive which has induced me to come to these remote habitations to visit you, and because I wish not to hold you intent on the desire to learn truly who I may be, know, wise men and ladies, that I am one of the nine damsels whom the lofty and sacred heights of Parnassus retain as on-dwellers.

"My name is Calliope, my office and condition is to favour and aid those divine spirits, whose laudable exercise is in the marvellous and the never to be too much celebrated science of poesy. I am the individual who wrapped in fame eterne, the old blind bard, native of Smyrna, who will cause to live to all future ages the Mantuan Tityrus, till time shall be no more, and her who has kept in just repute the compositions of the veteran Ennius. In fine I am the person who patronised Catullus, gave renown to Horace, eternised Propertius, and have rescued in deathless fame the memory of Petrarca of world-wide renown, and who made to descend to the obscure regions below, and to touch highest heaven, the great Dante. It was I who helped to weave the varied lines of the divine Ariosto, I who in your own country made acquaintance with the subtle Boscan, with the celebrated Garcilasso, with the learned and sage Castillejo, and the artful Torres Naharro, whose genius and fruits so enriched your country, and I was satisfied. I it was who moved the pen of the clever Aldana, and who never deserted the side of Don Fernando de Acuña; am her who appreciated the strict friendship and conversation which I ever held with the beatified spirit of that body which lies in the tomb, whose obsequies, by you enacted, have not only rejoiced his spirit, which already is passed into the realms of space, and have so satisfied me, that compelled I am hither come to acquiesce in a so pious and commendable a rite, which is in usage amongst you.

"Hence I promise you in truth that in my virtue they may hope that in indemnity for the benefit which you have conferred on the ashes of my well-beloved Meliso, so to arrange it that on your banks there will never lack swains who will not surpass in the science of poetry all on the circumjacent banks. I will ever advance your counsels and guide your minds, so that you shall never confer a mistaken vow when you determine who is to be interred in your sacred valley, for it will not be right that an honour so particular and marked, and which is deserved only by white and melodious swans, should be enjoyed by black and hoarse crows; and thus it seems to me that it will be just to give you some notice now of those renowned worthies who dwell in your Spain, and those in the Indies, separate yet subject to her, who, if all or any of them, whose lucky lot should draw them to finish the course of their days on these banks, undoubtedly you might grant sepulture in this famous locality. Added to this I would advise you, that you do not understand that the first I have named to you are worthy the honours of the last, for in this I do not follow any order, for since I can reach the difference the one bears to the other, and the same to the same, I would rather leave this declaration in doubt, for your intelligence in marking the distinction of your people consists in exercise of which their works will give testimony. Hence I will cite them as my memory serves, that no imputation may lie against me, relative to special favour, by taking one before the other, for as I said to you, worthy swains, you may accord to each the justice which each merits. So that with less annoyance and trouble you may be attentive to my extended relation, I will arrange it so that you shall only blame the brevity of the story."

The heavenly nymph, on saying this, ceased, and incontinently seized a harp which was near her, but which had been seen by no one, and on proceeding to strike it, the very heavens began to clear up, and the moon with a novel and unaccustomed splendour illuminated the earth; the trees, in despite of a gentle breeze which blew, found their leaves unmoved, and the eyes of all who there stood durst not lower their lids, that the brief space which caused delay in upraising them might not deprive them of the glory which they experienced in gloating on the perfection of the nymph, and they even wished that their five senses should be converted into that of hearing alone. With so much peculiarity, with so much sweetness, with such harmony, she touched the harp of the graceful muse. She having sounded the strings awhile, with a voice sonorous past conception, then gave utterance to these stanzas :—

SONG OF CALLIOPE.

1. To the sweet sound of my attempered lyre,
   Oh shepherds listen with attentive ear,
   In my voice will you hear, in it breathes forth
   My sister's sacred inspiration too,
   How it suspends, astonishes, you will see,
   And with contentment fills your very souls,
   When upon earth I here relation give
   Of those great geniuses which dwell above.

2. I trust to sing of only those spirits
   Whom fate as yet has not severed the thread;
   Of those who worthily exalted are,
   And may be signalised in such a place,
   Who, in despite of all devouring time,
   Accustomed to laudable offices,
   A thousand years shall their renown survive,
   Their works of brilliancy, and revered names.

3. And he, who with just title well deserves
   To enjoy a high, honoured pre-eminence,
   Is Don Alonso, in whom flourishes
   Science divine, of God Apollo's art;
   In whom, with depth of light, resplendent is,
   Of Mars the courage, and the power the same,

Who bears De Leiva, for a noble name,
Illumining both Spain and Italy.

4. Another name identical, who sang
Arauco's wars, and Spain's achievements high,
Who the vast realms which Glaucus habited,
Traversed, and felt the fury of his wrath.
His voice was not, nor accent rough had he,
On both had nature grace extreme conferred,
So that Ercilla, in this cherished place,
A sacred, during monument deserves.

5. Don Juan de Silva, famous, now I say,
Who every honour, every glory claims,
As well for friendship with Apollo as
For every virtue which he justly boasts.
His labours all are testimonies of it,
In which his genius everywhere bursts forth
With brightness, dazzling crass ignorance,
And e'en the sharp wit of genius quenching it.

6. May the rich number of the accounts increase
The catalogue of all in heaven enrolled,
Whom Phœbus' breath sustains with potency,
With Mars, his valour here below on earth
A match for Homer, when intent to write,
Such is the flight of his adventurous pen ;
So that in truth to all is known the wit
Of Don Diego, styled, Osorio.

7. By ways so many speaking fame can sing,
Can celebrate a cavalier's renown,
Can scatter wide valour's illustrious acts,
A name conferring never-dying claims ;
His vivid genius his virtue inflames
More than a tongue, which, steeped in lustre's blaze,
Of time regardless, on its hurried wings,
Sings of Francisca de Mendoza still.

8. Diego de Sarmienta, happy, too,
And Carvajal, illustrious, produced
From the same quire immortal Hippocrene,
A youth in age, ancient in sentiment ;

From age to age will flow, in lustre bright,
Despite the waves of dark oblivion,
Thy name, associated with thy works, will fly
From tongue to tongue, from race to race consigned.

9. I would inform you by a sovereign power,
Of tender age and judgment quite mature.
Dexterity beyond humanity,
Courtesy, valour, and refinement too,
Who equally in Tuscan with his own
Language, can indicate talent so vast,
That in his song we recognise
Don Gutierre Carvajal, the bard.

10. Thou, Don Luis de Vargas, where I see
Judgment profound, the fruit of a short life,
Try to obtain the trophy enviable,
Which my loved sisters thee have promised.
So near thou art to it, that I believe
Already triumphed hast, essay by ways
A thousand, virtuous, wise, that thy clear fame,
A flame, resplendent, lively, may burst forth.

11. The beauteous banks of the clear Tagus' stream,
Infinite spirits are its ornaments,
Who make our epocha more fortunate
Than that of Greece or Latin processes ;
Of these, I think to say one only thing,
Worthy at once our valley and honour,
Their works to us do plainly indicate   ·
How they direct us towards the heavenly mount.

12. Two famous doctors, Presidents,
In sciences taught by Apollo, me
Seem to be effectually in their age,
In genius and in management the same,
Absent and present equally admired ;
And in such splendour do they both appear
By their profundity and breadth of wit,
.That all the world consent to give them praise.

13. And now the name which occupies my mind,
Which I, to praise with the other two, advance

Is the renowned Campuzano hight,
A second Phœbus surely might be styled.
His lofty mind and superhuman wit
To us discloses an entire new world,
Excellencies surpassing India,
As sciences supreme are over gold.

14. Doctor Suarez, also Sosa called,
His extra name a spirit following,
An artificial language, in its depth
Most pure, and he makes it his own in use.
Whoever in the fountain marvellous
Mitigates it, and thirst doth mitigate,
Will envy much the Grecian erudite,
Or him who sang of Troy's destructive fire.

15. Of Doctor Baza, if of him I may
Speak what I feel, and doubtless I believe
Would hold you all suspended—out of breath.
Such is his knowledge, virtue, and ornament,
The first I was to raise him from the quire
Of consecration ; I who had desire
To eternise his name precisely as
The Lord of Delos gives his light to earth.

16. If fame should on our ears a knowledge bring
Wonders of some far famed man of wit,
Conceptions lofty, order well arranged,
And sciences which stagger us to hear,
Matters which dwell alone in sentients,
And which no tongue can give expression to,
To entertain no doubt or contrivance,
Know that Licentiate Daza is the man.

17. Master Garai's dulcet, laboured works
Incite me justly to appropriate praise,
Thou, fame, which to light time superfluous,
Hold it an enterprise to celebrate him.
In him shalt see what fame thou coverest ;
Fame, which is thine in elevation
Who speaking of this fame in very truth
Hast to exchange the current breath of fame.

18. That very genius who all human skill
    Behind him leaves, aspiring to divine ;
    Putting aside the old Castillian,
    The heroic Latin verse pursues with zeal,
    The Homer new and the new Mantuan bard,
    The Master Cordova, who right worthy is
    In happy strain to be much celebrated,
    Where the sun rises and in ocean sets.

19. Of thee, Doctor Francisco Diaz, I can
    To these my shepherds all assurance give,
    With hearty purpose in true merriment,
    That praises would redound to their true gain.
    But if in them I find myself restrained,
    Owing to thee a greater sum of praise,
    It is 'cause time is brief, and I dare not
    Pretend to pay thee what is thy fair due.

20. Lujan, who wears the toga of desert,
    Art honoured in native and in foreign soil,
    And by the muse associated with thee,
    Ascendest to the summit of the clouds,
    After decease gain immortality,
    Effecting in a light and rapid flight
    The fame which your especial genius
    Transports from this pole to the opposite.

21. In lofty genius and its worth, declares
    So much a friend and a licentiate too,
    Juan de Vargara is his noble name,
    Honour to this our truly lucky age ;
    Open and clear the road by which he moves,
    I, myself, guiding genius and step ;
    And where he wends I compensation find,
    Being by his wit and merit satisfied

22. I wish to name another, for in esteem
    And honour holds him my adventurous song,
    Contributing due animation,
    And may I rise to the much coveted end ;
    Now this both forces and oppresses me
    In speaking sole of him, essaying so much,

As to the greatest geniuses is due,
Alonso Morales, licentiate.

23. Unto the difficult height in the ascent   .
     To fame's proud temple, near in the approach,
     Is seen a generous youth, who quite breaks through
     The opposition which should terrify.
     As soon as he arrived is, we learn
     That in a prophecy already fame
     Chants of the laurel, which for licentiate
     Hernando Maldonado is prepared.

24. Now the respected laurel's learned front,
     You'll recognise as due to him, who in all
     The sciences and arts is conversant ;
     Whose just renown is through the world diffused.
     A golden age, epoch most fortunate,
     Whose fate has been to claim him for their own.
     What age, what epoch so renowned can boast,
     Marco Antonio de la Vega, bard ?

25. A certain Diego to my memory comes,
     Mendoza is his other appellative.
     Worthy alone to indite history,
     Such as will reach his great extent of fame.
     Virtue and wit in him, specialities,
     Encompassing the wide world's circled orb ;
     Absent and present praising him alike,
     Nations remote and near enriching too.

26. A well known worthy Phœbus entertains,
     Why should I give this epithet ? a true
     Friend, with whom private entertainment is,
     The treasurer of all the sciences,
     Industriously reserving to himself
     Which may or not be all communicated,
     Diego Duran, in whom long will last,
     The virtues of courage, staidness, self-respect.

27. Whom do you think is he, who in sweet voice,
     His deep anxieties chants regularly ;
     In whose illumined breast Apollo dwells.
     Orpheus the wise, Arion prudent most,

Whom from the eastern portals of the globe
Unto the drooping west's circumference
Is known, is loved, and estimated too,
The famous Lopez Maldonado hight.

28. Who could give commendation due, shepherds,
Your shepherd true, beloved and recognised,
The best of all who are acknowledged best;
De Filida his appellation is;
Ability, science, prime qualities,
Uncommon genius, courage elevated,
To Luis de Montalvo is assured,
Glory and honour while the heavens endure.

29. The gilded thistle (acanto) on Iberus' bank,
The verdant ivy, with the olive white,
Is ornament, and in gay canticle
Its glory and its honour ever lives.
His ancient valour elevates so much,
. That from the fruitful Nile his name deprives
Of Pedro de Liñan the subtle pen,
The sum and substance of Apollo's wealth.

30. Of Alonzo de Valdez me incites
The rare and lofty genius that I sing;
Shepherds, to you declaring, he transcends
The best of authors, going far beyond.
This has he proved, and ever still he proves,
In elegance and easiness of style
Which the deep wounded breast discovereth,
Lauding the violence fierce love has made.

31. Admire the talent in which is comprised
All that desire enabled is to ask;
A genius, though it dwelleth here on earth,
From heaven draws its strength and ornament,
Treating now of peace and now of war
So much do I admire, listen and read,
Of Pedro de Padilla's excellence,
Awakening in me taste and wonderment.

32. Thou, famous Gaspar Alfonso, hast ordained,
Aspiring ever to celestial heights,

That thee with difficulty I celebrate,
Should I be bounded by your true merit,
The ever-fertile, sweet produce of plants,
Which our famed mountain in its bosom hides,
All offer laurels of the richest growth,
To gird and honour thy temples alone.

33. Of Christoval de Mesa, sure I say
The consecrated valley he can raise
To honour, well in life as in his death,
So may we him a just laudation give.
The symmetry of his heroic verse
His grave, exalted style on him confers
A high and honoured name, though I should be
Oblivious of his fame, nor all record.

34. Well, well you know how he your banks adorns,
Enriches them, Pedro de Ribera hight;
To him, O swains, accord a just reward,
And be I first the tribute due to give.
His dulcet muse, his virtue offereth
A proper subject, in the which his fame
A thousand fold may revel and expand,
In doing justice to his extreme worth.

35. Thou who the treasure singular in use,
Transportest in new form to this the bank
Of the rich river, where the milk of gold
So famous is in its depository.
With due applause, and with decorum too,
Benito de Caldera, hail to thee!
Your genius unapproached I promise
With bay to honour, with ivy to crown.

36. Of him who Christian poesy has lodged,
In such a seat of honour has it placed,
May fame and my still faithful memory
Secure it from oblivion's limit dark.
From when 'tis born, to the very day it dies,
Let science be, goodness notorious,
Which to Francisco de Guzman belongs,
In Mars and Phœbus' arts equally skilled.

37. Of Captain de Salcedo it is clear
That his divine intelligence mounts up
To the highest point, in use rare and acute,
As lofty as imagination can.
If he's compared, it must be with himself,
As no comparison will touch the sum
Of his vast virtue, for the measure is
Bereft of standard, or distorted quite.

38. Now for the singular intelligence
Of Thomas de Gracian, licence I crave:
That I a seat in this vale may assign
To virtue, courage, science equivalent.
Should he attain to his deserved reward,
To such a step and high pre-eminence
Will he ascend, that equals few he'll find ;
His virtues are of such validity.

39. Now lovely sisters, unexpectedly
Baptista de Vivar commands our praise,
Yet with discretion, sprightliness, and guard,
That being muses we may justly laud.
Narcissus will not celebrate disdains,
Which cost so dear to Eco, solitary.
Bereft of cares, which all originate,
A joyful hope, oblivion sad, between.

40. A novel dread, new consternation,
Assists me and assails me at this point.
Only to see I wish, and yet cannot
Raise to the honour of supremest height
The grave Baltasar, who Toledo's styled,
For extra name, although presumption is,
That from the high reach of his learned pen,
He has attained empyrean's lofty top.

41. There shows a genius with experience,
Which in green years and mellowness of age
Its habitation has in science profound,
As in maturity, ancient and bald.
Into no argument will I embark,
Which truth so plain essays to contradict.

But should his fame reach to the auricular sense,
Lope de Vega's name I loud announce.

42. Encircled with the peaceful olive branch,
Ere my intelligence presents itself,
The sacred Betis much indignant is,
And of my inadvertence doth complain,
Requiring in my just commenced discourse
Of understandings rare, that I give 'count
Of those who herein dwell, and now in truth
My voice I'll raise to extreme echo's ring.

43. What shall I do, who in the early moves
By me made, find infinity of things.
Pindus and Parnassus thousand folds,
And quires of sisters yet more beautiful,
By which my ardent spirits are subdued.
And more in harmony with wondrous cause,
I hear an echo still reverberating,
When it reiterates Pacheco's name.

44. Pacheco is he with whom Apollo holds,
And the nine sisters, ever cautious,
Amity new, and entertainment wise
From the first hours of cradled innocence,
From that time forward even until now.
Through extraordinary, unaccustomed ways,
His works and wit I bear, which have attained
To honour's title most extolled of all.

45. In this position stand I, when I speak,
Thy praise, Herrera, noted for divine.
Advantage small to me though him I raise
To the fifth sphere in heaven's locality.
But if I seem towards him suspicious,
His learned works and veritable renown,
Hernando will proclaim in sciences,
Master from Nile to Ganges and the poles.

46. Another Hernando I would freely name,
Ycleped de Cangas, and in whom we admire
The soil, where lives and doth sustain itself,
The science aspiring to the laurel branch.

If to high heaven a genius is intent,
To elevate itself and seek success.
In this place set it, and will soon arise
Lofty results and most ingenious.

47. Of Don Christoval, who the surname bears
Of De Villaroel, and assured be
That his name never can the fate deserve
To melt in waters of oblivion.
His genius is admired, his courage strikes,
And both are recognised by men of fame,
In the extremest bounds of this round ball,
As far as sun extends and earth expands.

48. Rivers of eloquence which from the breast
Of the grave, antique Cicero were poured,
Those streams which Athens' people satisfied,
Shaking the arsenal, Demosthenes,
Wits whom time has fairly brought to naught,
Which were, in bygone days so celebrated,
Bow themselves down before the science of
Lofty, divine Francesco de Medina.

49. Oh, famous Betis, worthily you may
Precedence take of Mincio, and Arno,
And Tiber too, raising a sacred front,
Thyself expanding into unknown bays,
Since heaven requires it that you acquiesce,
Such glory, honour, deathless fame be given,
To your rich banks as is acquired to you,
From Baltazar del Alcazar, your bard.

50. In others you will see, and recognise,
The rarest science of Apollo stamped.
In many thousand subjects scattered wide,
Having a semblance of due gravity.
And in this subject more ameliorated,
Assisting in perfection's various modes,
Mosquera the licentiate is shown,
E'en as Apollo's self is celebrated.

51. Never disdains the prudent child of song,
Adorned with science, which his fertile mind

Duly enriches, to observe the font
Which in our mountain into clear streams grows.
In that bright current deemed incomparable,
His thirst he mitigates.   Where now flourishes
A name of brightness over earth diffused,
Domingo de Becerra, doctor styled.

52. Of Espinel, the famous, I would indite
Facts which exceed the compass of all wit.
Relating to those sciences begot
By Phœbus' sacred breathings in his breast.
I cannot, by my tongue, expression give
Less than the inspiration which I feel,
No more I say than that to heaven he looks,
His pen and lyre both yielding evidence.

53. If you would view, in equal balance set,
The ruby Phœbus and the blood-stained Mars,
Look at Carranza, justly styled the great,
From whom these deities cannot parted be.
In him both pen and lance are manifest,
With such discretion, art, dexterity,
That all subjected to divisions,
Form sciences reduced to closest art.

54. Of Lazaro Luis Iranzo, whose soft lyre
Has tempered been to sweetness more than mine,
To whose sounds are sung the good which it inspires
In heaven's high reach, courage generating.
Through the high ways of Mars and Phœbus too,
To mount aspiring, where fancy of men
Can scarce attain, of doubtfulness bereft
'Gainst fate and fortune the wished goal will touch.

55. De Escobar, Baltazar styled, who now
The banks of Tiber's famous stream adorns,
And by his absence long disfigures quite
The spacious continent of Betis' flood.
Fertile of wit, if he by accident
Return to his loved country, to his honoured
And youthful temples freely offer I
The laurel and honour, merit's rich tribute.

56. What dignity, what honour, laurel, palm
    Is due to Juan Sanz de Zumeta
    Styled? from India to the sunburnt moor,
    No other muse in excellence outstrips.
    His fame anew then here do I restore
    By barely saying, shepherds, who accepts,
    Shall from Apollo lustre, honour derive,
    Honouring Zumeta shall himself honour.

57. Fail not to give to Juan de las Cuevas
    His worthy seat, when you appointment make,
    Shepherds, desert and worth are really found
    In his loved muse and delicate intellect.
    I know his works from dark oblivion,
    In opposition and despite of time's
    Quick current, will his name deliver quite,
    Involving it in clear and deep renown.

58. My shepherds, should you see him, honour him,
    That famous wight whose virtues now I speak,
    Celebrate him in grave, sweet canticles,
    Such as himself excels competitors.
    Bibaldo, styled mighty, poets among,
    And Adan too, who gilds and illustrates,
    With his extensive florid genius,
    The existing race of earth's quick sons of fire.

59. As with variety and countless flowers
    The florid month of May is beautified,
    So with infinitude of sciences
    Established is Don Juan Aguayo's wit,
    Though I myself detain in his due praise,
    I shall add, too, that I do make essay
    Now, and another time I will announce
    Things shall be deemed miraculous to all.

60. Of Don Gutierrez Rufo, that clear name,
    I wish in deathless memory it should live;
    To wise and simple admiration, fear
    Composing history in heroicals.
    Give to him, sacred Betis, the renown
    Which his style merits; give him glory too,

All ye who know and can, may heaven yield
A fame equivalent to his sustained flight.

61. In Don Luis de Gongora I offer
A lively genius, unsurpassed by bard.
His works are my delight, and I enrich
Myself not only, but the world at large.
I therefore you demand for merit's sake,
Will so adjust it, deeply and profound,
In your due praises, that he long survive
Against light time, and death inevitable.

62. Bind fast the laurel green, the ivy too;
The oak robust, let it adorn the front
Of Gonzales Cervantes Saavedra,
Then will you bind a forehead worthy praise.
Apollo through him science nourishes,
In him Mars shews the burning liveliness
Of fury, measured with reason's nicest care,
That well beloved and dreaded is the bard.

63. Thou who of Celidon the sweet instrument
The name and fame made to resound so far,
Whose admirable and well-filed measurement
To laurel and triumph thee invites and calls,
Receive authority, sceptre and crown.
Gonzalo Gomez, he who loves you well,
A signal that your person merits too
To be of Helicon acknowledged lord.

64. O thou Darro, the well known stream of gold,
Now can you really signalise yourself,
And with new current and new ardour too,
Surpass remote Hidaspes in your stream,
For Gonzalo Mateo de Berrio
To honour you by genius, has procured
That thy name, published by diffusing fame,
By it through all the world's expanse be known.

65. Of laurel green now weave a coronet,
Shepherds to honour the front and divine head
Of the licentiate Soto Barahona,
In eloquence and wisdom one renowned.

And in the sacred stream of Helicon,
If lost should be sustained in that clear font.
Oh, wondrous fact ! recovery is made
As on Parnassus' lofty eminence.

66. From the Antarctic regions one might
Give immortality to the sovereigns wise.
If riches are created and sustained
So even may the superhuman mind.
This day these facts may well be demonstrated,
And in two days I would that hands be full,
One for new Spain, and bright Apollo too,
The other for Peru, united soils.

67. Francisco de Terrazas holds the one,
A name which is diffused far and wide,
Whose vein, in stock is a new Hippocrene,
Which to the country's venturous nest is given.
A glory equal to the other comes,
For his divine invention has produced,
In Arequipa an eternal spring,
Diego Martinez de Ribera styled.

68. Here, underneath the star most fortunate,
A light so signal now has emanated,
That of the illumination the small spark
An eastern name has given to the west.
When this light rose, uprose also, with it,
Valour, true form, Alonso Picado,
My brother rose, and he with Pallas joined,
In both we see the living copy too.

69. If we due glory render to thy name,
Alonso de Estrada, styled the great,
Now, worthy art, we sing not cursorily,
As if person and mind both foreign were.
By thee the land undoubted riches draws,
Infinite wealth pouring in Betis' stream,
Rendéring return unequal, for no wealth
Can satisfy a debt so fortunate.

70. As a rare pledge for this illustrious land,
Renowned Don Juan has heaven endowed us with,

De Avalo's glory, De Ribera's light,
Of native and of foreign soil the pride.
Fortunate Spain, who through the medium
Of many lights thy works declare, model
Of all that nature can in genius,
And singular nobility transcend.

71. Who, in this land delicious, is content
The waters pure of Limar to enjoy.
The famous bank and freshest blowing gales
Exciting with divinest melody,
Advance, and you shall see in this account,
Heroic liveliness and discretion blent,
Sancho de Ribera, in all parts
Apollo's friend and Mars' associate too.

72. This very famous valley of renown,
Upon a time on Betis did usurp
A Homer new—to whom we might accord
The crown of wit and of politeness eke.
The graces to his own measure he reduced,
And heaven proffered of her best to him.
In our famed Tagus had he a renown,
Pedro de Montesdoca was his name.

73. In all that true desire can arrogate,
Diego de Aguilar illustrious view
A very eagle, in whose flight I see
An elevation scarce attainable;
His wing thousands amidst trophies does gain,
Many before his flight retiring;
His style and vigour of what celebrity
Guanuco will declare, by proof made known.

74. Gonzalo Fernandez himself presents
Victorious Captain of Apollo's quire,
Of Sotomayor's patronymic proud,
A name heroic, made to conjure with,
In verse conspicuous, with wisdom fraught,
A just concession made from pole to pole,
And though his pen in just repute is held,
His martial weapons are no less renowned.

75. Enrique Garces, the Peruvian,
    That realm enriching, for with sweetest rhyme,
    With subtlety, with genius, and quick hand,
    The enterprise most difficult is attained.
    Into sweet Spanish, the great Tuscan bard
    Converted has, on him conferring new
    Language of praise, and who shall him transcend,
    Unless Petrarca be resuscitated.

76. Rodrigo Fernandez de Pineda,
    Whose vein immortal and whose excellence
    And rare ability, chiefly derives
    From consecrated stream of the Equine fonts.
    But what from it he wills no one discerns,
    Yet so much western glory he enjoys,
    Here also hath he maximum of praise,
    Such as his genius and his art deserve.

77. And thou, too, whom your native Betis holds,
    With envy full, complaining reasonably,
    That other skies and soil have also been
    Of your prolific songs the witnesses.
    Rejoice that your famed appellation,
    Juan de Mestanza, styled the generous,
    Shall be no second name upon the soil,
    Whilst a fourth heaven can its light diffuse.

78. All the condensed sweetness in pure vein
    One can distinguish, and in one discern
    How to sounds tasteful regulates the Muse,
    The ocean's fury, Eolus' swift course;
    Baltazar de Orena is he called,
    Whose reputation from the pole to pole
    Lightly transmits itself, from East to West,
    Imparting honour to Parnassus' height.

79. Then from a fertile and a precious root,
    It is transplanted to a higher hill
    Than any which in Thessaly swells up—
    A stem which many precious boughs hath borne.
    Shall I be mute how fame herself has sung
    The name of Pedro de Alvarado?

Illustrious, and yet the not less clear,
For his capacity to a learned world.

80. Thou also with a muse extraordinary,
Cairasco, warblest love essential,
And that variety of man's estate
Strengthening the weak, and trampling on the strong.
If from thy site you to Canaria
Should wend with ardour, and magnanimous,
My shepherds shall to your true merit give
Infinite laurels, and a well earned praise.

81. Who is it, ancient Tormes, who denies
That the deep Nile is not advanced by thee?
If the Licentiate Vega all alone
Than Tityrus more the Mincio can laud,
Damian, I know that your ability
Can reach the highest chord of honour's harp,
Being conversant from years' experience
In your great skill and virtues singular.

82. Although your genius and elegance,
Francisco Sanchez, obvious be to me,
Still should I hold myself inadequate
The praises to accord which you deserve,
A voice unique from heaven, competent
The extensiveness of your career to write,
Or to dilate in praises on your worth—
A task to human skill impracticable.

83. The rarest treasures, in a style quite new,
Which an endued spirit can raise up
In proofs ingenious as they are difficult,
Esteemed for wise, considerate, practical—
Such Don Francisco de las Cuevas doth;
By me let him be worthily glorified,
So that renown a sterling herald be,
With nothing to obstruct or course divert.

84. My song of sweetness I would now conclude
In such a season, shepherds, with the praise
Of such a genius as alarms the world,
Into ecstacy transporting it.

In the writing and the gathering up,
All is here shewn, and yet I have to shew
Fray Luis de Leon, of whom I treat
As one I reverence, and still homage pay.

85. What methods, means, alternatives, shall I
Seek to praise him who bears the noble name
Of Great Matias? may it live centuries,
Zuñiga for distinction, superimposed.
To whom may all my praise be proffered,
Though I divine be, yet is he a man
Who for his genius is divinely wrought,
Worthy of praise, honour, and reverence.

86. Now turn your pressing meditations towards
The lovely coasts of Pisuerga's stream,
Remarking how this rich account will swell
Mighty proficients who have honoured them,
Not they alone, but the wide firmament,
Whence shine in brightness stars innumerable,
This honour gives, when I attention call,
To those famed sons of poesy and truth.

87. Damasio de Frias, you alone
Can praise yourself, since so it cannot be,
Unless Apollo condescends his praise,
Who in just commendation is not slack.
The sure and certain polestar hast thou been
To him who ventures, by your guidance, on
The sea of sciences, a traject good,
Prospicious gales, and harbour surely found.

88. Andres Sanz de Portillo, you transmit
That inspiration with which Phœbus moves
My learned pen and upraised phantasy,
To thee I give the honour that is due,
That not my tongue without experience
By many ways holding and proving thee,
May find another such as I desire,
Subject for praises such as you deserve.

89. A genius happy, which to thee belongs,
Assisted by Apollo's bounteous gift,

Whose clearer light doth us illuminate,
Deflecting us from error's dangerous course,
You dazzle me with your bright affluence,
And hold my genius fettered in rebuke,
Yet give I thee the palm and glory too,
Which, Doctor Soria, thou hast given to me.

90. If all your works are still so estimable,
Renowned Cantoral, throughout the world,
Thy praises surely may be well excused.
Though neither with new art nor style I praise
With eloquence certainly qualified,
And with that power which genius me ordains,
In silence too I praise, and eke admire,
Advancing where no speeches can advance.

91. Geronimo Baca y de Quiñones, thou,
If any obstacle to thy praise has been,
Will pardon this my inattention,
In the indemnity I offer now.
From this day forward, in clear voice and acclaim,
In the concealed and the open parts
Of the terraqueous world I'll cause to shine
Thy name with flame and reputation too.

92. Thou green and fertile bank of juniper, (Nebro,)
Nor of the mournful cypress art enriched,
Exulting clear and well known Hebrus' stream,
Bedecked with laurel and the myrtle too,
Now in my power joyful I celebrate,
Also I celebrate the good assigned
By heaven to thy banks, for on them dwell
Poetic wits as clear as stars remote.

93. Witnesses of this two brothers are,
Two lights, two sons of poesy divine,
To whom kind heaven with open hand did give
As much of art as well may be possessed ;
Temperate age, reflection excellent,
Treatment mature, with modest phantasy,
Working eternal, worthy, laurels for
Lupercio Leonardo de Argensola.

94. With holy envy, competition, too,
    It seems the younger brother would aspire
    The elder to surpass, advancing strait
    And mounting where scarce human wit can rise,
    For this he writes, sings infinite success,
    With a so sweet and modulated harp,
    That Bartolome the younger merits well
    What to Lupercio the elder is given.

95. If good beginning and continuance gives
    Hopes the result will rare and excellent prove
    In every circumstance, my wit attains
    What yours has reached not, Cosme Pariente;
    So with assured confidence you may
    Promise to your wise, open countenance,
    The crown, a guerdon honourably due
    To your clear genius and unspotted life.

96. In solitude, by heaven accompanied,
    You live, O great Morillo, and evince
    That never quit your Christian character,
    Muses most sacred and most apt to sing,
    From my own sister's aliment you received,
    And for indemnity you us direct,
    And teach us how to sing of things divine,
    Grateful to heaven, to the soil profitable.

97. Turia, thou with voice sweet, formerly
    Did chant the excellence of thy favoured sons,
    If thou wouldst deign to hear my voice now formed,
    Neither invidiously nor in rivalry
    Shalt thou hear how thy fame is aggrandised
    By those I will rehearse, whose presence sure,
    Valour, and virtue, genius thee enrich,
    Gindus above, or Ganges thee enhance.

98. And thou, Don Juan Coloma, in whose breast
    Heaven has implanted so much of her grace,
    That envy self is compassed with hard chains,
    Creating numberless tongues for your fair fame,
    Which from the gentle Tagus to the realms
    Of wide fertility your name bear, growing great;

Thou, Conde de Elda, fortunate in all,
Hast Turia made than Po more celebrate.

99. What in your breast pours out and superabounds,
A fountain ever is of divine streams,
To whom the quire illumination brings
As to a Lord, bending obsequiously,
To whose unique name a deep debt is due
From Ethiopia to the Austrian race,
Don Luis Garceran, peerless exists
Montesa's master, master of the world.

100. He merits well in this renowned vale
A noble spot, a situation known,
Where fame would willingly a name concede,
Which his great genius worthily has earned.
Heaven be careful him due praise to yield,
By heaven it is his virtue is increased,
May heaven commend what I am powerless
Towards Don Alonso Rebolledo to do.

101. Doctor Falcon, you rise with so high flight
That e'en the eagle in the rear is left,
For with thy wit thou touchest heaven's point,
Thyself removing from this wretched vale.
This makes me dread, in just suspicion,
That though I praise thee, you complaints will make
Of me: for on this land by night and day
My voice and tongue continually dilate.

102. If I had that which fortune only holds,
The various wheel of sweetest poesy,
Light and more moveable than the moon herself,
Which neither is nor can in quiet be.
Should such a faculty as unchangeableness
Exist, to Micer Artieda it may belong,
Who occupies ever an exalted place
In science, wit, and virtue conversant.

103. Such praises, well deserved, abundantly
You give to genius rare, O Gil Polo,
These hast thou merited alone, and reached;
To me is this reiteration sweet:

Hold it with certainty, bound in by hope
That in this vale a mausoleum new
These hinds to thee will raise, well guarded too
Shall be your ashes, and name celebrated.

104. Christoval de Virues, advancing too,
Science and virtue adequate to time,
Do you these properties in verse embalm,
Whereby you have the world's deceit escaped.
Fortunate land, with plant well born and reared,
I will procure that in your native realm,
And foreign eke, your genius have its fruit,
Be known, admired, and be approved of all.

105. If, in conformity to the genius which
Silvestre de Espinosa shews, we had
To praise another voice more competent,
More time, more means, had then been requisite.
But since my voice to his intent is set,
I will bestow, as compensation full,
With riches which he holds of Delos' Lord,
The greater waters of the Hippocrene font.

106. These among, as I see Apollo come,
The world embellishing with his radiance,
I find the gallant Garcia Romero
A worthy name in a so worthy list.
Should the fair daughter of quick Peneus' stream,
Ovid himself the historiographer,
In plains of Thessaly discover him,
She had into him, not laurels, herself transformed.

107. Burst silence forth ; sacred interment burst ;
Piercing the air, to heavens raising up
De Fray Pedro de Huete, accent full
Of his divine muse, sacred, heroical,
By his exalted rare ability.
He sung of fame, in singing perseveres,
Raising astonishment, in a knowing world,
By works as testimonies of his pure strains.

108. Contemplating the end, the time is come
Which gave commencement to the highest aim

    I ever undertook, and which I hope
    Will move to crashing fury Phœbus' soul;
    For by a genius rustic and too gross,
    The double suns which Spain illuminate
    To Spain not only, but the world entire
    I would give praises, though the means should fail.

109. Apollo's sacred, honoured sciences,
    Discretion courteous in maturity,
    The well spent years, with sage experience
    Counsel consummate still assuring us,
    Wits' keenest point us advertising sure
    How to select, and dissipate the obscure
    Difficulty, encompassing us round,
    In these two sons of Spain alone are seen.

110. In them an epilogue, my shepherd friends,
    Of my extended canticle now I make,
    In it composing the due meed of praise;
    Such you have heard, not equal to their claims,
    For all man's wit justly their debtor is,
    Honourably I try to satisfy their due,
    And may the world the same aim meditate,
    Admiring them who draw from heaven descent.

111. With this 1 wish my canticle to end,
    Commencing with an admiration new,
    And if you think in it I do advance,
    Declaring who they are I overcome;
    For these men do I raise myself above,
    Wanting these men, I were and am ashamed:
    Such is Lainez, such Figueroa is,
    Worthy eternal and ceaseless applause.

Scarce had ended the charming nymph the last accents of her tasteful strain, when turning to unite the flames which were divided, they closed in the midst, and by degrees consuming themselves, in a brief period the burning element disappeared, and with it the discreet muse, before the eyes of all, just as the morning began to disclose its fresh and rosy cheeks over the skies, giving joyful indications of the coming day. Immediately the venerable Telesio, placing himself on the grave of Meliso, and surrounded by all the agreeable company there, borrowing of all complaisant attention and uncommon silence, in this wise he spake :—

"That which this night past in this identical spot, and you, with your own eyes, have seen, discriminating swains and lovely women, will be granted to you to know how acceptable to heaven is the laudable custom which we assign to yearly sacrifices and honourable obsequies, for the happy souls of those corpses which, by your decree, have deserved interment in this memorable valley.

"I tell you, my friends, because that henceforth, with more fervour and diligence, you may co-operate in this holy work, since you see how rare and exalted spirits the notice of the beauteous Calliope has awakened in us, that these are not worthy alone of your praises, but of all which may accrue to them ; and think not that it is a small matter and enjoyment that I have received the knowledge exactly how great is the number of those exalted geniuses which still breathe vital air in our Spain ; for it always has been, and still is, the opinion of foreign nations, that many there are not, especially in the science of poetry. This being contrary to the fact, for each one called by name by the nymph would show well in comparison of any stranger, and would establish the truth that in Spain poesy is estimated at its due worth. Hence the clear intellects which abound in Spain, though little appreciated by some, by their energy communicate lofty and unusual conceptions, without daring to publish them to the world, and I undertake to say heaven should arrange it so, for the world is not worthy, nor is our ill-conditioned age in a fit state to enjoy such fruits of the spirits. Yet it seems to me, shepherds, that the short repose of the past night, and our protracted ceremonies, have awakened in you fatigue and desire to sleep ; so it will be well if we fill up the measure of our intent, and that each return to his cottage or village, treasuring in his memory what the muse has inculcated."

This saying, he descended from the tomb, and turning to crown it with new and sorrowful boughs, he circumambulated the pyre three several times, all following him, reciting after him certain devout orisons.

This terminated, in the midst of all, he bent his solemn visage on every side, and bowing his head, indicating a smiling exterior, and loving eyes, he took leave of all the company, who dissolved on all sides of the four ways which radiated from the locality. In a brief interval all broke up, leaving only those of the hamlet of Aurelio, and with them Timbrio, Silerio, Nisida and Blanca, with the famous shepherds, Elicio, Thirsis, Damon, Lauso, Erastro, Daranio, Arsindo, and those unfortunate four, Orompo, Marsilio, Crisio and Orfenio, with the shepherdesses, Galatea, Florisa, Silveria, and her friend Belisa, for whom Marsilio pined.

These all united, the venerable Aurelio told them it would be well if they quitted that spot, and went to pass the siesta at the streamlet of palms, as a place best adapted for it.

All seemed very sensible, as Aurelio had said, and forthwith, with measured pace, off they repaired to the appointed spot. But as the bright vision of the shepherdess Belisa would not let the spirit of Marsilio rest in peace, he asked, if it were practicable and allowable too, to join her and remonstrate with her on her unreasonableness towards him ; but not to forego the decorum which was due to Belisa, he remained incapable of effecting his purpose.

These consequences and accidents did love cause in the souls of the two enamoured ones, Elicio and Erastro, each desiring to acquaint Galatea with what she already knew. Then spoke Aurelio :—" It does not seem consistent to me, hinds, that you should show yourselves so greedy, so that you will not correspond or pay what you owe to the larks and nightingales, and those little variously-plumed birds, which, amidst the boughs, in an unwonted strain, entertain and rejoice you. Tune up your instruments and elevate your sonorous voices, and show how, by art and management, you can excel nature, and with such an entertainment we shall less perceive the onus of the journey and the rays of Phœbus, which now threaten forcibly to strike the earth."

The suggestions of Aurelio were soon obeyed, for in an eye's twinkling Erastro awakened his rebeck and Arsindo his pipe, at the sound of which instruments, each giving a hand to Elicio, he started a song in this wise :—

ELICIO.

1. For the impossible I combat,
Should I wish to withdraw,
Nor pass nor way do I perceive.
Whether to vanquish or surrender,
Desire impels me behind thee to go ;
And though I know 'tis here imperative
Rather to die than conquer,
When I am more dangerous,
Then come I to acquire
A fuller faith in the uncertain end.

2. Heaven, which me condemns,
An advance favourable not to hope,
With a hand plenteous on me lets drop,
Without the works of hope,
Infinite assurances of pain,
Yet my valorous breast,
Which burns and dissolves itself
In a quick-loving fire,
In exchange reverts
To fuller faith in the uncertain end.

3. In constancy, firm doubt,
False faith, sure dread
The naked will of love.
These never love disturb
Which changes not from its integrity.
Quick-footed to me flies onward.
Absence or disdain ensue,
Evil grows, and quenched is repose,
Yet will I entertain for my own good,
A fuller faith in the uncertain end.

4. Is not madness recognised,
And obvious dotage too ?
Should I seek what accident
Denies me, and my destiny,
What fate assures me not ?
At all this alarmed am I,
There reaches me no delight,
And in so perilous a circumstance,

Deep love induces me to hold
A fuller faith in the uncertain end.

5. From my grief I ascertain
That to a certain end it is confined.
It reaches where love
And imagination
In part its rigour truly doth assuage.
Poor and necessitous,
To imagination I give up
A so painful solace.
Yet does the heart embrace
A fuller faith in the uncertain end.

6. More than ever supervene
At a blow all woes,
And the more to wound me
All being mortal wounds.
They me preserve in life,
But at last to a fine end
Our life in honour mounts.
My end will render me notorious,
For I in life and death have exercised
A fuller faith in the uncertain end.

It seemed, to Marsilio, that what Elicio had sung was so apposite to his case that he desired to pursue the same conceit. Not doubting but others would assist at the voice of those instruments, he prosecuted the strain :—

MARSILIO.

1. How easily inflates
The wind our hopes,
Which may be composed
Of vain affiances.
Such as imagination oft suggests
All ends, and achieves
Love's hopes.
The means which time proffers,
Still in the candid lover,
Alone surviveth faith.

2. And this in me such vigour doth attain,
   That in despite of that disdain
   With doubtfulness replete.
   It reassures a very precious good
   Which very hope supports.
   Though very love should fail
   In the most candid and impassioned breast,
   My woes augmenting sorely
   Within my breast, e'en to vexation's point,
   Alone surviveth faith.

3. Thou knowest love, that thou exactest still
   The tribute of my faith immutable.
   In this you by exaction overcome;
   My faith died not,
   For truly it regenerates with my works.
   Thou knowest well that diminishes
   My glory all, and my contentment too,
   The more your glory doth expand itself,
   And that in my soul, for a sure dwelling place,
   Alone surviveth faith.

4. Yet if it be a fact notorious,
   Without a doubt existing,
   That faith doth not on glory verge,
   I who without it will not live,
   What triumph hope I, or what victory?
   My feeling vanishes
   With the evil which is present,
   All good to flight is put,
   And in the midst of such misfortune still,
   Alone surviveth faith.

With a most profound sigh, the melancholy Marsilio terminated his canticle, and forthwith Erastro, seizing his rebeck, without let or hindrance, pursued the song :—

ERASTRO.

1. In the deep woe which doth beset me sore,
   And in the 'vantage of my sad sorrow,
   Is my faith of such estimation
   That it flies not from apprehension

Or rests itself on hope
Nor disconcerting, nor disturbing it,
To witness my undoubted suffering
In its ascent most difficult,
Nor do consume a life
Vivid faith, dead hope.

2. A miracle existeth in my woe,
The more so for my good,
And, if it happen, such a nature 'tis,
That midst a thousand 'vantages is assigned
For the principal the palm.
Let fame herself with expert tongue declare
Due notice to the earth
That constant love subsists
My breast within, where do support themselves
A living faith, dead hope.

3. Your rigorous contemptuousness
And my humble deserts
Me in such apprehension do detain,
That though I knew you wished it,
Nor utter could I, nor presume to act,
Open ever I remark
To my unhappiness the portal is,
Only gradually do I achieve,
For with you of small avail are
Lively faith, dead hope.

4. There touches not my fancy
A so foolish raving
As to conclude that I can e'er attain
The smallest of my coveted desires
By faith alone to reach ;
Oh, shepherdess, pray rest assured
That the restored soul attains
The very love which thou deserveth,
For in it wilt thou clear discern
A living faith, dead hope.

Here Erastro ceased, and without intervention the absent
Crisio, at the sound of the same instruments, gave voice to
his own state—

CRISIO.

1. If at times into desperation falls
   Of good the firm affection,
   Who in the career would droop
   Of the so amorous passion?
   What fruit or what advantage hopeth he?
   I know not who doth to himself assure
   Glory, satisfaction, good fortune
   By amorous impetuosity,
   If in it, and in the most fortunate too,
   No faith faith is, without duration.

2. In endless circumstances long since known,
   Are seen, and in amours
   The haughty and the bold,
   In the beginning conquerors,
   But finally among the vanquished found;
   He knows, who boasts discretion,
   That in continuance is purified
   The triumph of the battle,
   Discovering wheresoe'er it be
   That is not faith which is not permanent.

3. In him that would love
   Not by its contentedness alone,—
   Impossible to last
   In his vain thought
   The faith that he would guard,
   If in the greater misadventure too,
   My faith so firm and safe,
   And in it innate goodness not be found,
   Of it I would predicate
   That is not faith, the faith which not endures.

4. The impetuosity and the levity
   Of a young half-maddened lover,
   The wails and sorrows
   Are clouds which summer
   Can dissipate with speed.
   Love is not that which to extremity drives
   Sheer appetite and fatuity;
   For when he wills he doth not stoutly will,

Who dies not is no lover,
No faith faith is, without duration.

The order observed by the swains in their respective
strains seemed good to all, and with aspiration did they
await until Thirsis or Damon should begin. Hastily did
Damon fulfil expectation, for when Crisio ended, to the
touch of his rebeck he indited the following versicles :—

1. Ungrateful yet, oh, Amarillis fair,
Who can melt you
Should contribute to harden you.
Oh the anxiety of my complaint
And the fidelity of my desires,
Instructed well, ye shepherdesses, are ye
That in the love which I sincerely boast
Unto extremities I reach
For, after love to God,
My faith alone converges towards thee.

2. For since I mount so high
In loving a mortal thing,
Upon me my woes close,
E'en rising to the soul
As to its natural country.
By this am I in recognition full
Yet so remote my love
That entertaining it I die indeed,
But if in love faith be,
My faith alone converges towards thee.

3. The many years now past
In love-devoted services,
The sacrifices of my very soul
Of faith, and my solicitudes,
All obvious indications,
For this of thee I will not supplicate
A remedy for evils I sustain.
Should I come to supplicate
Amarillis, 'tis because
My faith alone converges towards thee.

4. In tne ocean of my torture
　Calm weather ne'er found I,
　And that cheering hope
　Whereby fidelity itself sustains,
　Is quite unreached as yet.
　Of love and fortune
　Do I complain, yet do not I come up;
　For them I come to such a point,
　Yet destitute of hopefulness,
　Alone that faith is faith which **towards thee bends.**

This poetic effort of Damon completely confirmed in Timbrio and in Silerio the good opinions already conceived, and the more so when at the instance of Thirsis and of Elicio, the free yet disdainful Lauso to the melody of the flute of Arsindo relaxed his voice into a corresponding vein of poesy.

LAUSO.

1. Disdain has burst thy chains,
　False love, and to my memory
　The same has restored the glory
　Of absence from thy pains,
　Who wills my faith may call
　A longing not a lasting one,
　In his opinion he may me confirm
　As seemeth to him good.

2. Let him aver that quickly I forgot,
　That by a so thin hair
　E'en that a breeze could snap it
　My faith suspended was,
　Let him add that feigned were
　My plaints, my sighs,
　And that the shot of love
　Beyond my vestments never did **extend.**

3. Not to be styled vain
　Or e'en capricious, me torments,
　In exchange for seeing exempt
　My neck from an insane yoke
　As to Silena I am well advised,
　And her unusual state

21—2

Which assures and yet betrays
Her peaceful serene face.

4. From her extraordinary gravity
And her submissive loving-looking eyes
There's not much but would despoil
Volition under every aspect too,
This at first sight
But after being known,
Not seeing her a very life confers,
And more, if more could be.

5. Silena, mine and heaven's,
Oft times have I her invoked,
All lovely stood she forth
As if from heaven she late descended were,
But now, mistrust aside,
Better shall I entitle her
Sirena, as water false,
No more the Syren she from heaven came down.

6. With eyes and with the pen,
With earnestness and jests
Of vain, hoodwinked lovers
To me the sum incalculable
The last is e'er the first,
Yet the most enamoured,
As badly hated is the unfortunate last,
As cherished is the first.

7. Oh how much more would sure esteemed be
The beauty of Silena,
Should her deportment and discretion be
Equal to her comeliness,
Discretion would not fail,
But in her is it undeveloped so
That only for a halter doth it serve,
And bold presumption chokes.

8. I speak not currently
But would impassioned be,
I speak not in disguise,
Offended without reason

Passion blinds me not,
Nor of diminution the desire,
Close my tongue hath ever followed
The boundaries of reason.

9. Her many various predilections,
Her mutable ideas,
Continually convert
Friends to be her opposites,
Hence many reasons justly do exist
Why foes Silena has.
Not wholly good is she,
Or they as evil wholly to be stamped.

Now came Lauso to an end, and though he conjectured that no one understood him under the covered name of Silena, yet more than three of the company knew it, and were surprised that the modesty of Lauso should be instrumental in offending any one, especially the disguised shepherdess, of whom he was so enamoured.

Still in the opinion of his friend Damon he was exculpated, for he knew all about Silena, and how Lauso had used her name, and wondered more at what he did not say.

However, as before said, Lauso finished, and as Galatea was cognisant with the voice of Nisida, he asked her for a song; hence, ere any other swain had made essay, giving signal to Arsindo that on his breathing into his flute she would proceed, at whose sweet noise she lifted up her voice and delicately warbled these stanzas :—

GALATEA.

By how much love invites and gently calls,
To the soul rendering apparent taste,
By so much more its mortal grievance flies,
Who knows the name which Fame confers on it.
The breast opposed to an amorous flame
With honourable resistance arms itself,
Nothing can hinder its inclemency.
Little its fire and rigour can inflame
Who ne'er was loved stands in security,
And never knew to love by that same tongue

Which in dishonour lessens and corrects.
But if to love and not to love causes
Dishonour, in what exercise will pass
Life, which doth honour more than life esteem ?

One could easily see that in the strain of Galatea there
was an answer made to the malevolent Lauso, which concurred with free spirits, but not with malicious tongues and
wayward souls, who in not attaining what they desire,
turn love, which from time to time they show, into an
odious and detestable principle, as appeared in Lauso ; but
he might have emerged from this error had the good condition of Lauso known it, and the froward state of Silena
been ignorant of it.   Immediately on the cessation of Galatea's stanzas, with words of courtesy she asked Nisida to do
the same, who, being as courteous as lovely, without further
repetition, at the sound of the instrument of Florisa, began
her song in this wise :—

NISIDA.

Well did I call valour to my defence
In hard assault, and amorous attack,
Well did I raise presumption up on high,
Against the rigour of the known offence,
So reinforced and so intense appeared
The battery, and my native powers so weak,
That without gathering up myself, surprise
In love, his power immense did make me feel
Valour and honesty, and gathering up,
Caution and occupation and coy breast,
With small reward is love the conqueror,
And to escape the victory, sure
Counsels were ever indispensable,
At sight this very truth I recognise.

When Nisida ended, and Galatea ceased admiring, as well
as those who heard her, they approached the spot destined
for the siesta.   But in that brief interval Belisa completed
what Silveria had asked, which was that she should sing
something, who, accompanied by Arsindo's flute, gave utterance to the ensuing strains in liquid melody of verse :—

BELISA.

1. From a free will exempt
   Awaits that reason
   Which doth our fame augment,
   Abandoning all vain affection,
   Parent of mischief;
   When the soul is freighted
   With some loving cargo
   'Tis something to its taste,
   A compound poisonous
   With juice of bitter Oleander too.

2. For the greater quantity
   Of acquired riches
   In value and in quality
   Never is given or sold
   Precious liberty;
   For who to its loss will expose himself
   For a simple quarrel only
   With an obstinate lover,
   Whatever else one may on earth possess,
   It is not comparable to liberty.

3. If it is grief insufferable
   In a disdainful confinement to hold
   A body free from love,
   To hold the soul in deep captivity
   Wil't not be greater pain?
   Truly it will, and of such character
   That remedy for such will, being strong,
   Is not in patience found,
   Not years, courage, not skill,
   In death alone doth it reside entire.

4. Move, then, my sound intent,
   From this fatuity afar,
   This false concealment fly,
   Directing my free will,
   My thought to reasons mode.
   My tender neck exempt
   Allows it not, nor yet does it consent
   To bear on it a yoke too amorous,

> For which repose itself is set at nought,
> And liberty disappears.

To the very soul of the wretched Marsilio went these free verses of the shepherdess, by reason of the slender hope that his words promised to improve his labours, yet so stout was the faith wherewith he loved her, about the notoriety even of her actions, of which he had heard that he still continued to favour her.

And now was at an end the path conducting to the stream of palms, and though they did not intend deviating from their intention of there passing the siesta, yet on viewing the commodiousness of the locality, it induced them to stay there. Hence they all arrived, and quickly the venerable Aurelio ordered that all should be seated adjacent to the clear and mirror-like brook which glided through the small herbage, whose rise was at the foot of a very lofty and antique palm, not another like it on the banks of the Tagus, save one adjoining, hence the place was styled the brook of palms, and after sitting down, with extreme will and liberality, they were served with juicy apples by the shepherds of Aurelio, and their thirst was assuaged in the clear and fresh fluid which the limpid brook supplied. The short and tasty refection done, some of the company divided, and sought a shady retired place, where they might pass the nightly hours in slumber. There only remained those of the company and of the hamlet of Aurelio, with Timbrio, Silerio, Nisida and Blanca. Thirsis and Damon, who appeared to be enjoying even a more grateful confabulation than they expected, and this was preferable even to sleep itself.

Divined, and almost known, was this Aurelio's intention, for he said to them, " Well will it be, sirs, that we who are here, as we have not yet surrendered ourselves to sleep, that, in fact, we should steal from sleep, so will we avail ourselves of what we like best, and what my idea is, and we can exact it from ourselves, is that each one, as best he may, should make manifest the power of his wit by suggesting some question, or enigma, to which the nearest companion should reply, by which device two things are achieved, one, that we pass with less *ennui* the time we must here remain ; the other, that we fatigue not our auditory faculties with laments of the tender passion, and love-belaboured ditties."

To this motion of Aurelio did they readily consent, and without altering their relative positions, the first who began to interrogate was Aurelio himself, and in this wise :—

AURELIO.

What is that powerful thing
Which, from the orient to the drooping west
Is known and is renowned?
Now strong and valiant,
Now timorous and weak,
Taking and giving health,
Virtue both shows and conceals
In more than a single time.
Stronger is in age,
And in the cheerful growth,
Changeth it doth in that which changeth not.
By some unusual pre-eminence
It makes him tremble who perspires,
And for the rarest eloquence
Can it to baseness and to silence turn.
With divers means,
It measures its being and its appellation,
Is wont to seize renown,
Such as is known in lands innumerable.
Armless itself, it yet subdues the armed,
And to be victorious is compelled,
Seeming directly vengeance to pursue
The most disgraced is,
A thing of wonder is it,
Which in field and city,
At the head of proof,
That any man may boldness feel,
Yet doth in the scuffle lose.

It fell to the lot of the shepherd Arsindo, who was standing near Aurelio, to reply, so having a little ruminated on the meaning, he finally gave utterance,—

"It seems to me, Aurelio, that an age impels us to become more enamoured of the signification of your question than of the most lively shepherdess we can meet, for if I am not in error, the powerful and well known of which you talk is wine, and in it are concentrated all the attributes to which you have adverted." "You say truly, Arsindo," rejoined Aurelio, "and I am rather vexed that I did propose a question so easily solved; but announce yours, which will require some eminent one to unloose its complexity." "I am delighted," said Arsindo, and the following was proposed :—

ARSINDO.

1. Who is that who loses colour
When he ought to revive?
And quickly to recover turns
A yet brighter and a better one?
Leopard in its birth,
Then besmeared with black,
And thus coloured,
Doth satisfaction to the sight impart.

2. Nor laws, nor customs doth it entertain,
Friendship with flames it holds,
The chambers visiting from time to time
Of sovereign lords.
Dead, it is styled a man,
Alive, as woman known.
The likeness of a shadow it holds too
With fire's bright condition.

Damon it was who was standing by the side of Arsindo, and scarce had Arsindo propounded his riddle when he said to him, "It seems to me, Arsindo, that your question is not quite so abstruse as would appear; for if there be no evil in it, coals is what, when alive, one calls man; inflamed and quick, it burns, which is the name of a woman, and all the rest agrees in the description; and if you rest in the same penalty as Aurelio, by reason of the facility with which your riddle has been understood, I would have you keep company in it, for Thirsis, whose business it is to reply, will bring us out all square," and then he propounded his riddle :—

DAMON.

1. What is the so polished lady
   Adorned and well arranged,
   Timorous yet bold,
   Shame-faced, yet dishonest,
   Exciting, yet unsavoury?

2. If there be many because he affrights,
   They change from woman the name
   Into man, and a sure law is it,
   That the king goes with them,
   And that each individual man takes them away.

"It is very well, friend Damon," said Thirsis quickly, "that your undoubted defiance comes out, and that you abide by the penalty of Aurelio and Arsindo, if any there be; for I would have you to know that I am conversant with what covers your riddle. It is the card and the fold of the card." Damon acknowledged what Thirsis said, and then Thirsis proposed his riddle :—

THIRSIS.

Who is that which all eyes is,
From the crown to the feet.
Occasionally his own interest without,
Is cause of amorous annoyances?
Accustomed is he quarrels to appease,
Yet neither goes nor comes,
And though possessing eyes so many,
Few children doth discover,
Of grief bearing the name,
Which is accounted mortal,
Both good and harm he doth,
Love moderates and inflames.

In confusion, the riddle of Thirsis was put to Elicio, it being his duty to reply, and in no time, almost, did he solve it. But jealousy arose, and Thirsis giving way on the very spy of the time, the moment of it did Elicio substitute the following :—

ELICIO.

1. Dark 'tis, yet very clear,
   Containing infinite variety,

> Encumbering us with truths,
> Which are at length declared.
> 'Tis sometimes of a jest produced,
> At others of high fancy,
> And it is wont defiance to create,
> Of airy matters treating.

> 2. Any man its name may know,
> Even to little children,
> Many there are, and masters have
> In diffcrent ways.
> There is no old woman it embraces not,
> With of these ladies, one
> At times in good odour,
> This tires, that satisfies.

> 3. Wise ones there be who overwatch
> Sensations to extract.
> Some run wild
> The more they watch o'er it.
> Such is foolish, and such curious,
> Such easy, such complex,
> Yet be it something, be it nought,
> Reveal to me what the said thing may be ?

Timbrio could not divine what Elicio's riddle purported to be, and scarce began he to run about to see if any reply was tendered, or if any idea was suggested, when soon they found that Galatea, who was standing near Nisida, said, " If it is consistent to break the order which is received, and that the first who discovers should be the first to speak, I say, for myself, that I have unravelled the propounded enigma, and am ready to announce it, should Timbrio grant me leave."

" Certainly, all lovely Galatea," answered Timbrio, " for I know that though I cannot, your clear wit can solve yet greater difficultics ; still, I would desire your patience until Elicio speaks. Should he not hit off the solution, I bow to the opinion which I entertain of my genius, and of yours too."

Elicio turned to proffer his riddle, and then Timbrio declared what his was, saying, " In the same sense which I thought your question was dark, Elicio, with the same too it seems to me that it enucleates itself, for the last verse says, ' Let them aver what thing the very thing is ;' and thus I answer your inquiry and aver that your question is, that that which is the thing, the thing is—and you will not be astonished—to find that I demurred as to the reply, for I should be more astonished at my wit, if I had answered yet more quickly, which will be proved how little artifice there be in my question, which is this—

TIMBRIO.

> What is that which to its displeasure
> Measures its feet by its eyes,
> Without discomfort causing,
> Making them quickly sing ?
> It is pleasant to extract them,
> Though ofttimes he who them fairly extracts,
> Not only does not his sure ill assuage,
> But more disgust conceals.

It appertained to Nisida to give response to this proposition, yet was it not possible tor her to divine it, or Galatea, who followed.

Now Orompo, discerning that the lady shepherdesses had fatigued their brains on the thought, said to them, " Weary not yourselves, ladies ; do not oppress your minds in the opening of this enigma, for, peradventure in all your lives you never saw the character comprised in this riddle. Were it otherwise, very certain are we in your understanding that in a less space of time you could have furnished solution to more difficult questions. Therefore, with your permission, I would reply to Timbrio, and announce to him that his riddle implies a man with fetters on his legs, since when he gets his feet away from those eyes who see him, it is either to be free or to get clear of punishment, for you perceive shepherdesses, if I had reason to imagine, that none of you have, during your existence, seen a prison or its tenants."

" Speaking for myself, I cannot say that I ever did see a prison," said Galatea. This was also asserted by Nisida and Blanca, hence Nisida proposed her riddle in this wise,—

NISIDA.

Fire bites, and the mouthful
Is the damage, and the profit of the masticator,
The wounded wight loses no blood,
Though he should be well slashed.
But if the wound is deep,
Its point the hand not hitting,
Death to the stricken party doth ensue,
And in that death stands life.

A brief space only did Galatea delay in reply to Nisida, for she soon broke out—"I know full well that I do not deceive myself, fair Nisida, if I advance that to nothing better can we assimilate your enigma than to a pair of candle-snuffers, and to the wick and wax which is cut off. If this be true, as it really is, and you remain satisfied with my reply, hear now mine, which with not less facility I hope will be enunciated by your sister, than I have composed thine, and directly I announce it, and it is this :—

GALATEA.

Three sons which of one mother
Were in perfection born,
And of a brother there a nephew was,
One and the other a father.
These three without remorse
Their mother did ill treat,
Her dealing a thousand blows,
Thereby evincing their science profound.

Blanca there stood ruminating as to what this enigma of Galatea could signify, when she caught sight of two lively swains who crossed to where they were standing, shewing by the force with which they ran that some matter of moment has impelled such haste, and in a twinkling they heard some mournful tones as of persons needing help ; and with this surprise all rose up and followed the guess where the sounds issued, and in a few steps they abandoned the delightful spot and entrenched themselves on the banks of the fresh-flowing Tagus, which here so softly glided along, and scarce did the stream loom upon them when something presented itself beyond imagination to paint. They observed two lady swains of gentle deportment, who held a shepherd down by the folds of his skin vestment, with all their available strength, with a view not to let the unfortunate wretch drown himself, half of his body being in the water. His head was above it, and he was trying with his feet to disembarrass himself from them, they hindering his desperate intents. However they almost wished to release him, seeing their power was inadequate to contend with the obstinacy of his defiance.

Fortunately two swains came up who had witnessed all, and, seizing the desponding man, dragged him from the water effectually. Being shocked at the strange spectacle, their grief was augmented when they knew that the shepherd who would drown himself was Galercio, Artidoro's brother, while the shepherdesses were Maurisa, his sister, and the fair Teolinda, who, when they recognised Galatea and Florisa, with tears in their eyes Teolinda dashed forward to embrace Galatea, ejaculating—

"Oh, Galatea, my sweet friend and lady, how has this unhappy woman accomplished the word which caused a return to see thee, and to declare to thee the news of her contentment!" "As to what you treat, Teolinda," replied Galatea, I shall be as pleased to serve you as you know my will is, but it appears to me that your eyes do not credit your words, nor do these satisfy me so that I should predict success in thy desires."

Whilst this was passing between Galatea and Teolinda, Elicio and Arsindo with the other shepherds had divested of his clothes Galercio, and while detaching his pelisse of skin, which, with the rest of his attire, was dripping wet, a little piece of paper fell from his bosom, which Thirsis gathered up, and opening it found it to contain some verses, and because they could not be read for the wet, he placed them on the branch of a tree, to dry in the sun.

They put on him a great loose gabardine belonging to Arsindo, and the luckless youth was quite amazed and was speechless, although Elicio asked him the cause which induced him to commit the rash act. However, his sister Maurisa answered for him, saying, "Lift up your eyes, shepherd, and you will see who is the occasion, and what

has brought my ill-fated brother to such a desperate extremity." Hearing what Maurisa said the swains turned
up their eyes, and saw on the top of a rock which overhung
a river flowing beneath, a buxom and pliant shepherdess
seated on this same eminence, looking on with an oblique
leer at what the swains were doing. This lady was discovered by all to be the cruel Gelasia. "This one, unim-
pressible to love, this unknown one," pursued Maurisa, "is,
swains, the mortal enemy of this my hopeless brother, who,
as all the bank frequenters know, and you also, loves her,
courts and adores her, and in exchange for all the uninter-
rupted services which he has done for her, and the tears he
has lavished, this morning, with the most coy and unloving
disdain that could be brought to bear, demanded that he
should depart from her presence, and never more return,
and so prompt was my brother to obey her, that on his own
life a dire defeat he made, not to violate her command ; and
if luckily these swains had not opportunely arrived, the end
of my joy had come, and the close of the days of my much
to be pitied brother."

Into astonishment did what Maurisa said throw all who
heard it, but into yet wider astonishment when they saw
that the cruel Gelasia without stirring from the place she
occupied, or taking the smallest account of any of the company, whose eyes on her were fixed with a most reckless
nonchalance and a disdainful elasticity, seized upon a little
rebeck from out of a shepherd's pouch, and moderating her
movements quite at ease, in a short period, with a voice
tuned to the extreme, began singing in this strain :—

GELASIA.

Who will forsake the verdant, shady mead,
The herbs so fresh, and eke the fresh fountains,
Who to pursue with steps so diligent
The upstarted hare or the wild boar so brisk,
Who, with a friendly and sonorous note,
Will not keep back the innocent feathered tribe ?
Who in siesta's burning hours will not
Seek in the shade the solace of repose,
Rather than follow fear, incendiaries,
The zeal, the anger, passion, death, and pains

Of love delusive, which so afflict the world?
My loves both are, and have been, in the fields,
Roses and jessamines my manacles ;
Free was I born—I ground on liberty.

Gelasia stood while singing, and in her movement, and the motion of her face disclosed her disenamoured condition. Yet scarce had she terminated the final verse of her canticle, when she uprose with a peculiar levity, and, as if she would fly some fearful object, began to make off for the rock below, leaving the swains in wonder at her state, and even confused with her running.

But quickly they saw what was the cause of it, at sight of the enamoured Lenio, who, with a jerking step, purposed ascending the same rock to arrive at where Gelasia stood. Yet would she not await him, her intention being to carry out her cruel device. The wearied Lenio touched the highest point of the rock, when Gelasia was at its base, and seeing that she did not slacken her pace, the rather with increased celerity she passed over the surface, with a fatigued breath, and spirit outworn down sat he on the identical spot so lately occupied by Gelasia, and then began with governless passion to curse his fortune and the moment he ever raised his eye to look on the heartless Gelasia. At that very time, as if repenting of his speech, he turned to bless his eyes, and to hold it for a fortunate occasion that he was so situated. Quickly irritated, and impelled by a furious motive, he hurled from himself his shepherd's crook, and stripping off his goat-skin gabardine, he delivered it to the clear waters of Tagus' stream, which rushed along the base. All which being observed by the by-standing shepherds, they thought he was beside himself by reason of his love's passion.

Now Elicio and Erastro began mounting the rock to hinder him from committing any other rashness which might cost him dearer, and as soon as Lenio perceived them to be on the brow he made no other movement save drawing from his satchel his rebeck, and with an unaccustomed tranquillity down he sat, and directing his face where he heard the shepherdess, with a voice harmonious, yet not exempt from tears, the following strain he sang—

LENIO.

1. Who thee impels, cruel, who thee diverts?
   Who thee withdraws from the beloved intent?
   Who in thy feet doth wings of speed create,
   Wherewith thou runnest lighter than the wind?
   Wherefore dost thou my true faith lightly hold,
   The noble power of thought depreciating?
   Why dost thou fly me, why abandon me?
   Oh, harder far than marble to my plaints!

2. Am I perchance of a so mean estate
   That your sweet eye disdains to look on me?
   Poor am I? Am I covetous? hast found
   Aught false in me since I knew how to look?
   My first condition is no way changed,
   From less than from thy tresses do depend
   My soul; why then do you elude me so?
   Oh, harder far than marble to my plaints.

3. Take warning, lest your pride superfluous,
   Should see my free will back again restored;
   See how exchanged my whole presumption is,
   Converted into amorous intent:
   Observe how love 'gainst nothing doth avail,
   Exemption none to the most careless life.
   Stop there, then, why dost thou still hasten on?
   Oh, harder far than marble to my plaints.

4. I saw myself as thou seest, and now see,
   And as I was, myself I trust to see,
   Such potency has over me desire;
   I wish in consummation not to wish.
   Thou hast the palm gained, and the trophy thou,
   Whereby love can me in his prison hold;
   You have restored me, and of me lament'st,
   Oh, harder far than marble to my plaints.

Whilst the luckless swain was giving note to his dolorous lamentations, all the other swains were reproaching Galercio for his evil design, blackening the deed which he had attempted. Yet did not the disheartened youth deign a reply, at which Maurisa did not a little disconcert herself, thinking, that on her abandoning him he would try to put into execution his ill-conceived purpose. In this conjuncture Galatea and Florisa stepping aside with Teolinda, asked her what was the reason of her return, and if by chance she had learned anything of her Artidoro.

To this she replied, weeping, "I know not what I may tell you friends and ladies mine, except that heaven wished that I should find Artidoro, to the end that I should entirely lose him; for you must know that that ill-advised and my traitorous sister, who was the origin of my misadventure, that same person has been the occasion of the end, and, I may say, the clenching of my contentment, for knowing, as when we came with Galercio and Maurisa to the hamlet, that Artidoro was on the mountain, not far hence, with his flock, without dropping me a syllable she started to find him.

"She did find him, and feigning herself to be me, (for this sole end heaven ordained that we should appear) with little difficulty she made him to understand that the shepherdess, who in our hamlet he had disdained, was her sister. In fine, she declared for hers all those acts which I for him had done, and the extremity of suffering which I had undergone. And as the sensibilities of the swains were lovewards, with much less than what the traitress affirmed was she credited by him, so that he believed her so much to my prejudice, that without waiting for fortune to interweave any new obstacle, incontinently he proffered his hand to Leonarda to be his lawful partner, in the conviction that he gave it to Teolinda.

"Here then, you see, oh shepherdesses, in what terminates the fruit of my sighs and tears. You see too, how is deracinated the root of my hopes; but what I most feel is that it has been by the hand who sustained her most. Leonora enjoys Artidoro by means of the deceit of which I have apprised you, and since he knows it, although he ought to have felt the imposition, he actually dissembles his discretion.

"The news of his marriage soon reached the hamlet, and with it came the close of my joy. He knew the artifice of my sister, who also asserted, in exculpation, that the seeing that Galercio whom she so much loved, was mad for love of

22—2

Gelasia, that it appeared more easy to reduce to compliance the enamoured Artidoro than the desperate one of Galercio ; and then the two were one as far as appearance and gentility went, and that she considered herself lucky, nay, fortunate, in the society of Artidoro. With this she palliated the matter, as I have said, the enemy of my glory, and I, not to see her enjoy my due, quitted the hamlet and the presence of Artidoro, in midst of the most sorrowful ideas one can conceive, I come to impart the news of my misfortune, in company with Maurisa, who also comes with an intention to recount to you that which Grisaldo did after he heard of the abduction of Rosaura, and this very morn, at sunrise, we met with Galercio, who, with affectionate and loving reasons, was persuading Gelasia to requite his love. Yet she with the most *outré* disdain and coyness ordered him to quit her instantly, and never more presume to address her. So the harmless swain pressed by this order, and by such unwonted cruelty, wished to carry it out by doing what you have witnessed.

" All this is what has passed, my friends, since I left your company ; judge now if I have more reason to wail than before, and if the occasion is not augmented for you to dispose yourselves in solacing me, if peradventure ill counsel admits."

Teolinda said no more, for the profusion of tears which gushed from her eyes, and the sighs which shattered all her bulk hindered the office of her tongue, and although both Galatea and Florisa tried to shew themselves expert, and even eloquent, in assuaging her, yet was their labour of small effect ; and while between the shepherdesses certain reasonings were passing, the paper finished drying which Thirsis had drawn from the bosom of Galercio : being curious to read it, he took it and saw that it was to this purport :—

GALERCIO TO GELASIA.

1. Angel with a human figure,
    Fury with a female's visage,
    A cold and yet a quick enkindling flame,
    At which my soul doth purify itself.

Listen to the gross unreasonableness
From thy insensibility to love,
Translated from my soul
Unto these melancholy-written lines.

2. I write not you to soften,
Since 'gainst this outrageous harshness,
Avail nor stratagems nor supplications,
No adjuncts holding place.
You I address that you may well discern
The unreasonableness towards me you exercise
How much soever evil you enact,
Yourself in plumes of valour yet array.

3. That you should liberty praise
Is very right and reasonable,
But have a care you do not it maintain
Solely with cruelty.
It is not just what you ordain
To seek, without being offended,
To support your free existence
By so many external sacrifices.

4. You do not count that it dishonour is
That all should wish you well,
Nor that in serving yourself of disdain
Your honour is laid down.
Contrariwise the rigour moderating
Of the assaults you make,
With slender love you satisfy,
Concealing great renown.

5. Your cruelty has made me understand
How savage beasts have surely you begot,
Or that the very rugged mountains formed
Your hard existence quite indomitable.
In these your recreations do consist,
These deserts and vales within,
Where 'tis not possible for you to find,
Who stimulates desire.

6. In a fresh thicket,
You seated once I saw,

And I exclaimed a statue is fashioned,
Statue of impenetrable stone.
And though a motion followed afterwards,
Subverting my opinion.
Yet in the existing state,
I loud exclaimed more than a statue 'tis.

7. Would thou wert a statue,
A stony statue ; so that I might wish
That heaven for me would change
Your entity, and to female convert.
Ne'er Pygmalion was
So much infatuated with his statue
As I with thee, and have been, shepherdess.
Nay, shall be evermore.

8. With reason and with equity,
With good and evil equally you pay
A punishment for all the ill I do.
Glory enacted have I for the good,
In the way you do me treat,
Such truth is known.
By your observation life infuse,
While your deportment me annihilates.

9. From this bosom which emboldened is
To elude the shafts of love,
The fire of my sighs
Would melt e'en snow itself.
Yield to my plaint,
No leisure tolerating,
Into agreeableness and mildness turn
The virtue of your metal.

10. Well know I that you will advise
That I myself emancipate, so think,
Cut thou but off desire
And I will readily my request abridge,
But as to what you give me,
As to what my demands,
Little to thee imports it
If more or less should be solicited.

11. If for your extravagant savageness
    I could thee sore rebuke,
    Mark out the very sign
    Which indicates our weakness;
    Noting your carriage, I should say
    'Tis not so one is taught.
    I charge thee bear in mind thou art the rock,
    And as a rock you must converted be.

12. Yet be thou rock or steel,
    The hardest marble or a diamond,
    A lover of steel am I,
    Rock I adore and covet it likewise
    If thou should'st be in disguise
    Or e'en a fury, for all certain is,
    For such an angel living would I die,
    For such a fury am I in sore pain.

The verses of Galercio appeared better to Thirsis than
the condition of Gelasia, and wishing to show them to
Elicio, he seemed so changed in his colour and aspect, that
he looked very like a spectre. He advanced towards him,
and when he sought to ask him if any especial grief bore
him down, his reply was not awaited to understand the
cause of his suffering, for incontinently he heard it proclaimed, amidst the bystanding swains, how the two shepherds
who went to the succour of Galercio were friends of the
shepherd Lusitano, with whom the venerable Aurelio agreed
to marry Galatea, who came to say how that in three days
the luckless shepherd would come to the village to conclude
the happy betrothal. And soon did Thirsis see that this
intelligence caused more new and extraordinary accidents
in the breast of Elicio; yet, with all this, he advanced
towards him and said, "Now, my worthy associate, it is
right you avail yourself of all the discretion of which you
are master, for hearts are plunged into greater peril, and I
assure you I know not who fortifies my mind that this affair
will not have a different result from what you contemplate.
Dissemble and be silent, for if the will of Galatea be .not
agreeable to acquiesce in all that her father suggests, you
will satisfy yours, availing yourself, too, of ours, and of the
concurrence of all the swains who frequent the banks of the

stream, as well as that of the gentle Henares; which favour
I offer you, for I well conceive that the desire which all
have known of my wish to serve you will force you so to
act that what I promise may not eventuate vainly." Elicio
remained inanimate on recognising the noble and solid offer of
Thirsis; he could neither reply, nor do aught but embrace
him closely, and say to him, "May heaven reward you, wise
Thirsis, for the counsel you have imparted, which, with the
will of Galatea, shall not deviate from my will, understanding, no doubt, that a so notorious offence as has been perpetrated on these banks in banishing from them the rare
beauty of Galatea should not pass unheeded by;" and turning round for an embrace, the lost colour returned to his
cheeks. Yet did it not return to Galatea, who heard of the
embassy of swains as though she heard sentence of death
passed upon her.

Elicio marked all this, nor could Erastro dissemble, nor
yet the discreet Florisa; the news was by no means tasteful
to any there.

Just now the sun declined in its wonted course, and as
well for this as for noting how the enamoured Lenio had
pursued Gelasia, and that nought remained to be done,
taking Galercio and Maurisa with him, all the company
bent their steps towards the hamlet, and on reaching it
Elicio and Erastro stayed in their cottages, and with them
Thirsis, Damon, Orompo, Crisio, Marsilio. Arsindo and
Orfenio remained with some others of the same fraternity.
All of them, with courteous words and offers, took leave of
them, the fortunate Timbrio, Silerio, Nisida and Blanca,
telling them that on the next day they thought of going to
the city of Toledo, which would end their travels; and
embracing all who still remained with Elicio, off they went
with Aurelio, with whom, too, went Florisa, Teolinda, and
Maurisa; and the mournful Galatea, so full of anguish and
pensive, that with all her circumspection she could not
refrain from betraying indications of her irrepressible dissatisfaction.

With Daranio went his spouse Silveria, and the delicate
Belisa. The night now closed in, and it seemed to Elicio
as if with it were enclosed all avenues to his taste, and
were it not to give agreeable entertainment to his guests

whom he lodged that night in his cottage, he would have passed the night so badly that he had despaired of again seeing the day.

Pains analogous to these did the mournful Erastro feel, yet with more cheerfulness, for regarding nothing, with lofty voice and words piteous and profound, he cursed his misadventure, and the precipitated determination of Aurelio.

Thus standing, whilst the shepherds allayed their hunger with some country fruits, and then surrendering themselves to the arms of tired nature's sweet restorer, balmy sleep, the delicate Maurisa came to the cottage of Elicio, and finding him at his own door took him aside and delivered to him a paper, stating that it came from Galatea, and that he should read it forthwith, and then that she, at a certain hour, would take it. The swain was amazed at the advent of Maurisa, and the more to see in her hands the paper of the lady shepherdess, and he could not refrain a minute from perusing it, so entering his cottage by the light of some chips of a resinous pine, he made himself acquainted with its contents, and found the effect to be as follows :—

"GALATEA TO ELICIO.—In the over-hastened determination of my father consists that which I have undertaken to write to you, and in the momentum which forces me to reach that particular point. Well know you what I am, and I know well I would wish to see myself in a better condition to repay you the much I feel is your due. Should heaven decree that I continue in this doubt, complain of that and not of my will. That of my father I would change were it practicable ; I think I discern, however, that it is not so, hence I do not essay to do it. If you imagine any remedy there, as in it no supplications intervene, put it into effect with the view that you owe it to your credit, and that you are beholden to my honour.

"Him whom they give for husband, and he who gives me a burial to-morrow will I shew. Little time remains for counsel, although sufficient is left for my repentance.

"I say no more, save that Maurisa is faithful and I wretched."

Into extraordinary bewilderment did the reasons in Galatea's letter throw Elicio. It seemed quite a novelty that it should be written, for it was never done before, that is finding a remedy for unreasonableness. Pretermitting all these things, however, he paused to imagine how he should fulfil the injunctions, though he should even jeopardise a thousand lives if needs were. No better remedy offering itself than what he awaited from his friends, and in full affiance he was emboldened to reply to Galatea in a letter which he confided to Maurisa, which ran in this wise :—

"Elicio to Galatea.—Did my strength but correspond to the wish I have to serve you, beauteous Galatea, neither that which your father does, nor what the world would do, could offend ; but as I wish that may be, you will now see if the unreasonableness proceeds, since I am not backward in realising your injunctions in the most salutary way the case exacts. Be assured of the faith which is in me, and make a good appearance under present circumstances, trusting to the coming good by which heaven has moved you to write to me, and this will give me courage to show you how I merit the reward you have given me; so that to obey you nor suspicion nor dread shall operate to divert me from putting into effect that which is most in accordance with your taste, and the more so as it imports me much. No more, save what necessarily appertains, shall you know by Maurisa, to whom I confide this account. Should your idea not conform to mine, let me know it, that time may not slip away and with it the conjuncture of our chance, the which may heaven ratify in a way your virtue deserves."

By this note, entrusted to Maurisa as before related, he intimated how he thought of uniting all the swains, and that all, collectively, should go to address Galatea's father, requesting him, out of mercy, not to cause the banishment from these meads of the beauteous Galatea, his child, and should this not suffice, he thought of imparting such an inconvenience and fear to the Lusitanian shepherd, that he himself would not be content with the project ; but should solicitations and craft not avail, he was resolved to use coercion and place her in liberty, and this with a view to evince how much he loved her.

With this resolution departed Maurisa, and all the shepherds who were with Elicio agreed, to whom he gave account of his thoughts, asking favour and counsel in a so arduous case. On the spur, Thirsis and Damon spontaneously offered themselves to be the party who were to speak to the father of Galatea. Lauso, Arsindo, and Erastro, with the four friends, Orompo, Marsilio, Crisio, and Orfenio promised to seek and to unite all friends by the following day, and to put into execution whatever plan Elicio had suggested. In treating of what more appertained to the question, and in taking directions, the best part of the night elapsed. On the morrow all the swains started to fulfil their parts of the promise, but Thirsis and Damon stayed with Elicio.

That same day Maurisa returned to tell Elicio how Galatea had determined to follow his views. Elicio took leave of her with new promises and confidence. With joyful mien and unusual commotion of the heart, she awaited the ensuing day to testify to the good or evil which fortune awarded.

The night closed in, and associating herself with Damon and Thirsis, at the cottage, nearly all the time was passed in deliberating on and adverting to the difficulties which might ensue, pending the negociation, if perchance the reasons which Thirsis proposed should not have sway with Aurelio. But Elicio to allow repose to the swains, sallied forth from his cottage, and ascended a little hillock which stood before, and there, with preparation for solitude, he revolved in his mind all he had suffered for Galatea, and all he yet feared and would suffer, should heaven not favour his expectations; so without diverging from this idea, and the murmur a bland zephyr which calmly blew, and with a voice gentle and low, he gave utterance to the sentiments—

ELICIO.

1. I from this yesty sea, and the mad gulf
   Which the wild tempest threatens in its might,
   I save a life from a so harsh affront,
   And safely reach to me so prosperous land.

2. In the high air upraising both my hands,
   With soul in humbleness and a will content,
   What love may I know and perpetrate; Heaven feels
   What thanks I render for its sovereign good.

3. Fortunate I account my very sighs,
   My tears I tender for acceptable
   Refreshment from the fire in which I burn.

4. I will admit the shafts of love are stiff,
   Sweet to the soul, to matter salutary,
   In which no medium is, all in extremes.

When Elicio had ended his song the dewy morn began to ope the orient gates with its beauteous and varied cheeks, enlivening the soil (aljoforando) embroidering with seed pearls the herbs, and painting the meads, at whose much desired advent the talkative birds saluted her with concert of chimes.

Up rose Elicio, and around he cast his wondering eyes at the spacious plains, discovering at no great distance two squadrons of shepherds, who seemed to bend their course towards his cottage, as in truth it was so, for quickly he recognised they were his friends Arsindo and Lauso with others also in the train ; and those others were Orompo, Marsilio, Crisio, and Orfenio, and all such friends as could with them unite.

Immediately known by Elicio, he ascended the knoll to receive them, and when they reached the cottage there stood Thirsis and Damon outside, who advanced to seek Elicio. Now all the swains came up, and with cheerful recognition mutually received each other. So Lauso turning to Elicio, said to him,

"In the company which attends us you may see, friend Elicio, if we begin to give signs of wishing to accomplish the word we tendered to you ; all here, whom you see, come with zeal to serve you, although in the service they venture their very lives. What is wanting is that you do but what is most suitable only."

Elicio, with the best reasons he knew, returned to Lauso and the rest appropriate thanks, and incontinently communicated to them all that had been concerted with Damon and Thirsis to do, for the realisation of the enterprise.

It seemed quite just to the swains all that Elicio had said, and so without more ado they bent their way towards the village, Thirsis and Damon preceding them, the rest followed after to the amount of twenty shepherds, all sprightly, blithe, and as well-intentioned as any that could be found on the water-banks of Tagus' stream, and all moved and animated with the joint intention that in the event of their arguments not prevailing with Aurelio, to have recourse to violence, and never to submit to Galatea becoming the wife of the strange shepherd. At which Erastro was so content, as if the good success of that demand redounded to his sole satisfaction, for in lieu of finding Galatea absent and discontent he held it for a piece of policy that Elicio should secure her, and that Galatea would remain in obligation as he imagined.

The end of the loving story with the successes of Galercio, Lenio, and Gelasia, Arsinda, Maurisa, Grisaldo, Artandro, and Rosaura, Marsilio, and Belisa, with other matters which happened to the swains herein enumerated, are promised in the second part, which, if with a cheerful recognition this first part is received, it will embolden the author to submit for judgment, to the eyes and intelligence of the public, the sequel.

THE END.